(In Free Fall)

ALSO BY JULI ZEH

Eagles and Angels

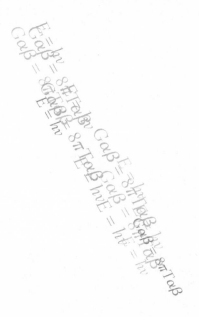

IN FREE FALL

A Novel

JULI ZEH

Translated from the German by Christine Lo

NAN A. TALESE | DOUBLEDAY

New York London Toronto Sydney Auckland

www.nanatalese.com

Originally published in Germany as *Schilf* by Schöffling & Co. Verlagsbuchhandlung GmBH, Frankfurt am Main, in 2007. Copyright © 2007 by Schöffling & Co. Verlagsbuchhandlung GmBH, Frankfurt am Main. This translation originally published in Great Britain in paperback as *Dark Matter* by Harvill Secker, the Random House Group Ltd., London.

LIBRARY OF CONGRESS CATALOGING-IN-PUBLICATION DATA
Zeh, Juli
[Schilf. English]
In free fall : a novel / Juli Zeh ; translated from the German by Christine Lo. — 1st ed. in the U.S.
p. cm.
I. Lo, Christine. II. Title.
PT2688.E28S3513 2010
2009042894

ISBN 978-0-385-52642-5

PRINTED IN THE UNITED STATES OF AMERICA

1 3 5 7 9 10 8 6 4 2

First American Edition

Few people master the art of fearing the right things.

CONTENTS

(*In Free Fall*)

[PROLOGUE]

WE DID NOT HEAR EVERYTHING but we saw most of what happened, for one of us was always there.

A detective with a fatal headache—who loves a theory of physics and does not believe in coincidence—solves his final case. A child is kidnapped but does not know it. A doctor does what he should not do. One man dies, two physicists fight, and a young police officer falls in love. In the end, everything seems different from what the detective thought it was, yet exactly the same. A man's ideas are his score, his life the twisted music.

It went, we think, something like this.

CHAPTER 1, IN SEVEN PARTS

Sebastian cuts curves.
Maike cooks. Oskar comes to visit.
Physics is for lovers.

[1]

AS YOU APPROACH IT FROM THE SOUTHWEST, at a height of about five hundred meters, Freiburg looks like a bright, worn patch in the folds of the Black Forest. It lies there as if it had fallen from the heavens one day, right at the feet of the mountains. The peaks of Belchen, Schauinsland, and Feldberg stand in a ring around it. Freiburg has existed for mere minutes in relation to these mountains, yet the town behaves as if it has always been there, next to the river Dreisam.

If Schauinsland were to ripple its slopes in a shrug of indifference, hundreds of people cycling, riding in cable cars, or looking for butterflies would die; if Feldberg were to turn away in boredom, that would be the end of the entire district. But the mountains don't do that. Instead, they turn their somber faces to the goings-on in the streets of Freiburg, where people set out to entertain. Every day, mountains and forests send a swarm of birds into the city to gather the latest news and report back.

The Middle Ages live on in the ochre yellows and dusty pinks of the narrow lanes where thick shadows gather. The roofs are dotted with dormer windows, ideal landing spots unless they are adorned with bird spikes. A passing cloud sweeps the brightness from the facades. A girl with pigtails is buying an ice cream on Leopoldring. Her part is straight as an arrow.

A few beats of the wings, and here is Sophie-de-la-Roche-Strasse, so leafy and green that it seems to have its own microclimate. There is always a light breeze blowing here, making the leaves at the top of the chestnut trees rustle. The trees have outlived by a century the town planner who planted them, and they have grown larger than he had envisaged. Their long-fingered branches brush the balconies, and their roots bulge beneath the pavement and dig their way under the walls of the canal that flows by the buildings' foundations. Bonnie and Clyde—one head of brown and one of green—paddle along against the current, quacking away, always turning at the same spot, and allowing themselves to be carried downstream. On their conveyer belt they travel faster than the people walking on the canal path, at whom they look up, begging for bread.

Sophie-de-la-Roche-Strasse radiates such a feeling of well-being that an objective observer might think its residents are all at peace with the world. Because the canal makes the walls damp, the front doors are wide open so that the walkways over the water look like tongues hanging out of gaping jaws. Number 7—in tasteful white stucco—is without doubt the most beautiful building on the street. Wisteria cascades down from it, sparrows chirp in the swathes of ivy on the walls, and an old-fashioned lantern dozes in the porch, waiting to be lit at night. In an hour or so a taxi will come around the corner and stop at this building. The passenger in the backseat will raise his sunglasses in order to count change into the driver's hand. He will get out of the car, tip his head back, and look up at the windows on the second floor. A couple of doves are already picking their way across one of the window ledges, nodding and bending, fluttering upward occasionally to look into the apartment. These winged observers watch Sebastian, Maike, and Liam closely on the first Friday evening of every month.

BEHIND ONE OF THE WINDOWS, Sebastian is sitting cross-legged on the floor of his study, head bent over something. He is surrounded by scissors and bits of paper, as if he were making Christmas decorations.

Crouching next to him is Liam—blond and pale like his father, a mini-Sebastian down to his posture. He is looking at a sheet of red card on which the laser printer has marked a zigzag curve, like an outline of the Alps. As Sebastian puts the scissors to the card, Liam raises a warning finger.

"Wait! Your hands are shaking!"

"That's because I'm trying hard to hold still, clever clogs," Sebastian snaps. Liam's eyes widen in surprise and Sebastian regrets his tone.

Sebastian is on edge, as he is on the first Friday evening of every month. As usual, he puts it down to having had a bad day. Little things can spoil his mood on the first Friday of every month. Today it was an encounter on the bank of the Dreisam, where he takes a break from his lectures at lunchtime. He passed a group of people who were standing around a mound of earth a little way off the main path for no apparent reason. In the earth was a pathetic-looking seedling held upright only by a construction of wooden sticks and rubber bands. Three gardeners were leaning on spades nearby, and a lanky man in a dark suit, with a little girl hanging on to his leg, stepped up to the mound of earth and made a small celebratory speech. The tree of the year. Black apple tree. Love for home and hearth, for nature, for Creation. Elderly ladies stood around silently in a semicircle. Then came the thrust of the spade and a pathetic shovelful of earth, and the little girl poured water from a tin can. Applause. Sebastian couldn't help thinking about what Oskar would have said if he had seen them. "Look, a herd of forked beings celebrating their own helplessness!" And Sebastian would have laughed and refrained from saying that he felt very much like the tree of the year, actually. Like a seedling dwarfed by its scaffolding.

"Do you know about the tree of the year?" he asks his son, who shakes his head and stares at the scissors that have fallen still in his father's hand. "It's nonsense," he adds. "The worst rubbish imaginable."

"Oskar's coming today, isn't he?"

"Of course." Sebastian starts cutting. "Why?"

"You always talk about strange things when Oskar's coming. And," Liam continues, pointing at the card, "you bring work back home."

"I thought you liked measuring curves!" Sebastian replies indignantly.

At ten, Liam is already clever enough to know not to reply to this. Of course he loves helping his father with physics experiments. He knows that the zigzag line marks the result of a radiometric measurement, even though he can't explain the meaning of "radiometric." The integral under the curve can be measured by cutting out the surface area and weighing the card. But Liam also knows that there are computers at the university that will give you the answer without cutting and weighing. This could definitely have waited till Monday. Sebastian has brought it home for Liam to have fun with and because he finds this activity calming late on a Friday afternoon. Even though the chopping board and the sharp knife that they need to cut out the tiny jagged bits are with Maike in the kitchen.

When Maike is cooking for Oskar, the kitchen utensils are hers and hers alone. Every time Maike tells Sebastian about the new dish she is trying out that evening, he wonders why Oskar's visits are so important to her. He would have thought that Liam's hero worship of the big-shot physicist from Geneva would put her off Oskar, not to mention the heavily ironic tone of voice in which Oskar invariably addresses her. Yet it was Maike herself who had started the tradition of dinners with him ten years ago, and she is the one who has insisted on them to this very day. Sebastian suspects that, consciously or unconsciously, she is trying to steer something in a controlled manner. Something that should be playing out before her very eyes, rather than developing unchecked in hidden corners. They have never spoken about what this certain something might be. Deep down, Sebastian admires his wife's calm persistence. "He's coming on Friday, isn't he?" she asks, and Sebastian nods. That is all.

The curve is easier to cut out in the middle, and it becomes more complicated again toward the end. Liam holds on to the card with both hands, cheering when the scissors have negotiated the final jagged cliffs and the zigzag cutting falls to the ground. He picks up the masterpiece carefully by the edges, and runs off to see if the kitchen scales are free.

MAIKE IS STANDING AT THE KITCHEN COUNTER chopping some unruly-looking salad leaves. She is wearing a white dress that makes her look as though she is about to be married for the second time. Her feet are bare, and she is absentmindedly scratching a mosquito bite on her left calf with her right foot. The window is open. Summer air is wafting in with the smell of hot asphalt, flowing water, and a wind that is juggling with the swallows high in the heavens. In the golden evening light, Maike looks more than ever like the kind of woman a man would like to ride up to on horseback and carry off into the sunset. She is unique, and not just at first glance. Her skin is even paler than Sebastian's and her mouth is very slightly lopsided, which makes her look a little pensive when she laughs. The small contemporary art gallery in Freiburg where Maike works has her to thank for a great deal of its success, for she is not only the artists' agent, but also their occasional model. Maike's aesthetic feeling has almost the fervor of religion about it. Surroundings furnished without care depress her and she is the sort of person who checks every glass against the light before placing it on the table.

When Sebastian approaches her from behind, she stretches her damp hands out in front of her, showing her shaved underarms. His fingers climb the staircase of her vertebrae, from her bottom to her neck.

"Are you cold?" she asks. "Your hands are trembling."

"Can't you and Liam think about anything other than my clapped-out nervous system?" Sebastian asks.

"Yes," Maike replies. "Red wine."

Sebastian kisses the back of her head. They both know that Oskar will have read the article in *Der Spiegel* magazine. Maike has no particular desire to understand the intricacies of the long-standing scientific disagreement between Oskar and Sebastian. But she knows what will happen. Oskar's voice will be threateningly quiet when he launches his attack. And Sebastian will blink more rapidly than usual while he is defending himself, and his arms will dangle limply by his side.

"I bought a Brunello," she said. "He'll like it."

As Sebastian reaches for the carafe of wine, a red point of light sweeps over Maike's breasts, as if a drunken marksman were aiming through the window. Fruit, oak, earth. Sebastian resists the temptation to pour himself a glass and turns to Liam, who is waiting by the kitchen scales. Cheek to cheek, they read the digital display.

"Excellent work, little professor." Sebastian presses his son against his side. "What conclusion can we draw?"

"Nature behaves in accordance with our calculations," Liam says, glancing sideways at his mother. Her knife taps a solid rhythm on the wooden chopping board. She doesn't like him to show off with sentences learned by heart.

Sebastian lingers at the kitchen door before bringing his graph back into the study. Maike will want to say that she will keep Liam off his back later. Off his back. She likes that expression. It reminds her of the battle of her everyday life, which she wins every evening. But Maike is not really the fighting kind. Before she met Sebastian, she was very much a dreamer. She used to walk through the streets at night, dreaming her way into every illuminated window. In her mind, she was watering strangers' potted plants, laying their tables for dinner, and patting their children's heads. Every man was a potential lover, and, depending on the color of his eyes and his build, she dreamed of living a wild or conventional or artistic or political life by his side. Maike's vagabond imagination had inhabited people and places as she encountered them. Until she met Sebastian. The moment she walked into his arms on the Kaiser-Joseph-Strasse in Freiburg ("On the Münsterplatz!" Sebastian would say, for there were two versions of their first meeting—one for him and one for her), her hazy reality became solid. It was love at first sight, precluding alternatives, reducing an endless variety of possibilities to a here and a now. Sebastian's appearance in Maike's life was—as he would express it—a wave function collapse. From that moment on, Maike had had someone whose back she could protect. She does so at every opportunity, and gladly, too.

"You two can talk in peace later," she says, brushing a strand of hair off her brow with her forearm. "I'll keep . . ."

"I know," Sebastian says. "Thank you."

She laughs, showing a glimpse of chewing gum between her molars. This does nothing to diminish her irresistible charm—all fair hair and childlike eyes.

"When is Oskar coming?" Liam pesters.

As his parents look at each other, he expresses his impatience by decorating the kitchen table with chunks of onion and cloves of garlic. Maike lets him get away with it because there is a seed of creativity in his cheekiness.

[2]

IT'S INCREDIBLE, OSKAR THINKS, that all human beings are made up of the same components. That the glands which give him a light rush of adrenaline can also be found in the autonomic nervous system of the delicately built Oriental woman with the Yoko Ono face who is distributing coffee and rolls. Incredible that her nails, hair, and teeth are made of the same material as the nails, hair, and teeth of all the passengers. That the hands pouring the coffee are being moved by the same tendons as those reaching for change in their wallets. That even the palm into which he—carefully avoiding any contact—drops a couple of coins has the same pattern on it as his own.

As she passes him the cup of coffee, the Oriental woman holds his gaze a split second longer than necessary. The train judders as it travels over a set of points and the coffee almost spills onto his trousers. Oskar takes the cup from the woman and looks down at the floor to avoid the beaming smile of farewell that she is about to give him. If only it were just the similarity of their hands that connected him to her. If all they had in common were hydrogen, oxygen, and carbon. But the shared elements go deeper than that, right down to the protons, neutrons, and electrons from which he and the Oriental woman are made, which also make up the table supporting his elbows and the coffee cup warming his hands. So Oskar is merely a random collection of matter from which the world is formed, containing everything that exists, because it is impossible to be otherwise. He knows that the boundaries of his person blur into the enormous whirl of particles. He can literally feel his substance mixing with that of the people around him. This is almost always an unpleasant feeling for Oskar. There is one exception. He is on his way to him now.

IF SEBASTIAN WERE TO TRY to describe his friend Oskar, he would say that Oskar looks like the kind of person who could answer every question put to him. Would string theory one day succeed in uniting the fundamental forces of physics? Can a dress shirt be worn with a dinner jacket? What time is it in Dubai? Regardless of whether he is listening or speaking himself, Oskar's granite eyes stay fixed on you. Oskar is one of those people who have quicksilver in their veins. One of those people who always stand at a commanding vantage point. People like Oskar do not have silly nicknames. In his presence, women sit on their hands in order to stop themselves from reaching out to touch him involuntarily. When he was twenty, people put him at thirty. After his thirtieth birthday, he seemed ageless. He is tall and slim, with a smooth forehead and narrow eyebrows that seem to be raised in permanent questioning. Despite shaving carefully, a dark shadow colors his slightly sunken cheeks. He always looks as though he has dressed with care, even when he is wearing simply a pair of black trousers and a sweater, as he is now. On his body, clothes can do nothing but fall in the right lines. For the most part, he holds himself with a mixture of apparent ease and inner tension that makes others look him in the face with curiosity. Behind his back, they cast about for his name, taking him for an actor they ought to know. Oskar is indeed well known in certain circles, but not for acting. He is famous for his theories on the nature of time.

Outside, summer speeds by in a band of green and blue. A road runs alongside the tracks. The cars follow the train as though they are glued to it. The pavement is flecked with flat pools of light. Oskar has just pulled out his sunglasses when a young man asks if the seat beside him is taken. Oskar turns away and hides his eyes behind the dark glasses. The young man walks on down the aisle. A brown puddle of coffee spreads on the foldaway table.

Oskar's aesthetic sense is often what makes life intolerable for him. Many people cannot stand their fellow men, but few are able to explain precisely why. Oskar can forgive the fact that his fellow human beings consist merely of protons, neutrons, and electrons. But he cannot forgive their inability to maintain their composure in the face of this tragic state of affairs. When he thinks about his childhood, he sees himself at fourteen, surrounded by boys and girls who are laughing and pointing at his feet. He had, without his parents' permission, sold his bicycle in order to buy his first pair of handmade shoes—three sizes too big, to be on the safe side. To this day he despises tactless laughter and avoids pompous people, show-offs, and the Schadenfreude of the stupid. To his mind, there is no violence greater than an offense against aesthetics. If he were ever to commit murder—certainly not something he has planned—it would probably be because his victim had made an importunate remark.

His schoolmates suddenly stopped teasing him when he reached a height of 1.9 meters at the age of sixteen. They began to vie for his attention instead. They spoke loudly whenever he was in earshot on the school grounds. When a girl raised her hand to answer a question in class, she would glance over at him to make sure he was listening. Even the math teacher, an unkempt person whose neck hair stuck out over his shirt collar, would turn to Oskar with a "That's right, isn't it?" when he placed the chalk-breaking period after a row of figures on the board. Yet Oskar was the only one in his class who had left school after the *Abitur* exam without a practical experience of love for his fellow man. He viewed this as a victory. He was convinced that there was not a single person on this earth whose presence he could endure for more than ten minutes.

When he met Sebastian at the university, the magnitude of this error made him quite dizzy. The fact that they noticed each other on the first day of the new semester was due to their height. Their eyes met over the heads of the other students, and they seemed to be automatically drawn to sit next to each other in the lecture theater. They sat in silence through the embarrassing welcome speech by the dean, then started chatting easily as they left the hall. Sebastian did not say anything even faintly naive in the following ten minutes, and he did not laugh in an irritating manner, not once. Oskar could not only tolerate his company, but even felt a desire to continue their conversation. They went into the dining hall together and continued talking into the evening. From that moment on, Oskar sought the company of his new friend, and Sebastian acquiesced. Their friendship had no preliminary stages—nothing had to grow and develop. It simply turned on, like a lamp when the right switch is flicked.

Any attempt to describe the following months runs the risk of getting lost in exaggeration. Ever since Oskar started at the university in Freiburg, he had appeared in public dressed always in a morning suit—long jacket and striped trousers—and a silver cravat. It was not long before Sebastian started appearing at lectures in a similar dandy's uniform. Every morning they walked across the lawn in front of the Institute of Physics as if drawn to each other by an invisible string—bypassing all the other students in various different years who seemed to exist only to get in their way—and greeted each other with a handshake. They bought only one copy of every textbook because they liked bending their heads over each page together. The seats next to them in the lecture theater remained empty. Everyone found their getup odd, yet no one laughed at them, not even when they walked arm in arm on the bank of the Dreisam in the afternoons, stopping every couple of steps, because matters of importance could only be discussed while standing still. In their old-fashioned garb, they looked like something from a yellowing postcard, carefully cut out and pasted—but not seamlessly—into the present. The ripple of the Dreisam punctuated their conversation and the trees above them waved in the wind. The late-summer sun was never more beautiful than when one of them pointed at it and said something about the solar neutrino problem.

In the evenings, they met in the library. Oskar strolled along the shelves, returning from time to time to their shared table with a book. Ever since Oskar had got into the habit of putting his arm around his friend while bringing his attention to something interesting in a book, female students of German literature had started gathering on the benches behind the glass walls of the reading room. At parties, when Oskar and Sebastian glided through the crowds separately, Sebastian, with a heavy heart, sometimes kissed a girl. When he lifted his head, he could count on seeing Oskar smiling at him from across the room. At the end of the evening, the girl would be led to the door and handed over to anyone passing by, like a piece of clothing. Then Oskar and Sebastian would walk together through the night until they had to part ways. They came to a standstill, the light from a streetlamp falling around them like a tent that neither of them wanted to leave. It was hard to decide on a suitable moment to say good-bye—this one, or the next? As the headlights of passing cars caused their combined shadow to rotate on its axis, the friends made a silent vow that nothing would ever change between them. The future was an evenly woven carpet of togetherness unrolling before them. When the chirp of the first bird sounded, they turned away and each disappeared into his half of the coming morning.

On the first Friday of every month, Oskar allows himself to imagine for a few seconds that the InterCity Express is bringing him back to one of those farewells beneath the streetlamps of Freiburg. Back to a heated discussion on the banks of the Dreisam, or at least to a moment over a shared textbook. He feels his lips curve into a smile, but immediately falls into a peevish mood. Clearly the Freiburg of the streetlamps no longer exists. What does exist is this: a circular underground tunnel in Switzerland where he makes elementary particles collide at nearly the speed of light. And the Freiburg where he has been invited by Sebastian's wife to dinner with the family. It was on a

Friday that Oskar had met Liam—tiny as a doll then—for the first time. It was on a Friday that he had learned about Sebastian's renown at the university. On Fridays, they look each other in the eye and try not to think about the past. On Fridays, they fight. For Oskar, Sebastian is not just the only person whose presence brings him pleasure. Sebastian is also the person whose slightest movement can turn him white-hot with rage.

WHEN THE TRAIN COMES TO A STANDSTILL on an open stretch of land, Oskar leans down to his bag to remove a rolled-up copy of *Der Spiegel* magazine, which falls open at the right page. He doesn't need to read the article again—he practically knows it by heart. He looks at the photo instead: it shows a forty-year-old man with blond hair and eyebrows, and clear blue eyes. He is laughing, and his half-open mouth has taken on a slightly rectangular shape. Oskar is more familiar with this laugh than with his own. He touches the photograph carefully, stroking the forehead and cheeks, then suddenly presses his thumb into it, as if he were trying to stub out a cigarette. He is worried about the train stopping like this. In the seats across the aisle from him, a mother in a flowery outfit is handing out sandwiches from a Tupperware container. The smell of salami fills the air.

"So it's four now!" exclaims the father, whose fat neck bulges over his collar. He slaps his newspaper with the back of his hand. "See! Four people have died now! Bled to death during surgery. The medical director continues to deny it."

"Four little Negro boys," a childish voice sings, "on the river Rhine."

"Quiet," the mother says, and she stops the song midflow with a piece of apple.

"'Is the pharmaceutical industry behind the experiments on patients?'" the father reads. He shoves out his lips crudely as he drinks from his bottle of beer.

"Criminals, the lot of them," the mother says.

"Ought to be locked up."

"If only."

Oskar puts *Der Spiegel* back into his bag and hopes that Sebastian will not smell salami on his clothes when they greet each other. He strides out of the carriage and almost stumbles when the train jerks into motion. Send all the stupid people to war, he thinks, as he leans against the wall next to the toilets. Let them burn to a crisp in some African desert or in an Asian jungle, it really doesn't matter. Another fifty years of peace and the people in this country will have regressed to the level of apes.

Outside, the first well-tended front gardens of the Freiburg suburbs have appeared.

[3]

"SUMMER IN FREIBURG IS JUST WONDERFUL."

Oskar is standing by the open window behind a half-drawn curtain, cradling a glass of wine and breathing in the scent of the wisteria that he had admired from the street when he got out of the taxi. He is wearing a dark sweater despite the heat, but he looks fresh as a daisy, as though sweating is not something of which he is capable. He hears the parquet creak behind him, and turns his head.

Sebastian is walking across the large dining room, arms dangling by his sides, deliberately relaxed, quite the opposite of his friend. His hair is as startlingly fair as Oskar's is dark. While Oskar always looks as if he is attending a formal celebration of some kind, Sebastian has something boyish about him. His movements have a playful openness about them, and though he dresses well—today in a white shirt and linen trousers—he always looks as if he has slightly outgrown his shirtsleeves and trouser legs. On him, growing older seems to be a mistake, and age has merely deepened his laugh lines.

He walks right up to Oskar and places a hand that he knows is warm and dry upon Oskar's neck. Sebastian closes his eyes for a moment as the smell of his friend sweeps over him like a memory. The calm way they stand so close together indicates habit.

“I’m going to murder someone in four days,” says Sebastian, “but I don’t know anything about it yet.”

Sebastian could have said that without telling a lie. Instead he says, “Summer in Freiburg is as beautiful as those who appreciate it.” His words strike a false note—they betray his uneasiness rather than conceal it. Sebastian’s hand slides off Oskar and falls into emptiness as his friend steps smoothly to one side. Below them, outside, Bonnie and Clyde have reached the start of the street. They turn and float past the house like flotsam and jetsam.

“Let’s get to the point,” Oskar says, his eyes resting on the ducks in the canal. “I read your outpourings in *Der Spiegel*.”

“I take it you’re congratulating me.”

“It’s a declaration of war, *cher ami*.”

“My God, Oskar.” Sebastian shoves one hand into his pocket and passes his other over his face. “The sun is shining and the birds are singing. It’s not a matter of life and death. It’s about a theory of physics.”

“Even a harmless theory like the earth being round cost a lot of people their lives.”

“If Copernicus had had a friend like you,” Sebastian replies, “the earth would still be flat.”

The corner of Oskar’s mouth twitches. He takes out a crumpled pack of cigarettes and waits until Sebastian, who doesn’t smoke, has found some matches and given him a light.

“And if Copernicus had believed in the Many-Worlds Interpretation,” Oskar retorts, the cigarette between his lips jerking as he speaks, “mankind would have been wiped out by idiocy.”

Sebastian sighs. It isn’t easy arguing with someone who is part of the greatest intellectual endeavor of the new millennium. Oskar’s goal is to unite quantum physics with the general theory of relativity. He wants to bring $E = h\nu$ together with $G_{\alpha\beta} = 8\pi T_{\alpha\beta}$ and thus make two views of the universe into one. One question and one answer. A single equation that describes everything. He is not alone in searching for a theory of everything. There are hordes of physicists working on it, all competing with each other, knowing that the winner not only will receive the Nobel Prize, but will also follow in the footsteps of Einstein, Planck, and Heisenberg in gaining a piece of immortality. The winner's name will forever be associated with a certain epoch—the age of quantum gravity. Oskar's chances of winning are not at all bad.

Sebastian's focus, to put it carefully, lies elsewhere. He is an experimental physicist in nanotechnology at the University of Freiburg and is regarded as brilliant in his field. But from Oskar's point of view, Sebastian is a mere bricklayer and it is theoretical physicists who are the architects. Sebastian is not engaged in fighting for immortality. His free time is taken up by the Many-Worlds Interpretation—whose very name, from Oskar's point of view, reveals that it is not a theory but a hobbyhorse. Sebastian is grazing in an empty field. The great physicists left it behind some fifty years ago. In Oskar's eyes, it is now of esoteric interest only, or for show-offs. A dead end.

Sebastian knows that Oskar is basically right. Sometimes he feels like a child who stubbornly persists in trying to make a lightbulb out of a preserving jar and a piece of wire despite his parents' objections. But in front of his less gifted colleagues, in front of his students, and, most of the time, to himself, he claims to be looking for a new approach to questions of time and space. An approach that would leave the Many-Worlds Interpretation behind. Ultimately it doesn't matter whether Sebastian still believes in it or not, for he has no choice but to continue on the path he has carved out. Even if he were to take it upon himself to join the race Oskar is in, he would never be able to make up for the ten years he had lost. The final push to find the theory of everything had begun once the existence of W and Z bosons had been successfully proved in experiments. Oskar and Sebastian had been in their twenties then, the age at which people have the best ideas of their lives, the age at which Oskar had his only idea. Oskar had devoted himself to his theory of discrete time, behaving like an obsessive lover. Hour after hour, week after week—for ten years he had pursued it, regardless of whether it would eventually yield to him. Sebastian had not wanted anything to do with it. At an appropriate juncture, he had turned his attention to other things—not only to another theory, but, above all, to another life.

THE MAN WHO HAD THE DUBIOUS HONOR of presiding over this turning point in Sebastian's life was called Little Red Riding Hood. He had earned the nickname because of the bald pate, glowing red from wine, that emerged through his threadbare fringe of hair. He always wore a shabby corduroy jacket, the shoulders of which were covered with a white layer of dandruff. Unlike many of his colleagues, Little Red Riding Hood was adored by his students. And while he took them seriously, and stimulated their intelligence with complicated assignments, the affection was not mutual. Little Red Riding Hood especially disliked students who challenged what he said.

He had a particular aversion to the two young men who stood blocking the entrance to the lecture theater every morning. Their arrogance was legendary and their friendship was the subject of gossip even among the lecturers. They were said to love physics even more than they loved each other, and they fought over it with the passion of rivals. Little Red Riding Hood could not bear listening to their bragging conversation. Their backs were far too straight as they stood there surrounded by a circle of listeners, reciting formulae like the verses of a libretto, ordering the universe with conductors' hands. Every now and then Oskar would turn his head to draw on one of his Egyptian cigarettes, doing so with an affectation that stirred his audience into nervous movement.

The entire faculty had long since been made acquainted with Oskar's view that the world was a finely spun web of causalities, with a hidden pattern that could only be deciphered either from a great distance or from up close. Recognition of the pattern, he intoned, was a matter of being at the right distance, and was therefore possible only for God and for quantum physicists. Normal people remained in the middle distance, blind to the nature of things.

Sebastian, who always spoke a little less loudly and also more slowly, called his friend a despicable determinist. He claimed not to believe in causality himself. Causality was, like space and time, a theoretical problem of cognition. To provoke Oskar and everyone around them, he cast doubt on the validity of empiricism as a method of establishing scientific findings. A man who stands by the river and watches a thousand white swans swim by cannot conclude that there are no black swans. Therefore physics is ultimately the servant of philosophy.

Little Red Riding Hood pushed past the arguing students impatiently. It was impossible to give a lecture any longer without hearing their intrusive voices. Sometimes he looked up grumpily from his notes, thinking that their whispering would drive him to the brink, only to realize that Oskar and Sebastian were not even present.

But they were very much present on the day that Little Red Riding Hood set a problem on dark energy, which could be solved only by the assumption of an Einsteinian constant that was not a constant. The next week, Oskar and Sebastian were not standing before the doors when Little Red Riding Hood arrived, but already sitting at their usual places, looking him in the eye. He summoned them to the board even before he had reached the lectern. They rose in unison. Oskar went to the right-hand side of the board; after a second's hesitation, Sebastian went to the left. They flung their frock coats over their shoulders, and each held his with one hand as the other hand scratched frenziedly with a piece of chalk on the board. They wrote like men possessed: Oskar from the right and Sebastian from the left. The lecture theater was silent apart from the squeak of chalk that accompanied the growth of the equation. When their hands met in the middle of the bottom line, all fell still. A few faces in the auditorium cracked into smiles. Oskar completed the final lambda and clapped his hands together to shake off the chalk dust. Little Red Riding Hood was standing behind them looking at the panorama of equations with his mouth half open, like someone gaping at an impossibly beautiful view. Oskar turned around and tapped him on the shoulder with the tip of his finger, as if he were striking a triangle.

"Do you know what we have just proved, Professor?"

His voice was loud and resonant, but Little Red Riding Hood was too deep in thought to reply.

"Physics is for lovers."

If Little Red Riding Hood made any retort, it was drowned out by the laughter and unrest that had broken out in the room. The sound of chalk breaking between Sebastian's fingers was also obscured. While Oskar drank in the admiration for their work of art, Sebastian was still standing in front of the blackboard looking thoughtful. He finally pulled on his jacket and left the lecture theater, unnoticed by his friend. What had shaken him was the certainty with which Oskar had stepped to the right-hand side of the blackboard while pointing him toward the left.

The knowledge that Oskar had in no way meant to overshadow him did not make it any easier for Sebastian. The feeling of his own unfairness mingled with his foolish sense of humiliation. Oskar reveled in the spectacle and the exhilaration of pulling off a performance together, but Sebastian wanted to be a good physicist more than anything else in the world. For Oskar, being right was never any effort—it was the natural state of things. He had simply assumed that, unlike himself, Sebastian would be unable to write the mathematical derivation from back to front. The worst thing was—he was right. The moment their hands met in the middle of the blackboard was a one-sided victory, and Sebastian felt the urge to punish Oskar for this. Only Oskar saw it as a celebration of their friendship and their brilliance. Sebastian saw it as proof of his own inferiority.

From that moment on, Sebastian froze in Oskar's presence. He was not able to explain to his friend why the laws that governed their friendship had suddenly lost all validity. When they argued, his rejoinders grew sharper, and he found less and less time for shared research. Oskar did not fight against any of this. His calm gaze beneath half-closed eyes followed Sebastian into his sleep. His friend's refusal to defend himself against this new aggressiveness made Sebastian even colder. In Oskar's room, he shouted and raged against narrow walls and limited worldviews until one evening Oskar told him quietly and calmly that he was a man devoid of aesthetic sense. That night, Sebastian walked through the streets punching lampposts and declaring to them that something was not right with the world, that there must be other universes in which things went differently. In which it would be impossible for a man like him to throw away his own happiness despite knowing better. In which he and Oskar would never lose each other.

When they were defending their PhD theses, they no longer met on the bank of the Dreisam, but only for the occasional whiskey, sitting on lumpy stools at a bar. They were no longer of one mind on anything, except when it came to which one of them was the better physicist. It was Oskar; and after this conviction of theirs was confirmed by Oskar's summa cum laude, Sebastian exchanged his morning jacket for jeans and a shirt, and got married.

The guests at the wedding whispered behind raised hands about the best man, who slid along the walls at the function room and whose presence seemed to be personally responsible for the shadows in the corners. From the expression on his face, it appeared that he had never been so amused about anything in his life. Instead of a veil, he told the painfully embarrassed guests, Sebastian should have put a green light on top of his bride's head. All emergency exits had them.

[4]

"I'LL BET A CASE OF BRUNELLO," Oskar says, "that they only asked for your article because of that time-machine murder."

Sebastian is silent. That this is the case is clear as daylight. It is even in the description on the contents page: "Freiburg professor explains the theories of the time-machine murderer." In his article, Sebastian has even tried to express certain things from the point of view of the murderer. After killing five people, the young man had explained that it was not murder at all, but a scientific experiment. He had traveled from the year 2015 to prove the Many-Worlds Interpretation. This theory considers time not as a continuous line, but as a vast heap of universes that expands minute by minute, like a kind of time-foam consisting of countless bubbles; so a journey into the past is not a return to an earlier point in human history, but a switch between worlds. Therefore it would be perfectly possible to reach into the past without changing the present. He could bear witness to the fact that all five of his victims were alive and well in 2015. In the world he belonged to, there were no murder victims and therefore no crime, and he did not feel subject to the jurisdiction of the year 2007, much as he regretted it. The advice of his lawyer, that he plead insanity, he had refused indignantly.

"So you end up writing something for *Der Spiegel*," says Oskar, "that goes even beyond the ideas of this lunatic."

"Is an insane person automatically wrong? That's news to me."

"What's driving you isn't even insanity. It's your desire to relativize a personal reality." Oskar casts the words into the room over his shoulder.

"Be quiet," Sebastian hisses. "That's enough."

At the far end of the dining room, Maike is leaning over and holding Liam by the wrists. She is talking to him and pulling him toward her, and he is turning his head this way and that. Her hair is hanging over her forehead as she looks up at Sebastian, smiling.

"I know just what you're talking about," she calls. "The parallel universe in which Liam is not refusing to set the table."

"Exactly," Sebastian says genially.

"And a universe in which Oskar doesn't stare so angrily."

"Let's hope so."

"And perhaps even one in which I am not your wife and Liam is not your son?"

Maike laughs because Sebastian looks put out. The potential semi-orphan of a parallel universe has pulled himself free and is running past the table. He disappears into the hall, with Maike in hot pursuit.

"You long for other worlds," Oskar says in a low voice. "For the notion that you might be able to be two different men at the same time. At least."

Sebastian forces himself to let go of the curtain he has been fingering all this time and has wanted more than anything to pull off the rail in one violent tug. Oskar's hand passes over his shoulder as he tosses his cigarette butt out of the window. Bonnie and Clyde race across two ripples, only to prod the sinking butt with their beaks, disappointed.

"Do you remember the world in which you said this to me?" asks Oskar: "'I want to be the ground that trembles beneath your feet when the gods take their revenge on you'?" As he quotes his friend, two lines appear around his mouth—brackets of irony.

Sebastian has not forgotten—of course not. He said those words on the night that he and Oskar, with the help of a bottle of whiskey, had cracked Little Red Riding Hood's assignment on dark energy. The chairs had been upended on the tables in the bar by that time, and the bartender had smoked his way through five cigarettes while waiting for them to leave. But the two of them had seen and heard nothing else—their eyes had been closed and their foreheads pressed together as their shadows on the wall accepted the Nobel Prize for the year 2020. That evening, over the talk of numbers, they had grown closer than ever before. Their minds had worked so perfectly together that they might have belonged to the same being. Sebastian had lifted two fingers to touch his friend on the cheek, and said the words that had come into his head: *I want to be the ground that trembles beneath your feet . . .*

"Not long after," Oskar says, "I heard something quite different from you."

Sebastian remembers that, too. "You overestimate your own importance," he had screamed at Oskar in his room. "You overestimate your own importance in general, and you overestimate your importance to me in particular!"

Oskar's aesthetic sense demands that he appreciate the sophistication of an attack, even one against himself. He had admired the precise sequence of behavior aimed at cultivating trust (*I want to be the ground . . .*) and the deadly blow (*You overestimate . . .*), so he simply stayed in his armchair and did nothing more than watch casually as Sebastian worked himself up.

"So many worlds," Oskar says now. "Sometimes I wish I could find a way of diverting you from that path."

"You're exaggerating."

"You used to be a good physicist before you went off course."

"I haven't gone off course," Sebastian says with utmost composure.

"I have simply not recognized the Copenhagen Interpretation as a final, binding truth. Even it is a point of view, Oskar. Not a religion."

"Not a religion, no. It is science. Quite the opposite of your Many-Worlds escapades."

"Let's be clear on one thing. I was not defending the Many-Worlds Interpretation in *Der Spiegel*, only explaining it. Because I had been asked to."

"If you're not even defending this garbage, that only shows cowardice on top of stupidity."

"Enough now."

"You need a good shake to wake you up. A slap in the face to bring you back to reality."

"What," Sebastian asks insolently, "is reality?"

"Everything," Oskar says, suddenly touching Sebastian's stomach with the back of his hand, "that is open to experiment."

Sebastian raises an arm helplessly, and lets it drop to his side again. His eyes flit from Oskar's profile to a pigeon fluttering upward, immediately disappearing from sight. His drooping shoulders and bent head signal capitulation. But Oskar does not notice. He has turned away, placed both hands on the windowsill, and is talking again.

"Perhaps you've read Orwell's *1984*. In Oceania, people learn under torture to see things as both real and unreal at the same time. They are forced to see only one possibility out of many. Do you know what Orwell called that?" Without looking around, Oskar makes a sudden grab for Sebastian. "Do you?"

Sebastian looks at the fingers wrapped around his wrist. In a moment, he and Oskar will look each other straight in the eye for the first time that evening. Neither will be able to tear his gaze away for a few seconds. Oskar's face will relax. Then he will hurriedly take out another cigarette and light it in silence.

The ground beneath their feet begins to tremble as Liam runs noisily into the room. He throws himself headlong against Oskar, wrapping his arms around his hips and placing a sock-clad foot on each of Oskar's polished Budapest shoes. Oskar's fingers have let go of his friend's wrist very quickly.

"Are you going to lay into me the whole evening simply because I've been in *Der Spiegel*?" Sebastian asks.

"With a photo, too," says Liam.

"Mais non." As Oskar strokes Liam's head, single hairs stand up, following the static electric charge in his hands. "I will enjoy being a visitor in your life, as I always do."

They exchange a fleeting glance while Liam tugs at Oskar's sweater to get him moving.

"Come on, quantum feet!" he shouts, smiling when Oskar laughs. They sway toward the table, a two-headed creature with only one pair of legs.

"By the way," Oskar says, turning his head to speak to Sebastian over his shoulder, "I have something for you. An official duel."

He walks Liam around the table an extra time, then lets Maike—who is sticking candles into holders—tell him where to sit, even though he knows already.

"A duel," Sebastian murmurs, still standing by the window. "And I know who will be choosing the weapons."

He looks up into the chestnut trees where the sparrows are chirping, and wonders if the twittering would translate into human language if it were recorded and played backward. Endless talk. A novel per bird, per day.

[5]

MAIKE SERVES ROCKET SALAD FROM A BOWL; her long arms are marked with tan lines from wearing a short-sleeved top in the sun. She blows a strand of hair off her forehead and gives Oskar a pleading look.

"How's it going with the particle accelerator?"

"Oh, Maik."

The first time he met her, Oskar refused to use the final vowel in Maike's name: since then, he has stuck to this short form. Every time Maike's eyes meet his, their faces brighten in mutual mockery. A casual observer might even think they were secretly in love.

"You know it took me ten years to get used to your existence on Bohr's earth."

Liam butts in. "What's Bohr?"

"A great physicist," Oskar says. "'The world belongs to those who can explain it.'" He brings his finger to his nose, as if he has to press a button to recover the thread of his thought. When he finds it, he points to Maike. "And if you had to exist, I thought eventually, you could at least look out for him. But what do you do? A pathetically bad job of it. He's disgracing himself in public."

Maike lifts her left shoulder in a half shrug, as she does whenever she is at a loss.

"Take a seat," she says to Sebastian, who has come up to the table.

Oskar is looking at her as if he knows a good joke at her expense that he is keeping to himself out of politeness.

Sebastian adjusts a strap on Maike's dress and smooths the hair on the back of her head before pulling up a chair. When Oskar is there he touches her more often than usual. This irritates him, but he can't stop himself. Right now, he even wishes that Maike would put down the salad bowl and walk over to the window so that Oskar can see the down on her cheeks lit from behind, and the silhouette of her body beneath the dress. He wants Oskar to see that Maike is a rare creature, a woman to be watched over and to be envied for. He finds these thoughts repellent. Even more abhorrent is the fact that his changed behavior in Oskar's presence doesn't disturb Maike in any way. Instead, she raises her eyes in a coquettish fashion, and her voice is half an octave higher than usual.

"Do start."

Oskar spreads his napkin over his lap, elbows raised as he does so, just as he used to fling his coattails back before he sat down.

"By the way," Sebastian says, deliberately signaling a change of subject, "my argument with Oskar is on a topic that is extremely current."

"How nice for you both." Maike folds salad leaves into tidy parcels with her knife and fork. "Then perhaps there are other people who know what it's actually all about."

"I think it's old news, actually," Oskar says.

"Not at all," Sebastian claims. "It's ultimately about science versus morality. That's always relevant. Think about that scandal with the doctor."

"I know nothing about it."

"Some heart patients bled to death during their operations at the university hospital. Charges were brought. Apparently, unauthorized drugs, which impeded blood coagulation, were being tested on these patients."

"Oh yes, the Mengele of Freiburg!" Oskar dabs his napkin on his lips after every bite. "Even the proles on the train are talking about it."

"What's a Mengele?" asks Liam, who is losing his fight with the salad leaves.

"Let's not talk about that now," Maike says quickly.

"Every time you say that, it's about sex or the Nazis!" Liam crows.

"Don't be too clever!" Maike says.

Liam throws his fork down immediately. "The Nazis strung steel cables across the streets to cut off the heads of the Americans in jeeps. I saw it on TV!"

"Eat your broccoli," Sebastian says.

"It's rocket," Maike says.

"I don't think it's about experimenting on patients," Sebastian continues, anxious to keep the conversation on track. "The pharmaceutical industry wouldn't be so bold as to do anything like that, what with the press uproar—"

"Do we have to talk about this?" Maike interrupts.

Oskar lifts his head, astonished. "*Ça va*, Maik?"

"Mama knows the murderer!" Liam cries.

"One more word and you're going straight to bed!"

"You're talking nonsense, Liam," Sebastian says. He has not eaten a thing yet, but has already finished his second glass of wine. "Mama knows a senior registrar in Schlüter's department." To Oskar he says, "Schlüter is the medical director who is under suspicion. He's probably going to be suspended. For manslaughter."

Oskar's face brightens. "Maik's cycling friend! The one who works at the hospital. What's his name again?"

"Ralph," says Maike.

"Dabbelink," Sebastian adds, casting a warning glance at Oskar.

If Maike had not been trying so hard to stop herself from blushing, she might have asked herself how Oskar knows about a cycling friend of hers in the first place. Dabbelink had certainly never been mentioned at their previous Friday gatherings.

But he had been mentioned on another occasion, which Maike knew nothing about because she had thought Sebastian was at a conference in Dortmund. Instead, he had been lying under an attic roof on an old sofa, resting on one elbow like a Roman at a feast, gesticulating with his free hand. This Dabbelink fellow, he was saying, was someone who had enough ambition in him to liquefy reinforced concrete. Apart from working crazy hours, he followed a training regime on his bike that took him to the peak of the Schauinsland in the early mornings or the late evenings, depending on his shift. He shaved his arms and legs in order to cut down on air resistance, and when you shook his hand you felt like you were touching a dead man. Sebastian had no idea why Maike had made friends with such a ghastly person, of all the people in her cycling club, and how she could bear to see him two evenings a week. At this point, Oskar's amused voice interrupted him: Two evenings a week? In tight-fitting cycling gear? With red faces and sweaty hair? Sebastian was at a loss for words.

Now he stands and walks around the table to pour more wine.

"Maike doesn't like talking about Dabbelink's involvement in the scandal," he says. His jokey tone falls flat, as if he has played a note on a badly tuned instrument. He almost crashes into his wife as she stands up, still chewing, to collect the salad plates. The muscles beneath her temples are tensing visibly.

"That's not funny," she says. "Ralph is Schlüter's favorite anesthetist. They get along well in operations and at conferences. Now everyone thinks that Ralph knows something about suspicious contacts with pharmaceutical firms. And that if he talks, the entire hospital will collapse."

"I see." Oskar's eyebrows are raised in sympathy. "Has the poor man been threatened?"

"Yes indeed, he has," Maike says. "When you try, you can even be quite sensitive."

She carries the pile of plates to the door, and all is silent until she tells them that they can have a cigarette before the next course. As soon as she leaves, Liam runs into the next room, where there is a plate of biscuits on top of the television. Sebastian watches him through the half-open door, while Oskar sits with his head thrown back, blowing smoke sculptures into the air. For a few minutes, the silence is tender and good.

"What I said before I meant seriously, *cher ami*," Oskar says now. "Our colleagues are laughing about your forays into popular science. If public attention is so important to you . . . "

Sebastian makes an angry gesture with his hand and Liam, who has come back with crumbs on his lips, thinks it is meant for him. He forces himself onto Oskar's lap with a cheeky grin.

"Aren't you getting too old for this now?"

"Not me," Liam says. "You may be."

"Do you know," Oskar says to Liam, "that every time you sneak a biscuit, another world opens up, in which you haven't stolen one?"

"Parallel universes." Liam nods. "When Mom asks if I've had a biscuit, I always say yes and no. But that doesn't work with her."

Oskar starts laughing, and has to wipe his eyes with the backs of his hands. "How right you are!" he says. "If you'll let me, I'm going to quote you tomorrow evening."

"Tomorrow evening?" Sebastian asks.

"What are you doing over the weekend?"

Sebastian gets up to fetch him an ashtray.

"He's taking me to scout camp on Sunday," Liam says.

"And after that," Sebastian says, crashing the ashtray down on the table, "I'm barricading myself in my study and turning our understanding of the world upside down."

"What's the work of genius going to be called?"

"'A Long Exposure: or, On the Nature of Time.'"

"That suits you." Oskar suppresses another fit of laughter. "And what's Maike doing?"

"Three weeks' cycling in Airolo. So, what's going on tomorrow night?"

Oskar waves his hand mysteriously.

"In Airolo?" he repeats. "Alone?"

"Did you think I was bringing my senior registrar along, too?"

Maike has come back unnoticed, and is placing a bowl of tortellini on the table. Sebastian raises a palm and she gives him a high five, glancing sideways at Oskar at the same time. Unhappy that he is no longer the center of attention, Liam kicks his legs impatiently and slides off Oskar's lap. Oskar stands up and, ignoring the ashtray, walks over to the window and watches as his cigarette butt falls into the canal and is carried away by the current. Bonnie and Clyde are nowhere to be seen.

"While we're on the subject of holidays, perhaps you need a break, too." Maike helps Liam light the candles—the flames are almost invisible in the evening light. "You don't look as well as you normally do."

Oskar strolls back to the table, hands in his pockets. "Insomnia," he says.

"I'll pull out the bed in the study for you. It's quiet there."

"The doctor has given me something." Oskar taps his chest on the left side, as if he were wearing a jacket with inside pockets.

"Me too!" Liam shouts, running out of the room before anyone can stop him. A door slams, and a drawer in the bathroom is pulled open. When Liam returns, he is carrying a little plastic case in his palm.

"Travel sickness," Maike says. "He gets as sick as a dog on longer journeys."

"One for the way there, and one for the way back," Liam says proudly.

Oskar looks at the tablets earnestly. "They look exactly like mine. Conditions like ours are the price to pay for extraordinary genius."

"Really?" Liam's eyes grow round, and points of light shine in his pupils.

"Enough of that," Sebastian interrupts.

Oskar has sat down. He spears a piece of tortellini and holds his fork up in the air like a pointer.

"*Mes enfants*," he says. "There are areas of thought that we do not traverse unpunished. Headaches and a bad character are the least we must pay. I know what I'm talking about, Liam." When he stretches his hand out, Liam places his own in it quickly. "Your parents are lovely. But a bit too normal to know what real genius means."

"Don't talk nonsense to him," Maike says heatedly.

"Tell me," Oskar says, chewing thoughtfully on his pasta. "Is there some rocket in this, too?"

[6]

IN THE TWILIGHT, the chattering of the titmice is growing louder. They have a lot to talk about. A cloud of midges dance around an as-yet-unlit streetlamp, clearly drawn to it by the memory of light. Two swifts jaggedly circling their prey share the same memory.

Inside, the late evening has painted the walls red. Spoons are clinking on dessert plates; the wine in the glasses looks almost black. Liam is no longer allowed to talk and his pouting lower lip is hindering the consumption of his pudding. Maike is resting her chin in her hand, turning a spoon as she licks chocolate cream from it.

Quiet moments are as much a part of the Friday gatherings as confrontation, diplomacy, and barely averted war. In the reflective moments, it is mostly Maike who speaks. She enjoys talking about cycling, about the relentless heat on steep inclines with no shade, and the cool embrace of the wind as she goes downhill. About the quick changes in temperature in the layers of air, and about what freedom means—to reach a speed at which one can escape oneself. She says every time that speed preserves youth, and not only because physicists think that time passes more slowly for bodies in motion.

While Maike is speaking, Sebastian gazes at her intently. It is only when she laughs that he darts a quick glance at Oskar, as if there is something to share. He absorbs little of what she is saying. He is thinking about how much he loves Maike, yet how happy he is that he will have some time alone beginning the day after tomorrow. The thought of the three weeks ahead, which he will spend at his desk in isolation, brings on a shudder of anticipation. On the first day, he will fill the Volvo to the roof with shopping and then not leave the house at all. He will pull out the telephone cord, turn the television to the wall, and leave Oskar's folding bed down in the study. He will lock the doors to the other rooms and thereby erase them from the map of his daily habits. It will be quiet. He will be entirely undisturbed for a few weeks—the greatest luxury that Sebastian can imagine. While thinking about space and time, images will form in his mind, not unlike the abstract brush strokes of Maike's painters, who in their naive way, Sebastian has often thought, do nothing other than get closer to the true physical nature of things with the help of shapes and colors. For three whole weeks, Sebastian will relish the growth of the chain of letters across the computer screen, filling page after page until finally coming to the sentence that he has long kept ready for this purpose, the sentence that will form the crowning conclusion: "Thus, there is no more to say."

Sebastian's head sinks a bit lower, and his supporting hand pushes the flesh of his cheek upward. Oskar glances at him from across the table, humming in agreement now and then to keep Maike talking. As he does, he smiles at Sebastian, who has finally lost the thread and is secretly occupied with a question of physics. Once, Oskar would have been able to guess what his friend was thinking about by reading the play of his eyebrows and the silent movements of his lips, but those days are gone. He sits beside Sebastian's thoughts as if by a river that he knows is flowing constantly, but can neither see nor hear. Despite this, Oskar still enjoys the presence of his friend's river of thought. This means a great deal to him. Ever since his teenage years, he has felt as though he stumbled into the wrong century and is living the wrong life, while elsewhere—and above all, at another time—people like Einstein and Bohr are missing him in their discussions. Before the great European wars, there had been not only the necessary intellectual capacity but also the will to think a few things through to the end. Oskar wonders with longing what it would have been like to have been born in 1880. He can reconcile himself to very little in the world today, a world in which stupidity, hysteria, and hypocrisy reign, turning life into a carousel, rumbling along to music and spinning everything important away from the center, rendering it secondary. Sebastian's presence is a consolation; but when he thinks about his friend, he grows impatient again. Sebastian is a renegade, a traitor to the cause of achieving a new intellectual revolution a hundred years after Einstein and Bohr. Every new departure from the path of theoretical physics is a departure from the possibility of their being together. If there is something that Oskar will never give up, it is his desire to get Sebastian back.

When Oskar realizes that Maike's stream of talk has petered out, and that Sebastian is doing nothing other than tracing lines on the tablecloth with the handle of a spoon, he breaks the sudden silence by telling a vague anecdote about a young research assistant. The man got it into his head that he could come up with a brilliant idea, just as Heisenberg had while walking across an island, and he spent his entire salary on journeys to Sylt. There he tramped endlessly over one damn dike after another until he finally found out that the uncertainty principle had come to Heisenberg not on the island of Sylt, but on Heligoland—and then Oskar no longer knows where he is going with this, especially as the story isn't even true; it had merely worked well once in another situation.

IT IS ALMOST DARK NOW. The streetlamp in front of the house has failed to go on, and will now stay unlit through the night. The mountains have sent a tawny owl as their nighttime spy; it is sitting somewhere in the branches of the chestnut tree, calling sorrowfully as if through cupped hands. Cutlery lies crisscross on the plates. Liam's head is nodding slowly to the beat of his drowsiness. With his legs crossed and his arms folded, Oskar looks as if he is posing for a black-and-white photograph. Before the scene can freeze into a tableau, he stretches his back and draws breath into his lungs. It's clear that he is going to make an announcement. He runs his hand through his perfect hair and taps another filterless cigarette out of the packet.

"Before, we would probably have met at daybreak in some forest clearing," he says to Sebastian.

Liam's head jerks up, curiosity stealing over his sleepy face, while Sebastian finds his way out of his own thoughts with some difficulty. Finally he realizes that the darkness in the room is not due to his confusion, tips back in his chair, and switches on the overhead light. Maike suppresses a yawn and begins collecting cutlery halfheartedly on one of the plates.

"Nowadays," Oskar says, looking at his unlit cigarette from all angles, "there are microphones and TV cameras in forest clearings."

"You're talking in riddles," Maike says, a yawn forcing its way out as she finishes her sentence.

Oskar puts the cigarette down on the table still unlit, folds his napkin, and continues speaking to Sebastian.

"TV," he says. "The media. You like that, *n'est-ce pas*?"

There is something frightening in his voice that finally wipes the dreaminess off Sebastian's face. "What are you thinking of?"

"ZDF started a new science show some time ago—*Circumpolar*," Oskar says, standing up. "I've agreed that both of us will go on it. We're going to Mainz tomorrow evening." He is by the door now, raising a finger. "At eleven p.m. exactly. It's live."

Liam's excited whoop gives Oskar the opportunity to leave the room. The boy runs excitedly around the table and grabs Sebastian by the shirt. At the same time, Maike has run to the open window. She is shooing a fluttering something back into the darkness.

"That was a tawny owl!" she shouts. "Did you see that? Unbelievable!"

"Daddy," shouts Liam, "are you going to be on TV?"

"It feels more like I'm going to war."

The bathroom door slams shut. Sebastian tries to catch Maike's eye but she is still hanging half out of the window, looking down at the impossible bird. The last thing Sebastian feels like doing is laughing, but then his stomach begins to twitch. A laugh rises up in him like bubbles of air and shakes Liam's small body, which is leaning on his. When Sebastian hears the sound of his own laughter, he realizes that the die has been cast. Oskar has reckoned with Sebastian's pride, and has engineered everything so that it is impossible to refuse the challenge.

"You scoundrel!" he shouts down the hall.

Why this ridiculous word has occurred to him, he cannot say.

[7]

THERE ARE THREE EMPTY WINE BOTTLES left on the table. The window is closed and moths are flinging themselves against the glass. The grown-ups have moved to the living room; two rooms away, Liam is practicing insomnia. Low music weaves through the smoke curling up to the ceiling. Sebastian is sitting on the sofa, cradling an amber splash of whiskey in a tumbler, relishing the burning sensation in his stomach, not knowing if it is due to the whiskey or to happiness. Oskar and Maike are dancing, limbs heavy from the wine and from fatigue. Her eyes are closed and her cheek is on his shoulder. Sebastian looks on, feeling himself sink into the upholstery. His free hand scrabbles in the sofa cushions, as if searching for a lever that will stop this moment from disappearing. It is the last evening of happiness in this apartment, and it is a mercy—for Sebastian more than for the others—that humankind is not able to see into the future.

CHAPTER 2, IN SEVEN PARTS

The first half of the crime is committed. Man is everywhere surrounded by animals.

[1]

IT IS EARLY EVENING ON SUNDAY, two days later. Under a sky like this, Sebastian thinks, the world looks like a snow globe lying forgotten on God's shelf, not shaken for a long time. His eyes and his arms are tired, so he has opened the car window a little. The breeze tugs at his hair and his shirt. Outside, meadows drenched in rich light roll by and utility poles stand proudly next to their long shadows. The winding road resembles a painted landscape, and it manages to look like ski country even in the summer. On the horizon, the slopes have been cleared—only a few pine trees remain in forlorn clusters. Wire mesh holds back the scree where the mountain encroaches upon the road. In the ditch lies a black cat who had the bad luck to cross the street from the left.

When Sebastian is not looking at the landscape, he rests his eyes on the line in the middle of the road. Its white dashes fly toward him, then strangely slow before disappearing one by one under the car. The longer he looks at them, the more he thinks he hears a sound like quiet footsteps—the passing of time.

Last night he slept no more than two hours. Having finally fallen asleep at about four, despite a pounding heart and sheets drenched in sweat, he was woken at six by a tetchy Liam demanding his full attention for the results of a calculation: In twenty-six hours, thirteen minutes, and approximately ten seconds at the latest, he shouted, he would be with the scouts in the woods!

Sebastian woke with the feeling that he had survived a disaster that he could not remember. But he had to smile at Liam's excitement, and at the "approximately." He could imagine how his son had sat down with pen and paper to work out the exact number of seconds, which, at the moment he recorded them, trying to fix them in place, became no longer right. As Sebastian swung his feet out of the bed and placed them on the floor, the memory of the previous evening returned and settled on his shoulders like a cloak of lead. The radio in the bathroom spat out a cacophony of sounds when he pressed the button, as if the noise had been stored up overnight. Fearful that he would hear his own name coming out of the speaker, he switched it off immediately. In the shower, he turned the hot water up to full. As the steam hit the glass, he told himself over and over again, arguing rationally, that nothing terrible had happened. *Circumpolar* had a relatively small audience, and his colleagues at the institute did not watch popular science programs. In any case, no one would take what had happened as bleakly as he did. Now no one could remember anything for more than a couple of days anyway, especially if they had seen it on television.

A stone's throw away from the road, a fleet of shiny boats with horned figureheads glides over a sun-dappled lake. After a moment of confusion, Sebastian suddenly sees some deer—"Look, Liam! On your left!"—walking through a golden field of rape. And they're gone. Trees hug the edge of the road Sebastian has taken. The air smells of mushrooms, earth, and a rain that has not fallen for weeks. Sebastian is gripped by the desire to keep driving toward the south, as if the south is a place one can reach. He tries to whistle a tune—*"I haven't moved since the call came"*—but the sounds from his lips bear absolutely no relation to the melody in his head.

[2]

HE CALLED MAIKE IMMEDIATELY AFTER THE PROGRAM. He had not said good-bye to anyone, but had gone straight to the cloakroom to get his bag and wandered the corridors of the television studio looking for the exit. When he finally got reception, he called the apartment in Freiburg and listened, astounded, to Liam's excited whoops and Maike's cheerful voice. "That was really something!" she laughed, but changed her tone as soon as she realized the state Sebastian was in. She searched for words of comfort, but did not grasp the seriousness of the situation. The noise on the set meant that Maike had noticed nothing more than a heated scientific disagreement. Sebastian was giddy with relief. He decided to drive back to Freiburg instead of staying the night alone in the hotel in Mainz. For three hours he drove blindly on the autobahn, his brain churning relentlessly in an attempt, after twenty years, to analyze Oskar's personality, Oskar's character, Oskar's state of mind, and his entire nature from a completely different angle. He did not get very far. He found it difficult to concentrate and kept arriving at the same conclusion, like coming up against a wall: people like Oskar see life as a game that they have to win.

Maike was waiting for him at the door to their apartment with a freshly poured whiskey sour and, to his surprise, a similar conclusion: it is not enough for Oskar to win—others have to lose as well. He doesn't even love you as much as he loves the fight. It seemed that they had not talked about Oskar for years; but they came to the same conclusion that evening. For hours Maike listened to her husband's hate-filled tirade, said over and over again that she loved him, and told him that an idiot like Oskar ought to just drop dead. When Sebastian was finally drunk, she put him to bed.

Now he is swerving into the oncoming lane to avoid driving over the flattened remains of a hare. A bird of prey is sitting on the guardrail, eyes dark.

Perhaps the whole thing was a stroke of luck, Sebastian thinks. A warning sign, a narrow escape, so that a real tragedy will not happen. Of course he realizes what he has in Maike. But since last night, he feels more keenly than ever before that he does not really deserve this gift. Wealthy patrons put their hands on her bottom by way of greeting, something he knows only because she tells him about it; he no longer attends her gallery receptions. When Maike stands in front of the mirror in the bathroom, painting herself a prettier face (or so she thinks), he leans into the doorway and says that physics is a hard taskmaster, by which he means that he, too, has to work over the weekend. As soon as she is gone, he sits down with Liam on the floor in his room and talks about the theory of the big bang. The walls of their apartment are hung with large, framed pictures, in which Maike sees things that he does not understand. Sebastian knows the young artists, who always seem too small for their trousers and their spectacles, and who speak in sentences consisting only of nouns, faces averted. He knows the collectors, who spend a fortune on suits designed to make them look impoverished. That Sebastian has no cause to feel jealous is due neither to the lack of opportunity nor to the respectable nature of the art world.

As soon as she had gotten to know Dabbelink, she'd insisted on introducing the two men. Sebastian had shaken the senior registrar's hand at the cycling club, and felt pity for the thin, drawn man, who had limbs like twisted cable and a face etched with exhaustion. Two large full-stops for eyes, a comma for a nose, and a mere line of a mouth, even when laughing. Sebastian borrowed a bicycle from the club and ignored the looks from the other cyclists, whose faces reflected the exact number of times Maike and Dabbelink had met.

The senior registrar overtook them at the first steep section of the Schauinsland. Maike good-humoredly accompanied her husband as he pushed his bike on foot. They met Dabbelink again on the summit of the mountain, which he had conquered in an incredible thirty-five minutes. He was lying on the ground with his calves on the seat of a bench, lifting his torso and alternately touching his forehead to his left and then his right knee. While they were having coffee, he gazed impatiently at the view, as if he was thinking about how many mountains it would have been possible to conquer during that time. The last Sebastian saw of Ralph Dabbelink that day was a back covered in yellow polyamide, leaning dangerously close to the pavement as he sped downward in a tight curve. Maike and Sebastian had taken their time, and had stopped at a good restaurant for a meal on the way back through the valley of Günterstal.

"Are you OK?"

Liam is too quiet.

[3]

SEBASTIAN ADJUSTS THE REARVIEW MIRROR so that he can see his son. Liam is leaning against a corner of the backseat with his head tipped to one side. His body is held in place only by the safety belt, a broad band across his neck and torso. The travel sickness pills are obviously working. When they left the house, Liam had waved as if they were off to sail around the world. Sebastian closes his window and reaches out to switch off the radio, which isn't even on. Sleep is definitely the best thing for his son at the moment.

The farther they get from Freiburg, the more freely Sebastian's thoughts flow. He locks his arms; a yawn pushes air into the farthest corners of his lungs. He will have plenty of time to be angry with himself over the coming weeks. He is angry not only because he had once again found it necessary to accept a challenge from someone stronger, but also because he had not felt himself to be above accepting a challenge from someone weaker. He writes articles such as the one in *Der Spiegel* because the scientific journals do not publish his work. He tells himself that there is nothing dishonorable about wanting to bring his ideas to a wider public. But when he thinks about Oskar reading these pieces, he flushes.

The Many-Worlds Interpretation, Sebastian wrote, was nothing less than an escape from the central paradox of human existence. From the viewpoint of classical physics, it was still impossible to explain why the universe was arranged for the needs of biological life with such astonishing precision. For example, mankind would not exist if space had expanded at a speed that was only the tiniest bit faster or slower. At the time of the big bang, the probability that a universe with the necessary conditions would come into existence had been 10^{-59}. That meant the existence of the earth was as unlikely as winning the lottery nine times in a row. From a stochastic point of view, mankind could be viewed as nonexistent. Man was completely overwhelmed by the improbability of his own existence, and this was precisely the cause of his urgent longing for a Creator.

Those who did not believe in God, he'd posited in the article, had to call upon statistics. If not just one universe had been created in the big bang, but 10^{59} different universes, then it was no wonder that one of them could support life. The only logical, non-theological explanation of human existence lay in thinking of space (and therefore time) as an enormous heap of worlds that was expanding minute by minute. A growing time-foam, in which every bubble was its own world. "Everything that is possible happens"—*Der Spiegel* had liked the caption.

Nothing in the article is wrong. Rather, such thoughts belong to a realm where "wrong" and "right" barely play a role. But that is exactly what provokes Oskar's biting mockery. *That's exactly how stupid people behave!* Sebastian hears him say. *They take a question of some kind, any old "why," hurl it against the world, and are amazed when they do not get a sensible answer.* Cher ami, *every bird on the branch that just twitters and refrains from this ridiculous questioning is cleverer than you!*

SEBASTIAN LIFTS A HAND FROM THE STEERING WHEEL and wipes the beads of sweat off his upper lip. Even worse than Oskar's contempt is the fact that his work on these theories is taking over his life. He has started shutting himself in the study almost every day after dinner. There he broods over his papers until some fragment of an equation starts whirling through his head like an abandoned LP. Some nights he does not dare go to bed, because the noise of his thoughts can increase to an intolerable level in the dark stillness of the bedroom. Maike came to him once, long after midnight. Her bare feet in the hall sounded like the footsteps of a little girl. When he looked up, she was standing in front of him in her nightdress, looking small and fragile. Stay with us, she said. Before he could reply she had turned away and vanished. Sebastian did not follow her, because he was not sure if he had really seen her at all.

After nights like those, he barely knows which world he is in when morning comes. At breakfast, he sat down not as a husband next to his wife, but as someone who is shocked to find two strangers in his own home. Liam suddenly seems far too old, his childish laughter false, his beloved face unfamiliar. Sitting with his family, Sebastian feels as if he has stumbled into an unknown universe by mistake. This terrible feeling of being a guest in his own life has been with him for a long time. Since Liam's birth, there have been many moments when he has felt like an impostor, as if he has cheated his way to some good fortune which was not his by right, and for which he would be severely punished. At times like this, he wants to put aside his skin like a borrowed coat, and destroy everything he loves before it can be taken away by some counterbalancing force of justice. It is only recently that he has begun to think that this feeling is not a personal problem, but a matter of physics.

He had once described these confused feelings to Oskar as the side effects of a big idea. Oskar had pointed an index finger at him sternly. *Don't trouble yourself with your neuroses*, he said. *You'll never be a great man. Everything that has meaning for you bears your surname. That's how you can recognize it.*

Sebastian was incandescent with rage about this remark at the time. Now he finds Oskar's words calming. As a child, he often lay in bed tortured by the question of whether, faced with a barbaric murderer, he would save his father or his mother. Now, if he had to choose between Maike and physics, or even between Maike and the rest of the world (with the exception of Liam), his wife would have absolutely nothing to fear, despite all his scientific and other obsessions.

He took her to the station in the afternoon. When the train drew alongside the platform, he grasped her arm and told her he loved her. She patted him on the back like a good horse, told him to take care of himself, and passed her lightweight racing bike to the conductor. She blurred into a light patch behind the carriage window, and Sebastian's arm started to ache with waving. He felt himself getting smaller, shrinking constantly until he disappeared behind the long curve of the tracks.

This holiday is an exception, he thinks now. After this, he will not endanger his family's happiness any longer in pursuit of a frenzied obsession. He will forget last night's pathetic TV program and complete "A Long Exposure." And he will ring Oskar and ask him not to visit on the first Friday of the month any longer.

As soon as he has decided this, he feels free, as if a thorn has been pulled from his flesh. He checks on Liam in the rearview mirror and looks at his peaceful sleeping face for a long time. A wide-tailed buzzard is tearing white intestines from the next piece of roadkill by the edge of the pavement. Since Sebastian started noticing birds of prey, he has counted more than fifteen of them. They sit in the trees, or even by the roadside, staring at the traffic with eyes unadorned by lashes. It seems to him that there are an unnatural number of them. Or, worse still, it is always the same one.

At Geisingen the Volvo leaves the country road and moves onto the A81.

[4]

THE PUMP GURGLES AS IF IT IS SUCKING PETROL out of the tank instead of filling it. While the digits race over the price display, Sebastian uses a sponge to scratch the yellow and purple bodies of flies from the windshield. He buys a chocolate bar at the counter and drops it into the side pocket of his door when he gets back to the car, as Liam is still asleep. He turns the key in the ignition gingerly, as if this will dampen the noise of the starting engine. The car moves slowly around the petrol station.

The parking lot behind the building is almost empty. A couple is sitting on camping stools next to a caravan, having their dinner. A young woman is walking her dog on the strip of grass, a light wind blowing her hair across her face. The sun is slanting through the tops of the trees; as the light hits the branches it breaks into mawkish stars. Sebastian stops the Volvo once again, next to some dirty trucks. He has started out of an empty blackness several times over the last few kilometers. Asleep for a split second. He needs a rest.

The air smells of axle grease and cooling engines. Swinging his arms and hopping from one leg to another, Sebastian goes over to the edge of the service area. The wind sings in chorus through the railings. In the valley there is an insignificant little south German town—its roads shine like rivers. Lake Constance is not yet in sight, but it will appear between the trees in half an hour at most. They will drive its length and cross the invisible border to Austria at the easternmost end before they reach their destination near Bregenz. Latitude 47°50' N and longitude 9°74' E. He has looked up the coordinates in an atlas with Liam. There is always a vast amount of information in the world, just not the information you might need in order to know what will happen in the next second. To avoid having to stop again, Sebastian decides to go to the toilet.

He is washing his hands when the phone rings. He dries his hands on his trousers hurriedly, wedges his mobile between shoulder and ear, and leans against the door to push it open. In the hallway a fat woman in a surgical green housecoat points at a plate with a single coin lying in the middle of it.

"Maike?" Sebastian ignores the toilet attendant and walks down the corridor with his head bent. "Did you get there all right? How is the hotel?"

"I'm sorry to disturb you. I'd like to ask you to stand still for a minute and listen to me."

The voice in the distance sounds familiar to Sebastian. It is young enough to belong to one of the few female students in the institute. He takes the phone from his ear so he can look at the display. Unknown number.

"Who is this?"

"Vera Wagenfort."

In his head, Sebastian goes through all the women in his faculty. There is no Vera. "Listen, this is not a good moment for me. I'm just leaving a public toilet, if you must know."

"I'm saying this for the last time. Stand still. For your own sake."

This woman is not trying to sell anything; she has also not dialed the wrong number. A cold shock cements Sebastian's legs to the tiled floor. There is a glass case in front of him, filled with colorful stuffed animals, watches, and toy cars. Liam loves these machines. One euro sets in motion a claw, which can be steered and lowered with two buttons.

It's generally possible to grab hold of something, but when the arm moves back, it bumps into the edge of the chute, and the prize almost always falls back into the case. Liam never lets lengthy explanations of the chances of success spoil his fun. If he were here now he would certainly be cajoling a stray coin out of Sebastian.

"First, I must ask you to keep calm at all costs. My employer thinks that you can do that."

The woman sounds as if she is reading from a piece of paper.

"The most important thing is: tell nobody. Do you understand? *No-bo-dy*. Leave the building now. I'll call you back immediately."

The line goes dead. Sebastian shakes the phone as if he is hoping an explanation will fall out of it. His eyes meet those of a pink toy dog, which seems to be looking at him pleadingly. He finally tears himself free, clears the final stretch of tiled floor, and opens the door to the outside.

Inside the air-conditioned service station, he has forgotten how warm the evening is. Images from the journey still fill his head. When he closes his eyes, the broken white line flies toward him, a bird of prey looks on, a dead cat is at the side of the road. Sebastian walks around the building and stands on the spot surveying the parking lot. There are the trucks. The caravan is gone. And the space where the Volvo was is also empty. Sebastian does not wonder for a moment if he might have parked elsewhere. He knows exactly where he left his car. The space is unbearably empty, emptier than anywhere else on the planet. It takes several seconds for him to understand this.

He walks in an arc across the asphalt divided by white lines, and although his stride gets longer with every step, he feels unable to move from his spot, as in a nightmare. It is only when he gets to the exit ramp, and is looking at the autobahn with its shiny cars disappearing at high speed over the hill, that the rise and fall of the occasional horn brings him to his senses. The frequency of sound waves, Sebastian often explains to his students, depends on the relative motion between the observer and the source. The Doppler effect. It's the same with light. If Sebastian's senses were a little sharper, he would register that the vehicles moving away from him are red while those coming toward him are blue. Every one blue, like the Volvo that he has lost.

He runs across the grass, past overturned bins and crudely made picnic tables. Some distance away, two truck drivers are standing next to the raised hood of an engine, cradling cups of coffee in front of their stomachs, watching him. For some reason, Sebastian has his hands in his trouser pockets, which slows him down as he runs. His mouth is already open and he wants to shout, but something clicks in his brain. *Tell no-bo-dy.*

"Lost something, mate?"

The fat one's voice is too high for his girth. Sebastian waves the question aside and forces himself to slow down to an innocuous stroll. He has to dictate every movement to his limbs and he almost stumbles; he must look like a madman. He comes to a halt again in the middle of that ghastly void where his car had been. His heart feels constricted in his body—it is looking for a way out through his left lung. Growing in the hollows of a manhole cover is a fleshy plant that Sebastian has seen in Japanese rock gardens. The parking lot swims around him in a blur. This is what the world looks like from one of the roundabouts that Liam preferred over everything else in the playground before he grew too old for them.

Sebastian's temples are cold as ice. Time is a card index with an infinite number of cards. He starts flicking through it, looking for the parallel universe in which he had not left Liam sleeping in the car. Or one in which Maike had not come up with the idea of scout camp. Or even one in which he had studied mechanical engineering and lived in America. He takes a step to one side to make room for the Volvo, which any moment now will emerge from thin air in the spot where it was parked before. Sebastian grips his forehead. The truck behind him shakes and rattles like a beetle before takeoff, angles its nose to one side, and rolls toward the exit. Vera Wagenfort. *Wagen fort*. Car gone. Jokers, jokers everywhere. All will be revealed.

A family is returning to its yellow Toyota. Two children climb into the backseat. The girl is Liam's age.

Sebastian's phone rings.

5

THIS TIME HIS BODY does not require specific instructions—it reacts before it has received any orders. Lips, tongue, and teeth crash together and scream into the mobile.

"What do you want? I can get anything!"

A hand lands over his mouth and stops him from speaking; it is his own hand. There is an uncertain pause on the other end of the line. A woman clears her throat.

"Herr Professor, I've been instructed to give you a message. A single sentence. I've been told you will understand. Are you ready?"

"My son," Sebastian groans.

"Excuse me, I don't know what this is all about. I just have to make sure that you understand the sentence. Shall we continue?"

It is the woman's friendliness that does it to him. He never knew that pain could come from so deep within the human body. He never knew how it could claw at his throat, desperately trying to reach his brain. Vera Wagenfort takes a breath. Then she says it.

"Dabbelink must go."

The sun has set behind the treetops and taken the shadows with it to preserve them till the next day. There are still a few cars parked here and there, but not a soul in sight. A random wind races over the ground, chasing empty paper cups in circles and flapping his trousers.

Sebastian looks at his watch as if he had an important appointment and no time for further chat. Just after nine thirty. The time tells him nothing. He has never felt so alone.

"Would you repeat that?" he asks.

"I've been told to add this when questions are asked: 'Then everything will be all right.' Did you get that?"

"You can't do this," Sebastian says. "I'm begging you."

"Apart from that, you probably know the rules: No police. Not a word to anyone. Not even to your wife."

There is a pause, as if they are in the middle of a difficult personal conversation and don't know how to continue. The caller's voice is not unpleasant. Sebastian imagines her to be a healthy young woman. Perhaps, he thinks, we would get along well under different circumstances.

"Go into the restaurant in the service station," the woman says, rustling her piece of paper. "Are you still listening?"

"Yes."

"There is a service station and a restaurant where you are right now, isn't there?"

"Yes."

"Sit down near the counter. Get a beer and a newspaper. It might be a while before I call again. Keep your phone on."

"Wait!" Sebastian shouts. "I will— We can—"

The buttons on his phone have always been too small for his fingers. At last he finds the list of calls received. Two calls from "Unknown number." He would have liked to ring back and explain that he has absolutely no experience with such things, that he needs a few tips. He also wants to ask why he of all people has been chosen. What he should do now. And how. And when. Just as Vera Wagenfort suspected, the rules are actually clear to him. They are shown several times a week on television in those badly lit thrillers Sebastian has never been able to stand. Absurdly, none of the films ever taught you what you were supposed to think and feel in such a situation. They also did not teach you what to do with a three-word sentence. It is always three-word sentences that change the life of a human being in a decisive manner. *I love you. I hate you. Father is dead. I am pregnant. Liam has disappeared. Dabbelink must go.* After a three-word sentence, one is totally alone.

Sebastian spends a while trying to remember the behavior of people with time on their hands. He widens his stance, folds his arms, and drops his chin to his chest. An empty paper cup rolls over the asphalt. Sebastian looks at it and waits for the merciful effects of shock.

When he raises his head after a few minutes, the surroundings look unnaturally clear to him, as if seen through diving goggles. His breath is even and his heart is not beating faster than once per second. He looks around (the swerving beam from a pair of headlights, a woman in a pink coat getting out of her sports car) and the innermost forces that hold the universe together are within his grasp now, if he felt like thinking about it. He thinks he knows now what they want from him. He even knows who did it. He can imagine how they pressed a chloroformed rag to Liam's mouth and nose as he slept, and brought him to some apartment or other, or perhaps straight to the intensive care unit of some hospital. It is easy for doctors to keep a child in an artificial coma for as long as they give Sebastian to complete his task. It would be just as easy for them to get rid of Liam forever. They know that he cannot rely on getting his son back, but that he still has no choice other than to follow their instructions.

If Dabbelink talks, Sebastian thinks, the entire hospital will collapse. A medical director has done something wrong, and now he needs not only the person who knows about it to die, but the right person to kill him. They have found that person. Sebastian's wife is close to the victim, and jealousy is one of the most common motives for murder. The kidnappers probably know that Sebastian understands all this. Intelligent people can be honest with each other. Sebastian starts laughing. He presses his clothing to his body with both hands to stop the wind flapping it as he walks through the dusk to the service station.

[6]

THERE ARE NO TABLES NEAR THE FOOD COUNTER, only a refrigerated display in which the same green apple glistens over and over again. Sebastian estimates the distances as painstakingly as a land surveyor until he is sure which seat is nearest the bar. He picks one next to a towering plant, which on closer inspection turns out to be made of plastic, and therefore out of countless plants. The weight of the earth compressed them over millions of years into a greasy substance until mankind was developed enough to extract it and make artificial branches and leaves. The chemical exhalations of the plant are so strong that Sebastian feels nausea rising. He marshals his thoughts as if he is whistling a pack of barking dogs into order, and stands up again to get a beer and a newspaper in accordance with his instructions.

The restaurant has windows all around. The dusk presses close against the panes of glass. Three tables away, a man in a suit is eating something brown with gravy, dabbing his mouth with his napkin after every bite and turning his wrist to look at his watch. Behind the next potted plant, the young woman in the pink coat is composing a long text message. All the diners in the restaurant look as though their cars are waiting outside. Without a car, Sebastian is a castaway among sea captains and will surely be recognized as such by the way he is glancing around wildly. The woman smiles when her mobile beeps. Perhaps she is waiting for a lover, with whom she will betray her husband on service-station furniture. Perhaps she calls herself Vera Wagenfort at these assignations. Strangely, Sebastian would not give a damn.

The first gulp of beer hits him like a dull thud in his arms and legs. As the shock wears off, so does the feeling that he has understood everything. Sebastian realizes that he was wrong in thinking he had fully grasped the situation. In physics, when an attempt is made to go beyond the limits of the knowable, mathematics takes over from the imagination. But the sentence "Dabbelink must go" cannot be expressed as a mathematical formula, so it stays outside the parameters of Sebastian's understanding. This has consequences. Until now, Sebastian has looked toward the future believing that he is looking out at an open prospect. From this day onward, he will be looking down at his feet. His new world is the little patch of ground beneath his next step. He won't run across exit ramps anymore. He will not even try to locate the perpetrators in his mind. He will simply do what is being asked of him. As cleanly as possible. Surgically. His blackmailers have chosen him because they need someone who will do the job properly. Sebastian will do everything to make sure he does not disappoint them. Resolutely he opens the newspaper to the contents page.

When the clock above the bar displays ten thirty, his mobile phone has only one bar of battery left. Almost as soon as he picks it up, a ring pierces the air. Tables and chairs crash into each other and settle down again as the woman in the pink coat stands, pressing her phone to her cheek. Nodding and talking at the same time, she walks out of the restaurant. While Sebastian is looking after her, there is another ring. He cannot muster the same sense of shock.

"Hello?"

"Sebastian, you won't believe how beautiful it is here!"

The sharp pain in his gut had died down with very little resistance after he had sat down in the restaurant. But Maike's voice brings back the pain. Between her words Sebastian feels he can hear his son, and he feels this so keenly that Maike must surely notice it. "In twenty-six hours, thirteen minutes, and approximately ten seconds, I'll be with the scouts in the woods!" Sebastian has to get off the phone and conserve his battery. Maike chats about misty mountains and little lakes looking up at the sky like blue eyes. She talks about swimming pools, the sauna, and massages. Cuba libres at the bar.

"Maike!"

That comes out harsher than intended. Sebastian does not have the patience to try for a specific tone of voice.

"What's up?" A faint reflection of his shock colors her voice.

"I have to get off the phone. The battery is low."

"Did everything go OK with Liam?"

"He slept through the whole journey."

"Are you back at home?"

"Almost."

"Are you sure everything is all right?"

"Of course! Maike, the battery . . . "

A little jingle sounds and the display shows two intertwined fishes. Sebastian has never understood what the phone manufacturer meant to say with this symbol. When he tries to turn his mobile on again, he gets as far as typing in his PIN before the display goes dead. He feels like letting his head sink into the open newspaper, only to realize it is already there. Three centimeters away from his right eye, a blond man is laughing out of a photograph. It is he. He knows the caption by heart. "Everything that is possible happens. Freiburg professor explains the theories of the time-machine murderer."

When someone calls his name, he does not even have the strength for astonishment. The cashier comes to the table—the yellow and red pattern on her apron swims before his eyes.

A woman rang but did not wish to speak to him. She just wanted to leave a message to let Sebastian know that he could return to his car when he wished.

[7]

THE STREETLAMPS AT THE EDGE OF THE PARKING LOT are wearing broad skirts of light. Without the trucks flanking it, the spot where Sebastian had parked is no longer a gap, just a random space on the black asphalt. Now everything is a gap apart from the Volvo, which is standing in its previous position as if it had never been gone. Sebastian's shadow hurries before him and casts itself against the driver's door; it is unlocked and the backseat is empty. Liam's bags are gone. The floor of the trunk needs a good clean.

The ignition does not react at the turn of the key. Sebastian bends down and finds a couple of wires hanging loose beneath the dashboard. As he twists the two ends together, the engine springs to life. When his shin brushes against the tangle of wires, the headlights flicker and the engine splutters. Sebastian spreads his knees as far apart as he can, gets into gear, and drives off.

There are a handful of cars on the A81, heading toward unknown destinations. After the first few miles, Sebastian turns on the radio. *I haven't moved since the call came.* He sings along quietly in a monotone.

CHAPTER 3, IN SEVEN PARTS

High time for the murder. Everything goes according to plan at first, and then it doesn't. Showing that waiting is not without its dangers.

[1]

THE HOUSE IS IN THE FARTHEST CORNER of a cul-de-sac and keeps its distance from the other buildings, proud to be the home of a single person. Even in the darkness, you can tell that children do not play in the garden and that the lawn is mown by hired help. There is a stone statue on the strip of grass by the driveway, a crane stretching its neck up toward the sky, prevented from taking off by the plinth on the ground. It has the blank air of an object that brings pleasure to no one.

Sebastian did not even have to ring directory assistance to find Dabbelink's address. He simply looked in Maike's address book. He has been crouching behind the trash cans for two hours with his back against the wall of the house. He has watched a glorious sunset through the gap between the bins (the sky a three-colored sea, mountainous clouds with a halo of gold) and is feeling melancholy, as one does after witnessing the optical phenomena of the evening sky. Heedless of his feelings, night has fallen, and Sebastian has spent the time since looking at the flickering windows of the apartments next door. At least three living rooms are watching the same film. There was a fire a little while ago, and then a shoot-out. And now the murderer is taking his time explaining to his final victim the meaning of the plot so far. There follows the hectic flicker of hand-to-hand fighting, interrupted by the colorful flash of an advertisement break. Sebastian thinks he knows who the murderer is.

He shifts his weight and stretches his legs out from time to time in order not to tumble into the driveway at the decisive moment. A snail is moving astonishingly quickly across the spade that Sebastian found in the shed. Every time he looks at the spade it seems a little bit farther away from him, and he pulls it closer.

From the long spells of pale light shining through the windows, Sebastian can tell that the neighbors are now watching the late evening news. The doors and windows of Dabbelink's house look as if they have been painted on. Just as Sebastian is starting to doubt whether the senior registrar will ever return to this place, the garden bursts into life. Headlights shine on a couple of trees and then cast them back into the darkness. Shadows scurry across the grass. The fence leans to the left and the crane revolves. Sebastian has tucked his legs under his body and is crouching in the position of a sprinter, three fingers of each hand pressed into the gravel. The gate slides open. The car stops a few centimeters from the house. The handbrake sighs and the headlights go out. Sebastian watches through the gap in the bins as Dabbelink gets out, yawns theatrically, stretching his arms, and turns to get his bag out of the backseat. There is no unexpected woman sliding out of the passenger seat; no one is walking past the gate. Dabbelink is alone.

Sebastian is basically a weak person. His friends and colleagues may say that he is strong-willed, but actually, he thinks, as he looks at Dabbelink, a strong will is precisely the mark of a weak person. For only the weak constantly desire things. They have to work and strive, experiment and practice, whereas strong people achieve things quite naturally. Some days, Sebastian can barely muster the energy to sit on a bench by the Dreisam and watch the river flow by in front of him. How much more energy he needs to reach out and clasp the handle of a spade! Sebastian puts the snail down on the gravel gently.

Dabbelink has been kind enough to stay in the same position while these thoughts have been running through Sebastian's mind. The sound of his own footsteps seems strange to him, as if someone else were walking in long strides across the driveway—a man whom Sebastian is duty-bound to follow as an invisible observer. The senior registrar has heard the crunch of the gravel, too. He stands up and looks at Sebastian uncomprehendingly. The spade is raised high and the blow falls with a dull sound. Dabbelink draws himself up instead of falling down, and his face is surprisingly relaxed. Sebastian draws back to make a fresh attack, turns the edge of the spade downward, and strikes his victim on the head with full force. Immediately, everything human is wiped off Dabbelink's face. There is a smell of grazed knees—sickly sweet and metallic. The car's central locking system clicks in five places as the senior registrar's hand clutches the key. Dabbelink falls over, catches himself, staggers, and holds on to his car with slippery fingers. The next blow makes his arms and legs jerk as if an electrical current were running through him. But his body still resists collapsing to the ground. He lurches to one side and Sebastian strikes into the emptiness; before he realizes what is going on, Dabbelink begins to run. Blindly, perhaps even heedlessly, he brushes against a fir tree, crashes into the gate, and manages to close his hands around the railing. He heaves himself up and over and falls into bottomless darkness. The televisions flicker luridly. Sebastian hears screams, shots, and the anxious whining of American police sirens. The reflections from the screens reach into the garden and move over the front of the house. The flickering takes on a regular rhythm—a blue light circling nearer and nearer. The air smells of freshly cut grass.

[2]

SEBASTIAN RUBS HIS EYES WITH HIS THUMBS: this is no good. Instead of coming up with a plan for murder, his imagination is coming up with schlock B-horror flicks. He washes his face at the sink and reaches for a tea towel, which has Maike's fabric softener in every fiber and so does not absorb any moisture but merely spreads it over his skin. Then he stands still, listening to the hum of the fridge, which with sufficient imagination can sound like the crashing waves of a distant ocean.

Quite unexpectedly, he slept for two hours during the night, waking only when the doorbell rang. Dabbelink was standing in the hallway in his yellow jersey, asking in a very friendly manner if he could borrow a pair of poultry shears. Sebastian woke screaming, soaked in sweat. He sank back into bed, closed his eyes, and tried to let the memory of the previous day trickle into his consciousness as slowly as possible. There was a vortex spinning deep within him, with a strong gravitational pull. This was fear. Sebastian realized that it was possible to be afraid of absolutely everything—getting up, staying in bed, the nighttime, and the day ahead. Most frightening of all was the thought that this fear would itself bring further misfortune. The thought of Liam was paralyzing. Sebastian had to avoid thinking about his son at all costs. He recast the situation in his mind: Liam was not there because he was at scout camp. Sebastian would take advantage of his family's absence in order to get rid of a rival. He had been assigned this motive by his blackmailers, and he was determined to follow their plans to the letter. Obeying them would bring freedom, he thought, it was his only chance. He was subscribing to a widespread fallacy, but it did not disturb him. He felt better for it, in fact.

When he opened his eyes, a man was standing at the foot of the bed. A paper bag covered his head. When Sebastian tried to escape, his feet got tangled in the sheets. He hit his head against the corner of the wardrobe, and woke up on the sofa in front of the television. The screen was filled with the very large mouth of a woman singing tunelessly. Sebastian padded around the apartment gingerly. The furniture cowered in the kind of muffled silence that comes with blocked-up ears. He touched the leaves of a potted plant cautiously, picked up stray letters and turned them over, and checked the books on the shelves and found they were in order. On the way to the bathroom, he glanced into the bedroom through the open door and noticed an unfamiliar bulge under the bedspread. Walking up to it quietly, he realized that the hump was rising and falling in time with his own breathing. He pulled the covers back and looked himself in the face, eyes torn open and lips stretched in a horrible grin. Time and space split apart in a sudden jerk, and Sebastian was lying in the place of his doppelgänger. He dug all ten fingers into his thighs, hit the wall repeatedly with his palms until they hurt, and finally got up and drew the curtains. A greenish strip of dawn was glimmering over the roofs of the houses.

THE SHOWER DID NOTHING TO CHANGE the impression of having woken too little, or too often, of being caught in a world where the rules have shifted. The worst thing was that there was absolutely no-bo-dy left who could help him out of this trap. He was to talk to no-bo-dy, and could ask no-bo-dy if he had merely dreamt the events of yesterday. Or if, on the contrary, at that service station on the A81, he had woken from a dream that had lasted decades. Reality, Sebastian thought, is nothing more than an agreement between six billion people.

He had been forced to unilaterally renege on the overarching agreement. So waking in the morning no longer offered any guarantees. He had no choice but to face the new day without a certificate of authenticity.

Cold water brought strength back into his limbs. Wearily, he suppressed an urge to rush into his study and destroy all his theoretical writings, which suddenly seemed to him the work of the devil—aiming only to turn time and space upside down and thus cast into chaos the conditions required for the survival of reason. At eight o'clock sharp, he rang the number of the scout camp in Gwiggen and said that his son had come down with a sudden attack of flu. A girl with an Austrian accent replied that the deposit paid for Liam could not be refunded. Sebastian did not scream or cry, but simply said good-bye.

After this success, he decided to take care of the damaged Volvo. He needed a reliable car and it felt good to occupy himself initially with an everyday matter. So he drove into town, past the backdrop of a perfectly staged Monday morning—young men in suits cycling through the streets with briefcases on their panniers, visibly exulting in the beautiful weather. On the way, Sebastian decided on three principles to follow: twenty-four hours' planning at most, the same for the execution of the deed, and a 100 percent guarantee of success.

Of course it would also be a question of leaving as few traces as possible, but that was just a vague matter of chance, not a necessary condition.

A mechanic with ponytail and steel-rimmed glasses tugged at the loose ignition cables and congratulated Sebastian on his good luck in still having a car at all. Sebastian did not enter into the question of whether he had been lucky or unlucky, but promised to return in an hour. At a high table in a bakery, he drank coffee. On the radio there was a report on the government's new plans for reform. The woman in the bakery was selling bread rolls with names that sounded like fitness products and discussing with her customers the imminent end of the world. The only advantage in Sebastian's situation was that none of this mattered to him any longer. He paid. He picked up his car—repaired and fully cleaned, too, thanks to a special offer at the garage that week. Even the trunk had been vacuumed.

IT IS JUST AFTER TWELVE. Sebastian hangs the tea towel on the hook and walks over to the balcony door. The sun has risen over the ridge of the roof, and casts a rectangle of light between the trees in the courtyard. A cat parades over the cobblestones, lies down on its side, and stretches one leg in the air to clean itself. The scene is simple and clear; the trip into town has done Sebastian good. But he is no nearer to his goal of coming up with a proper plan. Every imagined attempt to approach Dabbelink ends in fiasco. At least he feels no pity when he thinks of Dabbelink—only hatred. It seems to him that Dabbelink is, in some secret fashion, responsible for all of this. Sebastian is wary of this very useful conception on moral grounds. He is also happy that Dabbelink has neither wife nor children—not out of human kindness, but for logistical reasons.

He pulls open all the kitchen drawers for the third time, and also opens the little cupboard under the sink.

Bread knife and kebab skewers. A corkscrew and a potato masher. A hammer.

Although Sebastian knows that human beings like killing, he has never thought the process would be simple. He is annoyed by TV films in which a distraught woman reaches for the fallen pistol on the floor and kills her attacker with one clean shot to the head, despite the recoil and a lack of weapons training. The way Sebastian sees it, normal people can perhaps operate a gun, but will never hit their target. Normal people handle a variety of possible murder weapons every day—parcel string, plastic bags, rolling pins, not to mention kebab skewers (have these ever actually been used?)—but still wouldn't know how to employ them in order to kill.

Ethyl alcohol. Insecticide.

Sebastian seriously considers getting a professional to do the job. It would be simple for an anesthetist to get the necessary drug, then ring Dabbelink and tell him some cock-and-bull story. They would meet at his house for the handover. They would clink glasses of red wine. With luck, it would look like suicide.

Pastry fork. Duct tape. Poultry shears.

Right at the back is an old bottle without a label, filled to the brim with a clear fluid. Sebastian opens it and sniffs. Nothing. Absolutely, markedly nothing.

His mother had always kept the distilled water for ironing high up on a shelf in the laundry room. If you were to drink it, the dead water would seep into your cells, bloat them, and make you explode. A cool wind touches the back of Sebastian's neck. Dabbelink's racing bike is kept in the shelter in front of the cycling club. Two water bottles are beneath the saddle.

When Oskar was asked about his methods at the university, he replied that the art of thinking did not lie in finding the answers, but in teasing answers from the questions. Perhaps, Sebastian thinks, the human being is also a problem that carries his solution within him. Perhaps that is what those who study the humanities call fate. A machine, like Dabbelink, has to die cycling.

Bent over the computer keyboard in the study, Sebastian cannot stop thinking about Oskar. Oskar in the full glory of his infallibility. Perhaps he, too, would be unable to come up with a way out of this straight off, but he would know how to rise above by force of intellect. For a moment, Sebastian feels ashamed of wanting Oskar's support at this of all times. Then he found the right article on the Internet. Contrary to popular wisdom, drinking distilled water is safe. Some health fanatics even consider it good for you as it is sterile. Sebastian reads the article as if it is his own death sentence.

Immediately after this, he is sitting at the kitchen table once again, head buried in his hands. He is a physicist, not a chemist, and certainly not a criminal; he is probably not even very practical minded. They have chosen the wrong man. For a frenzied half hour, he imagines an alternative past peppered with if-onlys. If only he had not set his heart on a couple of weeks of undisturbed work. If only he had not immersed himself in useless theories. If only he had used his time with Maike and Liam fully and wrung every bit of happiness out of it. Now he is being punished for his inattention.

When he stands up to get a glass out of the cupboard, his spine bears the memory of his tensed posture. The distilled water tastes of nothing, a liquid corpse. Sebastian suppresses his revulsion and drinks. After the second glass he is able to cry. He drinks a third, and his tears flow into his collar. The sound of crockery rattling in the apartment below comes through the open balcony door, marking the boundary beyond which an alien everyday is progressing relentlessly. If it were within his power to do so, Sebastian would silence the clinking plates, the hands that are stacking them, the twittering of the birds, the distant grumble of car engines, and the entire, bright harlequin world outside with a single blow.

As he stands there motionless, letting his damp cheeks dry naturally, enjoying the brief moment of peace after his outburst, his exhausted brain tosses forth something else Oskar has said. *For you, my diligent friend, thinking is hard labor. A solution that is obvious the moment it springs to mind is best.*

Sebastian leaves the apartment and walks down the stairs to the cellar, where his seldom-used tools are kept.

[3]

SEBASTIAN HAD NOT NEEDED THE MOBILE PHONE alarm to wake him up. He had not taken his eyes off the clock on the dashboard. The Volvo is parked on a track in the woods. Darkness has turned the bored pine trees into a wall. When Sebastian leans forward he can see the shaft of Ursa Major against a little patch of sky. He has always thought that this constellation ought to be replaced with a new and more interesting one. When he opens the car door, the smell of the forest hits him: plants that suck up nourishment from the rotting wastes of past generations. His foot lands on springy subsoil, a contact so natural that the next movement follows from it. Sebastian takes the rucksack out of the trunk and sets off.

A forest considers various processes going on in it to be perfectly normal. It does not strike Sebastian as odd to be climbing a mountain away from the road at half-past three in the morning. He can concentrate entirely on not stumbling over tree roots, carefully untangling thorny blackberry branches from his sleeves, and fighting the fatigue that is tempting him to lie down on the cool ground and see in the break of day peacefully. When he reaches the edge of the forest, the night has already withdrawn between the tree trunks. Dawn is breaking over the broad, grass-covered hollow high above, which is hugged by the Schauinsland road. A cow raises its head, and turns back to its endless munching when Sebastian lays a finger on his lips. He climbs through the barbed wire and keeps a respectful distance from the animals. Just as he has crossed the meadow in a diagonal line and entered the cluster of trees opposite, sun slants across the crevice between the tops of two mountains. The air is clear as glass, casting every contour into sharp relief. Every tree is an individual, every pebble is in its right place. Shafts of light pierce the patches of even ground. Grass grows wherever there is room. Insects circle over sunny patches. From a distance come the workshop noises of a woodpecker. All creation belongs to the animal world at this time of day, and every man is like the first or last on earth.

Sebastian has already walked this route during the dress rehearsal, no more than three hours ago. But knowing the ground does not make the final leg any less difficult. There are dead branches to stumble over everywhere and thick undergrowth that forces him to make detours. Sebastian has to use his hands to help him up the steepest inclines. After five hundred meters he is soaked with sweat and sits down on a tree stump to rest. He has barely taken off his jacket and tied it around his waist when the midges land on his arms: three on the left and seven on the right. He slaps them dead but the swarm is instantly replaced. Hundreds of midges dance around him jostling for position, landing and sticking their nozzles into his skin. Only female midges bite, Oskar once told him on the bank of Lake Geneva. Females fight, feed, and sting. That is why "ant," "wasp," and "midge" are all feminine in German. Sebastian squashes the tiny bodies between his hands, mixing them with his own blood.

When he cranes his neck to look up the mountain, he can already see the bushes lining the road. Two wind turbines murmur in the distance, the placid rotors turning above the forest canopy, looking out over the whole of Freiburg. A group of scouts are whispering their way through the forest, carrying cooking equipment and folding spades on their narrow backs. They gather at the edge of a clearing two hundred kilometers farther east, so Sebastian knows nothing of this.

But as he takes a sip of dead water, out of the corner of his right eye he catches a glimpse of something moving. The ferns are rustling. Something large is coming nearer. Sebastian jumps up. His stretched nerves conjure images of brown bears. Suggestions for an appropriate reaction do not follow. He watches as a figure unfolds in the ferns, but it does not swell into the threatening mass of a bear, only the trim form of a little man. Agewise, he could be Sebastian's father. His face is hidden in the shadow of a floppy hat, his eyes looking around restlessly from under the brim. It is a while before Sebastian takes in this apparition. The man is festooned with equipment: a large net sticking up over his right shoulder, two cameras dangling from the left, a lantern-shaped cage in the crook of his arm, and a butterfly net in his hand. He purses and stretches his lips constantly, turning his head this way and that, as if he is greeting everything he sees with air kisses. Finally he stretches his arms out, as if he has realized that he was expecting to meet Sebastian here.

"Son!" he cries, rounding the "o." "Rare to have company at this hour. It's a good day. Look."

His Wellingtons wobble around his calves as he approaches, raising his knees as if he were wading through water.

"The best ones are always the most difficult to catch. They like being alone, prefer the shadows at this ungodly hour. And they show the world a mask, or perhaps a second face."

The butterfly net drops to the ground and the old man holds the lantern-shaped cage in front of Sebastian's face. Unprompted, Sebastian takes it in both hands. Through the transparent walls a fantastical face grimaces back at him, round eye-whites showing, a broad nose, cheeks with dark shadows on them, and a mouth with pink flews, like the jaws of a predator. Sebastian, who could not have spoken even if he knew what to say, feels as if the hideous face is looking right through him in the most unpleasant way.

"From the family of hawk moths," says the butterfly catcher, slapping himself on the thigh—not with joy but because of the midges.

"*Smerinthus ocellata*, a fantastic specimen. Look at this lady's real face."

When Sebastian turns the cage, he sees a miniature gas mask: bulging eyes and a trunk, feathery feelers sticking out of the sides like tiny fringes of fern. The hawk moth allows him only a cursory glimpse before it creeps into a corner and folds its wings together, transforming itself into what looks like a piece of bark. Sebastian passes back the cage.

"That's nature for you," the butterfly collector says. "A labyrinth of distorted images and trickery. Everyone deceiving everyone else."

He positions the cage contentedly in the crook of his arm and lifts his equipment. As he is turning to leave, he looks Sebastian in the eye for the first time. "What about you?"

It is only now that Sebastian realizes who is standing before him: the witness who always materializes at the end of a murder case. Instead of panic he feels an impulse to laugh, which he suppresses with difficulty. Murder is one of the few things that he has always been absolutely sure he would never do. The presence of a neutral observer suddenly brings home the absurdity of his behavior with full force, and he realizes that he has not come to terms with the meaning of what he is about to do. "Thou shalt not kill" is not enough to make a clear-cut judgment, and they've forgotten to add the list of exceptions to this rule. In any case, he has little time to come up with the answer to a much simpler question.

"Mushrooms," he says, rubbing his hands on his trousers as if he can rub away the absence of a mushroom knife and a basket as you would dirt. The butterfly collector sizes up his lack of equipment with amusement.

"A little early in the year."

"That's probably why I haven't found any."

The small man nods, seemingly pleased with this appropriate reply. He swings the hawk moth in the lantern-shaped cage in farewell and walks away. Sebastian shoulders his rucksack and continues his ascent. Soon he can no longer be sure if he has really bumped into the butterfly collector or not. In his exhausted brain, layered memories of the past forty hours and thoughts of the minutes ahead jostle each other. When he closes his eyes, he sees a hawk moth with the face of a cat. Distorted images and trickery, thinks Sebastian.

When he looks toward the direction in which the small man has disappeared, there are birds in the branches everywhere. Sebastian sees them sitting on the ground and swaying in the bushes. The longer he looks, the more numerous they become. Chaffinches, wood pigeons, jays, nuthatches, song thrushes. Sebastian wonders how he knows their names. And if it is possible that they, too, know his name.

[4]

HE FINDS HIS BEARINGS AGAIN EASILY once he reaches the road. Even though a dress rehearsal without the lead actor can hardly fulfill its purpose, he had taken things very seriously. He paced the road deliberately, calculated distances, checked lines of sight, and estimated the gradient and curvature of the corner. He examined tree trunks and finished with a walk around the area. At the Holzschlägermatte inn, he cast his mind over his day out with Maike and Dabbelink. There had been a fleet of shiny motorbikes in front of the dilapidated building that day. Swarms of cyclists had crawled up the mountain and raced down it with their tires singing.

He recognizes the right spot immediately. The road abandons the forest at the top of the hollow, and leads into a kilometer-long downward curve before disappearing between the trees again. The quality of the surface allows speeds of at least sixty kilometers an hour. A cyclist entering the twilight under the canopy of leaves immediately after the glare of the sun would be almost blind for the next hundred meters. During his rehearsal, Sebastian had sought out two trees standing on the left and right of the road like gateposts, and cut notches into the bark at a carefully calculated height, notches that he touches now with restless fingers.

A few meters up the slope, he finds a place from which he can watch the road unobserved. Then he sits down on the ground, unpacks his rucksack, pulls on a pair of plastic gloves that he has taken from the first-aid kit in his car, and lays out his tools in the order he has rehearsed. He has been able to plan up to now; he has no control over the next step. Dabbelink is either training early on Tuesday morning or not. If not, Sebastian will come again on Wednesday, Thursday, and so forth, for all eternity. Or, to put it precisely, until he is taken away and put in an asylum or in prison.

The rising sun dapples his shoulders with trembling points of light. The night air caught in the undergrowth cools his forehead and his neck. Despite this, moisture gathers in the fingertips of the plastic gloves, which Sebastian does not dare to take off. His rapid pulse doubles the length of every second. Half an hour passes without anything of note happening. The rustling and crawling between his feet increases. Some ants are sawing a caterpillar to bits, and carrying pale specks to the entrance of their nest. Sebastian enjoys watching the comings and goings of an entire society that hasn't the slightest interest in the concerns of larger creatures. From the ants' point of view, Sebastian's activities must seem just as surreal as the movements of the stars seem to human beings. He would gladly submit his application to join the ants. He would carry out his duties conscientiously and not step out of line. He would be not an unpredictable loner but someone firmly in the middle—a small cog in the system.

Looking up, he catches the glance of a roundish bird that also seems to be waiting for something. A bullfinch, thinks Sebastian. Suddenly the bird shakes itself and flies off. Perhaps the whirring has disturbed it. Now Sebastian hears it, too: rubber on asphalt. That is all. No human sound, no scraping of metal under stress. Professionals make very little noise.

A yellow back is working its way up the road. The biker sways slightly from side to side in time with movement of the pedals, long limbs tensed, fighting against gravity. Although the man cycles past only a few meters below Sebastian's position, the lowered face cannot be identified—it is hidden by a white plastic helmet. Sebastian calculates the probability of this being Dabbelink at 80 percent. Scientists are used to the lack of total certainty, it is normal for them. Through the trees, he watches as the cyclist passes the inn and works his way upward along the broad curve. Once the man is out of sight, Sebastian does not lift a finger for a further ten minutes. Then the forced calm uncoils into a frenzy of movement.

Holding his equipment in both arms, he runs down to the road. He uncoils the steel cable, slings it around the first tree, and threads the end through the eye of the clamping device. The clamp engages—Sebastian checks the lever a couple of times. The solid rasp calms his nerves. As he pulls the cable across the road, makes another loop around the second tree, and fastens it, his thoughts follow Dabbelink's climb to the summit. Now he is on the steepest part and now he is entering the final bend. Together they feel the blood pulse under the skin—both men have sweat running into their eyes. They are working together on a task that connects them intimately. Dabbelink gets to the faded line marking the end of the ascent. Perhaps he checks his time, pulls on a jacket, and allows himself a victorious look down into the valley from which he has risen in thirty-five minutes using nothing but his own muscle. Perhaps he merely puts one foot down on the ground, turns his bike around, and hurls himself into the descent.

Sebastian stands panting behind the last tree at the edge of the hollow, staring so intently down at the start of the bend that the colors swim before his eyes. He is concentrating so hard, he nearly misses the moment when Dabbelink's yellow jersey first flashes between the trees in the distance. The senior registrar is fast. At this speed, Sebastian barely has a minute to get under cover. In a few paces, Sebastian reaches the cable and tightens it to the maximum resistance. Then he stumbles into the undergrowth, making an effort to keep his legs from giving in to gravity and running on and on through the forest, over the meadow, and finally into the car. Sebastian forces himself to stop, lies facedown on the ground, and folds his hands over his head, as if waiting for an explosion.

The beauty of time is that it passes unaided and is undisturbed by what happens within it. Even the next few seconds will disappear, and what seemed impossible a moment ago will be over and done with. Waiting is not difficult. Life consists of waiting. Therefore, Sebastian decides, life is child's play.

The whir of the tires approaches. It grows louder and higher; it wants to move on quickly. Before the pitch can sink again in accordance with the Doppler effect as it rushes by, it is interrupted by a damp slicing. At the same time there is the sound of a human voice, the first syllable of a word that is not completed. "Wha—"

Hard pierces soft. A curious moment of stillness, then metal meets the road in screeching protest. Impact and the slide of a heavy body. Metal rods strike the road—tiny parts clattering in all directions. An object flops into the undergrowth, hopping and rolling, as if an animal is running away in great bounds.

Then there is silence. Something has crashed into this new day and sunk quickly into its depths: the concentric ripples have dispersed and the surface of time is smooth, like an impenetrable mirror in the morning light. Unmoved, the orchestra of birds resumes its interrupted performance. Sebastian looks up. The color of the light is unchanged; a slight breeze rustles the leaves. In such a simple way does a man leave this world: a gateway of trees, a little noise. Immediately after, everything is the same as it was. It has almost been fun, in the way that things can be fun when a little effort reaps a great reward. Good that it was Dabbelink and not someone nicer. The whole thing was a fantastic idea, Sebastian thinks, and his bile rises so sharply at this thought that he bends over and waits to throw up.

When he climbs toward the road again, he is swaying like a drunk. He has lost all control over his limbs. That was it: his only chance. He just wants to get away. The release of tension has opened the floodgates of exhaustion. He is now scarcely interested in whether the cable really caught Dabbelink or how severely. Decency alone demands that the trap be cleared away. Sebastian thinks that he owes that much to humankind; though why, he does not know.

A speed of nearly seventy kilometers an hour will carry an unrestrained body a long way. Hopefully way into the next bend or right into the town, Sebastian thinks, preparing himself for every possible sight. But when he steps into the road, he clutches his hand to his heart like a bad actor. Although he has prepared himself, what he sees exceeds his ability to comprehend.

There is nothing at all, only asphalt warmed by the sun, with leaves and branches casting art nouveau patterns upon it. The scene has been swept clean by the velocity of the act itself: every last screw has scattered into the undergrowth. The steel cable glistens like a taut guitar string, and the only change in it is a dark stain left of the center. Sebastian lifts the lever, loosens the clamp, and rolls up the cable, smearing himself with fresh red blood. The skin under his gloves is wrinkled, as if he has spent too long in the shower. He uses his last ounce of strength to pack his rucksack.

[5]

FEW PEOPLE MASTER THE ART OF FEARING THE RIGHT THINGS. Many a one boards an airplane with knees trembling but doesn't hesitate to climb a stepladder to change a lightbulb in the bathroom. When a bird drops dead out of the sky, people think the world is coming to an end. And when there is a real tragedy—which is never a general tragedy but a personal one—they believe that nothing worse can possibly happen, though the actual horror still lies before them. In the dark pit of despair, they sit in limbo, clutching their heads, which are pounding from the impact. They think that this is the worst it will ever get and plan to pick themselves up again after a brief period of recovery. They do not realize that they are in the waiting room for the actual catastrophe, which will come not as a blow, but as a free fall.

Shower doors all over town are being opened and closed. Naked men and women are stepping onto cold tiled floors, regarding their wet faces in the mirror with mixed feelings and toweling their damp hair. The time of day could lead Sebastian to believe that he has just gotten up and is getting ready for a perfectly normal Tuesday at the university. His exhaustion has evaporated. From the moment he changed his clothes in the car and tossed them—along with the steel cable and clamping equipment—into a trash can standing ready to be emptied, his head has felt light, as if he were about to rise to the ceiling like a helium balloon. He has bought bread rolls, parked the car, and brought the newspaper up to his apartment with him. He takes a summer suit out of the wardrobe and dresses as if for a celebration, head to toe in the colors of innocence. The parquet feels good under his bare feet and the freshly brewed coffee smells wonderful. Standing at the open balcony door, Sebastian is filled with a blessed certainty: his son is alive. A morning so bathed and clothed in breeze and filled with birdsong might be missing a crude creature like Dabbelink, but certainly not a little miracle like Liam. The same sunlight that is warming Sebastian's face must be caressing the hair of the sleeping child somewhere not too far away. A hint of the air that Sebastian breathes, Liam is also drawing into his lungs. Sebastian even feels his son's heart beating in his fingertips as he touches a spray of wisteria.

He pours coffee, out of habit not making any unnecessary noise, and sits down at the table with the newspaper. For a moment he allows himself the illusion that it is Sunday morning, and that Maike and Liam are still asleep in bed while he has woken too early once again and is relishing the gift of two whole hours to himself. The smell of the bananas in the fruit bowl is intense, as though they were planning their return to South America. Sebastian just wants to sit there and read the paper until he hears the pitter-pat of Liam's feet approaching in the hall. That would probably be the best, perhaps the only sensible way to get his son back—were he not lacking the last shred of belief. When a mayfly drowns in the coffee, he is almost distraught by its death until it occurs to him that these tiny flies are so similar and so numerous that they must surely be reincarnated, if only for practical reasons.

He carries a plate of cheese rolls and more coffee with him into the living room. He presses the remote control, feeling like he is waiting for his favorite film to come on while he has a picnic on the sofa. When he does not manage to interest himself in a program on the river flowing through his hometown, he switches from the regional channel to Channel One. He turns the volume up high to keep himself awake. After an hour, he switches on the radio as well. The coffee has grown cold and the bread rolls are practically untouched. Sebastian switches between channels and programs constantly; screaming voices intermingle. When the hospital scandal is mentioned, he listens. Some expert or other explains that the pharmaceutical industry makes no bones about testing drugs on human beings: new blood-clotting agents, for example, that are tested on heart patients during operations. But mostly in Africa until now, not in Baden-Württemberg. Apart from that, the mass media is filled with reports on seals in Canada, cancer research in Asia, and bands from Scandinavia, all without mention of a bizarre murder that has taken place in the immediate vicinity of the broadcast region. Images of war in the Middle East are punctuated by bad pop music from the radio. A woman reads out the stock prices to scenes from an American family sitcom. Everything has something to do with everything else; everything is connected. Only one thing is missing in the great web of connections—the news that a senior registrar at the university hospital has met his maker in mysterious circumstances.

Sebastian's rage at the unreliability of TV and radio programs is exceeded only by irritation at his own stupidity. What if the body is not found? What if Dabbelink's absence from work is insufficient proof of death for the kidnappers? Or what if the accident has not been fatal after all? What if he got the wrong man? A levelheaded person would not have left the scene of the crime so hastily, but tracked down the victim, established that he was dead, and then made sure that the body would be discovered immediately. Sebastian however, as he well knows, has been anything but levelheaded. What he has done was far beyond his capabilities.

The itch from the midge bites travels over his spine and neck and drills into his brain. Sebastian crosses his arms and scratches with his bent fingers, staring fixedly at the television, cradling his upper body like an institutionalized animal.

It is already early evening and Sebastian is just about to leave the apartment to return to the scene of the crime, like a garden-variety murderer, when he finally hears what he has been waiting for on a local radio station. Soon after, the television also knows about it. Sebastian sees flickering images of the patch of forest that he now knows only too well, but onscreen it seems to have little in common with his memories of it. Red and white police tape, bicycle parts lying in the ferns. Three cows chew their cud at the camera. A powerful zoom lens turns the colors to grainy specks. With some imagination, it is just about possible to make out the twisted limbs of a body lying between dead leaves and blackberry bushes. The palm of a policeman's hand covers the lens. The harsh evening sun has brought beads of sweat to the forehead of the excited reporter, who, while not wanting to anticipate the conclusions of the police, must mention here that the dead man worked in medical director Schlüter's department at the hospital. He presents the juicy details of his report with triumph. The police found the head of the corpse only after a long search. It was wedged in a forked branch above the heads of those looking for clues, and had followed the proceedings with wide-open eyes.

When the television falls silent, Sebastian feels as if he is sitting underwater. Every movement is slower, every breath he takes creates an eddy, and every thought is a bubble rising. He has carried out the task and thus lost his justification for existence. There are no plans to be carried out now, no reason for him to move. During the night he developed a theory of the meaning of life, a theory that appears clearly before him now in the underwater stillness of the apartment.

Like every other story, life flows backward toward its own cause. The meaning of existence is hidden to most people because human beings normally think things through from beginning to end. The man who recognizes and discovers the principle of the future purpose he serves is able to view every event between now and then as a part of his personal destiny. And so bear it all with equanimity.

Without a doubt, Sebastian's personal destiny is to save Liam. Among the events that he wishes to face with equanimity, he imagines discovery and arrest, Maike's horror and his parents' collapse, crises of conscience, and imprisonment for many years. He believes himself to be prepared for all this. He sits in the same position, with a rotten taste in his mouth—of industrial wastewater and a sky that has remained unchanged for too long—as it becomes impossible to hide his real problem from himself any longer. There are two telephones on the coffee table in front of him: his mobile and the cordless landline phone. Both have just been charged, and checked many times: they are ready. But they do not ring. Their manner of not ringing signals the final severance with reality. Nobody is calling—not the kidnapper, not Liam, not even Maike or the police. Scarcely has Sebastian understood this when the false floor is pulled away. Free fall begins.

[6]

IN HIS LECTURES, SEBASTIAN LIKES TO PRESENT A TYPOLOGY of waiting that he has come up with himself. Waiting (so he begins) is an intimate dialogue with time. A long period of waiting is more than that: it is a duel between time and the person who wishes to investigate it. Ladies and gentlemen, when you are next waiting in the student administration office for some information, do not bring a book. (Laughter.) Give yourself over to time, subjugate yourself, deliver yourself to it. Have a discussion with yourself about how long a minute is. Find out what on earth the instrument on your wrist has to do with you. Ask yourself what this waiting is meant to be: a betrayal of the present in favor of an event in the future? (Silence.) But what is the present? (More silence.) In waiting, you will establish that the present moment does not exist. That it is always over or not quite there when you try to grasp it. Past and future, you think, are directly connected. But where, ladies and gentlemen, does the human being find itself? Do we perhaps not exist at all, in truth? (Restrained laughter, dying down quickly.) Are we not really here at all, because the suit of time does not have holes for arms and legs? And think: man does not only wait for the never-ending lunch break of our department secretaries to be over. (A single laugh, followed by whispering.) You, for example, are waiting now for the end of my lecture. After that you will wait in the canteen for your lunch. During lunch you will wait for the start of the next lecture and during that lecture you will wait for your free time. Of course you wait the entire time for the weekend, and for the holidays. Waiting, ladies and gentlemen, consists of many layers. You are all waiting to pass your examinations, to finish your degrees, and to find jobs. You are waiting for better weather, happier times, and your one true love. We are all waiting, whether we want to or not, for death. We fill the layers of waiting time with all kinds of activities. Have you noticed something? (A long, artificially inflated pause.) Life consists of waiting; waiting is what we call "life." Waiting is the present. Man's relationship to time. Waiting sketches the silhouette of God on the wall. Waiting (Sebastian raises his voice at the end) is the stage of transition that we call our existence.

His lectures are popular. They give the students the impression that he has cracked the phenomenon, and that he will lead them out of their everyday ideas into a new understanding of time.

In truth, Sebastian has not even grasped his own typology of waiting. He has blithely overlooked an important category. It does not have much to do with time at all—at most, with the suspension of it. It is a waiting that is completely absorbed in itself and does not allow for any distractions: no watching TV or reading a book; no eating and no going to the toilet. This waiting consists of preventing reason from collapsing, and keeping the body from committing suicide. It is the waiting of one who is falling for an impact that does not come.

SEBASTIAN IS SITTING with his head tipped back against the sofa. His hands are lying on his thighs and his feet are shoulder-width apart. The body does not need a sense of equilibrium in this position. Even a dead man could maintain his balance. Through half-closed eyes he gazes at the upper half of a bookcase, the luxuriant tufts of a houseplant occupied with producing ten shoots a week, the top edge of one of the paintings that Maike has on loan from the artists in her gallery. Lots of red on a black background. He cannot remember the title of the painting. Even so, he is perfectly happy with what lies in his field of vision. Nothing is bothering him as his thoughts shuttle between two points to no avail. On one side, the conviction that continuing to obey instructions is the only right thing to do (no police, tell no-bo-dy). On the other side, the fear of endangering the life of his son through inaction. There is no room for other considerations. Not for asking how long it will take till they get in touch with him. Nor for the thought that he should at least be happy the police have not shown up: every passing minute gives him hope that he has managed to get away with the crude murder.

The sun has set; the air no longer smells of Liam alive somewhere. There is nothing to indicate that Sebastian's waiting is not the start of a lifelong vigil. His beard is growing, and his fingernails and hair, too. It is dark for a long time; then it slowly grows light.

THE RUMBLING IN HIS STOMACH STOPS just before noon the next day. The stores of sugar and protein have been used up, and the body is setting to work on the fat reserves now. The pain in his back had become unbearable at some point and finally disappeared. Sebastian is no longer sitting on the sofa, but has become part of it. He has blurred at the edges and is now a permanent part of the room that is part of this building, which is in a town in a network of streets, train tracks, waterways, and flight paths that stretch all over the earth, which revolves around a sun, which is part of the Milky Way, and so forth. Sebastian is in a state between waking and sleeping, interrupted by moments of consciousness in which he knows that, regardless of what the future brings, he will never again be the person that he once knew. That he can never return to what his life used to be.

The ring of the telephone has the force of a stroke. His body contracts and his left arm jerks convulsively. Sebastian first knocks the telephone off the table, then presses it to his ear, as if he wants to connect it directly with his brain. He conducts a conversation whose sense he understands only afterward. Maike once again talked about mountains, wind, and good weather, and asked if everything was all right. Laughing, she put Sebastian's halting replies down to his total isolation in the wasteland of physics. She didn't have much time, she was going out for dinner, and Sebastian did not want to speak for long either, he was in the middle of an important train of thought.

When the telephone is lying in front of him once again, he is trembling with rage. The wrong phone call has made the absence of the right one a hundred times worse. His agitation drives Sebastian to get off the sofa and walk through the apartment. His arms start jerking again, with a violence that increases the racket in his head to a mocking volume. Sebastian tugs one drawer after another out of the cupboard in the living room and throws them down to the floor until he has found his pocketknife. He scratches his swollen insect bites with the blunt side of the blade—the letting of blood brings relief. He drives the knife into the side of the armchair. He punches door frames and kicks over chairs. Newspapers fly through the air like startled birds. A vase hits the wall and leaves a water stain in the shape of a hand held up in defense. Sebastian beats his head against the stain until the room around him has turned into a monotonous hum. At some point he stands on the balcony sucking air into his lungs, clinging to the railing as if it is that of a ship racing into the oncoming night with breathtaking speed. When a pigeon lands in a flower box, he screams at it. Where is my son, you airborne rat, you scavenger, where is Liam?

He makes a grab for the bird and the tips of his fingers graze its tail feathers before the startled animal drops over the edge of the balcony. Showing that waiting is not without its dangers.

[7]

OSKAR PICKS UP THE PHONE AFTER THE SECOND RING.

"Forget it, Jean!"

"Who's Jean?"

"Sebastian!" Oskar's laugh of relief would certainly have made Jean, whoever he was, happy. "I've been waiting days for you to call."

It's clear that Oskar is still smiling during the pause that follows. A sofa creaks. Sebastian can imagine Oskar, wearing the black trousers and white shirt that suit him so well, stretching his legs out leisurely. He must have only just come home. At night, he had told Sebastian once, you can fish people from Geneva like trout from an over-full breeding pond.

Sebastian is sitting hunched over at the dining table, in the same place as the last time he had dinner with his family and with Oskar, not so long ago. His shirtsleeves are rolled up and his arms are crusted with blood. The pale material of his suit is also stained in many places. He can smell himself with every movement. The sweat of fear and sleeplessness and the stink of waiting—he can no longer tell how many days it has lasted.

"What time is it?"

Oskar's smile turns once again to laughter. "Have you rung to ask what the time is? It's three in the morning."

"My God," says Sebastian. "It's going to be light soon."

"You sound odd. As if you were a thousand light-years away and had been dead for a thousand years."

"That's about right."

There is a certain tone of voice, a darkly vibrating melody in the undertones, that sets in whenever Oskar and Sebastian speak to each other on their own. The sound of their voices together creates an intimate space cut off from the rest of the world. To create this space, Sebastian sometimes closes his office door and rings Oskar's work number. Then he asks him how his day has been, if he's making progress with his work, and what the weather is like in Switzerland. Now, too, he feels the desire to get Oskar talking, to ask him about how his night has been and to listen to him talk about who he has met and what he has been doing. Lulled by the familiar tones, he would put down the telephone after a while and surrender himself to the emptiness from which he has been trying to escape by calling Oskar.

"Why have you been expecting me to call?" Sebastian asks.

"So that you can tell me the end of the Many-Worlds fairy tale."

Sebastian has not thought about *Circumpolar* at all. In retrospect, his agitation over it seems so ridiculous that his forehead and cheeks grow warm with embarrassment.

"It's about something else," he says quickly. "I've killed a man."

"Oh?" Oskar says.

Sebastian is silent. This indifferent "Oh?" is a crime almost equal to his own, yet it is also a precious gift. It is a tiny but razor-sharp weapon that he can brandish in the face of his conscience whenever necessary from now on. Of course he might have expected this. Oskar is not the sort of man to jump up with fists clenched. He doesn't throw his hands up into the air or tear his hair out. His relaxed manner is not a front concealing a fearful nature—it is made of granite and its only boundary disappears at the very point that Sebastian's worldview begins. As always, Oskar is a fatalist, which is why Sebastian hates him most and why he is now eternally grateful to him.

"Dabbelink?" Oskar finally asks.

"How do you know?"

"His picture's in all the papers. The steel cable got me worried. You remember: Liam and the Nazis in the jeep."

"I'd forgotten that. I thought it was my own idea."

"One's own ideas are rarer than we would wish them to be."

While Sebastian sinks his head down onto the table in Freiburg, Oskar moves from side to side on his shabby sofa, trying to find a comfortable position. Compared with the flawless appearance of its owner, the state of the sofa is a scandal, but one that Oskar can well afford. He looks up through the skylight. The moon is bright as a spotlight in the theater, bathing the room in white. Oskar lights a cigarette and exhales languid curls of smoke from his mouth and nose.

"Jealous?" he asks. "Over Maik?"

"Nonsense!" Sebastian retorts, a little too indignantly.

"Then what? An escape attempt?"

"Oskar . . ."

"Or an experiment to prove the irreversibility of time?"

"Oskar! A man is dead. Don't you give a shit?"

Coming from the mouth of the murderer, this sounds like bad cabaret. Only the seriousness of the situation prevents Oskar from using this opportunity to tease his friend.

"*Cher ami.*" Oskar takes two more quick puffs, then stubs the cigarette out in the ashtray on the floor next to the sofa. "Life is merely an exception in nature. Did you like Dabbelink?"

"That's got nothing to do with it!"

"Answer me."

"No, I didn't like him."

"Does he have family?"

"Everyone has family."

"A wife and child?"

"No."

"Did he have style?"

"Now you're going too far!"

There is a rustling sound over the phone as Sebastian tugs his shirt out of his trousers to dab his forehead with the tails.

"Mon Dieu," Oskar says. "You're behaving like any old hypocrite."

Oskar has stood up and opened the skylight. He rests his elbows against the ledge and stretches his back, as though he is going to speak to a large audience. His fatalism is not entirely responsible for his calm demeanor, as Sebastian thinks. Ever since he read about Dabbelink's death in the newspaper, he has had time to consider every sentence in this conversation. The difficult part lies before him. From now on, every word must count. From now on, every word is a fiber in the rope with which Oskar wants to pull his friend over to him.

He wants to remind him that the entire universe owes its existence to a break in symmetry. Also that the existence of human consciousness is merely a result of this terrible breach, the space between its poles (big and small, hot and cold, black and white) spanned by thought. Without opposites there can be no distinctions, no space and no time; without opposites everything and nothing would be identical. Since distinctions are the basic condition for the material world, how is man supposed to believe in the moral validity of the distinction between "good" and "evil"? Why should one feel appalled about the extinction of a Dabbelink—when it was not even known if the man had style? Oskar laid particular importance on the first few words of the introduction: *Morality is the duty of the stupid. Intelligent people exercise freedom of choice.*

He has just drawn a breath when Sebastian cuts in.

"That's not all, Oskar. Liam has been kidnapped."

Individual stars hang on tight in the glow of light over Geneva. The city, thinks Oskar, is an enormous sack full of fear, sorrow, revulsion, and a tiny bit of happiness, tied up at the top.

"Liam is in scout camp," he says slowly.

"Listen to me," Sebastian says. "Dabbelink's death is Liam's ransom. Do you understand?"

The sofa is directly under the skylight, so Oskar merely has to turn around to sit down again.

"And . . ." Oskar does not normally break off midsentence. "And is Liam back?"

Sebastian covers his face with his fingers. This simple question would be reason enough to end the conversation and go back to lying on the sofa in the living room. Instead, he starts talking.

After a few coherent sentences (Sunday evening, service station, motion sickness pills) he starts losing himself in details. He talks about laughing truck drivers, ants carrying dead caterpillars, butterfly collectors, and an extended typology of waiting. Talking works well—everything can be described, everything consists of harmless details that add up to an event. When Sebastian has finished, he feels as if he has spoken for half an hour, but Oskar has smoked only a single cigarette in that time.

The silence that follows is a pause at first, then it grows intolerable, and finally becomes a matter of course. Sebastian has told Oskar everything he knows, and the speech that Oskar has prepared is meant for another situation altogether. The silent telephone line is like an open door between two empty rooms. In Freiburg, the first light of dawn is creeping toward Sebastian's fingertips. In Geneva, Oskar lights one cigarette after another. The twitter of lone birds waking can be heard in both cities. Merciful night dissolves and flows in all directions. In both places, the new day dawns—a rock with sharp edges, ready to peel the skin from the body of anyone who challenges it.

It is light when Oskar speaks again. His voice is a whisper that barely makes it across the distance between the telephones.

"Maik knows nothing?"

"Not yet."

"Go to the police."

"What?"

"I've thought about it. Go to the police." Oskar's breath hisses into the covering of the microphone. "Just tell them that Liam has disappeared. Once he's back . . . Sebastian? Liam will be back. Tell me that you heard that."

"Yes."

"As soon as he's back, we'll worry about the rest."

Very little has changed in Sebastian's posture, although the morning light makes him look even more pathetic than before. His face has lost its luster. The absence of light shows that he has just reached the bottom of the pit. Free fall has ended. Oskar's decision has exploded a world in which there is no demonstrable reality, and in which there is always the same number of reasons for and against every action. Sebastian stretches out to touch the armrest of the chair where his friend sat the last time they had dinner together, but he can't reach it—his arm is too short.

"Do you want me to come?" Oskar asks.

"What?"

"Do you want me to get on a train and come to you?"

"No."

"I'd have done it gladly. Think carefully about what you're going to tell them."

"Sure."

"Sebastian, I . . ."

The line is dead. Neither of them could have said with any certainty which of them hung up first.

CHAPTER 4, IN SEVEN PARTS

Rita Skura has a cat. The human being is a hole in nothingness. After a delay, the detective chief superintendent enters the scene.

[1]

RITA SKURA HAS A CAT. When she lifts the animal off the ground, it spreads the toes of all four paws as though it is preparing tiny parachutes for a fall. Rita Skura would never drop her cat, but the cat does not rely on that. If it were to fall one day, it would land softly and stroke the hair on its chin with a superior look on its face. That is exactly why Rita loves her pet. It possesses two qualities that to the end of her days she will never have: healthy mistrust and natural elegance.

As a child, Rita would believe anything, and became well known as the victim of playground pranks. It was Rita who looked up to see a UFO while someone kicked her in the shin. Rita climbed a chestnut tree in a short skirt to rescue a small bird while, below, sniggering boys discussed the color of her underwear. There was no trick too obvious for her. She was cheated out of all her coloring pens in a bet and spent hours waiting in a hiding place when no one was looking for her. Nobody wanted to have her on their team when they were playing cops and robbers.

Despite this, Rita already knew from the age of ten what she wanted to be. When the time came, her parents threw up their hands in horror. But one of Rita's strengths is an astonishing stubbornness. She stood by her decision, cleverly insisted on the truth of the paradox that people are always best at the things for which they have the least natural talent, and applied for the job.

At the interview, she answered half the questions wrongly: a result dependent entirely on the principles of probability theory. Flushed red, she promised to compensate for her unshakeable belief in normality and people's good intentions with extraordinary diligence and care. She got the job.

The training did not come easy to her. In criminology seminars she always had to play the role of the foolish witness who is led onto slippery ground with trick questions. Not a day went by in which she did not think about giving up—until she met an instructor called Schilf, who grasped her nature from the first hour of the lesson, and took her aside during the lunch break. He told her that she was ideally suited to a career in criminology as long as she followed one simple rule. She had to learn that her trusting nature was what her opponent expected; so she always had to assume the opposite of what she was thinking, and always do the opposite of what she felt.

From then on, it did not just become better. It became good. Rita's trusting nature was always so reliably wrong that when she followed Instructor Schilf's advice, she achieved an amazing degree of success. She had only to look at the photo of a suspect and take him for the criminal to be certain that he was innocent. When she read a witness statement and found it believable, she knew that the witness was lying. Rita's trusting nature transformed itself into a self-confidence so merciless that it seemed she was avenging all the humiliations of her previous life. She screamed at suspects, and her criminological sense exceeded that of not only her peers but also her instructors. When she was promoted to detective, the walrus-mustached police chief squeezed her hand; and Rita returned the pressure until this most senior officer winced in pain.

Despite this, Rita knows that her cat still has it in her to be a better investigator. Rita herself will never rise to be the stuff of police legend, though perhaps she might become the first female police chief in Baden-Württemberg. And that would be more than enough for her.

Her lack of elegance was not something that could be addressed with a simple reversal of assumptions. Although Rita's parents were normal people of average exterior, a genetic coincidence had turned their daughter into an anatomical exception. At first sight, her physique looked like a parody of a male fantasy. Her breasts are so large that they seem to pull her upper body forward. To walk is to fall; you can see that with Rita. Her shoulders and her waist are narrow and her legs are long, like those of a jointed doll. The young officers call her corkscrew curls a mane, even though none of them has ever seen a horse with a curly mane. Rita could explain straightaway why she reminds people of a horse, or perhaps a small pony. She has a little too much of everything: too much hair, too much leg, and too much mouth. She looks like someone who was fat as a child and who has been unable to forget that way of moving. She walks with long steps and sways from side to side like a buoy in a swell. The hands that protrude from her cardigan look like they have been borrowed from a man. Even her voice would have been better suited for a man: her most harmless comments come out sounding like insults.

Rita has gotten used to all this. She now means everything she says just as it sounds. She pulls the corners of her mouth down when she smiles. She breathes in, not out, when she says "yes," which sounds like a disapproving "huh" that makes everyone she speaks to lose all desire to carry on talking. And when she is angry she presses her lips together as if a word starting with "B" were stuck in her throat. Bullshit. Bluster. Balderdash.

Both men and women turn to look at Rita in the street, and she does not take this as a compliment but as a reaction to her physical oddity. She buttons her shirts and coats to the top in all seasons. In summer she wears flowery dresses that hang below the knee, a length no dressmaker would call fashionable. On Rita's body this type of dress has an effect similar to that of a campsite sticker on a Maserati.

A clever person has to laugh; stupid people get angry. Rita is fine with that. There are not many female detectives, and their colleagues claim they would faint at the sight of a drowned body. This is why Rita needs to package herself to display the superiority of mind over body. She wears ironic clothes and sarcastic sandals that are feared throughout the jurisdiction. When she enters a room at her workplace, all heads lower, as if the Latin teacher has just entered the classroom. If asked whether she has a sense of humor, she would answer that there is no sentence so foolish that a person could not say it in all seriousness. So why laugh?

The only thing that really interests Rita is police work. She is thirty-one, single, and childless. As a member of the murder squad, she encounters corpses every day and can examine wives battered to death, old people who have choked on their mashed potatoes, and suicide cases crushed by trains—without even thinking of fainting. She also has the young men in the police force well under control. At their morning meetings, she does not mince her words about their mistakes and failures. If anyone contradicts her, she points to a long list of cases in which she was right from the very start.

The cat is one of the few living beings whom Rita wishes well. When she holds the little animal on her lap, she can feel its warmth on her skin after a few seconds, unlike the warmth of a human being, which can take a few minutes to penetrate the clothing. Apart from that, the cat has a sensible job, unlike most people. It keeps the birds away from the windows of the ground-floor apartment. Rita tends to feel that she is being observed, and she can't bear airborne spies.

After devouring her third egg, Rita gets up and puts the purring cat down on the chair she has just vacated. In the kitchen, she fills the feeding bowl with the ground chicken that she has bought by way of apology. Since a senior registrar and his head parted company during a cycling ride, Rita has hardly been home. Last night she stormed out of her office after the walrus-mustached police chief had called, and she woke after a few hours' sleep feeling just as insulted. Even though she has very little experience of politically sensitive cases, she was not surprised when the police chief bellowed through the phone, explicitly demanding that she conjure up a miracle. She did not mind staying late in the office and going back to work at seven the next morning. What made her bile rise up was that they wanted to put a higher-ranking detective on the case with her. Rita Skura is young, she is a woman, and the steel-cable killing is actually the first time she has led a murder investigation. Even if the whole thing were to blow up into a real crisis, even if the chair of the bristle-haired home secretary were to wobble, Rita Skura does not need help. She must deliver concrete results by this evening, otherwise Detective Chief Superintendent Schilf, the very man to whose advice she owes her career, will be transferred from Stuttgart to Freiburg.

Schilf's guest lectureship at the police college had been anticipated with great interest. He was preceded by his reputation as a veritable prophet of crime. He was said to avoid working in a team and was seldom seen at headquarters, and he solved his cases more or less in his sleep. They expected a magician. When Schilf finally stood before the class, a chill wind of disappointment swept through the room. In his early fifties, he behaved like an old man. Beneath the worn jacket, his shoulders drooped as if he were trying to counteract his height. Colorless strands of hair that had once been blond hung in his face. Standing stooped at the blackboard, he snapped pieces of chalk between his fingers. He kept interrupting his lectures for no apparent reason, swaying from one foot to another and listening with a shocked expression to something within himself, as if hearing the echo of a thunderclap that had happened long ago. When he continued speaking, he spoke in sentences that no one understood. "I have no memory—that is why I can see into the future." Or, "Two contradictory statements are mostly right and wrong at the same time."

Or his favorite: "Coincidence is the name given to the greatest human error."

None of the students took his strange behavior as a disguise (they were right). Rather, they believed, they were faced with the pathetic remains of a man who had once been successful (here they were wrong).

At first Rita had thought of him as a genius damned. After he had turned her from an innocent to a skeptic in one fell swoop during the first lunch break, she called him a damned genius. When he said goodbye to her after his final lesson, he took hold of her hands without ceremony, gave her a piercing glance, and said, "Rita, child, what hefty mitts you have!" She pulled her fingers free and retorted, "And what a wrinkled visage you have!" They looked each other in the eye and laughed. Rita has not seen him since.

Of course, she had liked the half-mad Schilf. And precisely because of this—exactly as she has learned from Schilf himself—she does not trust him. If there is one thing she does not need right now, it is the presence of a genius, especially one who sees through her system of coming to conclusions. Next to him, her diligence and carefulness will count for nothing. Ralph Dabbelink is her most important case to date. His death, which could hold the key to the hospital scandal, belongs to her.

Although it is already remarkably warm at seven in the morning, Rita pulls on a cardigan over her dress before she leaves the house. In her lipstick-red Corsa she drives to Heinrich-von-Stephan-Strasse, holds up her pass to the card reader, and parks under the moss-covered, corrugated iron roof. Ignoring the back door, she walks around the building to enter it—with shoulders thrown back and chin jutting forward—through the brick front entrance as she does every day.

[2]

AT RECEPTION, A MAN IS STANDING with both hands on the counter, his forehead against the Plexiglas, as if he cannot keep himself upright any longer. Rita knows these blokes, and finds them repulsive. This one is tall and well built, someone who could easily have made something of himself. His hair is greasy, a dull street-dog yellow. His clothes must have cost a fortune; now they are smeared with blood and crumpled from head to toe. The man has clearly spent several days in them. Regardless of whether such people hand themselves over or are brought in, they cause the kind of trouble that never ends well.

Rita instinctively holds her breath to escape any whiff of alcohol fumes. The stranger does not even turn at the sound of her slapping sandals as she passes by. He stares ahead sightlessly. The duty officer raises his hand in greeting as he continues speaking into his telephone. Almost every morning, Rita climbs the stairs feeling relieved that she no longer has to deal with a certain type of everyday business.

She reaches her office on the third floor, a little breathless, takes off her cardigan, and falls into the black leather chair. Behind the frosted glass of her desk, she still feels like a child who is shuffling around the house in her father's shoes for fun. She doesn't mind. She knows very well that she has an office to herself at her current grade only because none of her colleagues wants to share one with her.

She loves this room, especially the under-floor computer cable that pops out through a hole in the carpet by a leg of her desk. Along with the rows of impeccably labeled folders on the shelves, it projects an atmosphere of professionalism in which Rita revels every morning, as if bathing in dragon's blood before setting forth to do battle.

A fan of letters to be dealt with is spread out next to the keyboard. The window was open through the night and has let in cool air, which will last for a while between the thick walls of the building. Far beneath, the usual pack of sparrows twitters in the hedges that a former graveyard gardener tends with great care. Rita looks smugly across the parking lot at the treetops. They are so far away that feathered parasites cannot look in on her. If her office were on the ground floor, Rita Skura would bring her cat to work.

She looks through Dabbelink's files for a bit. The photos have the most impact, and having seen them for a hundred times does not diminish their power to shock. Dabbelink's head, wedged in the fork of a tree. The same head again, lying on a stretcher next to the twisted body to which it had belonged only a short while before. There is a length of spinal column sticking out of the body, white and clean. The loose ends of the carotid artery, trachea, and esophagus look like the tubes hanging out of a broken machine. The report by the forensic expert stated that the victim had noticed the trap at the final second, and lifted his head in shock—otherwise the cable would have split his skull. In retrospect, Rita is grateful to Dabbelink for this noble gesture. His condition is already problematic enough.

One of the documents that has just arrived is a report from the forensic laboratory. Delighted, the detective claps her hands like a little girl when she reads the results. Only under protest did the men securing the crime scene carefully transport two square meters of the forest floor, agitated ants and all, to the laboratory. Now they have the genetic profile of a man, who has not yet appeared in any database, but who will shortly be found. Found by her. Apart from this, an indignant Freiburg woman has filed charges against the as-yet-unknown person because she found a pile of garbage in her compost bin on the morning after the murder. With that, Rita has almost everything she needs: the murder instrument and the murderer's shoes, trousers, and shirt. Everything except the murderer himself, whose continued absence is almost beginning to take on a physical form. The hairs that were found pronounce him blond, and his footprints indicate that he is 1.9 meters tall and weighs 85 kilos. Definitely a handsome and clever murderer, not one of the poor devils that one puts behind bars with regret.

Rita will spend the morning in the hospital and will continue looking out for a man who matches the description. In the cardiology department, there is a rumor going around that someone had been threatening Dabbelink. But no one will say who or how. In a combustible situation like this, practically everyone could have had an interest in Dabbelink's death: a pharmaceutical company with a priceless reputation to protect; a nurse who fears losing her job; Medical Director Schlüter, afraid that someone knows too much. Rita will grab hold of Schlüter once again before he can barricade himself in the operating theater. Ever since the university has started looking into disciplinary proceedings, Schlüter has been well-nigh invisible in his department. The criminal charges triggered by the hospital scandal were made anonymously. Schlüter claims that a rival heart specialist is trying to blacken his name.

Rita will question everybody she can get hold of today. In the afternoon she will drop by the cycling club once again. The detectives who are dealing directly with the hospital scandal update her around the clock. Rita tosses the documents onto the desk and stretches her arms. She thinks she will solve this case before Detective Chief Superintendent Schilf can buy his train ticket to Freiburg. At least she will not fail for lack of persistence.

She recognizes Sergeant Schnurpfeil's knock. As always, he waits for a clear "Come in!" before he opens the door slightly, sticks his head in, and smilingly waits for the invitation to be repeated. Only when Rita has said "Yes, come on in!" does he gather up his bulk and bring it to rest in the center of the room. Schnurpfeil is ten years younger than the detective and the only person in the precinct who, in his stoical manner, knows how to deal with her. The young female officers-in-waiting think he is the best-looking man at police headquarters. And yet he always seems uncertain, as if there were a frightened boy behind his mass of muscle, constantly worried that he will be asked to emerge one day. Even now, Schnurpfeil does not seem comfortable with the vantage point granted him by his height. When his colleagues ask him how he puts up with Rita Skura's moods, he shrugs and says that she is clever and also a good detective. He cannot say whether her hair looks like a horse's; and whatever else he thinks of her, he keeps to himself. The senior policeman is always sent when there is bad news. He knows that as well as she does. He stands next to the desk, twisting his cap in his hands. Rita has never yet offered him a seat.

"Schnurpfeil," she says, looking as if she is still checking something in the file, "are you driving me to the hospital?"

"Yes," Schnurpfeil replies. After some thought, he adds, "As well."

He looks up and tries smiling once again. What his colleagues will never understand is that he likes talking to Rita Skura. He doesn't mind formalities and thinks nothing of it when she addresses him in military fashion by his last name. After all, he is only a young senior officer, while she is an up-and-coming detective. He generally knows how to reply to her in a manner that will not agitate her, and he is proud of that.

"Break it to me gently," Rita says, pushing her heavy curls off her forehead.

Rita can't stand the summer, just as she cannot bear many other things. If it were up to her, it could be autumn or winter the whole year long. It's easier to think when it's cold and clothing is more sober.

"Three more senior doctors had their heads chopped off?"

Schnurpfeil avoids looking at her unshaven armpits. "A child has been kidnapped," he says briefly.

Rita's gaze lights on the senior policeman with hatred, as if he were criminal, victim, and witness all in one. "Say that again, if you dare."

"A child has been kidnapped," Schnurpfeil repeats.

Rita lets go of her hair and throws herself back in her chair, which tips gently. "The blond guy with the bloody shirt?"

"How do you know?"

She waves away his awed tones with a dismissive gesture. She should have known right away. Since she had taken the guy at reception for a tramp, he must be a professor at least.

"The father?"

"His son has been gone for four days."

"And he's only come in now?"

"The kidnappers stopped him. He didn't dare go to the police."

"Money?"

"No."

"Then what?"

"He doesn't know."

"What?" Rita jumps up and takes a few threatening steps toward Schnurpfeil, who clearly considers retreating, but decides against it.

"Until now," he says, "they have demanded absolutely nothing."

"But they've been in touch with him?"

"On the day of the kidnapping. They told him to wait."

"What a fucking story." Rita turns away and slams the window shut with such force that the glass rattles in the frame. She waves her large hands in the air a couple of times, as if brushing aside fog in order to see the senior policeman clearly.

"Doesn't sound like pedophiles," she says. "Probably something within the family. Has his statement been taken?"

"All done. He's sitting downstairs."

Rita suddenly lets her hands drop. "He's not a doctor, is he?"

"Professor of physics at the university."

"Thank you, Lord!" Rita shouts.

Schnurpfeil grins, as though this is meant for him. Rita leans back against the edge of the desk, which presses into her bottom slightly, and raises her index finger, which she always does when she feels overwhelmed.

"The press does not like child kidnapping cases," she says didactically.

"We'll separate them," Schnurpfeil says. "The press doesn't need to know anything about the kidnapping right now."

Rita nods, her shoulders relaxing. As is often the case, the senior policeman has thought of something that calms her down.

"Listen, Schnurpfeil. With the best will in the world, there's no way I can look into this personally."

"Of course. The chief suggests that Sandström could take on the case."

"Sandström is a total idiot," Rita says. "Tell him that."

Schnurpfeil reaches for a notebook.

"He should drive to the professor's home with him. Get the technical guys and the shrinks on board. Bug the telephone, the whole lot. And interrogate him for as long as he holds out. Family problems, friends, job. I'll drop by in the evening if I can."

Schnurpfeil puts his notebook away. "I'll just run down and let them know," he says, "then I'll drive you to the hospital."

"Good."

Rita Skura looks past Schnurpfeil at the bulletin board, on which there is a snapshot of her cat next to photographs of the crime scene.

"Four days," she says. "Makes you feel sorry for the man."

[3]

THEY HAVE TAKEN HIS CAR. They have taken his mobile phone. They have taken his shirt and his trousers and put them in plastic bags. He is wearing a suit made out of paper, which rustles with every step and makes him feel like a cross between a clown and a corpse. Right this minute he would have nothing against being laid out in an aluminum drawer with a tag on his toe, and being shoved into the wall. Cool at last. Quiet at last. To sleep at last.

They have taken the keys to his apartment from him, and now they are taking the apartment. Three plainclothes officers are on the street watching to see if the house is being watched. In the hall, a man wearing headphones is lying on his stomach, a black box by his side, fumbling in the telephone socket with a tiny screwdriver. Another man is leaning against the wall, making suggestions and flicking cigarette ash onto the parquet floor. In the kitchen, Sergeant Sandström is sitting at the table making himself a ham sandwich with gerkins and mustard. He had asked if he could "borrow" the Prosciutto di Parma. On the sofa in the living room, which Sebastian will always associate with the worst days of his life, a small woman shrouded in moss-green wool is crouching on thin legs, sticking her aristocratic-looking nose into the family photo album. A bird dressed in human clothing could not have looked stranger than she does. This is the experimental film that this apartment and I have been waiting for the whole time, Sebastian thinks.

When he had stepped into the Heinrich-von-Stephan-Strasse early this morning, the thought of letting the proper authorities deal with the situation made him nauseous with relief. The statement he'd feared making had turned out to be the simplest bit. He had been required simply to tell them what had happened (the grabber machine, pathetic stuffed animals, Vera Wagenfort); he'd kept only one sentence back from them: *Dabbelink must go*. After that, one thing had led to another. There was a practically endless stream of questions about anything and everything. Except whether he had killed a man.

But now what the proper authorities are doing is making him nauseous. They seem to be doing a great deal, but none of it seems to be directed at trying to get Liam back. Every time he tells himself that the police are following a tried and tested routine, the same retort sounds in his head: They are only human beings and can do nothing.

He stands in front of the open wardrobe in the bedroom, tearing the paper suit off his body as if unpacking an enormous present that he never wanted in the first place. He wants to lie down on the bed and lose consciousness, hand over the rest of his life to someone else who will know how to do something useful with it. As he gets dressed, he sets himself an ultimatum. He will give the police until midnight. Then he will tell them what the kidnappers really wanted from him. Tell them that they should ask Medical Director Schlüter where Liam is.

In the hall, the technician gives the thumbs-up—the interception circuit is almost ready. When Sebastian walks into the living room, the psychologist smiles at him, a horizontal gap opening beneath her bird beak. She has not said that Sebastian must be hiding a nasty family secret, but she is watching his every move from the corner of her eye and has been looking through that photo album for ages. Liam's first years are thoroughly documented. After that, there are only a few photographs of him here and there, in which Sebastian—who took the photos—is practically never to be seen.

"Almost done. Then we'll be off."

The psychologist has persuaded him that Maike should be the first person to be told about all this. If he refuses to tell her, the psychologist herself will ring Maike in Airolo. Their keenness to get the line bugged before this phone call suggests that they suspect Liam is with his mother. Sebastian knows that there are countless cases in which parents abduct children from each other. But he does not know how to make it clear to his guests that this is not the situation.

"All working now," the smoking technician says, as if his colleague has just repaired a broken toilet.

He beckons Sebastian over and passes him a telephone receiver with a spiral cord ending in the black box. Sandström brings his ham sandwich into the hall and smells of mustard. He wipes his nose with the back of his hand, pushing it upward at the same time, turning his face into a porcine grimace. The psychologist leans against the door frame, pushing her thumbnail between her incisors, constantly nodding at Sebastian in a friendly manner. If it were possible, he would ring Oskar instead of Maike and ask him to repeat what he had said the night before: *Do you want me to come to you?*

This time Sebastian would reply, *Yes*.

The old-fashioned receiver feels heavy in his hand. The policewoman's gaze bores into his back as he dials the number of the sports hotel in Airolo.

This was only to be expected. Maike is not there. She didn't go to the Alps to sit around in her room. She's on a cycling tour, isn't she? A hundred kilometers, right? No, definitely no mobile phone—true luxury is being out of reach. Isn't that right? A forced laugh. Yes, by dinnertime at the latest. She will return the call.

Sebastian asks the psychologist to let him have the sofa. He does not want to answer any more questions. He tells the technicians that they are not allowed to have music or the television on. Sighing, the policemen take books and magazines off the shelves and start leafing through them. The psychologist opens a window and listens to Bonnie and Clyde, who are in the stream below quarreling over the way things are progressing. Sandström's mobile rings in the kitchen. There's no news from the A81, where two police officers are questioning truck drivers, toilet attendants, and restaurant employees at the service station that Sebastian told them about.

Waiting. Sebastian has had so much practice waiting that it takes only a few minutes for him to lose awareness of everything around him. He lies with his head thrown back and stares at the ceiling—its white surface seems pleasantly in tune with his state of mind. His body seems to be sinking into a warm sand dune while his consciousness rises, circling gently around itself. Sebastian has the palpable sense of time becoming disjointed. The chain of seconds breaks down into tiny particles. His self dissolves, though leaves something behind that he can identify with. It is a kind of observation post outside body and soul. From this vantage point, Sebastian can think about why he held on so long to a theory that did not reflect in the least his feeling for space and time. They are not many, the worlds in which he moves. He is in a single cosmos, a great roar in which he feels the presence of other entities aside from his own. Names can be put to them—Maike, Oskar, and Liam—and they form a weave in which energy and matter are really the same thing: information. A human consciousness that consists of nothing besides memories and experiences is pure information. The observation post called Sebastian thinks that he could sit down at a desk and make notes. He should find out if Oskar's attempts to extrapolate from the big bang through the quantization of time are ultimately aimed at comprehending the world as one big information machine. Have they not been working on the same idea for years but from different sides: that time, not only in the philosophical but in the physical sense, is a product of consciousness and also identical to it? He should speak to Oskar straightaway, find common ground . . . he should . . . When the doorbell rings, Sebastian's daydreams collapse and leave a single sentence: Man is a hole in nothingness.

Someone enters the apartment. A female voice calls Sandström an idiot and asks what has happened that afternoon. It is a good question. Sebastian's watch indicates that he has spent five hours staring at the white surface of the ceiling. The woman comes in and bats the TV magazine out of the hands of the smoking technician. Sebastian has seen the woman before, that morning, when she was running up the stairs in the police station. He found her unsympathetic even from behind. Now her gaze flickers through the room as if she once lost something here and has come to get it. When she walks toward Sebastian, her curly hair is like a symbol of permanent agitation around her head. Under the tightly buttoned cardigan, the large breasts protrude more than is strictly necessary. With a paw of surprising dimensions, she crushes Sebastian's fingers.

"Rita Skura, detective."

At least she leaves him in peace and asks her colleagues questions instead. Sandström and the police psychologist are apportioning Sebastian's statement among themselves. They have barely finished speaking when Rita Skura tells them that that bastard of a medical director has not appeared in the hospital all day, and that the staff continue to protest their innocence. So there is basically nothing new in the case of the murdered senior registrar, and therefore the suits are having their asses kicked. While she is still cursing, the telephone rings.

The scene freezes, then chaos ensues. In the midst of the scuttling and chattering, Rita Skura takes control. She sends a technician to the black box, Sandström to the balcony, and the police psychologist to the phone with Sebastian.

"Pick up when I give the sign. Stall for time. Play dumb. Ask questions. Understood?"

"That will be my wife," says Sebastian.

Rita shakes her head impatiently and leans back against the wall with her arms crossed, maintaining eye contact with the technician. Sebastian is overcome by a desire to put a giant glass over her, push a piece of card under it, and throw the detective out into the courtyard like a twitching insect. When she clicks her fingers, the technician hands him the telephone receiver.

"Dad?"

Liam's voice is coming not only from the telephone receiver but from a box on which a spool of tape turns.

"Hang on, Dad. Hey, stop that!"

Liam is speaking to someone else. A giggle is heard in the background, and there is a bump and a bang. Then he's back.

"Sorry," he says, laughing. "There's only one telephone here and it only takes fifty-cent pieces. Philipp and Lena keep tugging my arm. They think it's funny or something."

"Liam," says Sebastian.

"Dad? Are you angry because I haven't called for so long? I really couldn't. We went off straightaway with rucksacks and tents. I was put with the oldest group from the start, because I talked about how to make a fire and about the bundling effect and exceeding the ignition temperature. And about how it's not flint but pyrite that you need, and then they took me with them on the hike right away—"

"Liam! Are you OK?"

Sebastian's broken cry interrupts Liam's stream of chatter. There is a hesitant pause, stretching out of the phone and wrapping itself around everyone in the room, filling the hallway like an invisible gelatinous mass.

"Of course. I'm great," Liam finally says. "Is something wrong, Dad?"

"No," Sebastian says quickly. "Everything's all right. I was simply . . . worried."

While Liam thinks about this, Sebastian pushes his fist toward his mouth and bites into the white knuckles to stop the heaving in his gut from producing any unwanted noises.

"Some of the kids are homesick," Liam says. "Maybe you're homesick for me?"

This is too much, Sebastian has to get off the phone. He covers the receiver, bashes his forehead against the wall, and takes another deep breath.

"Yup, you've got it!" he says in just the right cheerful tone. "Listen, Liam, I've got to go. We . . . I'll call you later, or tomorrow. I mean, I'll come to see you."

"No!" Liam's horror is unmistakable. "You can't do that! Tomorrow we want to . . ."

"OK, Liam, have fun! See you soon! Bye, Liam! Bye!"

The receiver falls and Sebastian with it. The technician presses a button and *click*, all is dark. A softness comes over his eyes, a jacket he doesn't recognize, it smells male. Someone allows Sebastian to slide slowly to the ground. The heaving in his gut forces out a scream.

[4]

SOME DAYS, DETECTIVE SCHILF KNOWS as soon as he wakes up that he will not be leaving his apartment through the front door. Quickly and quietly, he slips into the army-green cargo pants that he buys in a work-uniform shop, and which he wore long before they became fashionable with young people. He pulls his travel bag out from under the bed and leaves the room, holding the door handle with both hands in order to close the door quietly. He stands at the breakfast bar for a few moments with a glass of Coke that is much too cold, and looks around his own apartment as if he is seeing it for the first time. For fifteen years these rooms have been somewhere for him to stay, but not a home. He feels especially out of place in the kitchen, as if some prankster has plonked him in an advertisement for modern living. He is surrounded by brushed steel and expensive kitchen equipment that he cannot operate. Even as a young lout sitting on a bar stool seemed laughable to him. *A real single person's kitchen*, his landlord had declared when he moved in; and the rent is very reasonable for Stuttgart. Schilf had stuck a couple of postcards onto the fridge out of a sense of duty. They show Majorca, Lanzarote, and Gran Canaria. He had gotten them on vacation. The backs of the postcards are empty. He puts his Coke down, takes the bread bin, the unused fruit bowl, and a pile of newspapers from the windowsill, and opens the window.

To the east, the retreating night splashes the eastern sky with color, interspersed with graffiti made of clouds that the sun will soon have washed from the walls of the dawning day. Through a gap between buildings, Schilf sees a road junction. It is empty, as if cars have not been invented yet or have already been consigned to history. A lone pedestrian is creeping along by the buildings. A shift worker or a sleepless artist, the collar of his jacket turned up even though the nighttime temperature has not fallen below seventy degrees.

The detective turns his wrist: four thirty on Saturday morning. Perhaps he should take out a patent on this time of the day. Getting up early has long ceased to bother him. He can open his eyes at any given time and get out of bed as if nothing has happened, as if sleep does not exist, nor dreams, in whose corridors human beings waste a third of their lives. Rising early without difficulty is one of the few things that gets easier with age. When he was young, Schilf liked to claim that he would never grow old. The only thing old people had left to wait for was their meals.

He smiles and puts both feet down on the metal grating of the fire escape, which starts clanging like a large gong even though he has been careful. Why he leaves the building in this way on certain days, climbing like a burglar into his own life, he cannot explain. Sometimes it seems to make sense to slip around reality and all its preposterous vagaries and take it by surprise. He looks into the apartment one more time before he pulls the window closed from the outside. All is still. The apartment looks as if the detective were alone.

When Schilf looks back on his life, he thinks he was a perfectly normal person about twenty years ago. He had a job and a roof over his head, he had passions, possibly even family. Then came the fracture. While on duty, the young Schilf shot a man who was only reaching into his pocket to get his car key. Or perhaps Schilf had been driving out to wine country one weekend when a suspect forced him off the road—his wife and young son had been in the backseat. The detective insists that he cannot remember. "The fracture" is the name of a catastrophe that his bad memory conceals.

The fracture called for an entirely new person. From the remnants of his life, Schilf picked out the bits that were still functioning. This included his work, which he was good at, better than most in equivalent positions. He got up in the morning. He ate at regular intervals, availed himself of public transport and the small pleasures of life, and he knew where his bed was. But he waited in vain for these things to make him into a new, complete person. His problem was that he could not find it in his heart to end his life simply because the man leading it had reached the end. At some point, he realized that it was a matter of carrying on. The detective became a master at carrying on. Until, barely a month ago, two things happened that upset his mastery: a woman and a death sentence.

He received the death sentence on the obscenely squeaky, sweat-inducing leather of a Chesterfield armchair. This armchair stands in a study decorated in the English style, to which Schilf's doctor leads his patients after he has shone a flashlight into various orifices. There is a thick rug on the floor and the walls are paneled with dark wood. In a gesture of ludicrous excess, gold-tooled volumes of the classics can be reached by means of a mobile librarian's ladder.

The woman whom Schilf met is to some extent the opposite of this study. She has lightly permed dark hair, a snub nose that seems quite implausible, flat eyes that reflect the scene around her, and a build more like a girl than a forty-year-old. The detective met her in the pedestrian zone of Stuttgart city center shortly after the fatal visit to the doctor. To be precise, she walked straight into him because he had come to a sudden standstill. The ground had opened right in front of him, a common occurrence of late. He looked down into a dizzying abyss, a state outside of space and time in which everything was connected.

Ever since he was a child, the detective has believed that there must be a kind of primeval reality beyond the visible world. Greater men than he have spoken of *the-thing-in-itself*, *being as such*, or simply *information*. The detective adds to this by calling it "the program code," by which he means something lying behind the visible and practical desktop of the everyday. He likes this concept because it allows him to compare reality with a man-made machine, an intelligent product of intelligence. In his opinion, reality is nothing other than a creation born second by second in the head of every single observer, and thus *brought into the world*. A long time ago, the detective developed a method by which he attempted to read the program code. This is how he solves his cases. The fact that the ground sometimes opened before him—that, and unbidden and repeated headaches—was the reason for his most recent visit to the doctor.

Plastic bags rustled behind him. Then came a cry and a blow to the back. The impact ought to have pushed him into the abyss. He imagined himself falling, but felt no fear, only a great longing, so great that when he had taken a step forward and found firm ground beneath his feet, he turned to his attacker with an expression of deep disappointment. The woman laughed when she saw his face, shook her head cheerfully, and did not apologize. Instead, when the detective set off again, she followed him.

He had neither extended his hand nor introduced himself. He pulled her like a drag anchor all over the city center. After his visit to the doctor he had intended to do something normal, like buy a slice of pizza. But now all he wanted was to get rid of his new friend. She was carrying plastic bags in which—as became clear later—she had everything she needed to survive, and she followed the detective without asking why they kept walking past the same spots. Schilf had too little imagination, and the pedestrian zone was too small, to make such a long walk more varied. While they were waiting at the same traffic light once again, crossing the same streets, and glancing into the same shopwindows, the woman spoke unaffectedly about herself in a constant stream of chatter.

She had started modeling for life-drawing classes when she was sixteen, and soon earned so much money from it that she did not see the need for a so-called decent education. Over time, the painters became more famous and the wages higher. She had quickly realized that she was not being paid for her nakedness but for a feat of strength—her ability to remain motionless for hours. She perfected the control of physical pain in utterly dull rooms, enlivened only by the scratching of charcoal, the sharp intakes of breath, and the occasional sighs of the artists. To the delight of the painters, she was able to stand in a kind of acquiescent trance for a whole afternoon in the attitude of someone who had just received a shock. Word of her talent got around and she was never short of work. There were so many pictures of her that she never had to ask herself who she was. While other people crouched over desks in gloomy offices, she sat with her cup of café au lait in the garden of her favorite coffeehouse, feeling the breeze on her cheeks. She admitted to the detective that she had not really reckoned with having to change anything about this extremely comfortable lifestyle. That is, until an orthopedic surgeon had told her that she must never model again if she wanted to prevent the constant holding-still from ultimately destroying her back, her knees, and her elbows.

What did the detective think of this story? the woman asked as they stopped in front of the glass doors of the McDonald's on Schlossplatz, as if by mutual agreement. The detective had not realized that her tirades had constituted a story. A person who does not have to ask herself who she is can have little talent for the art of storytelling.

He had said this out loud, and the woman liked it. She laughed. At their feet, sparrows hopped after sweet wrappers and cigarette butts that were rolling away; it was a windy day. The long walk had exhausted the detective so much that the prospect of something edible and a cup of coffee made him feel intensely happy. They walked into McDonald's together in the best of moods. Schilf held the glass doors open for the woman, sensing that the people coming toward him on their way out were looking at him strangely, and followed the determined steps of his companion to a table in the corner. She slumped onto the bench and shrugged off her jacket with a smooth movement of her shoulders. After the orthopedic surgeon's diagnosis, she said, her savings had barely lasted for a couple of weeks. Like the cricket in the fable, during an endless summer she had not bothered herself with thoughts of the harsh winter days to come. That was why she was now looking for someone to take care of her.

The detective understood what was going to happen. He sat down, stood up again, and asked if he could get her something. A hamburger, perhaps, an apple pie, or chicken scraps in oily batter. With a reproving yet almost tender look, the woman asked him to sit back down again like a civilized person and look out for a waiter from whom they could request a menu. Now the detective not only knew what was going to happen. He was overcome by the firm suspicion that this woman, who had been sent to him quite by chance along with the death sentence, really did not exist at all. Someone who asks for a menu in McDonald's fitted too well into the strange form of his imaginative power. In her position, nothing would be easier than simply to go mad, the woman said, still looking at him with those eyes that reflected everything. But what life had to offer was still more appealing to her than insanity.

Even before the detective walked up to the counter to order a meal for two from a pale girl, he had given the woman his address and the key to his apartment. When he came back from work that evening, she had tidied up, vacuumed, made the bed, and cooked some soup. As they ate together for the second time that day, she revealed her name: Julia.

That was four weeks ago. Since then, of course, the detective has tried his best not to make any noise when he gets up early. His new girlfriend lies asleep in bed.

[5]

SCHILF CAREFULLY PUTS ONE FOOT IN FRONT of the other on the clanging metal grate. He sucks the excessively warm morning air through his teeth and gazes at the facades of the buildings around him. People are sleeping behind all these dark windows, in layers beside and above each other like pupating maggots. This image does not exactly make him feel any keener on today's continuation of his existence. Just as he is halfway down the steps, the inner observer starts talking.

Once again, Detective Schilf left the apartment by the fire escape, the voice in his head says. *He was not keen on his new case.*

Schilf has known this voice for over twenty years, ever since the fracture that divided the story of his life into two halves. From time to time the urge to comment off-camera on all his actions overwhelms him like a chronic disease. Then there is no longer a present tense in his head, only a narrative preterit, and there is only the third person instead of "I." His thoughts suddenly start sounding as if someone in the future were talking about him and this early morning, which is fastened to the wall of the building by a zipper of metal grating. Schilf has learned not to defend himself. It is possible to run away from many things, but not from what is going on in one's own head. He has christened this voice the "inner observer," in the way that human beings give names to things they do not understand. Sometimes the observer's visits last only a couple of hours. At other times, he stays close for weeks and turns the world into a radio play without off-switch or volume control, with Schilf as writer, speaker, and listener all in one. The observer keeps silent about some things, but then goes into great detail on other occasions. He can always be relied on at the beginning of a difficult case. He loves nothing more than to repeat what the detective is thinking.

The last thing I need is a beheaded cyclist, the detective thought, the detective thinks.

Two days ago, the walrus-mustached police chief had honored him with a personal phone call and—a sign of the estimation in which he is held—canceled the holiday Schilf had planned. "The Freiburgers can't cope," the chief had shouted into the telephone. "The hospital scandal is driving the whole town crazy. First four heart patients die, then a senior registrar is murdered. Even the blockheads in the press can see the connection. Take your vacation later, Schilf. Clear up this Dabbelink business first."

In other circumstances, Schilf would have obeyed the chief's orders without resistance. He obeys now, but his resistance is enormous. When he considers the matter carefully, there is a problem asleep in his apartment, and another problem (perhaps even the same one) that has inhabited his head for quite some time. The detective does not want to go to Freiburg now. He feels repelled by the thought of the tiny police apartment not far from Heinrich-von-Stephan-Strasse. He is not interested in dead anesthetists or the megalomania of a medical director. He has worked nonstop for years and he needs a break. Right now, there are more important things than this Dabbelink, who is in the safe mitts of Rita Skura.

Schilf considers smoking a cigarillo on an empty stomach, and abandons the idea. For a while he peers into the stillness of the courtyard. Slowly a cat walks across the cleanly swept flagstones. When Schilf starts moving again, it flees into the nearest building with one leap.

Some days there is just no choice other than to leave through the back door, the detective thought, the detective thinks.

He walks down the groaning metal steps. Ignoring the creaking in his knees and shoulders, he climbs sideways over the gate at the end of the fire escape and jumps the final one and a half meters down to the ground.

BARELY TWO HOURS LATER, Schilf leans his head against the cool, vibrating glass of a window, feeling his terrible headache subside. The air-conditioning is blowing into his face through a vent. In a broad curve the train rounds a small town, which with its church tower, half-timbered houses, and tidy meadows looks like an exhibit in an open-air museum. As the rear of the InterCity train comes into view, Schilf thinks, as he does on every train journey, what a miracle of human endeavor he is sitting in. What powerful masses are accelerated by mankind, what pains it takes to wrest materials from the earth in order to forge them into something that serves a great idea. And how it strives toward a goal that, despite thousands of years of philosophical efforts by the cleverest of men, is still utterly unknown.

When the next stretch of forest wraps itself around the train, he turns his gaze away from the window and the world becomes a blur in the corner of his left eye.

Schilf managed to miss the five o'clock train to Freiburg even though he had reached the Stuttgart station with plenty of time to spare. A magazine held him up—it was lying on the platform and he nearly slipped on it. He picked it up out of the wind, which was riffling its pages, and read where it had fallen open.

The article, by a professor of physics, was about the theories of the time-machine murderer—the case that had brought Schilf a promotion to first detective chief superintendent and, moreover, secured him a modest place in police history. As he devoured the article, he felt as if it had been written just for him. He stood reading in front of the departure board, did not move aside when someone asked him to, did not hear the announcement about the train's arrival, and was quite unable to tear his eyes from the article. When he had finished, he looked up at the departing train in astonishment, ready to believe that he was sitting in his reserved seat—number 42 in coach 24—and was traveling, split from himself, on another train track into a parallel universe. His right hand fingered his temples as if he were looking for a lever to reverse his little mistake. He had simply looked up from the magazine too late, and not jumped onto the train. Such a detail could surely not have buried itself in the world's memory so quickly and so irrevocably.

Schilf stood alone, lost in thought in the nighttime quiet of the platform, and remained in the same spot for one hour, without moving. When the next train drew in, he had not even started waiting.

The InterCity train in which he now sits is exactly the same as the one he has missed. Doggedly, Schilf sits in seat 42, coach 24. He places his feet to the left and the right of his bag, puts his hands on his knees, and stretches his back. In this position, he is able to stare off the headache that has resurfaced and also forget about his spine for a while. As he has known for some time, aging does not only bring the ability to wake at four in the morning without being able to go back to sleep. Aging is above all a continuing rendezvous with one's own body, a dialogue with pipes, filters, hinges, and pumps that have been doing their work behind the scenes for years, but now suddenly impinge on the consciousness with their demands for attention. Mapping the self is equivalent to dying; to have totally grasped oneself is death, the detective thinks, sitting upright like a statue, swaying gently with the rise and fall of the train. Once again he says to himself that his badly constructed replacement life has finally been turned upside down. He feels ridiculously happy at the thought. Mentally he feels sharper than he has for a long time, precisely here: at the outer limit of his strength.

Outside, the landscape interrupts its hurried progress; a few passengers get off and on. Schilf lifts his bag onto the seat next to him so that nobody will sit there. The magazine that has gripped him sticks out of a side pocket willfully. If Schilf has understood correctly, the physics professor's statements seem to confirm the theories of the time-machine murderer. But it is not entirely clear if the professor is defending the Many-Worlds Interpretation or merely explaining it. The detective turns to the contents page once again. The square photo shows a blond, laughing professor. He looks happy. Schilf likes the caption: "Everything that is possible happens." Somehow this fits with his hazy ideas about the program code for reality, even though the time-foam model seems much too clichéd.

EVEN AS A CHILD, he loved the idea that the world could really be quite different from the way human beings perceived it. In summer, the little detective lay on his belly in the garden behind his parents' house talking to a butterfly about whether the nut tree by the wall was really a single object or, as seen through the compound eye of the insect, a conglomeration of two thousand nut trees spliced together. There was no conclusion to the discussion, for both the little detective and the butterfly were irrefutably right. From this butterfly, from echo-sounding bats, and from mayflies, Schilf has learned that time, space, and causality are matters of perspective, in the truest sense of the word. Lying in the grass, distracted and focused at the same time, he did not find it difficult to let go of the guide-rail of familiar perception for a few moments and to float free over an unimaginable chaos. How nicely he chatters away to himself, said one delighted parent to the other. Whereas the detective came close to losing his mind at the age of ten.

His childish efforts have developed into a method of working now, except Schilf can no longer lie in the garden. With painful concentration, he bores holes into the desktop made up of crime scene descriptions and witness statements until it is porous enough to allow for conclusions about the program code, about reality. He sees coincidences as metaphors and contradictions as oxymorons, and the repeated appearance of details as leitmotifs. When Schilf gets a hollow feeling in his stomach, as if he were on a trajectory at the very apex of a parabola, he reaches out instinctively to hold on to something (the corner of a table, a door frame, the edge of the sink) and reaps the reward for his efforts: premonitions, daydreams, feelings of déjà vu.

No one in his office understands how he works; they see only his successes. His colleagues shake him by the hand, call him a fantastic clairvoyant to his face and a lucky bastard behind his back. When the case of the time-machine murderer was solved, they said that he had done nothing more than sit around quietly for days until the murderer had contacted him and politely asked him to take down his confession.

THE DETECTIVE HAD ACTUALLY SPENT WEEKS breaking down the cage of his perceptions into pieces in order to find the threads that connected him with the person he was looking for. He combined the study of files with meditation as he waited for a clue that would tell him where and when the coincidence that he urgently needed would occur. At some point the telephone rang and a woman who had dialed the wrong number kept asking for someone called Roland. That same afternoon, a bird crashed into the window of the conference room and dropped onto the window ledge as if it was dead, but when a young female officer tried to pick it up, it flew off, perfectly unharmed. A little later, the detective stumbled in the hallway and broke the glass of his watch against a door frame. In the watch department of the Karstadt department store, two young men were standing in front of him in line, one of them resembling the third murder victim. They were chatting and laughing about how a life without watches and clocks was not only possible but actually more pleasant. The detective decided not to repair his watch and went back out into the street, where he accepted a flyer for a performance at the Panorama Café in the Stuttgart television tower. That evening, he turned on the television and landed on *Vertigo*, a film about a dead woman returning, with an ending that the detective did not understand.

The next day, Schilf sat for hours in the café in the television tower, eating plum cake and looking at the cars far beneath him negotiating their complicated routes through the pattern of streets, and at the Black Forest shrouded in mist on the horizon. He had put his broken watch down on the table. When a young man sat down at the table next to him and started scribbling busily in a notebook, a bird crashed into the large window. In his surprise the detective knocked his broken watch from the table. The man at the next table put his pen behind his ear and picked up the watch for him. They started talking. The young man was wearing a blue shirt with white trousers, and his mobile phone was in a leather pouch on his belt. After two hours of animated conversation the detective said he had to make a quick phone call. The young man lent him his mobile phone, and Schilf walked a few meters away from him out of politeness and called his colleagues at headquarters. It was only later that he found out the surname of his new acquaintance was Roland.

Schilf would never forget the accusing look of the murderer as he was arrested. The young man had trusted him at first glance. He had told Schilf that he came from the future, and that he had landed in this time in order to conduct a few groundbreaking experiments. He was working on nothing less than a solution to the grandfather paradox. He wanted to prove that changes in the past had no effect on later events at all; so a time traveler could kill his forebears without endangering his own existence in the future. Schilf continued listening with interest for another half hour before two plainclothes officers walked in and arrested the young man so courteously that none of the other people in the café noticed.

During the trial, the murderer had presented a file detailing the lives of his victims up to the year 2015. Desperately, he had assured the court over and over again that the victims were alive in the future, some of them were married and had successful careers. Moreover, they had agreed to the experiment. He himself was not like everyone else, he shouted. He did not live here, he was only a guest, on a work trip to a world without consequences, and therefore was not responsible for any actions, however strange. In the jungle of time, the time-machine murderer screamed as Schilf was leaving the room, every moment was itself the next one.

Schilf leaned against the wall in the corridor outside the courtroom. He knew that the jury would convict someone who would not learn, someone lonely, someone innocent in the tragic sense.

6

THE DETECTIVE RUBS BOTH HANDS OVER HIS FACE. When the InterCity train takes the next curve, he becomes aware of whirling flecks, as seagulls seem to follow the train like an ocean liner. Although the speed of the train clearly rules out the possibility of seagulls, which must be an optical illusion, he can even see their orange beaks and the black feathers on top of their heads when he squints.

Gently he strokes the smooth surface of the rolled-up magazine. It is not actually the contents of the article that fascinate him so much, but the feeling that he recognizes the voice of the person who wrote it. While reading, he could hear it in his head, as if the professor of physics were speaking to him in person. As to a friend. The detective is sure that this article has been written by someone who does not believe in what he is saying. Someone who doubts reality, despairs of it, as one who is lost in a labyrinth. The detective superintendent learned something else from the butterflies with their compound eyes: those who believe in nothing also know nothing. Without a reliable cure for doubt, there can be no cognitive orientation. Schilf would give anything to speak with this Sebastian about it. Perhaps he does not need a doctor, but a physics professor for the yawning abyss that has started opening up in front of him at the most inconvenient moments. His doctor had not done much more than ask him a load of questions. He had asked about Schif's successes in his work and the ever-increasing price he paid for them—memory loss, headaches, a loosening grip on reality. The following week the detective was shoved into a scanner like a loaf of bread into the oven, so that magnetic fields could throw the atomic nuclei in his head out of balance. Sometime after that, he sat once again in the wood-paneled study and the assistant brought him a coffee so that he would have something to stir. Schilf dropped one lump of sugar after another into the cup and kept on stirring. While he was doing this, the doctor told him about the secret subtenant in his head. Name: *Glioblastoma multiforme.* Age: definitely a few months, perhaps even several years. Size: 3.5 centimeters. Place of birth: the frontal lobe, a little left of center. Function: causing memory loss, chronic headaches, and a loosening grip on reality.

The sugar in the detective's cup melted into the cooling liquid, forming a saturated solution. He had to stop stirring so that the doctor could pat him on the hand. On the table in front of him were the results of the MRI scan, photographs in tones of gray that Schilf found so attractive that he considered getting them framed. *Glioblastoma multiforme* sounded like a rare tree or a deformed insect, so he gave his subtenant a new name: *ovum avis*—bird's egg. As the doctor was writing down the name of a specialist for the detective, Schilf rose and said farewell. He did not intend to return. And he would not go to the famous specialist. Anyone who regularly attends postmortem examinations does not expect much from having his own skull sawed open.

"ARE YOU STILL THERE? Can you hear me? Damn."

Smiling, the detective shakes his head and stretches his spine until he hears a crack. Two rows behind him, someone is furiously pressing the keys of a mobile phone. The advent of the mobile has finally given human beings a means of expressing their metaphysical isolation and their deep-seated doubt about the existence of other life-forms. *Can you hear me? Are you there?* Who could claim with any certainty that the other person was really there and could hear you speaking? All sentient beings are necessarily solipsists and therefore occupied with ignoring that very fact throughout their lives, the detective thinks. He himself would have every reason to take his mobile phone out of his bag, dial the number to his own apartment, and wait to see if his new girlfriend picks up the phone—he still does not quite believe that she exists if she is not in front of him. *Are you still there?* He could ring himself or the bird's egg in his head and ask the same question. If the doctor is right, Schilf has only a few weeks, at most a couple of months left of the rendezvous with the self that people generally call their existence. He would need this time for an investigation in which he himself would be the chief suspect. The connection between his new girlfriend and the bird's egg had to be cleared up. Perhaps the time-machine murderer is an accomplice and the physics professor a valuable witness. The detective would also have to bridge larger gaps—to find out how the fragments of his life could make a whole. With some patience he would find a solution, one that at least he alone understood. After all, it is not every day that one is declared dead and then called the love of someone's life within a few hours. Before he finally signs off, the only thing to be done, surely, is to make himself whole.

Somewhere in the growing distance, Julia rolls onto her other side and sighs in her sleep because the narrow room is slowly growing too warm for her. When Schilf thinks about her, about the soft-skinned being heavy with sleep in his bed, who quite naturally spends the day tidying his apartment and reading his books and glows with cheerfulness all the time like a puppy, his stomach contracts with a mixture of fear and happiness. He does not believe in the redeeming power of love, and therefore does not plan to connect his desire to live with the tingle in his stomach. Nevertheless, he does not want to die—so far he has gotten no further than this with his musings. The only thing certain is that Schilf and the detective must hurry at all costs if they still want anything in particular from each other.

[7]

AFTER CHANGING TRAINS IN KARLSRUHE, the detective decides to put his musings aside. From his bag he takes a leather pouch, and from this a matte-silver object no bigger than a pack of cards. His new girlfriend has given it to him. She thinks the game of kings suits him and that if someone were to write a book about him one day, he could be the chess-playing detective, just like Sherlock Holmes was the violin-playing detective. Schilf refrained from pointing out that Holmes was not really a detective and that the violin was not a game of strategy, and accepted the gift with thanks. When he presses the "on" button, the display lights up in shades of blue like a new day dawning. Schilf learned the rules of chess thirty years ago from a friend at school, without mustering any enthusiasm for the game. But he has hardly been able to put down the electronic game since he received it. This pleases Julia. She perches on the side of his armchair looking over his shoulder while he taps away at the blue screen, and her hair tickles him until he has lost and goes out for a meal with her.

The game that was interrupted the previous evening appears at the touch of a button. It is the detective's turn, as always. The computer never needs more than a couple of seconds to make its move, but he takes half an hour over every one of his. It waits patiently for him. He is unable to work out the simplest algorithm in his head, so he ties himself into knots with his calculations until he finally makes an incredibly clumsy move after rallying himself to "just give it a go." The gadget lets him make his own fateful mistakes, so at the end he is plagued by the feeling that he has not been beaten but has checkmated himself.

At Offenburg, Schilf's bishop embarks on a daring attack on the queenside, which he feels he has prepared for by advancing a phalanx of pawns. His little soldiers have marched determinedly against the enemy and are now looking the opposing queen full in the face. Just for fun, Schilf imagines that she has Rita Skura's face. In the background, a couple of agitated officers are occupied with a plan that is too cunning for their own good. It has not fooled any grandmasters. It has also never worked.

Schilf's army is literally fighting for its life when the train arrives in Freiburg. On the platform, waiting passengers drop their bags and press their hands to their ears. An infernal screeching of brakes suspends time for three whole seconds. The detective gathers himself and his things quickly.

As he shuffles along next to his greenish reflection on the long row of train windows, he asks himself for the umpteenth time why he plays chess against a stronger opponent as if his life depended on it, without ever once pressing the button to reverse a mistake. In real life he would reverse any number of mistakes without hesitation. He would have given the most personal match of his life—which ended with the fracture, a disastrous checkmate—a new twist. *Perhaps the "touch-move" rule applies less to chess than to character, thought the detective*, thinks the detective.

AT THE END OF THE PLATFORM, a woman in a flowery dress and a cardigan is waiting for a cup of coffee from the drinks machine. She does not bother to turn around.

"Schilf. Congratulations on your promotion."

Rita Skura watches the final drops of coffee drip into her cup, giving Schilf enough time to recover from his shock. She takes the cup from the drip tray and sips from it before extending her right paw to the detective, a gesture that in defiance of several thousand years of cultural history has something threatening about it. She grabs the straps of his bag and tries to take it from him, but he resists indignantly. They tug back and forth a few times until Rita Skura suffers the first defeat of the day, as is evident from the look in her eyes. They walk side by side without another word. Secretly the detective steals a glance at his former student: the deep furrow above the bridge of her nose and the pursed lips, with which she sips from the cup as she walks. He is glad to see her again. At the police college he liked her ambition, her chin quivering constantly with tension, a testament to how seriously she took the world around her—it was rather touching. He almost envied her sincerity then. When he looks at her furrowed brow, he is nearly sorry that he had destroyed her childish trust in appearances with a single piece of advice. He had not remembered how short she was. Her bouffant hair barely reaches his shoulder.

Rita Skura takes long strides, and the skirt of her flowery dress swings around her legs like a sail whipping in a storm. She overtakes him on the steps up to the pedestrian bridge and waits at the top, visibly pleased at the opportunity to look down on him.

"Miss your train?" she asks. "Didn't get out of bed on time?"

"Delay tactics," the first detective chief superintendent pants as he walks up the steps. "To prolong the anticipation."

Rita snorts derisively. She has waited on the platform for an hour and God knows she has no time to waste. When Schilf reaches the top step, she looks at him properly for the first time. Her gaze flits over him with an expression of suppressed rage. The detective wonders why she is not pretty, why all the female qualities in her do not make a pretty woman, but simply Rita Skura. The veins on the backs of her hands are prominent and look like satellite images of deltas in the Amazon River, but that cannot be the reason. She tosses the coffee cup into a trash can decisively, pinching her nose with the other hand at the same time to clear her ears. As if she is crashing in an airplane, Schilf thinks, feeling a ripping sensation in the cortex of his brain, going from his left temple down to his ear. The two of us have arrived in this world like seasick fish, he thinks, but he does not know what this means. He reaches for the knob on the handrail and closes his eyes as the pain rises and swells. He hears the people behind him cursing as they have to maneuver past, and he sees Rita slipping her foot out of her flat shoe and wiggling her toes to rearrange the holes in her stocking. But he cannot actually see anything with his eyes closed, and Rita Skura is not wearing stockings.

Schilf tears his eyes open again and stares Rita Skura in the face, shocked because what she is saying comes through to him only after some delay. Her lips are moving like those of an actress in a badly dubbed film.

"You don't have to act the invalid with me," she says. "I know you better than that."

"That's what I'm counting on," he gasps in reply.

The headache disappears as quickly as it arrived. Schilf wipes the sweat from his brow with his shirtsleeve. Rita stares at him with knitted brows, turns abruptly, and walks on, shoveling air aside with both arms. Schilf has to make an effort to keep up with her. At the station exit he insists on having a sandwich, not knowing whether he is really hungry or simply wants to annoy his colleague. He will find out that these feelings are astonishingly similar.

Standing with their elbows on the sticky surface of a table, they listen to the soft squeaking of mozzarella between Schilf's jaws.

"I'm burning in hell," Rita says with a mixture of derision and wonder, "and you're eating cheese."

Broad shafts of sunlight suddenly fall through the glass front of the station, turning the people in the concourse into slivers of themselves. In the midst of this biblical light show, an unimpressed Rita Skura counts off the hell she is talking about on her fingers.

"Scandal at the hospital. Beheaded cyclist. And to top it off, a lunatic who is claiming that his son was kidnapped, though the son knows nothing of it."

Schilf lowers his sandwich. "Oh?"

Rita picks up a piece of tomato that has dropped onto the table and puts it in her mouth. "Some family nonsense. The man reports a kidnapping and as soon as the phones are bugged, the boy calls from holiday camp, safe and sound."

"And the father?"

"Apologizes profusely, withdraws his report, and assures us that no further investigations will be necessary."

"That's not for him to decide."

"I know. But the case will peter out anyway. We have more important things to do."

"Oh, the cyclist," Schilf says. "You shouldn't worry so much about him."

Her index finger is pointing like a weapon at his head—directly at the bird's egg, he thinks, feeling a faint pulsing.

"Don't play Superman with me," Rita says.

"I meant well."

"In case you failed to notice when you read the file, this cyclist was the right-hand man of Medical Director Schlüter. Strange coincidence, isn't it?"

Schilf suppresses a yawn, passes her the rest of his sandwich, and wipes his hands on a paper napkin.

"The press is roasting us on a spit," Rita says with her mouth full. "People don't like it when the gods in white are under suspicion."

"And you come to the station yourself and wait an hour to welcome me in person?"

Rita shoves the last piece of bread into her mouth and chews for far too long. She does not object when Schilf takes a pack of cigarillos out of his pocket.

"I wanted to talk to you without being disturbed," she says in an unusually quiet voice.

"This is a no-smoking station!" the sandwich man calls from behind the counter.

"And this is a smoking madman with good friends in the health and safety inspectorate!" Rita shouts back.

Schilf blows smoke through his nostrils and observes the play of light on the wisps as they rise through the air. The sandwich man starts wiping his counter.

"Experimenting on patients," Rita says. "Horrible stuff, don't you think?"

"The kidnapping guy," Schilf says. "What does he do?"

"He's a professor of physics," says Rita. "But that's not what this is all about. Just try proving that a doctor has done something wrong. They're all stonewalling. That's where you come in. Detective Schilf?"

Schilf is no longer listening. He has wedged the cigarillo between his teeth, picked up his bag, and has already walked a few steps toward the exit.

"Come on," he calls over his shoulder.

Behind the glass doors is a solid wall of heat. It shimmers in the air above the lipstick-red Corsa in the no-parking zone. In a sudden fit of respectfulness, Rita opens the rear door for Schilf. Moved by this, the detective climbs into the backseat. He had hoped for air-conditioning, but there is none. While a cursing Rita attempts to ease the car into traffic, Schilf finds time for a move with his knight that has occurred to him as a final opportunity for salvation. His defense is in tatters, his queen barricaded in by her own officers. Fleeing forward is his only option, moving another piece into the disputed area of the enemy kingdom. A gap opens up for Rita. The car moves forward in fits and starts. Her eyes seek out the detective's gaze in the rearview mirror.

"Let's get to the point, Schilf," she says. "I wanted to suggest that you call the police chief."

He has made a mistake that is stupid even for a beginner. The move was so irresponsibly rash that Schilf can hardly believe it when his knight disappears with a brief flicker of the screen. In the heat of battle, he has omitted to protect a particular square. He sinks back into the synthetic upholstery, exhausted. Rita's Corsa is one of those cars that will always smell like new. The detective considers abandoning the game, tipping his own king over and surrendering. He looks out of the window in a rage. He sees light patches on the grassy banks of the Dreisam. Snowdrifts or seagulls that are lying on their fronts with their wings spread wide, or sleeping sheep, if sheep ever sleep—he is not entirely sure on this point. Rita clears her throat.

"Listen, Schilf. Tell the chief that you are urgently needed for the hospital scandal. And leave the cyclist, who you don't think is important anyway, to me." She casts him a wary look in the rearview mirror. "The cases are closely connected. We would be working together either way."

Schilf saves the game for later. He thinks longingly of a world in which he has not made that stupid move with his knight and in which he wins every game against the chess computer, which is why he must always lose in this world: for there is no victory or defeat and no right or wrong; rather: victory *and* defeat as well as right *and* wrong.

"Are you even listening?" Rita asks.

"No," Schilf says. "But you can keep the cyclist. And the rest of all that nonsense. I'll take on the physics professor. Now look where you're going."

"Why?"

"Because of the traffic light!"

She slams on the brakes, and a treble C rings out. The detective's slack body folds around the seat belt. He rubs his stomach, groaning.

"But why," Rita says suspiciously as she reverses the car out of the intersection, "why don't you want to do the job on account of which you've come here specially?"

On account of which. Schilf knows why he liked Rita Skura from the moment he met her. In her own way, she is as lost in this world as he is. He aims a wintry smile at the rearview mirror. He's going to be sick if they don't get there soon.

"At my age," Schilf says, "you no longer judge crimes by their prominence."

"Not according to your most recent successes."

"Listen to me, Rita. You can have Dabbelink."

Rita does not quite manage to hide her pleasure. She turns into Heinrich-von-Stephan-Strasse with a flourish, lifts her pass up to the machine at the entrance, and parks in the shade of a tree, for the places under the corrugated iron roof have long since been taken. She rests her hands on the steering wheel. In the sudden silence, the birdsong is surprisingly loud.

"I have never forgotten that I must proceed from the opposite of my own convictions," Rita says. "Going by this rule, I will actually have to trust you."

"You are a good child," Schilf says.

The moment of weakness passes. Rita kicks open her door, plants her feet squarely on the ground, and waits with her fists pressed into her sides for Schilf to emerge from the car.

"This is how it's going to be," she says. "For as long as you're here, we'll be sharing an office. *My* office."

She locks the car and holds the detective back when he starts walking toward the building. He looks down at her and feels the hint of a fatherly smile on his lips.

"Two more things," she says. "First—no tricks."

"I have a new girlfriend, by the way," the detective says.

"Are you sure she isn't a social worker who visits you regularly?"

"Not at all sure," says Schilf. "I'll get the file on the physicist and pay him a visit. You can look after my bag in the meantime."

"Second!" Rita screams after him. "No smoking in my office!"

The detective's laughter is visible in his receding back.

CHAPTER 5

The detective superintendent solves the case but the story does not end.

[1]

FREIBURG IS ONLY HALF AWAKE at ten o'clock on a Saturday morning. The lanes are still in shadow, and the tables and chairs of the pavement cafés around the cathedral bunch together as if they fear the weekend crowds about to descend. The waitresses walk between them like shepherds, shooing chairs into place, patting tables on the back and putting ashtrays on them.

The detective has never much liked Freiburg. The people seem too happy to him, and the reasons for their happiness too banal. It smells a little of holidays, especially when the sun is shining. Students are lifting their behinds onto hand-painted bicycles. Married women festooned in batik make their way to their favorite boutiques. A traffic jam of strollers has already formed outside a health food shop. No one here seems to feel the need to ponder the meaning of life. The detective superintendent sees only one face with a skeptical expression. It belongs to the blue and yellow macaw in a large cage next to the postcard stand outside a photo shop. The bird gazes at the detective so piercingly that he chooses a wicker chair nearby.

"My name is Agfa," the parrot says.

"Schilf," the detective says.

"Look out," the parrot says.

The detective waves away a schoolgirl with green hair who is asking him for a euro even though she is wearing designer jeans and has a Dalmatian on a leash. Schilf is about to tell her that one cannot enjoy the practical advantages of wealth and the moral advantages of poverty at the same time, but the girl tells him where, in her opinion, he ought to go. Schilf grimaces. In ugly towns like Stuttgart, people at least admit that they have struck the jackpot in the lottery of life.

"We're not open yet but you can sit there," a waitress calls to him. She is placing menus on the tables with mechanical movements.

Schilf waves a hand casually in thanks. The waitress is not much older than the schoolgirl. She is wearing a headscarf with skulls printed on it, flip-flops, and a miniskirt so short that her pink underwear shows when she bends over. Schilf unrolls a bunch of papers and spreads them over the table. In her office, without a word, Rita had slammed down the physicist's file onto the corner of the desk she had designated as Schilf's workspace by pulling up a plastic chair. Schilf handed the papers to a passing officer to photocopy so that he would not have to take special care while reading them.

Despite years of experience, Schilf feels a slight shudder at the sight of a human fate turned into paper. Every file he opens is an intersection of his life and that of an unknown person. It will never be possible to untangle the threads that weave themselves together from the moment he starts reading.

Not for one second has Schilf doubted which Freiburg physicist was involved in the kidnapping case. The photo of a smiling Sebastian lies in front of him as he reads through the statement taken by Sandström.

The car had not simply disappeared. It had metamorphosed into a nothingness of a certain kind, into the terrible bequest of an event that should not have happened. Did you know, Herr Sandström, that there is an astonishing number of things that we believe will never happen? We are as convinced that these events will not happen as we are that the earth revolves around the sun. Our own death is one of these things.

And the disappearance of a boy like Liam is another. When something like that happens, the world goes out of kilter. (A comment in Sandström's nervous handwriting: *The witness starts screaming.*) You, Herr Sandström, you have to fix that. That's your job. Do you see?

Schilf is certain that Sandström has not understood the witness. But he, on the other hand, does understand him. Sympathy wells up when he thinks about those words—cries for help, really—coming from the same brain that produced the sober phrases of the scientific essay. The physics professor was used to bending the world with the power of his intellect. So this was how he spoke after waiting three days for news of his son.

The waitress has finished distributing the menus. Now she starts on the tea lights—symbols of uselessness in the bright morning sun. A customer walks up to the photo shop and knocks on the bars of the birdcage.

"Pretty please," the parrot says.

Schilf only skims the rest of the file. Sandström's handwriting shows the increasing strain he is under. The brief report from the police psychologist states that Sebastian is not suffering from schizophrenia. The forensic team notes that the Volvo was professionally cleaned the day after the kidnapping.

"What can I get you, sir?"

Schilf lowers his papers. "You have to understand dialectics," he murmurs.

"What did you say? You're diabetic?"

Under her knitted brow, the waitress's clear, green eyes are slanted. She is probably wearing tinted contact lenses to give her the transparent, all-knowing gaze of a cat. Schilf has to admit that it works.

"Look out," the macaw says.

"Could I have a newspaper, please," the detective says. "And a café au lait."

"Yes, you can have that," the waitress nods. "There's no sugar in it."

She comes back with a newspaper and a tall glass layered with coffee and milk in different shades. Deftly, she places a long-handled spoon down next to the glass and puts the accompanying sachet of sugar into the pocket of her miniskirt. Schilf lets her have her way, even though he prefers sugar in his coffee. He opens the newspaper. The headline is underlined in red, and stretches across the whole of the front page. "MURDERER IN WHITE." An enormous question mark detracts from the finality of the headline. The waitress stands idly by the table, watching a group of tourists gawping at the cathedral spire with their heads thrown back. Under the headline, large photos show an angular man in a yellow sports jersey frowning as he holds a trophy up for the camera, and a bald doctor in a white coat who has not quite succeeded in pushing his hand between himself and the onlookers.

"It's only a church tower, after all," the waitress says maliciously. Then she makes a vague gesture in the direction of the newspaper. "It's all nonsense."

"What's nonsense?" Schilf asks.

"This one didn't kill that one," she says, pointing first at one photograph, then the other. "You're not from here, are you?"

"My girlfriend and I live in Stuttgart."

Schilf recognizes the expression on people's faces when they are sizing up a crazy old man—it's a sure sign that he's on the right track. The waitress nods, her eyebrows raised, and starts justifying her presence by wiping the edge of the table. Her movements are precise, like those of a machine. Now that the detective thinks about it, the parrot with his painted headdress also looks mechanical, and the group of tourists is being hustled out of the picture as if on a conveyor belt. *Perhaps I'm the only creature made of flesh and blood here, the detective thought*, the detective thinks. *And I'm trying to investigate crimes among the robots.*

"But he has a motive, after all," Schilf says. "This senior registrar must have known about the experiments on patients, and blackmailed the medical director."

He lifts his head to confirm that the waitress is looking at him suspiciously. He feels her catlike gaze on him as a physical sensation, especially on his forehead and temples.

"All nonsense," she repeats stubbornly.

"How do you know?"

"Intuition."

She taps her pirate headscarf and Schilf nods approvingly because she has located her intuition in the depths of her brain rather than between her diaphragm and pancreas, like most other people.

"Someone like him," she says, pointing a false nail at Schlüter's half-covered face, "either does things properly or not at all. It was pure coincidence that the botched job with the steel cable worked."

Schilf suppresses a comment on the nature of coincidence, and hurries to ask his next question. "Who did it, then?"

"My name is Kodak," the parrot says.

"Agfa," Schilf corrects.

"That bird is a pain," the waitress says. "Either Schlüter got someone to do it . . ." She sinks into thought.

Schilf is afraid that her battery is dying. "Or?" he prompts.

"Or the death of that one has absolutely nothing to do with this one. We have stuff without sugar if you want something to eat."

She turns away and walks toward the entrance of the café with precise movements in time with the rhythmic slapping of her flip-flops. They ought to install etymological dictionaries on their robots' hard drives, Schilf thinks. But other than that, they seem to work very well.

"Look out."

Schilf has the impression that the bird is trying to tell him something. He gazes at the parrot thoughtfully as it nibbles away at a stalk of millet. When nothing else happens, he puts the file away and takes out his mobile phone. The rail information service informs him that the first train from Airolo won't arrive in Freiburg until eleven o'clock that morning.

[2]

MAIKE IS ONBOARD THE FIRST TRAIN from Airolo, feeling like a passenger on a ghost train. It judders its way along a labyrinthine course while a series of dioramas passes before the windows. White goats on shiny green—one of them raising and lowering its head. Cable cars gliding in front of a panorama of mountain peaks. An old man swinging an ax next to his wooden hut. Well-fed cows advertising political neutrality. In small countries the monstrous lies in the details.

When Maike is especially happy or unhappy, she makes lists. She has a list of the best days in her life (her wedding is number one), her greatest disasters (not many entries), her most important successes (founding the Gallery of Modern Art), and her most embarrassing moments (a new cleaning lady throwing a pile of broken chairs out onto the street shortly before a gallery reception). Maike ranks favorite dishes, most annoying people, and her dearest wishes. Her memory is a well-ordered storehouse in which an archivist categorizes every new event. She can say exactly how she feels about almost everything that has happened to her. Keeping lists is her own way of making an inventory of her memories. As of yesterday evening, there is a new list: of puzzling telephone calls.

After the receptionist had put the call through to her room, it had taken Maike an entire minute to realize that the stammering caller was her husband. He said to stay calm so many times that Maike finally started panicking. It was only when she sternly told him to stop it that he told her his confused story. Liam had been kidnapped but was perfectly fine in scout camp after all. Sebastian would pick him up early tomorrow morning. Maike had better break off her holiday, too. It wasn't actually necessary, but you never know. Perhaps the police might want to ask her a few questions.

Sebastian's outpouring ended midsentence, like a broken tape. There was a white noise over the line while she remained silent. Oskar had once said that the whole of space was filled with white noise. Maike had heard from someone else that such noise was caused by bugging devices. For a crazy moment, she wondered if they both meant the same thing.

When she had calmed down sufficiently to ask what on earth had happened, she heard Sebastian gulping hard on the other end of the line. He asked her to believe him—first he begged her, then he suddenly started screaming. He could call Oskar instead, Oskar would stand by him. Maike's shock turned to rage. She demanded that he pull himself together. She got no reply. Finally she realized that Sebastian was about to fall asleep while on the phone. This shocked her more than anything he said. She promised to take the first train to Freiburg in the morning. He swore that nothing had happened to Liam, then the line was cut.

Maike leans back across her seat and stretches her legs. In the seat opposite, a nun has wound her rosary so tightly around her hand that it has left red marks on her knuckles. The nun tries to engage everyone walking past her in conversation, as if she wants to prove to the poor Lord Jesus that mankind has no desire to be left in peace. Love thy neighbor. Maike shudders. When the dapper conductor speaking pretty Swiss German checks her ticket, she thanks him profusely.

She did not sleep well the previous night and spent a great deal of time imagining all kinds of different scenarios. A failed kidnapping attempt, perhaps, or maybe Liam got lost in the forest and has been found. Or perhaps Sebastian had had a nightmare and called her still half asleep, and would be thunderstuck when she walked through the door.

As morning approached, her imagined scenarios lost their definition, her theories grew wilder, and her questions led nowhere. Her thoughts began to work in images and to revolve around a night ten years ago, as if it were still the cause of every dark, incomprehensible part of Maike's life. It was the evening of the day that stood at number one in her list of favorite memories.

A function room misty with cigarette smoke. Happy crowds swaying to music. Friends, family, and an angular figure among them who wanders the room aimlessly, anxiously, conspicuously, like a shadow that has lost its master. Maike's feeling of delighted terror (or is it terrible delight?) every time this shadow bumps into the newly minted groom in the crowd. Proud and cold, the two men look each other in the eye. At some point Maike—incredibly drunk by then—tugs the sleeves of their frock coats and tries to get them to dance *à trois*. The guests clap and hoot. Oskar tears himself away and leaves the party without a word. A close-up of Sebastian's face as he kisses Maike with mouth wide open almost as soon as Oskar has left.

In the first year of their marriage, Maike was constantly prepared for something to break free and rise from the depths of the man who smiled at her every morning across the breakfast table. Something that could not be conquered by goodwill and understanding. But nothing of the sort happened. From an anomaly, Sebastian had turned into a good husband and a loving father. He was the youngest professor on faculty at Freiburg University. Maike opened her gallery and made sure that Oskar came to dinner regularly. The family got wrapped up in the everyday.

For a long time now, Maike has thought of herself as part of a happy family. Regardless of how well or how badly their life together is going, there is one thing she has never doubted since Liam's birth: she and Sebastian inhabit the same world. And she is prepared to do anything to keep it that way.

Perhaps, thinks Maike, looking at an Asian woman who is pushing a metal trolley down the aisle, perhaps this is what is waiting at home for me. The disaster I have feared more or less consciously for so many years. Perhaps it even has a woman's name, like a hurricane. Perhaps my own name.

Her thoughts are about to tip over into the abstruse again. She buys a coffee from the Asian woman. The cup is so hot that she can barely hold it in her hand. Two border guards appear in the carriage and the German one holds Maike's coffee for her so that she can dig out her ID card.

She feels her worry like a thousand pinpricks in her side. But whatever is waiting for her in Freiburg, she can be sure of one thing: if Sebastian swears that all is well with Liam, then it's true. Everything else can be borne. One of the reasons Maike loves cycling is because she enjoys estimating her own strength correctly. She drinks, burns her lips, and takes another sip anyway. The Swiss idyll has been left behind on the other side of the border; outside, a pale sun is conducting the overture to another relentless summer day. Let's see what happens, Maike thinks. Later, she will say the same to the detective: Let's see what happens. Long before that, she will see the face of her friend Ralph Dabbelink on the newspaper racks in Freiburg Station. It will be the beginning of a new list: the most terrible days of her life. And the detective will take second place on the list of people she is most suspicious of, just ahead of Oskar, who has topped this list for years, and just behind Sebastian, the new contender who has jumped straight to number one.

[3]

THE SUN GLINTS ON THE SNOW-WHITE STUCCO. Front doors and balcony doors are open, and a state-of-the-art racing bike is leaning against a streetlamp covered in ivy. The building is lovely to look at and perfumed with the scent of wisteria, but it resembles empty packaging. All this beauty cries out for happiness, and the people who live here are no longer happy. To the detective, everything looks wrong and empty, as if the entire street has been turned into a postcard, a memory of itself. When he steps onto the footbridge, Bonnie and Clyde swim up to him on the anthracite-colored canal. From his bag, Schilf takes out a currant bun he bought on his leisurely walk through the town center. The ducks paddle against the current so that the pieces of bread drop down directly onto their beaks.

"Back, back, back," they chorus.

"Look out," the detective calls to them. "Look out."

But Bonnie and Clyde clearly don't know what to make of the parrot Agfa's words. They turn like two synchronized swimmers and paddle swiftly down the canal. Schilf brushes crumbs from his hands and walks into the entrance hall, studying the names by the doorbells. Just as he finds what he is looking for, a thunderous bang causes the building to rumble. Up above, someone has slammed a door. Quick steps clatter down the stairs and a woman rushes out of the front door, straight past the detective. He touches his fingers to his forehead so as to raise an imaginary hat. He does not recognize the woman. Her blond hair waves around her head and falls over her eyes as she bends over to unlock her bicycle. The detective watches, transfixed. She is wearing a sleeveless shirt and cotton shorts; the morning light turns her tanned arms and legs into polished wood. In contrast, her blond hair seems far too bright, as if she had borrowed it from another pale person. The woman is livid—she hurls her bike around, swings a leg into the air, and, already moving at speed, shoves her feet into the straps on the pedals. A few seconds later, she has disappeared around the corner at an impressive angle. It occurs to the detective that he has never seen a more beautiful person.

He avoids pressing the buzzer, and climbs the stairs to an apartment on the second floor. It is apparent that someone is listening behind the door. He approaches and presses his ear against the wood in imitation. The tension is electric. Two men, separated only by a piece of wood, are straining with all their senses toward each other, as if they want to blend into a single creature. The door is wrenched open.

Sebastian is standing there with the remains of an interrupted fight on his lips—his lungs are pumped up, his mouth tensed for a scream. Helplessly his gaze moves across the detective's face.

"Do you have a trash can?" Schilf asks.

He stretches out a scrunched-up paper bag toward his host-to-be, and bread crumbs fall out of it. Sebastian slaps the ball of paper out of his hand.

"Get lost!"

The detective has, of course, already put his foot in the door. They look each other in the eye through the narrow opening. Instead of cursing and tussling over entry to the apartment, they are suddenly standing very close together, as if enveloped in a bubble of stillness in which something beyond language is happening. An encounter. A pause, at the intersection of two different kinds of chaos.

The definitive entanglement of our lives, the detective thought, the detective thinks.

The dripping of a tap behind Sebastian's back marks the passage of time. A jackhammer in a distant street marks the passage of time. There will probably be many questions. Why each of them feels the other has come to help him. Whether it is possible to stop a life from falling apart. How to patch it up in retrospect. If there is such a thing as mutual recognition at first sight between two strangers.

But they cannot stand like this forever.

"Professor," Schilf says softly, apologetically, "I'm from the police."

Sebastian immediately opens the door fully and walks down the hall with stiff legs. Without turning to look at his visitor, he drops onto the sofa in the living room, puts his elbows on his knees and his head in his hands.

"I'm sorry," the detective says as Sebastian finally looks up and rubs his reddened eyes, "but I'm still here."

Stillness seeps into the room again, but this time it does not feel intimate. It is like the silence between two travelers waiting on a platform for different trains. While Sebastian stares at the ceiling as if there were something to see up there, the detective looks around the room. The furnishings have lost their tasteful unity. They stand around indifferently like extras between takes.

Within seconds, Schilf thinks, everything here has become the past.

He listens for the echo of a scene that the room must have heard, for objects don't have ears they can block. The shadow of a man still passes over the walls, pacing up and down, trying to find a way out, his arms raised to protect himself from something heavy that is threatening to fall on him. A woman's screams still echo in the leather of the armchair.

This is a film! This *is not* reality!

Her manicured fingers have upset the pile of magazines on the side table; she had wanted to fling them onto the floor, but hasn't after all.

Ralph *dead*? My son *kidnapped*? And I am cycling happily in Airolo, not knowing any of this?

Happiness and not knowing are the same thing, dear Mrs. Physicist, Schilf thinks.

The sofa shakes with the impact of a man's fist.

Look! At! Me! I couldn't ring you, for God's sake!

A pause, a deep breath.

Keep your voice down!

The man's laughter makes the curtains tremble.

Don't worry. He's dead to the world. The motion sickness pills.

The laughter trails off. The print of a woman's hand on the glass of the side table fades away.

Something is . . . wrong . . . I can't . . .

And what about *me*?

The man's voice rises, driving the walls apart, transforming the room into a cathedral in which every word hangs in the air.

Do you want to know what *I've* been through? This is what it feels like, like this!

The armchair judders to one side as a small body falls into it, shaken roughly by the shoulders.

Let me go, Sebastian!

The final cry is like a bolt of lightning and the slamming door thunder. The quiet after the storm is what remains. Naked scorn. The neighbor's dog barks with three voices: soft, medium, and loud.

"Do you know what it's like to have lost everything?" Sebastian asks.

"More than you can imagine."

"What's your name, anyway?"

"Schilf." Sebastian slowly takes his gaze from the ceiling and repeats the name, which feels good in his mouth. Schilf.

Their eyes meet. Somewhere in the apartment an object falls to the ground but neither of them turns his head. The detective wonders why it is suddenly so dark. The headlights of a passing car lift the room and turn it on its own axis; Sebastian sits on the sofa, Schilf in the armchair, then Schilf on the sofa, Sebastian in the armchair. Then the car is gone. They nod to each other. The combine harvesters are working in the fields outside the town; somewhere Julia is sighing in her sleep. The detective wheezes air out of his lungs once (*ovum*) and twice (*avis*). A sharp beak is pecking the shell of the bird's egg. It is bright again, midday in summer, with dusty shafts of light by the window. Sebastian looks at Schilf with a mixture of suspicion and interest. He leans forward, almost as though he wants to take the detective by the hand.

"I want no further investigations," he says.

"You don't want to know who kidnapped your son?"

"I want to forget."

"Bad idea. You'll only realize when it's too late."

"I'm not interested in too late. I'm interested in now. I don't know what the word 'future' means anymore. There are situations where you have to draw the line. Do you see?"

"Even before you started going into detail," the detective says.

When Sebastian raises his arms to brush his hair out of his face, they both see how badly his hands are trembling. The skin beneath his rolled-up sleeves is thickly covered with scratched insect bites, some moist and inflamed and others crusted with yellow. Sebastian buttons his cuffs.

"Can I get you something to drink?"

"Yogi tea."

"Sorry, what?"

"Look in the kitchen. A woman like your wife will have something like that."

"How do you know Maike?"

"She just ran past me."

Sebastian pauses for a moment before he gets up and leaves the room. Schilf listens to the rustling in the kitchen cupboards, which stops when Sebastian finds the box of tea. The detective stands up quietly and crosses the room as carefully as if the floor were littered with dry twigs that might snap beneath his feet. He has no problem finding the study. Books fill the shelves and lie in piles on the floor. The computer keyboard on the desk is covered with a strangely shaped piece of red card. Schilf rifles through a pile of papers with practiced fingers.

"The Problem of Precision in the Constants of Nature," "The Purpose of Absurdity," "Materialism and the Metaphysical Landscape"—*We cannot ascertain that the universe was created with regard to a living observer . . .*

Or by an observer, the detective thinks.

He opens and closes drawers. A Yogi tea has to be brewed for about fifteen to twenty minutes on a low flame.

Pencils, used paperclips, letterhead paper from the university. Right at the back of a drawer, there is a photo of two young men in formal suits, slim as whippets, hands casually shoved into the pockets of their striped trousers. Although the faces are turned toward each other, their gazes are lost in the middle distance. Schilf puts back the photo. A normal detective would find a decisive clue among such documents. Schilf finds nothing.

When Sebastian brings in the tea, Schilf has been sitting in the armchair for some time. The scent of ginger and cardamom fills the room.

"This doesn't taste too bad." Carefully Sebastian puts down his cup; his hands have steadied.

"Do you collect art?" Schilf asks, pointing at two knobbly paintings whose thickly applied explosions of color in red and black portray a throbbing headache. Clearly the artist takes a different view; he has marked the titles of the paintings in crude letters across the canvas: *Blackmail I* and *II*.

"My wife runs a gallery."

"And likes cycling?"

"Is this the start of the interrogation?"

"Not an interrogation." Schilf waves his teaspoon dismissively. "Just asking some questions."

"What's the difference?"

"You. You are not a suspect, but someone who has reported a crime, and also a witness."

Sebastian laughs, and does not reply.

"If you're ready," Schilf says, "I would like to ask you a few questions."

"About the kidnapping?"

Now the detective laughs.

"No. About the nature of time."

[4]

"YOU'RE A STRANGE KIND OF DETECTIVE. It's not that I don't want to talk about the nature of time. That's my job, after all. But do you really want me to speak to you as I would to my first-year students? That would be like a journey into the past. As if all this was over. Would you like to do me a kindness? Shall we talk as if nothing has happened? You're looking at me like a doll without a brain."

Sebastian takes a sip of tea, a second sip, then a third before he continues.

"When I was at school I once wanted to write a story in which a man finds out that he is surrounded only by dolls. I've no idea what happened to that story. I never wrote it down. So I'm going to talk to you as if I am talking to a doll, Detective. As if I'm talking to . . . a friend.

"Do you know what materialism is? The love of money? No. Or perhaps it's that, too. The materialism I am talking about is a worldview that links everything back to one principle: that of matter. Seen this way, even thoughts and ideas are merely manifestations of the material. Dreams, for example—they're a biochemical product.

"This view of the world is very popular. It has pushed religious belief aside, and replaced it, in fact. The Commandments of materialism are simple and threefold. Thou shalt not doubt the material nature of the universe. Thou shalt trust blindly in the chronological causality of all events. Thou shalt honor the objectivity and uniqueness of tangible reality.

"These statements of belief anchor materialists in the world better than God ever could. There is of course the odd phenomenon that contradicts the principles of materialism—or seems to—and therefore remains inexplicable, at least for the moment. But there is an unfailing remedy for such doubts. You simply paste labels over the holes in this view of the world. An example?

"Not even the most brilliant scientist has any idea why an apple falls from above to below. He simply calls this lack of knowledge 'gravity.' Coincidence is another of these labels. Possibly déjà vu and intuition, too. The unknowable pinned down by the act of naming. Do I hear you say that ninety-nine percent of all concepts are such labels? You may be right. If I were able to unite all the sciences, something that has existed for a long time would emerge from the process: language.

"I've never liked labels. When I was in school, I found it hard to believe in teachers who wrote numbers on the blackboard but could not explain what gravity was. Instead of continuing to listen to them, I waited until I was old enough to read Kant. I had always suspected my mind of doing secret things—I had an inkling that it added something to my cognition, that it brought everything I perceived into a ready-made order, creating a world that it could understand. Kant was able to prove that—he showed me time and space as forms of human perception. It was not a matter of whether or not I believed him. I *felt* that he was right.

"All paths lead to enlightenment and none lead back! For a long time, I was tormented by the fact that my research was clearly not related to the tiniest particles and the laws which govern them, but to the physicist who studied them. At some point I came to terms with the question of whether the scientist is striving for truth in a world of objective reality, or in a world of apparitions. Instead of torturing myself further on this question, I annoyed my colleagues by claiming that we're engaged in psychology rather than in physics. It's just a matter of definition, isn't it? There's no cause for despair as long as there's logic, that long-standing barrier between us and the bottomless abyss. Perhaps the people who called me esoteric were not wrong after all.

"Please do light up! That way you're one of two people who are allowed to smoke in this apartment. Here's the ashtray—you can believe in its material nature or not, but it will fulfill its function in any case.

"It's very much the same with time. Time fulfills its function, and we don't know much more about it than that. It's generally accepted that time is a strictly regulated process with a necessary order of cause and consequence. The only things that humanity shares willingly are its mistakes!

"Take this building, for example. They started work on it in 1896. The hammering of carpenters echoed through the streets in 1897, and soon after that the building was finished. What do you think was the reason for its construction? A lack of living quarters in the Wilhelminian period? Or an aesthetic love of the neo-Gothic and neo-Baroque styles? Let me tell you this, Detective Schilf. The reason for its construction was its completion.

"You smile. But it goes some way toward proving my theory. What are the chances of an architect's plan actually beaming a house? Have a guess. Eighty percent? Good. The probability of a finished building being preceded by an architectural plan is nearly a hundred percent. The construction *enables* the existence of the building, but the building determines its own construction. Therefore the likelihood of a building being the cause of its own construction is significantly higher than the opposite assumption.

"You're still smiling. I ask you this: What is time when we can prove that an effect logically precedes its own cause? Now you're laughing. I think that you have understood me from the very beginning. I see it in your blank look.

"Don't say anything. Forget this little play of thoughts. It was only to shake the gates of your imagination. Please don't use the saucer, Schilf. I've brought you an ashtray specially. Or can't you see it?

"Let's get to the Many-Worlds Interpretation. You must know that God is guilty of its creation—or rather: its nonexistence. Stupidly, human life all comes down to a miracle, by which I mean an impressive instance of coincidence. During the big bang, the universe could have developed in an infinite number of ways. The number of possibilities that allowed for biological life was infinitely small. Despite this, the path that led to our existence was chosen. All the constants of nature that we observe are exactly calibrated to enable an unimportant cluster of biomass called the human being to exist among them. Given the tiniest deviation from the laws of physics we would not exist.

"Savor that thought, Detective: You are improbable. I am improbable. We are a coincidence, with a probability of one in ten to the power of fifty-nine. A ten with fifty-nine zeros after it, Schilf! You would have to throw the dice that many times for your existence to happen at least once.

"Do you feel ill at the thought of numbers like that? Dizzy? I wouldn't hold it against you. How stupid it was to get rid of a god who had been specially conceived of as the clockmaker of this precision machine called the universe! Abandoned, the physicist elevates his own existence into a matter of doubt and investigates against himself. What if the big bang had brought not just one, but ten to the power of fifty-nine worlds into existence? At least one of them with the right conditions for human beings to live in? Detective Schilf, that would turn the question of God into a problem of statistics.

"You've read that somewhere already? And I wrote it. So we nearly have something in common.

"Ever since quantum mechanics led to the discovery that—before the instant in which they are observed—the smallest particles exist not just as single bodies but as multiple layers, the Many-Worlds idea has become not only a philosophical convenience, but a consistent interpretation. Apart from that, it also leaves human beings their free will. For as long as we can call forth new worlds through our actions, it doesn't matter how much we are affected by the cause-and-effect mechanisms within each world. So we remain free in our decisions.

"Those are the advantages of the Many Worlds. Their disadvantages turn even the most peaceful physicists into bad-tempered know-it-alls. They mutter that this is nothing other than a tortured attempt to circumvent the notion of an intelligent designer. Exactly, I say! The know-it-alls complain that the theory goes beyond verifiable assumptions. And again I say, exactly! They are right—the critics of the Many-Worlds Interpretation just as much as its advocates—and they are wrong in the same way. All of them. Because they are all—listen carefully—all materialists.

"I see amazement in your eyes. I'm trying to bamboozle you: I don't give a damn about the Many-Worlds Interpretation.

"You remain impassive. You're tough, Detective. In an interrogation—yes, I know, you're just asking a few questions—everything has to come out, doesn't it? I'll tell you what I'm really working on. I'll bet that you didn't cotton on to any of the intellectual crimes committed daily at my desk while you were searching it. Yogi tea—a nice touch!

"Please record my confession herewith. I am a scientist, but not a materialist. What I am, I still do not know. In any case, I see not only space and time but also matter itself as the product of a collaboration between mind and reason. My world does not consist of fixed objects but of complex processes. All states of being and continuous forms are simultaneous and therefore timeless. What we see of them are merely clips, scenes from a spool of film running through the time projector inside our heads. They show us reality as a dance of concrete objects.

"Try this experiment, Schilf. Pack a camera and go to the top of a tall building one night. Choose an exposure of a few seconds and take a photograph of a crossroads. What do you see? The lights of cars and streetcars as straight or wavy lines. A network of lines. The longer the exposure, the denser the network.

"Take this cup. Imagine that you can photograph it from high above, with an exposure of a million years. It will not show as a cup, but as an impenetrable mesh. There will be a frayed, lighter patch in the middle where clay is formed in the earth. Around it will be the traces of the human beings who mine the clay and work it into porcelain. The forming of the cup. The transport of it. The use of it. Its disintegration. The material it is made of going back into circulation. You also see—we're very high up and we have the ultimate bird's-eye view of things—you also see the stories of how all the people involved in producing and using the cup come into existence and fall away. And the stories of their forebears as well as all those who are descended from them, and so on. You would see—no, don't look away, look at the cup! You would see that this cup transcends time and space and is quite simply connected with everything, because everything is quite simply part of the same process. And if you were able to increase the exposure to an infinite degree, and the distance from which you view it to an infinite distance, you would see reality as it really is. Everything flowing into everything else, outside of both space and time. A tightly woven carpet by the bed of a god who does not exist. Amen.

"Are you still there? Can you hear me? I didn't want to alarm you. Do you have a headache? Should I get some pills?

"Of course it's fine. It always is. That is one of the things I've learned in the last few days.

"Allow me a final comment. A couple of words on coincidence, the mention of which makes your eyes light up. If you, Schilf, as I suspect, are also not a materialist, you will be able to make something of the following connection.

"Let us assume that a human being stands before reality like someone walking along the shore of a peaceful lake. The smooth surface of the water reflects a familiar world and hides what is beneath. Now a large bough floats to the surface, and only the tips of two separate branches emerge from the water in different places. The person by the lake will not perceive this as a bizarre coincidence. He will quite rightly assume that the branches are connected to one another beneath the water. Without realizing it, he has understood what coincidence is.

"You haven't drunk your tea, Detective. Are you about to go?"

[5]

THE DETECTIVE, WHOSE EYES HAVE OF COURSE been anything but blank throughout, thinks it quite unlikely that Sebastian has said all this. But the professor would certainly have said something, and Schilf has filled in the rest himself. He had stirred his tea through the entire lecture, as if expecting to hear another death sentence. Now he stands up, swaying lightly, like a doll struggling to maintain its balance. Fighting his headache, he waits for one of the questions that are the purpose of his visit to surface.

"Who described you as esoteric?" he finally asks.

"Oskar," Sebastian says.

He looks at the detective through pale eyes. He has some color to his face now, and the way in which his fingers are playing a piano sonata on his lap shows that the talking has done him good.

"Who's that?"

"That's an excellent question."

Leaning his head back, Sebastian listens, as if he is trying to pick out the right answer from the song of the titmice in the wisteria. *Favorite person*, they twitter, *favorite person*.

"A great physicist, who is working on a new particle accelerator in Geneva. If you're interested in physics, you should go. The very bowels of the universe are studied there."

"By materialists, I assume."

"You've got it." Sebastian laughs. "Although I'm not at all sure about Oskar any longer. I was wondering only yesterday if we haven't misunderstood each other all our lives."

The detective looks at him for a moment longer than necessary before he nods. "Does the particle accelerator have any practical use?" he asks.

"Its by-products do, Oskar would say. For example, accelerated particles are used to irradiate tumors in medical science."

"Look."

Schilf is swaying even more than before. He makes a grab for the armchair and his fingers catch hold of a Swiss Army knife that has been driven into the leather of the chair. He puts it on the side table. There is blood on the blade. Schilf's headache is suddenly gone, as if someone has thrown a switch.

"You've been very helpful," he says.

Sebastian looks at the knife thoughtfully and wonders if it's a sign, and if so, of what. In an instant he feels completely drained, and when he finally looks up, the detective is already in the hall. He is not walking toward the door, but farther into the apartment.

"The door's that way!" Sebastian calls, following him.

"I'd like to meet your son before I go."

"But he's sleeping."

"Not anymore."

His eyes blinking like someone emerging from a matinee into the daylight, Sebastian stays in the hall while Schilf walks toward his son's room and turns the doorknob.

LIAM SITS ON A CHAIR that he has yet to grow into, with an open book that he is not reading. The room is dim and so small that the furniture seems to be jostling for space. A ray of light coming through the curtains gilds his head with silver and gold. An angel with a crown of sunshine. Schilf swallows to suppress his emotion.

"Hello," he says after clearing his throat. "I'm from the police." And when Liam does not respond, he says, "I'm a proper detective, like on TV."

The book is clapped shut and Liam turns his chair around.

"I'm little, but I'm not stupid," he says. "You can talk to me quite normally."

Looking at Liam's worried face, Schilf wonders how old the boy is. His soft hair has been pressed down by sleep and his scalp shows through in some places. The face beneath is serious and attentive. Schilf suddenly wonders if this child with his sharp ears can hear the voice of the observer who is asking himself if the sharp ears of a child can hear the voice of the observer. And if that is why Liam is looking at him so strangely.

"Are you in pain?" the boy asks.

Schilf looks around for somewhere to sit and settles on the edge of the unmade bed.

"No," he says. "Not at the moment."

Liam puts his book down, which takes three years off his appearance, and turns the chair a bit more so that he is sitting directly in front of Schilf, their kneecaps almost touching.

"What are you doing here?"

"I'm investigating your kidnapping."

Liam looks at his hands in silence, as if he is wondering whether his fingernails need cutting.

"Yes," he says finally. "The kidnapping."

"Are you angry about leaving scout camp early?"

"What do you mean, angry?" He rubs his eyes so hard that Schilf feels like taking hold of his wrists to stop him. "My father just picked me up early this morning. He was acting very strangely, and he didn't tell me what was going on."

"I know the feeling," Schilf says. "No one tells me what's going on either. But there have to be people like us, too."

A smile spreads across Liam's face, making him look pleasant as well as precocious and intelligent. There is something helpless in his eyes, like a small animal looking into the face of an approaching disaster that it can do nothing about.

"Will you clear this all up?"

"Most probably."

"Promise?"

"Promise."

The boy looks down at the floor to hide the glimmer in his eyes, and Schilf puts a hand on his shoulder.

"Liam," he says. "Were you kidnapped on the way to Gwiggen?"

"Did my father say that?"

"Just give me an answer."

"My father doesn't lie. He loves truth above all else."

"He loves you first," the detective says. "Then the truth."

When Liam lifts his head, he looks like a shrunken adult again.

"If I were to say that I wasn't kidnapped, and my father says the opposite, can we both be telling the truth?"

"Yes," the detective says quickly.

"Then I'll say that I don't know anything about a kidnapping."

"Who took you to Gwiggen?"

"My father."

"Are you sure?"

"I was asleep. And when I woke again, it was dark, and I was in a strange bed. Isn't that what it says in the file?"

"More or less." With a swift movement Schilf wipes the laugh away from his mouth and chin. "But it's my job to ask about things that I already know. Could it be that you were sleeping very soundly?"

"Children are like that," Liam replies earnestly. "Besides, the motion sickness pills make me drowsy."

"Can I have a look at them?"

"I only had one for the way there and one for the way back."

The detective nods and looks over Liam's head at a diagram in a glass frame on the wall. The solar system is depicted in the bottom right-hand corner, on a dark blue background. An arrow indicates the sun and its planets as a tiny point in a group of twenty fixed stars. Another arrow points from these stars to a barely discernible particle vanishing into the starry mist of the Milky Way. And the Milky Way itself is a fingernail-sized blob in a wider collection of galaxies, which, together with untold groups of other galaxies, form a supercluster. This supercluster is depicted as nothing more than a small patch of mist in the known universe, which is shown as a large hazy layer covering the diagram like a lid. Above it is a sentence: "Galaxies are to an astronomer what atoms are to a nuclear physicist."

When Schilf changes the focus of his gaze, the glass covering the dark background reflects his face. He feels as if this picture is the only window through which he can look out of this room into the world.

"Does your father tell you about his work?"

"He thinks it's good that I don't understand everything yet, because explaining things helps him to think."

"And you're interested in what he does?"

"I research time as well. I often used to lie in bed and try to catch hold of a second. I lay in wait and then suddenly whispered *'Now,'* but the second was either not there yet or already over. Now, of course, I know that time is quite different. And that they"—he points at the alarm clock ticking next to his bed—"are all lying."

"And what is time?"

Liam turns and rustles in his desk drawer with unexpectedly lively movements until he has found a piece of paper and a pen. Schilf bends over him so that he can see better, smells the child-smell of the unfamiliar head, and starts breathing through his mouth. Liam draws two red circles a hand's breadth apart.

"What's that?" he asks.

"No idea," Schilf says.

Liam taps his pen on the paper impatiently.

"Do they have anything to do with each other?"

"They look similar. I can't say anything more."

"Very good. And now?"

He puts the tip of his little finger down in one circle and his thumb in the other circle.

"Now they are connected," the detective says.

"Just imagine that you and I are the circles and that the piece of paper is a three-dimensional space, and that my hand has come from an unknown, higher dimension."

"You're talking about coincidence," Schilf says.

"No," Liam says indignantly. "I'm talking about the fourth dimension. You asked about time, after all."

"Your hand is a coincidence to the circles. Or a miracle."

Liam thinks about this.

"Yes, possibly."

"Did you think all that up yourself?"

"Almost. My father helped a little. He always says he is basically trying to solve quite simple puzzles."

"What a pity that the two of us," Schilf says, tapping himself then Liam on the forehead, "are only small red circles on a flat surface."

Liam's laugh does not yet have lines to flow along, but must carve out new paths on his face—yet it emphasizes his strong resemblance to Sebastian. He pushes both hands through his hair exactly like his father does. His forearms do not have a single mosquito bite on them.

"When you were little," he asks, "did you like researching things, too?"

"Yes," Schilf says. "I liked talking to insects."

"But that's got nothing to do with physics."

"I used to stand next to the rain barrel for hours, saving bees that had fallen. I used to think about what that meant to the bees."

"Did you want to be a vet?"

"For the bees, my hand was fate. And a kind of fourth dimension."

"You're a freak," Liam says.

The detective tweaks the boy's nose playfully, and the laugh they share comes easily this time. Schilf goes to the door. He feels lighthearted.

"Will you remember your promise?" Liam says.

"Do you know Oskar?"

"Yes, Oskar's cool."

"Do you think I should visit him?"

"Definitely."

The detective raises a hand in farewell and Liam waves back.

Sebastian is still out in the hall. He hasn't moved at all. He is overcome with confusion after hearing murmuring voices and laughter coming from Liam's room. Schilf walks past him on his way to the front door.

"Good-bye," the detective says and then repeats, "You've been very helpful."

As Schilf shambles down the stairs to the street, tiles start coming off the roof above him. Beams and rafters and joists fly apart in all directions. The rapid crumbling of the walls runs along the top of the whole building like stitches unraveling in a sweater. The foundation disappears and the earth closes over. A pencil sucks up the lines of an architectural drawing until the piece of paper is blank. The idea of a four-story building in the Wilhelminian style evaporates into mist in the head of the architect. Somewhere in the distance, a cockatoo flies up into the air with a shrill cry of warning.

[6]

"ARE YOU ALL RIGHT NOW?"

"Yes. The heat. Thank you for the water."

The detective has spent a lot of time recently telling people how he is feeling and thanking them for something or other. It is probably part of getting old, like waking up early.

The young woman bending over him has hair dyed a synthetic shade of red, and reminds Schilf of a film he saw some years ago, in which a girl is running all the time. He means to preface his next question with a gallant gesture, but it turns into a clumsy wave because of the way he is lying on the floor.

"Can you tell me where I am, please?"

"In Freiburg," the young woman says. "Or were you asking about the name of the planet? Or the galaxy?"

Schilf tries to laugh but stops immediately, because his brain is sloshing around in hot fluid.

"I'm familiar with the constellations. What kind of shop is this?"

"This is the Gallery of Modern Art."

"Very good. That's where I was heading."

"That's probably why you walked in the door."

"Very likely. Is Maike here?"

"She's in the courtyard with the birds. Do you know her?"

"I'm a friend of her husband."

Schilf allows the young woman to help him up, even though he feels quite steady on his feet by now. Her hair smells of mango, and the fair-skinned arm that she offers him smells of coconut. They pass affronted paintings, bad-tempered sculptures, and a few hostile installations; they get to the back door and linger at the threshold. Schilf feels as if he is looking into a piece of paradise. The walls of the small courtyard are covered in moss, and beams of light slant down through the leaves of an overhanging chestnut tree. The sunlight conjures up the familiar metallic shimmer on the head of the woman who is leaning over the hatch of a large aviary, just as she bent over to unlock her bicycle earlier. The caws of the parrots turn the courtyard into an exotic place, a bit of outback hidden in the midst of Freiburg's town center.

"Maike, you have a visitor."

Maike shakes seeds from a box into an earthenware bowl and distributes peanuts on little dishes as if she has heard nothing. Three of the yellow-faced birds flutter to the bottom of the cage and watch her. When she has finished feeding them, she stands straight.

The detective thought he was prepared for anything, but he is nevertheless shocked. Maike's eyes are expressionless, her lips pressed together. Her face is stretched over her cheekbones like a mask that has grown too small. Her obvious reluctance to engage in conversation allows the detective a few seconds in which to feel moved. There is a shadow over her bright surface, and it seems to Schilf as if it has the shape of a tall man. Suddenly he wants to do everything possible to protect Maike. He wants to sacrifice himself in order to divert catastrophe from her, even though he has come here as catastrophe's master of ceremonies. Maike stands stiff as a post in front of him—she is nothing more than the wife of a witness, a mere accessory to a case. Not for the first time, Schilf curses his job. The investigator does his work behind a glass wall, he frequently says in his lectures at the police college, always behind a glass wall. Other people's lives are like his own past to him: he can look at them, but not enter them, and it is always too late to change things.

Schilf will address Maike with the formal *Sie*, ask her questions, and not reveal the tightening in his throat. He can't speak clearly anyway.

I've got nothing against emotions, but they really don't have to hit me with full force every time, the detective thought, the detective thinks.

"Why are you looking at me so strangely?" Maike asks.

"I'm watching you exist."

"Who are you?"

"Schilf," says Schilf.

"He says he knows Sebastian," the redhead explains, disappearing into the gallery.

Maike raises her eyebrows, astonished. "Just don't tell me any bad news."

"It's about paintings," the detective assures her hastily.

Maike's eyebrows return to their usual place. "I'll just quickly give the birds their water."

They walk by the aviary together. Another parakeet uses its curved beak to climb down a pole at the side of the cage. It stops level with Schilf's face. Its cheeks are adorned with two red circles like over-applied rouge.

"Can they talk?"

"Not in our language."

"This morning I spoke to a parrot in town."

"That must have been Agfa. *Look out, look out*?"

It is a good opportunity for them to smile at each other, but Maike does not use it. She pushes the nozzle of a watering can through the bars of the cage and fills the water dish.

"What's he called?"

"He's a cockatiel parakeet, from the cockatoo family."

"I mean, what's his name?"

The bird in front of Schilf's face has finished his assessment and climbs farther down the cage to nibble at the peanuts. Maike pauses for a second before she answers.

"He's called Ralph."

"And those two there"—Schilf points quickly at a couple kissing on a perch—"they're in love, aren't they?"

"They're both male. They're kissing to stimulate their brains and their gonads."

"Is that what male friendships are good for?"

"Among cockatiels, yes," Maike says, unmoved.

Beneath her light eyelashes, her eyes are slightly puffy and stiff, as if she has forgotten how to blink. Expressionless, she looks the detective in the face.

"Let's go inside," she says. "We can talk about paintings there."

The two chairs that Maike leads them toward are in the middle of the room, and too far apart for a proper conversation. They are red, and twisted into themselves, so that the back supports not the spine of the person sitting on it, but their right shoulder instead. Schilf sees the creative urge of the designer floating around the chairs like a colored cloud, and sits down only with some effort. He is unable to find a suitable posture. Finally he leans forward with his elbows resting on his knees, like a hooligan at a bus stop. He puffs out his cheeks when he sees that Maike has crossed her legs elegantly on her contorted chair, and thus turned herself into the most beautiful of all her works of art. A giant photograph covers the wall behind her. Although it contains no recognizable objects, Schilf knows immediately what it depicts. A crossroads at night, taken with an exposure of a few hours.

Schilf doesn't have a clue about visual art; only in a moment of insanity could he pretend he was a serious buyer. Sweat trickles through his hair down onto his neck. The way Maike is sitting in front of him—unapproachable, hyper-real, radiating coolness like the canal in front of her house—she is the only work in this room that Schilf would like to acquire on the spot, chair and all. He would display her in his apartment. She would never be allowed to move or talk, certainly not while he was at home, anyway. No wonder Sebastian loves her, the detective thinks. Questions about the laws of nature pale into insignificance next to a woman like Maike. She would be present in every imaginable parallel universe, and always herself.

Maike is also looking at a bright red, sinfully expensive Girome chair, not with a work of art on it, but with a shapeless, sweating person who is casting her strange glances. In her head, a dead Ralph Dabbelink and a kidnapped Liam are struggling to expand themselves into something that could explode any minute. Maike is a victim—she has done nothing other than go on vacation. She is guilty only of being away for a few days, at the end of which she had to witness her husband turn first into a stranger, then into a monster who shouted at her, grabbed her by the shoulders, and threw her to the floor. The fight happened barely three hours ago, but has already become unthinkable to her. She has reckoned with a disaster of some kind, but one she could point to, not a situation in which she could no longer understand a single word in her own language. The list of the most terrible days in her life has begun to grow—each consecutive day will push the one before it out of pole position, and Maike senses that this will go on for a while.

The man in the Girome chair is sweating as if he wished to dissolve into water and then disappear from the surface of the earth. He is sweating too hard for a collector and certainly too much for a normal art lover looking for a deal. Only his eyes are cool. Maike sees something unapproachable in them, hyper-real, a reflection of the most beautiful of all works of art, which this man would buy on the spot if he could. This work of art is she herself. As she returns his gaze, she grows calmer and calmer, almost as if she is approaching an inner death without any fear of dying. She can hold this gaze longer than he can. She will not blink for all eternity. She has the form that is always able to outlast the content.

"How can I help you?"

Maike's question comes out perfectly. The redhead is sitting at a desk by the entrance, wearing a pair of large glasses and flipping through a file in slow motion. The detective shifts his weight on the chair. His next position, with one arm resting on the too-high back, is just as uncomfortable as his first.

"I've come about *Blackmail I* and *II*."

Maike's face is a blank surface. "You've been to my apartment?"

"Just briefly."

"Strange that you mention those paintings."

The voices of the parakeets come through the door from the courtyard—they are starting to comment on the scene. Maike crosses her legs the other way.

"When I came back from vacation today, there was a water stain in the shape of a hand on the wall next to *Blackmail I* and *II*."

Schilf does not reply. He noticed the stain.

"My husband threw a vase against the wall because . . . Excuse me." Maike shakes her head. Her lips begin to stretch into a smile for the first time. "It's not a good day. Signs everywhere."

The smile spreads and makes the detective's heart lurch.

"There's a sad story behind those pictures. The world is full of them."

"Of pictures? Or sad stories?"

"Perhaps they're the same thing."

"You could be right."

"Do you want to hear the story?"

"Absolutely."

"IT'S THE FINAL WORK BY THE ARTIST. He put forty pounds of oils on the canvas. Painted as if he were using up his supplies. Then he retired from painting."

Maike speaks quietly and quickly. The artist, a favorite of the Muses, and Maike's very own discovery, fell in love one day with a young boy, who soon moved in with him. The relationship was of the kind that turned every park bench into the stage for a Greek tragedy. There was nothing remarkable about the artist's appearance apart from a pair of incredibly bright eyes, but his boyfriend seemed to be made according to the sketches of a Michelangelo. Slender, dark, and supple. Pure body, no soul.

At gallery receptions, the young man strolled gracefully through the rooms, intent only on distracting the guests from the exhibition. Both men and women gazed after him. If the evening went well, there was more talk about him than about the paintings. He did not like his lover's work. He did not like art at all. He thought that art existed only to detract from the beauty of life, by which he meant, above all, his own beauty.

"Do you know what jealousy is?" Maike asks.

"From hearsay," says the detective.

Two years passed. The young man showed off his bruises proudly. When the fighting could escalate no further, he set an ultimatum. It was either him or the paintings.

"The artist chose love," Schilf guesses.

"Wrong," Maike says.

The artist chose art. He sent his lover packing and expressed his despair in color, creating *Blackmail I* and *II*. After that, his muse left him, too, and followed his boyfriend.

"He never painted anything of note after that," Maike says. "Sometimes love is a kind of destructive rage."

She raises her little finger to the corner of her eye as if trying to brush something away. Neither of them feels that the next sentence is their responsibility. While Maike looks down at her feet, the orchestra of thoughts in Schilf's head plays a polyphonic symphony of questions to ask and statements to make. Philosophical remarks about the architecture of fate. Queries about the price of the paintings that he is supposed to be interested in buying. Banalities about breeding parakeets. When he finally opens his mouth, he has assembled the most deadly collection of words imaginable.

"How are you coping with Ralph Dabbelink's death?"

Maike jumps up almost before the name is out of his mouth. She looks around as if she has come in here by mistake and stumbled into a conversation among strangers.

"How do you know Ralph?"

"From the newspapers."

"Did they say I was friends with him?"

"I know that from Sebastian."

"You're lying!" Maike shouts.

She is right, for it was not Sebastian who told the detective about Maike's friendship with Dabbelink, but Maike herself, or, to be precise, her racing bike, combined with the paleness of her cheeks, on which her tan looks artificial. She has pushed both hands into her pockets, and is kneading the fabric of her trousers.

"Who are you?"

"I'm sorry."

"Please go."

Maike walks over and looks directly down at him. Schilf rises clumsily. He can see that she is struggling for composure and losing it. Her self-control is falling away like a broken facade; an expression of naked fury is coming to the fore. When she lifts a pair of touchingly balled fists, Schilf does not feel that her aggression is directed at him. It is Sebastian's chest that she is punching, Sebastian's skin that she is digging her nails into. It is also his arm that she is holding on to, and it is even his voice that makes comforting noises. They sink into an embrace that the detective has not sought. He feels the fat of his stomach yielding to Maike's weight, the softness of his body. It takes only seconds for Maike to push him away from her and re-create some space. The redhead looks over, indifferent as a machine that has not been programmed to deal with occurrences of this kind.

"I'm here to warn you."

The detective hears the sweet whispering of a rejected lover; it comes from his own mouth. Quickly he pulls back the hands that for some unknown reason are reaching toward Maike.

"You have to stand by Sebastian no matter what happens. He . . ."

"We'll see," Maike says.

She wipes moisture from her face and smooths her hair. In another five seconds, she will have changed back into the untouchable gallery owner, curator of strangers' fates, saleswoman of sorrow turned into paintings. Three more seconds.

"Don't make a mistake. Leave everything else to me."

"Get lost."

She does not shout, but turns the words into a polite request. The detective obeys. The doorbell chimes the "Ode to Joy." Maike goes to the window and watches him as he walks down the lane, taking small steps and lifting his knees up high as if to avoid invisible obstacles. He takes an intolerably long time to reach the corner, where he does not turn, but simply dissolves into air.

[7]

RITA SKURA IS HAVING A SHITTY DAY, one of those days that get worse and worse with every passing minute. At around two o'clock in the afternoon, she sinks down into one of the armchairs that are on every floor for anyone feeling faint. Even with her eyes closed she can see the figures in dressing gowns shuffling down corridors, and hear the slapping of the slippers dangling from bare feet. All morning she has been surrounded by a cloud of disinfectant that ought to spread cleanliness, but which merely reminds her of flaking scalps, bedsores, and open ulcers. The light of the fluorescent tubes pursues Rita just as doggedly. It turns even healthy faces into grimaces of misery, and makes the summer's day outside look like a mocking stage-set, no more real than an Alpine panorama on a billboard advertising chocolate.

Rita Skura is young enough to think that good health is simply a matter of having the right attitude. She is a stranger to a place like this. She has always found the idea of people drilling bits of metal into each other, or cutting each other up into bloody sections, more tolerable than the exhibits of decline that accompany what they call a natural death. At such an endpoint to the glory of human life, the following question arises: Why does someone like Rita Skura devote all her energy to hunting down people who have done nothing more than replace this tortuously slow decline with a quick exit? No one can put the real criminals—illness, mortality, and the fear of both—behind bars.

Thoughts like these do not pass through Rita's mind as she leans back in a soulless, artificial leather armchair and pulls her cardigan tight around her—of course not, she is not the type to think like this. She is worrying instead about wasting time. She has not been in the business long, but she knows immediately when she is not making progress. And if Rita hates anything, it is dead ends.

On this wasted day, her only success so far has come from brazenly taking Medical Director Schlüter by surprise and forcing him into a brief interview. Early that morning, she swept past reception confidently, took the elevator to the cardiology department, and hid behind an aluminum cupboard in the corridor. When the medical director appeared during his rounds, followed by a flock of white coats, she stepped out in front of him at the door to the nearest patient's room. Schlüter did not seem surprised. Without saying a word, he grabbed her sleeve. His familiarity with body parts not his own was evident in the firmness of his grip and the indifference he showed to Rita's anatomical particularities. He dragged her through a glass door that he shut behind them. The senior registrars and the nurses locked outside immediately started up a conversation, looking through the glass with the studied indifference of goldfish.

Rita and Medical Director Schlüter found themselves in a section of the utility passage, surrounded by buckets, cleaning carts, and discarded wheelchairs. Unusually for Rita, she hardly got a word in. Schlüter did not raise his voice, and his lecture lasted less than five minutes.

The police had been plaguing him for two weeks—him, who had taken the Hippocratic oath not just as a matter of form but to his very heart—with the most absurd accusations. He was not sure if a thick-skulled civil servant such as Rita was able to appreciate what it was like to continue carrying out his very complicated duties under these circumstances. Some patients were refusing to take medication because they were afraid that they would be poisoned by doctors testing unauthorized pills on behalf of the pharmaceutical industry. Even less could Rita imagine that the gruesome death of his anesthetist affected him, Schlüter, most of all. He would not put up with it any longer. If Rita and her friends didn't immediately stop treating him like a murderer in public, they would find themselves charged with libel and facing a massive police scandal. He did not think it necessary to list the influential persons he played golf with on a regular basis.

At the end of this speech, face impassive, he presented an alibi for the night of Dabbelink's death. A short break with friends at the Montreux Palace Hotel on Lake Geneva. The dates tripped off his tongue with such confidence that Rita immediately decided to delegate the task of checking them to Sergeant Sandström. Schlüter wished her good day, waved his attendants over, allowed a nurse to open the door for him, and marched down the corridor toward the room of the patient he was scheduled to visit.

Too proud to run after him, Rita had stayed put, ground her teeth, cursed her job, and realized too late that the glass door could be opened only from the other side. She had far too little evidence to name Schlüter as a suspect. He was not even a witness whom an investigating judge could summon to give a statement.

Rita Skura had spent the rest of the morning on the hospital ward, annoying nurses, patients, and junior doctors with questions, all without obtaining a single useful piece of information. All of them had genuinely liked Dabbelink, who had been a competent senior registrar and a pleasant colleague. Sadly, no one knew him well. Unmarried, childless. Willing to be on call during weekends. All were shocked by his terrible death. Rita finally lost her cool in front of an innocent-looking trainee nurse. She sawed through the air with her large hands until the girl burst into tears. Then she had to take the girl in her arms and comfort her because an irate detective had been beastly to her.

Rita watches a patient have a sneaky cigarette on a balcony. The staff of this damned hospital, she thinks, is behaving like a family of rabbits gone to ground after a bird of prey has snatched one of their number. In truth, she cannot find fault with their behavior. Murders and other terrible things are happening outside, but inside the hospital nobody has enough time to spare from the business of saving lives to even glance up from their conveyer belts.

She snaps her mobile phone open and rings Schnurpfeil, whose obedient voice gives her peace of mind even in the most awful situations. Of course he will come to pick her up, in half an hour, yes, and with great pleasure. In the meantime, he adds shyly, she should order a turkey sandwich in the hospital canteen, so that she doesn't forget to have lunch again.

Rita gets into the elevator, and as it descends she stares at her neon-gray face in the mirror. If the Freiburg police force fails to deliver any results of note over the weekend, the press will give the bristle-haired home secretary hell, and he will give the mustachioed police chief a roasting, and so on. Rita is, as she knows, at the bottom of the food chain.

WHEN THE DOORS OF THE ELEVATOR OPEN, she is greeted with a sight not calculated to raise her spirits. There is not much happening in the wide expanse of the reception area. Visitors cross the room with hurried steps and there is a splashing noise from a nihilistic indoor fountain complete with a few goldfish. The usual potted palms add to the impression of freshly scrubbed futility. To the left of the entrance is the canteen with its red, yellow, and blue chairs.

First Detective Chief Superintendent Schilf is sitting in the middle of this garish splendor, exactly at the spot where two waves of the pattern in the tiles meet. He is hunched over on a particularly yellow chair, tapping away on the display of a small gadget that he is holding close to his face. Like an old man who has stumbled into the play area in a shopping center. His gaze follows a patient carrying a plate with three slices of cake on it. He looks as if he is looking out for someone he knows.

Rita watches from a distance until her desire to spray him with disinfectant and watch him die like a large bug on the floor has grown into an alarmingly vivid fantasy. Schilf barely seems to notice her when she walks up to him.

"What the devil are you doing here?"

"Playing chess," the detective replies without raising his head. "One of mankind's most elegant attempts to forget itself."

"Is it working?"

"Neither the game nor the forgetting."

He sighs. Until now, Rita Skura had quite understandably thought that he was here to get in her way, to snoop over her shoulder, and, worse still, to help her. When he sighs for a second time and looks around anxiously at the dull thud of a pair of crutches, she is no longer sure. Schilf seems to have come on personal business.

"Are you looking for someone?"

He shakes his head as if he has been caught out, straightens himself, and tries to look serious.

"Oh no," he says. "I'm probably afraid I'll discover a second Schilf here, shuffling around the corner in a shabby dressing gown."

"If I ever have to stay in a hospital," Rita Skura says, "I'll only wear evening dress."

"That's what everyone thinks, Rita, my child. But when it actually happens, they always turn into a down-at-heel shadow of themselves."

"How do you know?"

"One of the most important qualities of a good detective is omniscience."

Rita snorts with irritation and goes up to the counter, where she orders dead bird on bread. The waiter does not laugh; and it was not intended as a joke.

"How's it going?" Schilf asks when she sits down at his table.

"Wretchedly." The sandwich falls apart at first bite. "Doctors will sell their grandmothers before they betray one of their own. It's not impossible that this piece of wisdom comes from you." Rita licks mayonnaise from her wrist. "And by the way, we have an agreement. A clear division of labor. At the risk of repeating myself: What the devil are you doing here?"

"What would you do if you knew you were going to die soon?"

The sandwich stops in midair.

"What are you on about, Schilf?"

"I'm trying to have a conversation with you. We don't always have to talk about work."

Rita is ready with an acerbic reply, but she thinks better of it, and pauses to consider.

"I'd find a new home for my cat," she says. "And travel around to visit all the people I love."

"Would that be a long journey?"

"Fairly short."

Schilf nods. Two visitors have met at the hospital entrance and started a conversation. You can't give up hope, one of them says. Yes, hope, the other one says, that's the last thing to die. Both laugh, but stop immediately. They are standing in the path of the sensor for the automatic doors, which open and close busily.

"It would have to be a ground-floor apartment," Rita says, "with a garden. For the cat, I mean."

She pinches scraps of turkey from the plate, shoves them into her mouth, and swallows without chewing. More than anything, she would like to go home right now, draw the curtains, and stop up her ears with cotton wool to block out the twittering of birds. She would lie in bed, stroke the cat, and ask herself why she hadn't listened to her parents.

"This hospital is not good for us," Schilf says to her lowered head. "Let's talk about work again instead."

"Great," Rita says. "And how's it going with you?"

When Schilf reaches for her plate, she picks up the remaining piece of bread and bites into it defiantly.

"The usual," Schilf says. "As far as that goes, I'm quite the old hand. A real Stalin of investigative methods."

Rita looks at him, bewildered.

"By the way, I've found your cyclist's murderer," the detective says.

Rita nearly spits the piece of bread across the table. She looks at the remains of her pathetic lunch and waits for rage to fill her. It does not come. She just feels tired, with an air of finality.

"I warned you," she says lamely. "You mustn't cross me."

"But you're empty-handed."

"But they're *my* hands!"

As proof she shows the detective the palms of her hands, which despite her size are most elegant.

Schilf stands up, puts away his chess computer, and takes out an old-fashioned fountain pen. The nib tears the paper napkin as he scribbles down a telephone number.

"I still have to check on one detail. Call me if you want to know the outcome. In the meantime, I'm going for a walk in the woods."

Just as Schilf is leaving the table, Schnurpfeil appears at the entrance and looks around. Conversation ceases at neighboring tables with the appearance of the policeman in the perfectly fitting uniform. Schilf goes straight up to him. He pushes the senior policeman, who is gazing imploringly at Rita, back onto the street.

Exit Schilf, the detective chief superintendent and Rita think at the same time.

CHAPTER 6, IN SEVEN PARTS

The detective superintendent crouches in the ferns. A witness who does not matter appears for the second time. Many a man travels to Geneva.

[1]

THE THINNING HAIR ON SCHILF'S TEMPLES is lifted by the cool stream of air coming from between the front seats of the car. He does not find it unpleasant to feel a little cold, even though the air seems to be wafting from Schnurpfeil's rigidly hostile back. The senior policeman has turned the air-conditioning up high and turned the police radio up loud. Hissing and mumbled speech drowns the conversation that they are not having. Schnurpfeil is looking the detective in the eye through the rearview mirror, and Schilf is directing him through the city with minimal movements of his fingers, a photo from a newspaper balanced on his knees. It shows part of a road and two trees directly opposite each other.

As they pass the last houses, the light and shadow of the Günterstal woods playing on the dashboard, Schnurpfeil breaks his frosty silence.

"You could have just said straight off that you wanted to go to the scene of the crime."

"Oh dear," Schilf cries. "You've seen through me. So you know where it happened?"

"Everyone knows. And I was one of the crime scene officers."

"That's a piece of luck."

The detective tears up the photo, opens the window, and lets the scraps whirl out. Contentedly he breathes in the warm air rushing through the window. It smells of rosemary, thyme, and oregano. After two deep breaths, Schilf sees himself standing in front of a pretty stone cottage, pruning roses. The walls of the house glow in the evening light as fleet-footed geckos disappear into the gaps between the old stones. When this fictional detective pushes the brim of his straw hat back, an ugly surgical scar running straight across his forehead is exposed. Just as he is about to pour himself a glass of wine from a clay jug, the window closes. Schnurpfeil's finger is pressing a button. The South of France vanishes.

"When the air-conditioning is on, the windows stay shut," Schnurpfeil says. "Besides, I know that you're not in charge of this crime scene. Detective Skura is."

Schilf leans forward and pats him on the shoulder.

"You Freiburg people love your crimes. It's as if you've committed them yourselves."

For a while he looks at Schnurpfeil's thick head of hair. Beneath this primeval forest, a brain is struggling with the thought that First Detective Chief Superintendent Schilf would need to use no more than a few calories to end the career of a young police officer. Schilf is glad that Schnurpfeil is loyal to Rita in spite of this. He would be happy to explain that, although petty territorial fights have their pleasures, he is not at all in the business of taking anything away from the sparring Rita Skura. On the contrary, since this morning—or, more precisely, since the smiling physics professor in the square photograph entered his life—he has felt a new and quite irresistible drive to make everything all right for everyone.

Schnurpfeil, he wants to shout, can you imagine that a case I didn't even want to board the train for early this morning is really beginning to captivate me? I feel as if I've been given one last chance. As if I have the opportunity to repair a great breakage by putting the life of a physics professor in order. Schnurpfeil, there's suddenly someone I have to rescue! A man whose theories sound as if he is sitting in the middle of my head and formulating my thoughts better than I ever could myself. But Schnurpfeil, Schilf wants to continue, can it be that I have to bring misfortune upon this man in order to help him, to prevent someone else from doing it, someone who might not treat the subtle dissonances of this case with the necessary caution? What do you think, Schnurpfeil? Goddamn it, it's a classic dilemma!

And Schnurpfeil would shake his head and reply: You're sick, go see the doctor and leave those in good health to continue their work in peace. Or he would say nothing at all because he would have understood nothing; because for him, there would be nothing to understand, and nothing to say.

"Don't worry," Schilf says instead of all this. "I'm still working on the child kidnapping."

The muscles in Schnurpfeil's neck twitch. At the Schauinsland cable-car station in the valley, Schnurpfeil switches on his hazard lights as requested. The car climbs up into the forest with its nose held high. The sun flashes through the trees like a strobe light. The detective wonders whether to call his girlfriend that evening and discuss his classic dilemma. For one dizzying second, he thinks that he does not know Julia's telephone number, until he realizes that her number is also his own, because she lives with him. Right now she is sitting with a cup of tea at the breakfast bar, where she looks perfectly comfortable, unlike him. She is reading old case files or one of his books. The final few minutes of the journey pass easily.

"Here we are," Schnurpfeil says, when the car stops at the side of the road.

"Final stop, scene of the crime. Everyone off!" Schilf calls in a fit of good humor. "Show me the trees."

Schnurpfeil looks straight ahead of him like a soldier, and stays put behind the steering wheel, making no move to leave the car. Let him choke on his loyalty to Rita Skura, Schilf thinks, not feeling inclined to give an official order. Back first, Schilf climbs out of the police car. Even without help, it is easy to pick out the two trees. They flank the road like gateposts, separating two seemingly identical worlds. The forest rises up into the sky on both sides, like a three-dimensional puzzle.

How easy it is to distinguish the two halves from each other, Schilf thinks. Here and there, before and after, life and death. You could do it anywhere, with nothing but a cable.

The air tastes clean, drinkable like water. The birds twittering incessantly. *We should do more open-air investigations, the detective thought,* the detective thinks.

AFTER A CURSORY GLANCE AT THE MARKS left on the bark by the steel cable, he pushes his way into the scrub. He crosses the ditch, lifting brambles carefully from his shirt, and slides down into the undergrowth with one hand on the ground. The traces left by the forensic team are clear to see: bits of plaster from casts of footprints, earth that has been dug up, and branches that have been sawn off. Schilf parts the ferns with both hands and ducks under the green surface in a moment that seems fleeting. Squatting down, he looks around him. He is surrounded by hairy branches with brownish rolled-up leaves like snail shells.

The descent was hot work. His shirt sticks to his back and he tastes salt on his upper lip. Schilf rolls up his shirtsleeves and waits. He is convinced that this place will have something for him, something the forensic team could not find, because it does not consist of flakes of skin and hair. It is the story of how a boundary was crossed. A story about how thin the membrane is that holds a human life together. Schilf wants to know what it is like for one man to wait for another to die. Ants form a dark pile on top of a caterpillar, which twitches clumsily as its body is carried off in pieces. Apart from that, there is nothing that can help the detective's understanding.

A whining noise drills into his ears. Here are the mosquitoes to give the witness statement that Schilf still needs in order to be certain of what he thinks. Seven mosquitoes land on his right forearm and sting immediately. The detective jumps up and beats at them. The survivors launch a new attack without hesitation, and reinforcements come from invisible colleagues; they tickle his neck and sting his arms and hands over and over again. Schilf rolls his shirtsleeves down quickly, shakes his trouser legs, and wipes his face. When he has calmed himself, he notices a small man standing some distance away as if rooted in the ferns, watching him perform the dance of St. Vitus. When their eyes meet, the paunchy man starts moving toward him.

"Miserable bloodsuckers, aren't they?"

The butterfly collector approaches, raising a didactic finger.

"They're the rats among the hexapods," he says. "Insects with six feet," he adds, when Schilf does not respond.

The detective looks at the backs of his hands, where the first bites are swelling. He wonders what would happen if he were to scratch them with the blade of a knife until they were bloody, and then walk into the office of the leading public prosecutor with his arms outstretched proudly, proclaiming, "Look, here's the decisive piece of evidence!" He begins to laugh quietly. It would surely be the first case in criminal history to be decided on the grounds of an intolerable itch.

"Are you laughing at my equipment?" The butterfly collector is still. "A collecting net. And here is a storage net, which is just like life. It's easy to enter and difficult to leave."

The detective is busy spreading spit on his forearms.

"There's been a lot going on here recently," the butterfly collector says. "The police are frightening away my customers." Lots of tiny lines on the man's face add up to a great worry. He points accusingly at a lantern-shaped cage. "See—empty!"

"What are you looking for?"

"Six-legged specimens." The little man stretches out his hand. "Franz Drayer. Pensioner and amateur lepidopterist, on the path to immortality. And what are you looking for?"

"A two-legged specimen."

"Tall, blond, friendly face?"

"You saw him?"

"He was sitting in these ferns a couple of days ago. Almost at the same spot as you."

"Thank you," the detective says. "You've been very helpful."

"You can read about me in the relevant journal!"

Schilf nods farewell and leaves a witness who does not matter to infinity.

Puffing and cursing, he reaches the road. He is combing his hair with his fingers, removing small twigs, when a ringing sound disturbs the peace of the forest.

"All right, you bastard. I'm listening."

"Rita Skura in top form! Delighted. Sadly, my price has risen in the meantime."

"What do you want, you miserable blackmailer?"

Schilf allows himself an artificial pause and plucks a final burr from his trousers. The police car is parked a few meters away, looking like an uninvited guest amid nature's anarchic profusion. Schnurpfeil is sitting behind the windshield, pale and stiff as a waxwork, loath to even glance at him. Schilf turns away and looks at his feet. He needs all his concentration and persuasive powers for the next sentences, and not a resentful police officer.

"Listen, Rita. I need a little more time to clarify the matter. I'll give you the name, to take the wind out of your bosses' sails—otherwise, come Monday they'll be setting the special forces on us. Are you still there? Still listening?"

"Stop blustering, Schilf. Tell me what you want."

"I want my man to remain free. Don't take him in until I close the file. And no press."

This statement does not pass unnoticed. It's half an eternity before Rita is able to reply. When she does, she sounds utterly uncertain.

"We're talking about a murderer. I think you're losing your marbles."

"And you don't have them all yet, Rita, my child. And I mean all the people who count as suspects in your case. Where are you right now?"

"In my office."

"Are you waiting for the next call from the police chief?"

"You bastard. You know full well I can't guarantee what you're asking of me."

"Oh yes you can. Call me again when you've made up your mind."

Schilf hangs up. He takes loping strides toward the police car, slides into the backseat, and taps the frozen Schnurpfeil on the shoulder.

"You can drop me off at the police apartment. Then go to HQ and pick up my travel bag from Rita Skura's office. You'll probably be the only person to come out of there alive today."

The senior policeman starts the engine with a roar and puts his foot down. As they snake toward the valley through narrow bends, Schilf hums a sentence that is stuck in his head: *You have to complete something before it's all over.*

[2]

WHILE SCHILF SLEEPS IN HIS CLOTHES and shoes on the sofa of the police apartment, looking like a corpse in one of his murder cases, Sebastian is standing in his kitchen where every drawer handle is an expression of Maike's aesthetic sensibility. He is preparing an elaborate dinner. The day on which he embraced his son in scout camp, on which his distressed wife ran through the door only to storm out again after a terrible row, and on which a detective wanted to discuss physics—this horror of a day still stubbornly refuses to come to an end. Sebastian has spent the afternoon looking out from the balcony, concentrating on not calling the gallery because he wanted to give Maike time to get used to the situation. When he was unable to bear the silence in the apartment and Liam's polite reserve any longer, he went out to buy groceries for dinner.

Now he is cooking a Thai meal, following a recipe in a cookbook that he found at the back of a cupboard. It was still wrapped in plastic—an unwanted gift. Sebastian stands at the work surface, hunched as if he is trying to express humility before the highly specialized kitchen equipment in front of him. Even the simplest can opener fulfills its function better than Sebastian has fulfilled his.

To be a good physicist. To live a happy life. Not to upset the people he loves.

It is quiet like the eye of a tornado. Sebastian enjoys following the instructions in the cookbook. No pros and cons to weigh up, no decisions to make. He pounds coriander seeds, peppercorns, and cumin seeds into a rough paste with a heavy pestle and mortar, tosses slices of chili and ginger into the food processor, and almost forgets to thaw the prawns in water. Every now and then he bends down and takes another ingredient out of the two shopping bags that lie at his feet like obedient pets, losing some of their girth each time. Liam came into the kitchen ten minutes ago, and has been fighting his usual impatience before dinner by carrying glasses and plates from the cupboard to the kitchen table one by one, refilling the salt shaker, and constantly asking for other tasks.

"Why are we eating in here?"

"It's cozier."

In truth, Sebastian would not dare to attempt sitting down together in the familiar environment of the dining room.

"You can set the table," he says for the third time.

The washed vegetables glow in appetizing traffic-light colors, reaching their visual high point just before they sink into a reddish mass along with the prawns. When Liam comes up to the stove to peek into the pans, Sebastian strokes his head and swallows hard as he realizes how perfectly the curve of the child's skull fits into the cup of his hand. He snatches a sidelong look at his son, who does not notice. He looks at the boy's smooth forehead, the delicate nose with its arched nostrils, the pale eyes, which hint at depths as appealing as they are dangerous. As he looks at Liam, he gets a heavy, sinking feeling in his stomach. He is shocked by the strength of this love, which is capable of sending a grown man—with all his complex memories, convictions, hopes, and ideas—to a place outside of space and time, a place in which nothing except the laws of love apply. As Liam twiddles a wooden spoon with a wagging motion of his finger, Sebastian experiences, with painful clarity, the potential "no longer being" that is inherent in all creatures and things. From now on, Liam can also be seen as the absence of Liam, and that is hard to bear. Sebastian is irretrievably tied to an anti-Liam, whose visible body is a door, the entrance to hell, a door that is not closing properly. Ever since Sebastian has gotten his son back, it has cost him enormous effort not to send him out of the room.

"Damn!"

It was stupid of him to rub his eyes with his hands. The chili and onion take effect, sending Sebastian to the sink, where he washes his face with cold water.

Maike smells the food as soon as she unlocks the door and steps into the hall. It smells of appeasement. Sebastian is standing at the stove with puffy eyes and a red nose, and Liam is doubled over with laughter, pointing at him. The spit between Liam's teeth is green from secretly nibbled peppers. Maike stands in the door frame and wants to laugh with Liam and cry with Sebastian. She asks herself why she washed the floors of all the rooms in the gallery on her hands and knees in order to put off coming home.

"What's going on here, then?" she asks, dropping to her knees to catch Liam as he rushes into her arms.

"Dad's got Thai in his eyes!"

Liam puts up with a kiss and runs back to the stove. He stands on tiptoe and devotes himself to stirring the rice, as though the viscous mass on the wooden spoon could bind him to normality.

"How was your day?" Sebastian asks. For a second, it really seems as if everything were as usual.

As Usual is the worst thing that can happen to Maike right now. She drops onto a chair and smiles helplessly into the growing silence. She feels as though she has been gone not for a few days but for years, and is now returning to a life in which she can participate only as a spectator. Sebastian, who is screwing up his eyes as he tastes his curry, seems as alien to her as an actor who has stepped out of character without warning. She wants to take hold of him and shake him and scream at him, or perhaps hug him and stroke him and smell him, too—whatever it takes to get her husband back.

Since this morning, however, it has been impossible for her to make any movement in his direction, so she can only sit and look and think. It is not only Dabbelink's death that has driven her half out of her senses. Nor Liam's mysterious kidnapping. It is the coincidence of these two things as well as the fact that, in some final way, she understands nothing. Emptiness is not an opponent, and it is impossible to defend a family without an opponent. If Maike had experienced a little less happiness and a little more unhappiness in her life thus far, she would know what to call this empty feeling: fear.

"A strange day," Maike says after clearing her throat, a very necessary action. "A funny guy came to see me in the gallery."

"As tall as Dad?" Liam asks. "Only old? Bulging tummy, and a face like an elephant?"

"How do you know?"

"That's our detective."

"You're joking."

Maike has grown paler than before, if that were possible. Her patched-up calm is crumbling at the edges.

"Almost done!" Sebastian calls to her in an artificially cheery voice, like a TV chef. Maike ignores him.

"Are you saying," she says to Liam, "that this guy works for the police? And that he was here with you both?"

"Just after you left," Sebastian says in a low voice.

"I can't bear this any longer," Maike whispers.

"He promised to make everything OK." Liam's voice breaks with desperate enthusiasm. "He's clever."

"Everything *is* OK, my darling," Maike says to Liam. And to Sebastian, "What did you talk about?"

Sebastian brings a pan to the table and ladles curry onto the plates.

"About the nature of time."

He asks Liam to serve the rice, and wipes the hot ceramic stove top with a cloth. A burnt smell rises. Sebastian opens the balcony door slightly.

"The nature of time," Maike repeats, scornfully.

She mixes rice with the curry and adds salt and pepper without tasting her food.

"Is he coming again?"

"Hopefully," Liam says.

His wife and child are sitting in front of their plates with their cutlery raised, so Sebastian looks at them encouragingly, fishing prawns from his plate and stacking two of them on his fork, by way of demonstration. Maike glances around the kitchen as if she is looking for something: a spoon, a napkin, an answer.

"With a serious crime, you can't just withdraw the charges," Sebastian says. "They're investigating the kidnapping. It's a matter of routine."

"Have the police been to Gwiggen?" she asks. "Have they questioned the staff? Found out who took Liam there?" Her voice sounds as if someone were dictating to her. "Have they been to the service station? Did they look for clues? Find witnesses? Question the petrol pump attendant?"

"Maike," Sebastian says. Nothing more, but he repeats it. "Maike."

Not far from the balcony, a group of blackbirds is conferring in the chestnut tree. It is clear from their bickering that they are discussing something urgent. Do blackbirds even perch at the tops of trees? Do they spy on apartments in old buildings, or are they earthbound birds who leave their accustomed surroundings only in exceptional circumstances? And what constitutes an exception?

When a magpie lands in the branches the blackbirds fall silent.

"A pity it's Saturday already," Liam complains. "Otherwise Oskar would be here."

Sebastian bends down to him and presses his arm.

"There, there," he says, "it's all right."

Liam loads his fork with curry and shoves it into his mouth. He chews once, twice, and then sits still looking at his plate as his eyes fill with water.

"Still too hot?" Sebastian asks.

Liam shakes his head and swallows with a gulp. "Spicy," he says quietly.

"I'm sorry." Sebastian lowers his hands as Maike pushes her plate away from her. "You don't like it either?"

"I do," she says, "but I'm not hungry."

"I can eat the rice," Liam says. "The rice is good."

After a few more mouthfuls Sebastian puts down his fork and knife too, because the kitchen seems to be filled with the sound of his chewing. Maike is drinking water and Liam is trying to spear grains of rice on the tines of his fork. A drop of water falls from the tap and hits the stainless steel sink.

"The morning after the kidnapping," Maike says, "you rang the camp in Gwiggen and told them Liam was sick, didn't you?"

"Do we have to do this now?" Sebastian asks.

"And no one at the camp wondered about this illness, even though Liam had actually arrived there sometime before?"

"I've told you everything I know."

"Do you wonder, perhaps," Maike says, her voice rising in a spiral of hysteria, "why your super-detective hasn't cleared up this point yet?"

"No."

"Then *I'll* tell you why."

Sebastian resists the impulse to press his hands over his ears. He has never heard his wife speak in these shrill tones before. He has thought of Maike as a strong person ever since he met her, and he has never wondered what the conditions for this strength are. Just as Maike wants to grab hold of him and shake him, he, too, feels the urge to torment the figure on the other side of the table, the figure on the verge of a nervous breakdown, until it releases his wife. Until the usual, cool, collected Maike, stylish and composed to the last, appears again. Sebastian does not want to hear the next words. They have been in the room for some time, and are just waiting to be spoken by one of them.

"The police are not investigating," Maike says, "because they don't believe you."

"I'm going to my room now," Liam says.

No one stops him. Sebastian sits hunched on his chair, his arms hanging heavily by his side. He looks at Liam as if he were watching a departing train. The food on the table is no longer steaming, and there is a wrinkled skin forming over the curry. *This is what a farewell dinner looks like*, Sebastian thinks, or, more precisely, something within him thinks—a new, unknown voice, as if spoken by an observer in his head.

"The problem," he says, amazed at his own calm, "is that *you* don't believe me."

Maike finishes her glass of water, but does not know what to do with her hands after that.

"Sebastian," she says quietly, "have I ever given you cause to be jealous? Over Ralph?"

Sebastian's knee crashes against the table as he stands up abruptly, and curry slops off the plates onto the tablecloth. He stands with his back to the room, facing the glass door to the balcony, searching for the faint reflection of his face. He looks himself in the eye in order to know what to do next. Silently, he practices the sentence that he must say, a sentence that includes the words "truth," "trust," "I," and "Dabbelink." It is probably the only chance to save himself and Maike. A new feeling keeps him from speaking. It is the conviction that it is too late, and he finds it strangely uplifting.

"Please, Sebastian! I'm asking you, please!"

When he turns around, Maike's eyes implore him. Sebastian feels like sliding down against the wall and dropping his head between his knees. That would probably have been a good idea, certainly better than the uncertain journey on which he has embarked. At the kitchen doorway, he looks at Maike again properly, the way she is sitting there, her frame slighter than usual, thin and hunched. He smells the fear that makes her hard and strange. He sees her eyelids fluttering and her agitated hands clawing the tablecloth. Sebastian does not know how anyone with such small hands can survive in a world like this, or bring up a child, or love a man like him. He shares Maike's conviction that she and Liam are simply victims. He bears his guilt alone and out into the hall.

"I'm taking your car," he calls. "Mine's been impounded. See you later."

He has never felt the weakness of mankind so clearly as during these few steps out of the apartment. The affectation of walking upright, the power of speech and free will, is suddenly exposed as a laughable hoax. Here are the car keys, the stair landing, the cast-iron streetlamps, the trees and the buildings, and here is Maike's little car on a side street. The world is a signage system he just has to follow.

A liberating sense of clarity divides Sebastian's thoughts into squares on a grid. The voice in his head tells him that he has just made an unforgivable and probably irrevocable mistake. In the continuous chain of horrible events that his life has become, walking out of the kitchen is the crowning glory. It wouldn't be difficult to turn on his heel, climb back up the stairs, and steer the story a different way. But the observer in Sebastian recognizes that unforgivable mistakes are not the result of inattention, error, or not knowing better.

What distinguishes them is that they permit no alternative, even in full knowledge of the circumstances.

The central locking clicks. Sebastian feels the vibration of the engine in his arms and legs. He is a perfectly normal person driving a small car through the neighborhood in which he lives, shops, and works. He crosses the main road leading out of town, which is busy throughout the day regardless of what is happening in the world at large, and enters the enormous network of junctions, intersections, and connections that span the planet like the synapses of a giant brain. It's amazing how little it takes to make a ruinous decision, Sebastian thinks. Soon after, he is on the autobahn.

[3]

IT CANNOT BE SAID THAT RITA SKURA and Detective Schilf have absolutely nothing in common. Like Rita, Schilf hated birds as a child. He had his reasons. They gobbled up the butterflies with whom he conducted epistemological debates beneath the walnut tree. They had immobile faces that showed neither pain nor joy. They stared at him fixedly, concealing a knowledge, which, in his opinion, they did not deserve. He thought it was unfair that they alone surveyed the world from above. If he had known then that it is always the observer who creates reality, he would have despised the birds even more for being the creators of a failed world.

Birds were also the source of nerve-racking noise. They didn't give a damn about other living things who wanted to think, play, or sleep. Often the little Schilf went to his parents in bed in the middle of the night. I can't sleep, he would cry. The birds are screaming in the garden, and trampling on the roof!

His parents laughed about that for years after he had left home, but Schilf didn't find it funny. All those nights he had been unable to sleep, they had assured him that not a single bird could be heard for miles around. From then on, he had believed them to be on the side of the enemy.

Schilf has not thought about this for a long time; it must have turned up in his dreams. He awakens with the feeling that the sharp edge of a beak is boring into the soft inner sanctum of his skull. If only he could be left in peace to think, he would be able to ask himself what the little detective would have said about the bird's egg in the big detective's head.

Confused, he lies in a gloomy room, and it takes some time for him to realize where he is. The shadows around him are the furniture in the police apartment, and the shrill sounds that are tearing at his nerves are not coming from the throats of birds but from a ringing telephone. Schilf presses on the buttons of his mobile to no avail until he hits on the idea of getting up from the sofa to answer the landline.

"Is that you, Rita?"

A sunny laugh comes down the line.

"Sorry, there's no Rita here. It's me."

There are not many *me*'s in the detective's life. Most of the people he gets to know well disappear behind the bars of a penal institution sooner or later. So he doesn't have to think for long.

"How did you get the number of the police apartment?"

"You gave it to me."

Julia is right—for every "me" there is a "you." Schilf's new girlfriend has not been wrong about a single thing since he met her, and she seems to find that perfectly natural. The detective can see her now, sitting in the armchair next to the coffee table, hooking her finger into a hole in her sock.

"Did I wake you up?" she asks.

Schilf has not had the chance to switch on the light yet. Impenetrable darkness lurks behind the open doors of the kitchen and the bathroom, as if night were being produced for the entire country there.

"No," he says. "What do you want?"

The laugh comes down the line again.

"To ask how you are."

This is not an unusual request, but it surprises Schilf. Julia is ten years older than Rita Skura, but to him she stands just as clearly on the other side of the divide between young and old as Rita does. She is part of a new informal generation, a generation that treats everyone like a good friend. With someone uncomplicated like her, Schilf, with his respect for the infinite complexity of things, can relax and feel like a relic from a bygone age. A person like Julia, who can barge her way into a stranger's life with the words "Don't have a job, don't have any family, and I don't like the benefit reforms," is perfectly capable of ringing just to ask how he is.

"Good," Schilf says, which is true and false at the same time, and therefore needs elaboration. "I've found the murderer. Now I've got to protect him from the police."

"I thought you worked for the police."

"That doesn't make things any easier."

"Have you fallen in love with the murderer?"

Now it is Schilf's turn to laugh. He wishes he could see life through Julia's eyes, just for once. It must be like a building with a very straightforward design. Not your everyday detached house—that would be too boring; but perhaps a circus tent with an entrance, an exit, benches to sit on, and a roof. The detective can practically smell the sweet scent of the sawdust.

"Not exactly," Schilf says. "For me, the murderer is a great man, the kind of person we owe something to. I owe him a thorough investigation of this case. Anything else would destroy him."

"But it's your job to destroy the lives of murderers."

"There are subtle differences."

"The good policeman saves the poor criminal! Sounds romantic."

The length of the telephone cable and the size of the apartment allow Schilf to reach the balcony door. The balcony is so small that there is barely room to stand. People only ever want to save themselves, the detective thinks. The difference lies in what they want to save themselves from.

"I would do everything I can to help this man," Schilf says, "whether you believe it or not."

"I believe you," Julia says tenderly. She has interpreted his long silence correctly. "I believe everything you tell me. I have to, for structural reasons."

"What do you mean?"

"Don't you understand?"

"No."

"I love you."

The detective shakes his head involuntarily. There it is again, the notion that his life is completely out of control. The distant throbbing of a headache announces itself. Schilf suddenly thinks about Maike and realizes at the same time that he has skipped lunch and slept through dinner. He lights a cigarillo and inhales. The nicotine sets free a couple of endorphins somewhere in his body—he feels a slight dizziness and a gentle release. That's what dying must be like, smoking a cigarillo on an empty stomach.

"So you'll be staying a few more days," Julia says.

"Looks like it."

"Great. I'll come to visit."

"I'm not free tomorrow," the detective says quickly. "I have to do something."

"The day after tomorrow, then."

A group of young people are walking in the street below, and their voices carry up to Schilf. Young men, rendered soft and bloated by the love of their mothers, and young women who have made up their eyelashes like spiders' legs. They slap each other's backs, tug each other along, lean over parked cars, staring into the dark interior. They seem aimless, incidental, a mere episode in history. At the sight of them, Schilf finds it hard to believe what human beings can achieve on this earth when they join forces. The females are still wearing shoes that are impossible to walk in.

"What would you say," he asks his girlfriend, "if I had to go on a journey sometime soon? On my own?"

"Schilf," Julia says, with an earnestness that takes the detective by surprise, “you haven’t asked me about my past. I won’t ask about your future. That’s what they call a deal.”

“OK,” Schilf says, using a word he detests, but which suits her “deal.” Perhaps life would be a circus tent, thinks the detective, if people had the right concepts. Concepts like rubber gloves, so you could touch things without getting your hands dirty. Julia has a lot of such concepts.

“OK,” he says again. “See you the day after tomorrow, then.”

They send kisses through their telephones, but Schilf purses his lips clumsily and makes smacking noises that are far too loud. He puts the receiver down on the windowsill and finishes smoking his cigarillo. The monotonous beep of the busy signal blends with the darkness. His inner observer has not said a word during the entire conversation with Julia. A wave of exhaustion that the detective cannot explain sweeps over him, and he decides to go back to bed.

4

THE SUN HAS SET INTO THE HAZE OVER THE CITY, and has taken with it not only the light but the heat of the day. Night has come out of its hiding place at the bottom of the lake more quickly than usual, and crept into the lanes. It is cool and humid, as if summer is ending today. The air already smells of poorly lit pavements, hunched shoulders, and damp hats.

Maike's car is parked near the lake. Sebastian is sitting behind the steering wheel, trying to imagine where he will be in the winter. What he will look like then, what he will be eating, whom he will be talking to, and about what. He can't imagine it. He remembers the feeling of never being able to think beyond the next couple of hours because every day held the possibility of turning him into someone else altogether: that was how he lived as a child. At the time, he felt so at home in the present that it seemed normal to him that it was not time passing but he himself. Although that was a happy state of being, Sebastian is not thrilled to have lost his future in his early forties. For a grown-up, the absence of time is clearly a kind of homelessness.

He looks out over the black expanse of the water, which reflects the lights on the promenade. He has not chosen to stop here; he is simply stranded, with no strength left for the next step. He could take out his mobile phone and look in the address book for a number that naturally he has long known by heart. Or turn on the engine and take the familiar route to a certain apartment. Or take the key out of the ignition, get out of the car, walk along the Quai des Eaux-Vives, and then drive back home.

Since leaving Freiburg and the horror of the last few days behind him, he has been in the grip of an exhaustion that feels like the flu. The symptoms are similar: burning eyes, a scratchy throat, and aching limbs. Sebastian barely knows how he has managed to get here, let alone why he has come in the first place. When he closes his eyes, the autobahn zooms through his head with unrelenting speed. The windshields of the cars in the oncoming lane are flecked with the pink of the evening sky to the north. Wilted sunflowers beside the autobahn turn their faces down toward the earth into which they will soon sink.

The car swerved a few times on the way here. Sebastian breathed more quickly and pinched his thigh. Because nothing helped, he thought of Dabbelink. He led himself through a series of scenes depicting blood, bones, and bicycle parts, all captioned: "This is what I did." The effect was weaker than expected, a twitch in the stomach that was barely enough to keep his eyes on the road for five minutes. The more he tried, the less it worked. After fifty kilometers, the memory of Dabbelink left him completely cold.

Now he knows why murderers like to return to the scene of the crime, as the detective novels maintain. It is not the irresistible lure of evil, nor a desire for atonement or the secret hope of being arrested on the spot. It is their inability to believe that the murder has actually happened. A murderer returns to the scene of the crime so as not to continue thinking of the victim as a living person. If Sebastian could turn back the clock, he would not undo Dabbelink's murder. He did it to save Liam, and he is sure that he would have done plenty of other things merely for the illusion of saving Liam. But he would not leave the scene of the crime without having looked for the remains of his victim.

Sebastian realizes that even a minor player like Dabbelink cannot be shoved off the stage without consequences. He knows that he is lost. But this knowledge is suspended in midair as long as he thinks of his crime in terms of television images. Everything that awaits him—arrest, a torturous murder trial, perhaps a prison sentence, the loss of his family—his future misery seems to have arisen from another world altogether, a world that has no rightful claim on him. Whoever does not believe what he has done is in no position to understand what is happening to him and around him. The best thing about being at Lake Geneva is that it prevents him from pounding on the doors of the forensic department of the Freiburg police, demanding to see the head of his victim.

As if something had been decided with this realization, Sebastian starts the engine and turns the car around.

ON THE RUE DE LA NAVIGATION, he signals his name with the doorbell—short, long, short-short—and knows within seconds that Oskar is out. He wraps his jacket tightly around him and takes up his position in the entryway. Exhaustion has given way to restlessness. Newspapers tumble through the streets, a cyclist flaps past, and a siren sounds somewhere. Sebastian normally loves the anticipation that accompanies his visits to Oskar in Geneva. Despite all the changes in their lives, he and Oskar have kept a piece of the past here that seems like it will live forever. Sebastian has come here over and over again like an addict because, up there in the attic apartment, he is a god, in control of all the fulfilled and unfulfilled potential of his life. That attic is the source of his strength and life force, and also of the restlessness that now has him shifting from one foot to the other.

When a rowdy bunch of nocturnal revelers approach, bound by some giant embrace into a single being, and shout at him in German, asking where to find the best nightclub, he pushes himself away from the wall and disappears into the darkness.

The blue circle of neon lights that serves as the sign for Le Cercle Est Rond is not complete. One of the lights broke years ago, so the circle is open on one side. The bins shoved into the middle of the pavement, and several stray cats, keep the tourists away; since the red-light district was recommended as an insider's tip in several travel guides, Oskar has been talking about looking for a new apartment. He often says that those who go to the Cercle are the last people left on the planet who go out in order *not* to be recognized.

The room is lit by candles jammed into empty bottles, and the light sketches the souls of people and objects in flickering shadows on the walls. The tables seem to be more for beer-drinking card players than for the well-dressed men who sit at them in twos or threes, drinking red wine. The men speak in low voices and move cautiously, as if they are trying not to frighten each other.

Sebastian pushes aside the leather curtain at the entrance. The bartender, who is washing glasses under the only electric light in the room, does not even acknowledge him with a glance, though they have known each other for a long time. Oskar is leaning back against the bar, and a lanky young man wearing round-rimmed spectacles is standing in front of him, talking eagerly in the direction of his own feet. It is not possible to tell if Oskar is listening to him as he stands there with his legs crossed and his elbows bent, motionless. His hands are dangling beside him in an attitude of courtesy mingled with lordliness, as if he were allowing a beringed finger to be kissed. In this position, he looks like he could be leaning against a tree trunk in a forest clearing in the morning mist, his white shirt open at the collar, holding a pistol in his hands.

He allows himself little more than an arch of the eyebrows when he notices Sebastian. But Sebastian can see that his friend is shaken to the core. He almost expects Oskar to clutch his hands to his heart and sink to his knees. He has known this man for half a lifetime, and he has never seen him so shaken.

The bespectacled young man has not noticed that anything has changed. His eyes dart here and there behind his glasses as he is speaking, and when he finally raises his head because he has not received a reply to a question, his age nudges eighteen. Sebastian knows these young geniuses who come from afar to discuss the theory of the quantization of time with its renowned originator. In a pub in Geneva, they meet a man who adorns his intellect not with white hair and a face furrowed by thought, but with a classically handsome profile and a smile proclaiming the right to ownership. Oskar puts his mouth close to the young man's ear and whispers something. The boy immediately raises his hand and walks off toward the restroom.

Within seconds, they are standing opposite each other. It is Oskar who stretches his hand out first. No one can keep himself afloat day after day all on his own. The mingling of their scents is an invisible home. It houses the pain they feel about the space they share, a space that knows only biting cold and blistering heat, but not the conditions for human survival.

Oskar takes the "Reserved" placard off the table in the corner and sits Sebastian down facing a kitsch reproduction of a still life. It portrays a pheasant in its dress of feathers, its neck hanging broken over the edge of a bowl. Sitting opposite Sebastian, Oskar has a view of the whole room. Unbidden, the barman brings over two glasses and a bottle of whiskey that is as old as the bespectacled youth who has left the Cercle after his visit to the restroom. They clink glasses and drink. Oskar is outwardly calm. He does not tap his feet, or pick fluff off his suit trousers. He looks at Sebastian intently.

Sebastian is tracing the grain of the table with a finger, concentrating on not counting the years, not asking how many times he has sat in the Cercle filled with a delicate mixture of happiness and fear. Seen from here, his normal life seems like the memory of a film in which he, Maike, and Liam play the touching lead roles. Every time he has left Freiburg on the weekend for a supposed conference, Oskar has been waiting for him with eyebrows raised—mocking and acerbic, but not angry.

Perhaps Oskar's supreme quality is not his intelligence, thinks Sebastian, but his patience, which has the force of a natural law. "How time flies" is never a statement for Oskar, always a question.

And perhaps, Sebastian thinks, Maike and Liam's supreme quality is their boundless trust, while his own is the ability to abuse this trust without scruple. "Can that really be true?" is never a question for Sebastian, but always a matter of physics.

His index finger traces the grain of the wood on the other side of the table and when Oskar reaches out to grasp it, he gives him his hand.

"It can only be days now," Sebastian says.

"Hours," Oskar says.

"A detective is onto me. Either he understands nothing—or everything."

"Everything, probably. Or were you foolish enough to hope that they wouldn't find you?"

"Hope is the last thing to die," Sebastian says lamely.

"And honor never does."

Oskar drinks from his glass, then puts it down on the table.

"*Cher ami*," he says, "there is this thing called life and there are stories. The curse of the human being is that he finds it difficult to distinguish between the two."

"Say it again."

"What?"

"When I told you about Dabbelink on the phone, what did you say?"

"'Oh?'" Oskar says.

"I've been surviving on that 'Oh?' for forty-eight hours."

Oskar presses his hand.

"Is that why you came?"

Sebastian does not reply. He turns in his seat and looks around the room.

"I've made inquiries," Oskar says. "It's known as coercion. Anyone blackmailed into committing a crime cannot be held responsible."

"I'm responsible, without a doubt."

The bartender is drying glasses and the customers are talking among themselves. No one is paying the least bit of attention to the table in the corner. Amazingly, everything looks normal.

"That's the first time I've heard you say that," Oskar says. "Are you afraid that they won't believe you were blackmailed?"

"It's not that."

"Maik?"

Sebastian nods.

"Does she know?"

Sebastian shrugs his shoulders.

"You haven't told her . . . everything?"

Sebastian shakes his head. He pulls the bottle toward him and empties his second glass in a single gulp. Peat and a touch of honey, it's a good make. Oskar lights a cigarette and looks toward the window, which merely reflects his own face back at him. Sebastian's hand grows numb in Oskar's grip, and he pulls it away.

"She thinks I'm a murderer," he says.

"Not without cause, if I've understood everything correctly."

"It would be simpler to tell her the truth if she wouldn't anticipate the result."

"Aren't you expecting a bit much?"

"Oskar." As Sebastian presses his hands over his eyes, he feels the effect of the chili again. "She won't stand by me. I'll lose her, and Liam, too."

Oskar stubs out his cigarette and lights another one; this is faster than he normally smokes.

"You won't give up," he says.

"What's absurd is that I feel as if I've staged the whole thing myself. Not in practice, but in theory."

"Are you talking about your Many-Worlds Interpretation?"

"If something can happen and not happen at the same time in a microworld, the same thing must be possible in a macrocosmos, too. Haven't I always said that?"

"Let's put it this way: you cultivated a somewhat casual approach to the difficulties of moving from quantum mechanics to classical physics."

Sebastian wipes his streaming eyes with his cuffs.

"Liam was kidnapped and also not kidnapped at the same time. Since then, everything has lost its validity. I now live in a one-man universe. Its name is guilt."

The coffee machine behind the bar hisses. Someone laughs politely. The pheasant's neck still hangs over the side of the bowl.

"Pull yourself together," Oskar says. "You're talking nonsense."

"No I'm not!" Sebastian turns his red-rimmed eyes to look his friend full in the face. "If I hadn't been so obsessed with getting a few days of uninterrupted work done, I would never have taken Liam to scout camp. That's causality. You like causality, don't you?"

"To hell with it," Oskar says.

"I'd left the Many Worlds behind me long ago." Sebastian's voice grows louder and more urgent. "I wanted to use physics to prove that time is nothing more than a function of human perception. I wanted to pull the rug out from under your feet."

Oskar catches the finger Sebastian is pointing at him and places it back on the table.

"Sooner or later," Sebastian says, "you will prove through quantization that time and space share most of the properties of matter. That will be the next turning point after Copernicus, Newton, and Einstein. You no longer know the craving to achieve something groundbreaking. Inside that craving lies guilt."

His glass clinks hard against Oskar's and they drink, holding each other's gaze.

"Even if that were true," Oskar says, "my achievement would have been only to add to the endless series of errors that we call human history. That's all. You know nothing of guilt."

"I'm going to put it to you simply," Sebastian says. "You have chosen physics and you are loyal to it. I chose two people, and I have not been loyal to them."

Oskar blows smoke across the table.

"You've really changed. I quite like it."

"Oskar, is there anything more important to you than quantum physics?" Sebastian asks.

The armrests creak as Oskar jolts back in his chair with a laugh that changes his face completely. Sebastian has witnessed this laugh a thousand times, but it still astounds him. The corners of his own mouth turn up, and they are suddenly smiling at each other, sitting wrapped in a cocoon of warmth and mellow light that the outside world cannot touch. The moment passes as quickly as it came.

"Are you really sitting there asking me that in all seriousness?"

Sebastian examines his empty glass intently and pushes it aside.

"Let me tell you a story," Oskar says. "The day after the kidnapping you called me on the phone. After work, I drove straight to Freiburg, and got there very late. We sat up talking the whole night. I drove back to Geneva at about six in the morning and turned up at the institute more or less on time."

Sebastian's mouth is hanging open slightly.

"You're mad," he says.

"And you should start protecting yourself."

"In my statement, it says that I was alone in the apartment the whole time after Liam disappeared."

"Maik wasn't supposed to find out that you called on me for support instead of her."

"What were you really doing that night?"

"Nothing that anyone I met would remember."

Sebastian is gripping the edge of the table with his hands. The whiskey is going to his head and he feels as if his skull is getting ready to detach itself from his shoulders.

He pauses, then says, "I don't want an alibi."

"*Bien*," Oskar says. "How about another story." He looks at his reflection in the mirror again and smooths his hair. His hands are trembling. "We're in Switzerland. That gives us a couple of days. I can get my affairs in order within two weeks."

"What are you talking about?"

"This," Oskar says, knocking on the table, "is not the only continent on this earth."

"You want us to run away? Go into hiding? Live with the Bedouin?"

"Not exactly." Oskar leans forward. "There are research centers in China. And in South America. At my level, certain irregularities will be mere trifles. We would be welcomed with open arms."

It takes Sebastian a few seconds to register the meaning of these words. He lets go of the table, shifts in his seat, tries to prop himself up on one elbow, and sits still again.

"What about Liam?" he asks.

"We'll take him with us. As far as work goes, you'll have to stay in the background for a bit. You'd have time for him."

"You're not serious," Sebastian whispers.

"Yes I am," Oskar says. "For you, the last few years have been all about your wife. About your family. About physics. For me . . ." He places his cigarette packet and his lighter in parallel before he continues. "It was only ever about us."

Their knees touch under the table. Oskar reaches out with his hands and pulls Sebastian's head toward him until they are bent over the table, forehead to forehead, breathing the same air. Sebastian leans forward with his whole weight, concentrates on the warm point where their heads meet, and wishes he could flee his own body through this point and find refuge under the crown of his friend.

Of course. It would work. It even had a certain logic to it. Running away, not the first time, but the last. In retrospect, it would give the long series of small escapes a goal and a cause. Everything would acquire an order, even start to make sense. He would be no longer just the ball in the game, but the master of his own misfortune. This time he would kidnap Liam himself and acknowledge what he has long been: a criminal. The passage of time would help him to regard the exceptional situation as normal.

And normality as the past, Sebastian thinks.

Only when their foreheads crack painfully together, because he is shaking with violent sobs, does Sebastian notice that he is crying.

"You know I have always . . ."

"Let's not talk about it," Oskar says. "This isn't a good moment."

"When I look at Liam . . ."

He finds it hard to speak. He is clasping his friend around the neck, holding tight to keep himself from collapsing onto the table.

"When I look at Liam," he says, "it's impossible to regret anything."

"I can't regret anything either," Oskar says. "The past is a stingy beast. It doesn't relinquish anything, especially not decisions."

Oskar takes a handkerchief out of his pocket. He dries Sebastian's eyes and cheeks before pushing him away and sitting him upright again.

"You've had a few drinks," he says. "Are you driving back anyway?"

Sebastian nods.

"That's a terrible shame."

Sebastian turns away and presses his lips together.

"This way or that," Oskar says, "it will pass. After that, you'll be a new person. Not a better person, but still there."

His unfiltered cigarette has burned down to a stub in the ashtray. Oskar flinches as he burns his finger trying to put it out.

"Do tell me why you came to Geneva tonight," Oskar says.

"To tell you that we won't be seeing each other anymore."

The man who looks up at Sebastian as he rises from the table no longer looks like himself. His face has no greatness, no beauty, and no aristocratic air. It is suddenly so helpless that the changing expressions on it look like blueprints. The sketch of a smile, a diagram of mockery, a draft of exhaustion. The anatomy of sadness.

"Do me a favor," Sebastian says. "Stay there and don't watch me as I leave."

The pheasant has opened its eyes and is gazing into emptiness. Glasses clatter behind the bar. Outside, the night is waiting. The streets of the city are filled with mist. It smells of rain.

[5]

THE DRUMS HAVE BEEN CALLING TO HIM for an hour now, sounding the beat to which he should march. He knows they are right, that it is time to finally make a move. Nonetheless he hesitates as if he still has something important to do, something to verify and to understand. Then a scream, piercing like a battle cry.

The digital display of the alarm clock shows a four and two zeros. The detective often wakes exactly on the hour. There is no end to the scream, which turns out to be the cry of a baby in the apartment next door. The drumming, on the other hand, is coming from the rain falling against the window with the relentlessness of a machine. Schilf swings his legs out of the bed. He feels more rested than he has for a long time, and is startled to find that the day is far from beginning. He presses the light switch to no effect and walks over to the balcony door. Drops of water are racing across the glass in horizontal lines, as if the building were traveling through the night at speed. Outside there is a darkness that has no place in a city. The streetlights are not working, and only the yellow glow of a blinking warning light illuminates the hell outside. There is a tree lying in the road, and another has fallen on top of three parked cars. The storm tugs at the branches, still dissatisfied with its vanquished opponents. Schilf enjoys watching chaos that, for once, has not been created by human beings.

Shivering, he turns away and sits down at the desk. He finds a stack of postcards in the drawer. By the flame of a lighter, he writes on the back of the first one: "Dear Julia, When you come to visit, bring this card with you as evidence that you exist. Urgent [in capital letters with three clumsy-looking exclamation points]. Schilf."

He burns his thumb on the lighter and lowers his head over his second card: "Dear Maike, Whatever happens, you must not stop believing. You have no right to destroy Sebastian. Please [a splotch of ink where he strikes out three exclamation points]. Yours, Detective Schilf."

Content with his work, he addresses the first card to his own apartment in Stuttgart and the second to the Gallery of Modern Art. As a precaution, he takes the last two pills that the doctor prescribed him for headaches, then sits down on the sofa with the chess computer.

He has paid too little attention to his king from the start. He has watched pale-faced but unwavering as his major pieces died heroes' deaths. A large proportion of foot soldiers have also fallen victim to Schilf's fanaticism. He is sending his last pawns, rook, and knight to lay siege to the opposing king, who is barricaded behind a standard defense, bored and probably smoking one cigarette after another. Schilf pictures him with his shirt half open, holding a pistol in his limp fingers. If the detective were to grant his opponent a pause for breath, if he doesn't force it to move to save its king, he is finished. Even as he brings up the game, he is filled with rage against the superior enemy force, against its solid formation and distribution of pieces, which are always in the right place at the right time. The computer catches every one of his attacks in a net of calculations. Schilf is fighting against a determinist, an ultramaterialist who with precise knowledge of a situation and the laws that apply can determine past and future, and whose most important ability consists of predicting the moment and the manner in which everything that wishes to live will die.

The detective decides to beat the computer using its own weapons.

He lifts his feet up onto the sofa and sets to work calculating every possible move and countermove.

By the time it grows light, he has not shifted one centimeter from his position. His deliberations are now being accompanied by the whine of an electric saw, which is biting into solid wood on the street below. The rain machine has shifted down a gear or two, and glaring light that leaves no shadow makes everything in the room look washed-out. At about eight o'clock the detective stretches his legs and massages his neck. He has not made a single move. But he now has a vague idea of where the next attack against his opponent should be made.

Out on the street, he walks over a carpet of wet sawdust. It smells like a circus ring. He steps over branches that have been torn off in the storm, and drops the two postcards in a mailbox on his way to the streetcar stop. Onboard, strangers are telling each other about the damage done in their neighborhoods. Their eyes are shining with the happiness that is only ever brought about by a natural catastrophe representing the comeback of a half-forgotten god.

Schilf gets off the streetcar near the Institute of Physics and takes a detour along Sophie-de-la-Roche-Strasse. The peaceful canal has been transformed overnight into a muddy torrent filled with leaves and plastic bottles. Bonnie and Clyde are nowhere to be seen. Schilf manages to duck behind a parked car just as Sebastian appears from around the corner. Sebastian's arms are wrapped tightly around his body. He does not have a jacket, a bag, or an umbrella. He looks like a man who has spent half the night on the autobahn and then slept two hours on the swivel chair in his office at the institute.

So you've come back to us, the detective thought, the detective thinks.

With difficulty he suppresses the impulse to follow Sebastian.

NOT LONG AFTER, he is standing in front of the locked glass door of the natural sciences library looking at the posted opening times. It is a while before he realizes that it's the weekend, so he will have to wait another hour. Resigned, he follows his own wet footsteps back through the Gustav Mie building and goes to the cafeteria, which is empty but open. He calls out in a loud voice for a double espresso before he sits down at one of the freshly wiped tables. He puts his mobile phone down and places his hands on either side of it. Barely five minutes pass before it rings.

"Miserable criminal!"

Schilf is happy to hear that Rita Skura avoids repeating herself when she dishes out insults. It is good to hear her voice.

"I have you to thank for the most ridiculous Sunday morning of my life," she says.

She sounds relieved. Schilf wedges his phone between his shoulder and his cheek.

"Good morning," he says. "Lovely weather, isn't it?"

"Of course I had to lie," Rita says, undeterred. "Sooner or later I could have brought in the murderer by other means."

"Of course," Schilf says. "Sooner—or later."

Rita's snort makes the diaphragm of the speaker vibrate.

"Do you know the chief public prosecutor?" she shouts. "Have you tried dictating terms to a guy like that?"

Schilf not only knows the man but can also visualize him, hunched into his own body fat, perched behind a desk of presidential proportions. When the newly appointed chief public prosecutor had the immense piece of furniture delivered at his own cost, the laughter of the Freiburg judiciary had been heard all the way to Stuttgart.

This colossus of a man hates being on call during weekends. And he also hates summer. In summer, women like Rita Skura walk around in flowery dresses while men have sweat running down their buttoned-up shirt collars. The chief public prosecutor has probably not invited Rita Skura to come in. The door was wrenched open the very moment she knocked. She has already ruined the previous evening with her phone calls; now she stands before him like a Joan of Arc from Baden, offering herself up as her heaviest cannon, the hands on her hips a challenge. As she speaks, the chief public prosecutor plucks at his hair, observes her for a moment, and visualizes her floating to the ground. All the while he grinds his jaw incessantly, as if he were chewing on something. As soon as Rita has finished, he heaves himself out of his armchair with a groan and closes the window. What he has to say does not need an audience.

"Listen," Rita says on the telephone now. "No forty-eight-hour remand if he makes a full confession. That's all that was possible. I had to swear to God that he is not a flight risk."

"If he were a flight risk he would be long gone. It's not far to Switzerland."

"If it were that simple," Rita says, insulted, "why didn't you explain it to the public prosecutor yourself?"

A fat woman with dyed red hair and plucked eyebrows approaches in her apron and puts a cup down on the table.

"It's normally self-service here," she says.

"Because it's your case after all, Rita, my child," Schilf says. "Excellent work. You'll be police chief in no time."

He puts twice the required amount into the serving woman's outstretched hand and looks away to avoid her death stare. The coffee is surprisingly good. It's a good day all in all. The detective is doing the right thing and getting what he wants.

"Toady," Rita says. "Of course it's my case. And it's the last one that you'll be interfering with."

"Believe me, I've only been sent in the name of God. You'll never have the misfortune of accepting my help again."

"Glad to hear it."

The detective thinks he would like to bottle a few of Rita's snorts to tide him over in bad times.

"Now hand the guy over," she says.

"How do you know it's a man?"

"Women don't decapitate their victims."

"The New Testament would have it otherwise."

"Wrong, Schilf. Salome *asked* for John the Baptist to be beheaded. That was secondary liability at best, or just incitement."

"You know your Bible," Schilf says in acknowledgment, "and the basics of German criminal law. What would happen if Salome had blackmailed the murderer into doing the deed, though?"

"This isn't a seminar on criminal law!" Rita growls.

"Coercion," Schilf says. "Extenuating circumstances according to the prevailing view?"

"Who . . . is. . . . it?"

With every word, Schilf thinks he hears Rita chopping the air with the side of her hand. Rita had been an astonishingly good shot during her training. You could tell from her hand, the detective thinks. He would quite happily stand in front of her while, feet shoulder-width apart, arms outstretched, she aimed a Walther PPK at him. The bullet would bore a hole in his forehead, pierce through the bird's egg in his frontal lobe, and drill painlessly into his brain. Schilf sees himself falling to his knees and collapsing onto his side, as he has observed other men doing a few times over the course of his career. Set free by Rita's hand, he would fly out through the hole in his forehead and finally mesh with the network of the universe, where there is no time and space, and would enter the state popularly known as "the past."

What a lovely dream, the detective thinks.

"The physicist," he says. "The one with the kidnapped son."

He lights a cigarillo and enjoys the first puffs in total peace. Not even the sound of breathing comes from the telephone.

"Good," Rita finally says. Her voice is businesslike, if a little husky. "I thank you."

"Wait." Schilf takes the cigarillo out of his mouth and bends forward, as if Rita were sitting on the other side of the table. "He was blackmailed."

"At least," Rita says slowly, "the case seems to have nothing to do with the hospital scandal."

"You don't know that yet," the detective superintendent says sharply. "Were you listening to me? I said: Sebastian was blackmailed."

"The police chief will cry with joy."

"Rita!" The detective barely notices that the woman in the apron is beside him again. "Have you asked yourself why I'm telling *you* who it is? So that the case won't be taken away from you! You're the one with the most sense in that whole pigsty. Don't tell me that I've been mistaken!"

"All right, Schilf."

"The man is innocent," the detective says.

"Surely. The main thing is, there's no connection to the hospital scandal."

The conversation is over. The line is dead.

"You're not allowed to smoke here," the woman in the apron says.

"Damn," Schilf says.

"Absolutely no smoking here."

The detective looks into her doughy face and flashes his police ID at her.

"Another espresso," he says.

As the fat woman waddles hastily back to the counter, he drops his head into his hands. It's practically impossible, inconceivable that he has just made a serious mistake. He is holding the cigarillo between his thumb and his index finger, and ash falls past his right temple onto the table. There is the smell of singed hair.

[6]

THERE IT IS AGAIN, THE DOUGHY FACE. Plucked eyebrows and dyed red hair in the shape of a cloud. This time the woman is a kind of librarian who is looking at the detective in an unfriendly manner. Her fleshy fingers are tapping away continuously with great precision on a computer keyboard. The familiar pounding has started behind Schilf's temples.

"What do you want?"

It is not easy to answer this question. Schilf probably wants a new Rita Skura, one who is not thinking of her own career or of the walrus-mustached police chief, but only of how she can help the first chief detective superintendent in his mission for truth and justice. And he wants a slim librarian with hair that has been combed back, and a large room whose walls are lined with shelves of oak that go right up to the ceiling. He wants absentminded scientists who climb ladders to reach the volumes on the very top shelves. He wants green lampshades on antique desks.

Schilf is nauseated by the smell of the freshly cleaned carpet underfoot. Metal shelving divides the room into cells containing dark computer monitors. He is the only visitor. The conversation with Rita feels like rheumatism in his bones. He longs for a living being, for understanding and support, or perhaps just for the warmth of a freshly run bath.

"What do you want?" The librarian repeats herself slowly and clearly. She probably has to deal with confused foreign researchers quite often.

"Quantum physics," the detective says.

The woman's face shakes with silent laughter, and Schilf realizes that he has made a joke. He does not join in.

"Go ahead," she says.

Schilf does not bother with the rows of books whose covers threaten investigations of the cosmological lambda term or the missing-mass problem. He sits down at one of the computers and types Sebastian's name into the catalogue search function. The list is long. Schilf chooses two publications whose titles contain more familiar than unfamiliar words. He writes down the classification codes on a piece of paper and walks back to the desk. The librarian perches a pair of spectacles on her wide face and waddles over to a shelf of journals. The prim design of the booklets she pulls out would warn off any normal person from trying to read them. The librarian pats him encouragingly on the shoulder as she hands them over, and Schilf is left with his booty.

"Everett's Many-Worlds Interpretation as the Foundation for Quantum Cosmology."

"The Fluctuating Scalar Field, i.e.: The Eternal Return of the Same."

Schilf makes a concerted effort not to wonder about the sense of this undertaking and whispers encouraging words to himself: Let's just see, piece of cake, this. He starts reading the first article.

Since his phone call with Rita, he has been plagued by the feeling that he has no time left, and that whatever he does, he is neglecting something else far more important. His method does not work in such a situation. In order to look through things, to lurk and listen and wait for something to rise from the cellar of reality to the surface, he needs one thing above all: inner peace. Now he can only struggle to understand things with the usual tools of the trade, which will bring an average rate of success at best. His startled brain races along the words stretching across the pages like worms, staggers then falls, catches itself in the barbs of a semicomprehensible sentence ("Applied to the cosmos, the quantization machine leads to an assumption of general wave function"), and slides across the slippery ground of the next clause. It stumbles over a familiar phrase ("everything is possible and happens somewhere") and ends up standing in front of the impenetrable wall of string theory and supersymmetry.

Schilf does not understand a word. He does not have the faintest idea what Sebastian is writing about. The pounding of his headache has turned into hammering. He puts the journal aside and rouses the computer. On the home page of the search engine he discovers a report on the re-arrest of the former chess world champion Kasparov. He feels a little better after reading this short article without any trouble. Filled with hope, he types Sebastian's name into the gateway to the virtual world.

Two photographs immediately pop up under the heading *Circumpolar*. There is Sebastian's boyish, laughing face, next to a striking man whom Schilf would have immediately cast as Mephisto if he were directing a film of *Faust*. The detective looks at the two men for a long time: the laughter and the silence, the wanting and the waiting, the white king and the black king. A two-headed oracle, the detective thinks. It is some time before he realizes what the Web page is actually offering. You can download an episode of the science program *Circumpolar*, subtitled "The Clash of the Physicists." Schilf pulls his chair closer to the screen and clicks on "Watch Now."

Sebastian and Oskar are seated on protruding chairs in the narrow prison of a small screen. The show's host is sitting between them in a deliberately casual manner, leaning forward with his elbows on his knees as he introduces the program.

Twenty-first century. Challenges that no one had ever expected. The intersection between science and philosophy.

If the host had been alone onstage, he would have looked like everyone's picture of the kindly professor: spectacles, beard, and uncut hair. Next to his lofty guests, he simply looks untidy. Oskar lets an arm dangle over his chair's armrest, and examines the polished tips of his shoes. On the other side, Sebastian is looking straight into the camera with a defiant expression, and he winces when it is his turn to speak. He twists the microphone in his hands for such a long time that the detective feels nervous watching him. Finally, without any preamble whatsoever, Sebastian begins to speak.

"The parallel universe theory rests upon an interpretation of quantum mechanics, according to which a system assumes all circumstances that are possible within the specific probabilities. The elementary particles are the basic building blocks of our world. Their existence determines our existence. That can mean that we and everything visible around us are adopting all states at every moment."

By his sharp intake of breath while lifting the microphone gently, the host signals that more than three long sentences in a row are unthinkable even for the audience of a public broadcasting station. Sebastian refuses to be thrown off track. The detective nods at him across everything that separates them.

"We can imagine it visually," Sebastian says. "There is a universe in which Kennedy did not travel to Dallas on that fateful day, and was not shot. And one in which I didn't have cheesecake on my birthday but chocolate cake."

There is the sound of grateful laughter in the studio. Only now does the camera swing around to show that the three men on the stage are not alone in the room. The detective realizes that "LIVE" is displayed in tiny letters in a corner of the screen. Transfixed by the notion that the Sebastian onscreen has no idea yet of the reversal of fortune that awaits him, Schilf misses the next few phrases and just catches Sebastian gesturing with his hand that he will stop after his next sentence.

"Everything that is possible happens."

The audience claps. Sebastian's fervor makes his statement sound like a promise of salvation. Even the host pretends to clap as he asks Oskar to give his opinion. Oskar has listened to Sebastian with a smile on his face, more amused than mocking, as if he is a grown-up listening to a precocious child.

"What Sebastian has described," he says, holding the microphone very close to his mouth, in a voice that makes the detective shudder, "is a cozy attempt to circumnavigate God."

There are murmurs and subdued laughs. Sebastian looks offstage, as if the whole thing suddenly has nothing to do with him.

"You'll have to explain that," the host says, when Oskar does not continue.

"It's quite simple."

In the dead silence of the studio, Oskar takes a sip of water. It is clear that he is in control of the situation on the stage.

"According to the Many-Worlds Interpretation, a creator never need make a decision. We exist simply because everything that is at all possible exists somewhere."

Ever since his conversation with Sebastian, the detective has been working on a formulation that he himself does not fully understand: *The world is the way it is because there are observers to watch it existing.*

Schilf regrets that television programs don't permit interruptions.

"That is a cheap response to a question of metaphysics," Oskar says. "Totally unusable as a scientific viewpoint."

"Why unusable?" the host asks, raising a hand to shush another murmur rising in the audience.

"Because other universes avoid experimental examination."

Oskar leans back as if he has had the last word for the evening. In the same instant Sebastian bends forward and speaks into the microphone.

"That's how it is in theoretical physics," he says. "Even Einstein's ideas were partly worked out on paper to begin with, and then proven later in experiments."

"In the words of Einstein himself," Oskar replies calmly, " 'Only two things are infinite, the universe and human stupidity, and I'm not sure about the universe.' "

"What I'm talking about here," Sebastian says, "has been described by many reputable physicists: Stephen Hawking, David Deutsch, Dieter Zeh."

"Then Hawking, Deutsch, and Zeh have just as little an idea of physics," Oskar says.

As the audience protests, a close-up of Oskar's laughing face is shown. The arrogant expression has disappeared and he looks like a schoolboy who is delighting in pulling off a successful prank. The camera turns to Sebastian, who is shaking his head and lifting a finger to show that he has something to say. Schilf leans forward so that his nose is practically touching the monitor. Don't let yourself be wound up by him. Don't defend anything that you don't believe in. Tell them that there is no time and space. That Many Worlds and one world are all the same, even if matter is nothing more than an idea in the observer's thoughts.

The host calls for silence so that Sebastian can speak.

"The discussion here doesn't seem to be about the intersection between physics and philosophy," Sebastian says, "but about the intersection between physics and polemic."

Laughter from the audience shows that they are on his side again.

"Much as barbed language can be fun—"

"By the way," Oskar interrupts, placing a finger on his cheek as if something has just occurred to him, "according to your theory, it is not just the Creator who does not have to make any decisions. Nobody else does, either."

"On the contrary," Sebastian says. "One of the philosophical advantages of the Many-Worlds Interpretation is that it can explain the free will of mankind. In linear time—"

"Now it's getting esoteric!" Oskar laughs.

The camera is too late to catch Oskar, reaching him only as he waves away the host's admonishment. Schilf, who is watching the screen so intently that his eyes are burning, notices that Oskar's left foot is twitching.

"In linear time," Sebastian says, "our fates are determined from the earliest past into the most distant future. Our decisions are nothing more than biochemical processes in the brain that are subject to the laws of cause and effect." He leaves a dramatic pause before continuing. "Now imagine that every conceivable causal sequence exists at the same time in parallel universes. The way every individual universe develops may be predetermined, but our freedom consists of being able to choose one of these many worlds with every decision."

"Ladies and gentlemen, justification for the freedom of will through physics," the host says exultantly. His glasses reflect the spotlights, and he looks incredibly happy, as if he can see his program director's beaming face as he speaks.

"And that holds true, although science and determinism normally—"

"Then I would like to know," Oskar interrupts, "why we can't simply exercise an act of will to choose a universe in which the Second World War never happened. That would be nice."

The blood has risen in Sebastian's face. He slides forward and sits upright.

"That's because we are subject to the principle of self-consistency," he says. "And you know that only too well! Otherwise, according to the second law of thermodynamics, we could dissolve into a state of cumulative chaos."

"And that's exactly what we're doing," Oskar says. "Looking at you, one might conclude that this dissolution can sometimes happen all too quickly."

He gives Sebastian a challenging look and taps his finger on his forehead.

"Excuse me," the host says, "we can't . . ."

The uproar in the studio drowns him out. Oskar makes an impatient gesture with his hand to wave away any further disturbance, and turns his perfect profile to the camera, looking past the host, straight at Sebastian. The twitch in his left foot has grown more violent. His relaxed manner suddenly seems a poor front. He looks like a man whose smooth facade conceals boundless rage.

"If every decision is accompanied by its opposite," he says, "then it is no decision at all. Do you know what your justification for free will is? It's a license to behave like a swine!"

"Please . . ." the host says.

"That's . . ." Sebastian attempts.

"*One* universe," Oskar says. "With no possibility for escape. That's what you should be researching. That's where you should be living. And where you should take responsibility for your own decisions."

"That's not a scientific argument," Sebastian says, barely managing to control himself. "That's moralistic dogmatism!"

"And a good deal better than immorality legitimized by physics."

"Not one word more!" Sebastian screams.

"In your double worlds," Oskar says with feverish intensity, "you live a double life. And you pretend that you can do something and also not do it at the same time."

There is a merciless close-up of Sebastian's Adam's apple rising and falling as he swallows heavily. The unrest in the audience has increased again. One man raises his fist, but it is not clear against whom or what.

"Let me put it in Orwell's words," Oskar says, standing up.

He has left the microphone on the glass table. He points his index finger at Sebastian and says something that cannot be heard in all the commotion. The host's mouth is opening and shutting helplessly.

Oskar says something else that cannot be heard, and then the picture freezes.

The detective has grown warm. He has grabbed hold of the mouse to pause the clip, and is looking for a way to play the last few seconds again.

"That's not allowed," the librarian says.

Schilf gives a start, as though someone has stabbed him in the neck. A shadow falls over the workstation.

"You can't download films here. The computers are here for research."

This country is made up of prohibitions just like a house of cards is made of cards, the detective thinks. Perhaps I ought to have applied for something on the other side back then.

"This is a scientific program," he says out loud. "I'm from the police."

"And I'm enforcing the rules," the librarian says. "Do you have a search warrant?"

Without waiting for his reply, she leans forward and closes every open window with a rapid tap of the keys. Schilf has to get up from his chair in order to create some distance between himself and the woman. Her eyelids are covered with a thick layer of purple eye-shadow.

"Can I help you in any other way?"

"No thank you," the detective says. "I was just about to go."

On the street, he stands under a lowering sky and does not know where to go next. Cars pass in both directions and people stride toward secret destinations. Pain drills into his lower jaw. Schilf puts both hands to his face to prevent it from falling apart. He has to keep watching the cars so that they will continue moving, has to lean against the wall so that it won't collapse. He has to watch the passersby so that they won't crumble into dust. He is a pillar of the sky, a generator of time, the perpendicular in the earth's axis. If he closes his eyes the earth will no longer exist. Only the headache.

Not yet, not now, the detective thinks.

His next few steps land on firm ground, small paving stones that are exactly the same size as the soles of his shoes. He takes out his mobile phone and gets through to international directory assistance. He asks for a number in Geneva.

[7]

BIRD FLU HAS SCURRIED INTO EUROPE on its clawed feet. Migratory birds spread the virus to the farthest corners of the world. Seagulls are dropping dead from the sky near the coast of Hamburg and mankind is preparing for an epidemic. Everything that flies is being executed. Soon the last feather will float to earth in a forest clearing. After that, Detective Schilf will be carrying the last surviving bird's egg in his head.

He puts down the crumpled newspaper that he found on his seat. Bird flu. As if there were no other problems. He has used up the doctor's painkillers, and has managed to get only ibuprofen in the pharmacy at the station. Sitting opposite him is a mustached man in his mid-fifties, who is busy copying the train schedule into a notebook with a marker. The barren stomp and jangle of twenty-first-century music is forcing its way out of a girl's headphones. Two rows down, a train conductor is rebuffing an angry woman's accusations. Please let me finish what I am saying. The staff is doing its best. Everything that is possible happens.

Outside, the gray ceiling of sky stretches westward. A successful performance of late autumn in July.

When the train starts moving again, the gentle eyes of a few lost calves glide by. They are the reason the train has been held up in this field for almost an hour. A trampled-down fence, men in orange protective suits doing their work.

Wet calves are a good omen, the detective decides. They are the opposite of black cats, crows, and hooting owls. The ZDF television station has agreed to send a video recording of *Circumpolar* to him today. Schilf rubs his hands together and tries to calm himself down by breathing in and out slowly. He cannot shake the feeling that he has missed something, as if he has made the irrevocable decision to be in the wrong place. Suddenly he sees a cat in front of him, and he recognizes it as the cat in the photographs on Rita's bulletin board. It is sitting behind a patio door cleaning its front paws with a knowing expression on its face, as if it were responsible for the two wrists being roughly pressed together in an apartment at the other end of town. A boy's fair head appears in the gap of a half-opened bedroom door. A look from those eyes, widened in shock, drives a splint into the father's brain. A metallic click as the handcuffs snap shut. A hysterical blond woman runs down the hall, dissolving. She is not trying to scratch the people in uniform but the man in the middle.

You have a son!

The scream performs somersaults and is cut off by the crash of a door slamming shut. Blue light flashes rhythmically over the backdrop of an overcast day. The cat leans its head to one side and scratches itself behind an ear.

The series of pictures does not stop when the man in his mid-fifties packs his markers and leaves the train.

A woman in a flowery dress and a cardigan pushes her thick curls back. Sitting opposite her is a man, now free of handcuffs, but with a gray face. A lovely couple. The hatred between them spreads swiftly, like a gas diffusing through the room.

Do you know why you are here?

Where is Detective Schilf?

I am the one heading this investigation.

The woman's look suggests a score of over 90 percent in the shooting range. The man grows paler. Schilf clutches at a suffocating feeling in his chest. The woman laughs through her nose and switches on a recording device. She tells the man about his right to remain silent, to lie, or to hook up with some crooked lawyer. The man does not want to know about his rights.

He dictates his confession and says that he was blackmailed. The cat stops moving when a sparrow lands on the patio. The woman lets the man talk and updates him on the investigation. There are no traces in the car. The son knows nothing. The people at the service station know nothing. There are only those two calls to his mobile from withheld numbers, and he could have made those himself, if he doesn't mind her saying so. The sparrow decides to look for another spot to rest. The cat feigns indifference. The man says something now about rights and justice. The woman flips through her papers and then she says:

You may go now.

The man is at a loss.

What did you say?

Don't leave town, and be prepared.

The woman assumes an official air and takes notes. The man does not move.

Kindly put me on remand.

The cat smiles. The train drills into the next wall of rain.

If you're going to rip my life to shreds, the man screams, then please at least keep hold of the remains!

The woman in the flowery dress takes a deep breath and bellows so loudly that her voice echoes throughout the corridors of the police department:

Out!

The train has drawn into a station, so Schilf steps outside, paces up and down the platform angrily, and lets the rain cool his face. His heart tells him that it would have been better simply to have taken

Sebastian out of the country, but his head tells him that it was right to follow the path of law.

So Schilf stands in the rain and says to hell with head and heart, in equal measure.

The good news is that he has gotten out of the train in Basel, where he has to change trains anyway. In the InterCity train a man in his mid-fifties with a handlebar mustache is sitting opposite him, looking down at a book without moving his eyes. By the time they get to Delémont, he has not turned a single page. He looks exactly like the man with the markers.

If it is my consciousness that is creating the world, it clearly doesn't have much imagination, the detective thought, the detective thinks.

He gulps down two more ibuprofen. See you again soon, the man with the handlebar mustache says in Geneva.

THE WATER OF THE RHÔNE HAS BEEN SCULPTED into blades of black that sweep into the city in long rows. It is unusually dark for nine thirty on a summer's evening. Yellow light runs from post to post along the embankment and over the bridge toward the city center. In this bad weather, the detective is practically alone with the elements.

Schilf tries out an *Où se trouve* on a taxi driver, and is rewarded with the dour pointing of a finger that takes him directly to the right alley. He steps into the entryway and presses the doorbell with his wet finger. He takes his time with the stairs. Light streaming through a door left ajar takes the place of a greeting from the host. A stack of rugs prevents him from opening the door fully.

Schilf realizes what he expected to find behind this door only when he is confronted by its opposite. This is no minimalistic penthouse, there is no picture window, no Japanese furniture on shining parquet. Instead he finds an overflowing Aladdin's cave that has not been cleared out since its occupant's youth. Schilf obeys an impulse to take his shoes off. He steps with stockinged feet into a room stuffed with furniture like an antiques shop. Postcards and newspaper cuttings cover every available space on the walls. Shelves bow beneath jumbles of books. There are porcelain figurines everywhere, wristwatches without hands, glass paperweights, and foreign coins. From the ceiling lamp hangs a stuffed crow whose wings can be moved by pulling on a cord. On a sailor's chest beside the leather armchair is a child's drawing: a small stick figure with yellow hair and a taller one with black hair; a great big smile shared between them; signed with a clumsy "L."

The master of the house sits cross-legged on a cushion in the middle of his private museum, waiting patiently for the detective to finish looking around. In this environment, his carefully combed hair and his white shirt are a kind of self-parody. When Schilf finally sinks into the upholstery of the battered sofa, Oskar lifts his chin, opens his mouth, and speaks.

"Surprised?"

"I have to admit I am, yes."

"I don't see any point in cleaning up after my own past. Cumulative chaos is a way of measuring the passage of time."

He leaps to his feet with predatory agility.

"May I offer you something to drink?"

"Yogi tea, please, in honor of a summer that has suddenly died."

Oskar raises an eyebrow.

"There is nothing that cannot be had in this apartment."

Almost as soon as he has left the room, Schilf struggles out of the sofa cushions and slips into the room next door. Under another petrified mass of objects is a desk with its top drawer pulled out. The photograph is in a silver frame of the type in which other men keep pictures of their wives. Sebastian can't be older than twenty and is wearing a silver cravat and a frock coat. His laugh is a challenge, a gauntlet thrown down to the observer.

"A lovely boy, *n'est-ce pas*?"

Oskar has entered silently over the stack of rugs. When Schilf turns around, they nearly clash heads. Schilf sees himself in the other man's black eyes. The master of the house takes the picture out of his hand gently.

"There are few things that are sacred to me."

"I felt a fondness for your friend right away," Schilf says. "And I think he felt the same about me."

"That is the fondness of the bird food for the bird. Come with me."

Oskar puts the photograph back in the drawer and bundles the detective out of the room. The steaming cups of tea on the side table prove that Schilf has spent at least a quarter of an hour gazing at the photograph. Oskar pours a dash of rum from a white bottle into the cups.

"None for me," Schilf says.

"I make the rules here."

The fumes of alcohol prick the detective's nostrils like long needles even before he takes his first sip. Behind his forehead, something contracts and then expands to twice its original size. Schilf drinks. He feels the alien heartbeat in his head more clearly than ever before. The crow hanging from the ceiling lamp flaps its wings and shadows glide up the walls. Oskar's face is a solid plane in a web of intertwined curves. Say something, the detective thinks.

"Has Sebastian confessed?" Oskar asks.

"If not, you've just betrayed him."

"Surely not, Detective. I know that you're not as stupid as your profession would suggest."

"Did Sebastian tell you that?"

"If you've come here hoping that I'll incriminate him . . ." Oskar leans forward. "I'd rather rip out my tongue with my bare hands."

"Now *you're* the one playing dumb," the detective says.

The next sip of tea is better than any medicine. The pressure in his head eases off and the alien heartbeat becomes a monotonous buzz that affects his hearing but not his ability to think clearly.

"I've handed the murder case to someone else, by the way."

Oskar does not permit himself the slightest flicker of surprise. He looks at the detective's mouth expectantly and lights a cigarette, which Schilf counts as a success.

"I've seen you on television. I was impressed by the program. May I ask you something?"

"Go ahead."

"Do you believe in God?"

It is impossible not to like Oskar when he laughs.

"Sebastian was right," he says. "You are an unusual detective."

"So he did talk about me." Schilf blushes—perhaps it is the alcohol. "Will you answer my question?"

"I'm a religious atheist."

"Why religious?"

"Because I believe." Oskar blows smoke off to one side politely. "I believe that the existence of the world cannot be conclusively explained to us. It takes a truly metaphysical strength to accept this."

"A strength that Sebastian does not possess?"

"You're touching on a sensitive point. The grown-up Sebastian you have met is actually still the boy that you saw in that photo. Like all boys, he longs for a world in which one can be both a pirate and a bookworm."

"What do you mean?"

Oskar watches as Schilf pours himself more tea and pushes the bottle of rum across the table.

"Sebastian loves his life," Oskar says, "but he still wishes he had not made a certain decision many years ago. Back then he leapt over a wall to save himself."

"What's behind the wall?"

"C'est moi," Oskar says. "And physics."

"A tragedy of classical proportions." Schilf blows at the steam rising from his cup.

"Irony doesn't suit you."

"I meant that seriously."

"Then you've understood what I am talking about."

They hold each other's gaze until Schilf looks away and takes his cigarillos out of his pocket. Oskar stretches across the table to give him a light, and stays in that position.

"Intelligent people," he says, "often pour their despair into scientific formulae. In order to be happy, a man like Sebastian would need a second, a third, perhaps even a fourth world."

"So that everything that is possible happens," says Schilf.

Oskar's features soften into a laugh again, and he runs his fingers through his hair.

"You really are good," he says, letting himself sink back. "So you'll understand why the idea of several contradictory things happening at the same time is very attractive to some people. And why it's like a nightmare, too."

He looks intently at the glowing tip of his cigarette, takes a final drag, and stubs it out in the ashtray. The stuffed crow has swung nearer. To Schilf, it looks like it is hanging directly over Oskar's head.

"Thinking like that negates the validity of every experience," Oskar continues. "It negates us."

"Perhaps Sebastian has realized that now." Schilf lets ash fall onto the carpet. "After the kidnapping, which he's constantly talking about."

The remains of a laugh play in the corners of Oskar's mouth.

"Yes," he says, "perhaps."

"Sebastian and his family," the detective says, "are an equation with one unknown. Someone has adjusted one of reality's screws. It's the right way to create a false picture. When a person deludes himself into thinking he is in charge, reality puts her fat arms on her hips and leers at him. On the contrary, a good lie is the truth plus one. Don't you think?"

"To be honest, you're talking rather confusedly." Oskar's eyes bore into Schilf's face.

This time it is the detective who laughs.

"You may be right," he says. "Do you know that your friend doesn't really hold to the Many-Worlds Interpretation at all, but is pursuing advanced theories on the nature of time?"

"Did he tell you that?"

Schilf nods.

"That doesn't matter," Oskar says, suddenly brusque. "He's looking for new ways to escape himself."

They are silent until the final echoes of the last sentence die away. Schilf's body fills the corner of the sofa like a soft mass that would feel comfortable in any given position, while Oskar sits with his legs stretched out before him, looking ahead with hooded eyes.

Finally the detective speaks. "Do you love Sebastian?" he asks.

"A good question," Oskar says, still sitting in the same position.

There is a pause, and Schilf stands up. With his cigarillo in the corner of his mouth, he walks over to the dormer window, where for a moment the view takes his breath away. The steps to Oskar's apartment have taken him right up to the sky. From this bird's-eye view, the city is a circuit board of twinkling lights. Rows of diodes connect up into a network of communicating lines, like letters of the alphabet.

Blackmail, more or less, the detective thinks. Perhaps Sebastian has jumped over the wall a second time by murdering Dabbelink. Perhaps he had secretly hoped to find Oskar still waiting behind the wall, but was shocked to the core to find that he was right. And now he is escaping into nowhere.

Since the fracture that separated the detective from himself, he has wondered often whether people are not somehow responsible for every conceivable twist of their own fate. Whether it isn't that people only ever blackmail themselves.

He recognizes the glowing patches of the Place de Cornavin, Place de Montbrillant, and Place Reculet, the dark ribbon of the Rhône, the colorful twinkling lights of the Quai du Mont-Blanc, and the devouring darkness of Lake Geneva beyond it. As if on cue, the pain starts nagging between his eyes again. It grows hot and bright and draws the city closer to him, bathing it in a glittering light.

Three people, tiny as toy figures, are walking across a pier toward the Jet d'Eau. Two of them are close together, probably arm in arm. The third, smaller person is running ahead like an excited dog. All three have blond hair. The detective sees them in unusually sharp detail in spite of the distance; he can just see their outstretched index fingers, and the happy faces turned up toward the sky to take in the whole height of the white gleam at the end of the pier. The tower of water splits the sun into all the colors of the rainbow.

"Look, Daddy! The lake is throwing itself up into the air!"

The spray soaks their clothes. It is warm.

The detective is looking at a holiday snap, a postcard like the ones on his fridge. But there is one essential difference. The other side of this particular card is not blank. There is writing on it: "It's fantastic!" or "We were here!"

Schilf decides to take this card with him. Sebastian would certainly not object. A man, a woman, and a happy child. He will hang it over the hole in the story of his life. A life is so fragile. Something lurches out of its tracks, and instead of three people there is one, and only half of that person, too. The detective had practiced remembering for a while, then he had trained himself to forget. It had been unbearably sad to think about the life of his that had ended. Now he realizes that there is nothing easier than calling another person's past to mind.

Anyone who wants to die has to be whole, the detective thought, the detective thinks.

Oskar speaks in the room somewhere behind him. "Knowing Sebastian has taught me to fear the whims of the gods."

Schilf has closed his eyes. His fingers close around the edge of the windowsill as if holding on to the crow's nest in a storm-tossed ship.

"Yesterday, I would have claimed to know one thing for certain," Oskar says. "That I would give my life for him."

"And today?" Schilf asks through clenched teeth.

"Today I am an old man."

Oskar takes a breath. When he speaks again, his voice is even deeper. Cold.

"Did you know that Sebastian was with me yesterday evening?"

"I suspected it."

"I asked him to leave the country with me."

"And he refused?"

"He turned down everything that I had to give. It seems that he has finally made his decision. I can do nothing more for him."

"You're wrong, Oskar. You will do something for him. I promise you that."

When the detective opens his eyes, the city has returned to its former self. It is night and there is no man, no woman, and no happy child. Even the pillar of water from the Jet d'Eau cannot be seen from here. Only the stubborn wind is still there, rattling the beams of the roof. Schilf turns around. Oskar is standing in front of him with his arms stretched out, as if he wants to embrace him. The detective would take a step backward if it weren't for the pitched roof behind him, and behind that an abyss, a free fall. Their eyes meet.

There is a wave of human scents. Starched cotton, expensive aftershave, and a strange happiness. An arm is draped across the detective's shoulders. Oskar pulls him close.

"Come. Let me help you."

He conducts the detective back to the sofa, nudges his head onto the armrest, and presses something cool and moist to his neck. When Schilf looks down at himself, he sees a large red patch decorating his chest. He touches his face: nosebleed. There are flecks of red on Oskar's white cuffs.

"I've messed up your shirt," the detective says.

"Anyone wearing a white shirt is a doctor." Oskar wipes the blood off his hands and passes the wet cloth to Schilf. "That's what I thought when I was a child, anyway."

"You've helped me a good deal." The detective tries to sit up, but falls back down again. "Will you do me another favor?"

Lying down, he gropes in his back pocket for the chess computer. When the display lights up, Oskar kneels down next to the sofa.

"What have we got here?"

He looks at the sixty-four squares intently. Schilf knows exactly what he sees: a catastrophic situation in which everything that is still alive is pressing into one half of the playing field. Oskar scrutinizes the screen for a long time before he looks up.

"Interesting," he says. "You're playing black against the computer."

"Certainly not," Schilf says. "I'm white."

Oskar knits his brows and looks at the game again.

"I repeat, Detective," he says. "You're an unusual person. You seem to love destroying yourself for the narrow chance of victory. Did you mean to tell me something with this game?"

Schilf shakes his head in which a slowly cooling mass rolls from side to side. He passes Oskar the stylus.

"You want me to finish this thing for you?" Oskar twirls the stylus in his fingers. "You want to watch me win this game for you?"

Schilf does not answer. Oskar strokes his chin and looks around. Finally he puts the chess computer on the detective's stomach and props him up so that he can see the display.

"The knight goes here. The black queen is forked, and now your castle can move." The stylus taps the display. Every move jiggles the small chess computer against the detective's shirt buttons. "The pawn reaches the final row and is converted. Check. The king has to move. The rook moves in next to him. *Et voilà*."

Congratulations, the screen flashes.

"The black king is mated," the detective says.

"Yes," Oskar says. "Mated."

"You're a genius."

"Don't tell me that this wasn't planned."

"I've only been playing for four weeks."

"In that case," Oskar says, squinting as if he is trying to focus on a particular point behind Schilf's forehead, "it is most certainly *you* who are the genius. Can you get up now?"

Schilf wipes his face one more time and gives the cloth back to Oskar. With one hand on Oskar's shoulder, he gets up. When they are standing in the middle of the room, he reaches for the cord hanging from the crow's stomach.

"That's been broken for a long time," Oskar says.

In the hall, Schilf puts on his shoes but leaves the laces untied. Oskar has tugged the front door open over the rugs, and is holding it for him.

"I think you know everything that you need to know," he says.

The smile they exchange in farewell is tinged with mild regret.

THE WIND HAS SUBSIDED. The lake looks so smooth and solid that the detective feels like trying to walk on water. The gravel crunches in greeting with every step he takes. Schilf stretches an arm out to one side and imagines that Julia is leaning her head on his shoulder as they walk, saying something lovely about the clouds parting and the stars twinkling. A bird utters a shrill cry of warning, but when nothing happens it lapses into silence and invisibility again. The detective walks to the station: there is just time to catch the last train.

He has left the small chess computer on Oskar's sofa. He doesn't need it anymore.

Life is a story with many floors, Schilf thinks. Or one with many chapters that close one after another without a sound.

CHAPTER 7, IN EIGHT PARTS

The perpetrator is hunted down. In the end, it is conscience that decides. A bird soars into the air.

[1]

FROM THE FIRST DAY THAT SCHILF MET HIS NEW GIRLFRIEND, when she expected a waiter and a menu at McDonald's, he had decided never to introduce her to anyone he knew. Not that he'd be ashamed of her. But he fears that she might not survive the gaze of a third person, and would simply dissolve into thin air. He views her visit with mixed feelings.

Although Schilf has pulled himself together and is striding forward purposefully, his progress is slow, as if he were walking the wrong way along a people mover. He arrives at Freiburg Station a few minutes late. A woman runs toward him on the concourse. When he steps aside to make way for her, she stops in front of him. The detective clasps her hands and feels a pang of guilt. At first he did not recognize her. Without knowing it, he had actually been expecting to see Maike. He scrabbles around and finds one of the simple words that Julia likes so much: "Hello."

She laughs and puts her arms around his neck. She does not have any bags with her, but she has brought him flowers, or something similar. Three brown, velvety bulbs swaying on stalks. They look like microphones that have accidentally got into the frame.

"Schilf," Julia says, poking him in the ribs, "somewhat older than before."

"Do you have the postcard with you?"

"Did you write to me?"

"Yesterday. It was important."

"Yesterday was Sunday, Schilf. How could I have received the postcard this morning?"

She is right, as usual. The detective is relieved to realize that the result of his postcard experiment matters less and less to him the longer Julia is standing in front of him. He puts his arm around her shoulders, just like he practiced on the shore of Lake Geneva, and lowers his head to breathe in the scent of her hair. He remembers hearing somewhere that it is not possible to dream smells.

The sun breaking through the clouds turns the town into a silvery landscape. It must have rained again in the night; the puddles glisten like molten metal and Schilf has to screen his eyes against the sudden flashes from passing windshields. An old man in torn trousers calls out an airy greeting toward the other side of the road, where there is nobody at all. A young girl is standing at the corner of the street, motionless, holding on to an umbrella, her head tilted, as if she has forgotten where she wanted to go.

The detective decides to feel happy because it is delightful that there is someone who got up this morning to come visit him. It makes him happy to look at Julia's face and watch her funny hands with their short fingers moving constantly. Looking at those hands, he understands why some people believe in the goodness of human beings. A species that includes someone like his girlfriend can be driven to do dreadful things only through some enormous misunderstanding.

Schilf's good mood evaporates when he sees Sebastian's face behind the clear screen of a newspaper dispenser. He sees "Hospital Scandal" and "At Large" in the headline, and quickens his step involuntarily.

"How's your case going?" Julia asks, in the tone of a repair person come to solve a problem.

To Schilf's own surprise, he has to pause to think before he can reply. Sebastian, Oskar, Many Worlds, and a decapitated cyclist arrange themselves into a pattern that seems almost logical and then falls apart again in a colorful whirl. The detective knows the murderer and the kidnapper, but the stupid thing is, Dabbelink's death still does not make sense.

"There's just one detail missing," he says as he unlocks the door of the building that houses the police apartment. "Unfortunately, it's the load-bearing column in the whole thing."

"We'd best have a look," Julia says.

The small apartment has cast off its civil servant's demeanor today and taken on a friendly air in the zebra shadow of the slanted Venetian blinds. Julia strolls in as if she has just come back from town, empties a bottle of water into the sink, and puts the bulbs into the bottle. The detective steps into the middle of the room with his arms spread wide and shouts "Welcome!" a little too late, and feels foolish. Only that morning, he had found the words to describe his dark tear sacs and the network of lines around his eyes. *Elephant face*. It is not easy for a man with an elephant face to be charming, he thinks.

But Julia laughs the way she always does, and pulls the detective onto the sofa. She clasps his right hand with both of hers and presses it to her lips as if he had just died.

Since the fracture, Schilf's interest in women has limited itself mainly to their credibility on the witness stand. Julia's appearance in the final few meters of his journey has not changed things very much, though his body has come to an arrangement with hers that both parties find fulfilling. He likes looking at her when she undresses: she unbuttons her top as unself-consciously as other women open their handbags. Schilf is freed from any obligation to feel shyness or reverence by the countless pairs of eyes that have gazed intently at Julia's body for years. He can simply look at her.

When her clothes have been carefully folded and draped over the back of the chair, her nakedness touches Schilf more than it arouses him. But as soon as she nestles her body against him, he makes love to her with all the passion and gratitude that he is capable of. He makes love to her so completely that everything comes to a standstill: all the pain, all the brooding, the whole human impulse toward a permanent internal report on one's own existence. From the beginning, Julia had been able to silence the observer. There is peace for a few minutes. Infinite as the color black and beautiful as a harbinger of death.

AFTERWARD, THEY RAISE THE BLINDS and drink coffee next to the closed balcony door, clinking their cups against the glass to toast the Monday morning. On the street below, a child skitters past on steel roller skates, the kind that haven't been made for decades. Two doves fight over a walnut that neither can open. Schilf squints into the bright light until the two doves are unmasked as crows, winter birds, birds of doom that have slipped in through a tear in the colorfully painted curtain that calls itself summer. For a few seconds he sees the trees as black skeletons against a pale sky, and he sees a large plain on which thousands of crows gather; he sees them taking flight and the sun darkening. The interval is over, his head is the same as it always was.

With a contented sound Julia leans into his arm.

"Don't go," Schilf whispers.

"I was gone already," Julia says. "Now I'm here."

She looks at him with her ocean-deep eyes, raises her eyebrows, and stretches her mouth wide, like an actress in a silent film. Schilf puts a hand on her head, closes his eyes, and tries to read her thoughts.

"We'll soon be treating each other like a memory that is uncomfortable, but necessary," he says.

The doorbell rings and they collide. A young trainee police officer is standing outside, and she is looking keen to get away. Schilf realizes too late that he is not wearing any trousers. He takes the envelope from her and only just stops himself from giving her a tip. The word "URGENT" stands out in red letters on the package.

The buttons on the video recorder stubbornly change places until

Julia pushes the detective aside. The machine swallows the video obediently.

"Evidence?" Julia asks, making herself comfortable in front of the television with her cup of coffee.

Schilf nods.

"The murderer and his best friend," he says, as the *Circumpolar* set appears.

"And who is who?"

The detective does not answer.

He enjoys watching the program a second time. The presence of the two men is even stronger on the larger screen. Transfixed, Schilf notes every look and every gesture, observes Oskar's predatory elegance and Sebastian's nervous watchfulness, and registers the fluctuations in tension. Julia yawns and looks bored.

"*One* universe," Oskar says. "With no possibility for escape. That's what you should be researching. That's where you should be living."

When the discussion gets livelier, Julia sits up.

"What are they fighting about?"

"That's not a scientific argument," Sebastian shouts. "That's moralistic dogmatism!"

"Wait a minute," the detective says.

He turns the volume up. A glass of water hits the glass table with the force of a gunshot.

"In your double worlds you live a double life," Oskar says.

Julia presses both hands to her ears with a scream.

"What's going on?" she says angrily.

Sebastian's Adam's apple moves up and down in close-up. Schilf takes hold of his girlfriend's wrists and forces her to uncover her ears.

"Listen."

"Let me put it in Orwell's words," Oskar says.

As he stands up, the murmuring in the audience swells to a roar that makes the floor of the apartment vibrate. The rustling of clothing.

Oskar's leather soles on the wooden rostrum. *How dare he*, hisses the television host. Oskar's microphone is lying on the glass table and it is difficult to hear what he is saying. He is pointing at Sebastian with an index finger.

"Now," Schilf says, leaning forward.

The microphones in the auditorium have picked up Oskar's voice. He sounds as if he is speaking from a great distance.

"That is Dabbelink," the detective hears him say.

"Turn it off now," Julia orders.

Schilf has dropped the remote control; Julia reaches for it and pauses the tape. On the screen the host freezes with his arms raised; all three figures are united in one trembling statue. Next the host would probably attempt to point to the physicists' excitement as proof of his program's importance. Afterward he would continue the discussion. If Julia allowed him.

The detective's blood has gone to his feet. He feels his pale cheeks with his fingers in an unconscious movement.

"I don't get it," he groans. "My head is bursting."

Julia settles back into the sofa contentedly and takes her cup off the armrest.

"What strange methods of investigation you have."

When Schilf grabs her by the shoulder, coffee spills onto her bare legs and leaves a dark spot on the sofa cover.

"Hey!" Julia shouts. "Are you crazy?"

He lets go of her immediately and his elephant eyes look her in the face.

"What did the man say?" he asks pleadingly.

An artistic work of transformation plays over Julia's features: first indignation, then astonishment, and finally mockery.

"What do you mean?" she says. "It was perfectly clear."

She looks first into one of the detective's eyes, then into the other, before a glow of realization dawns on her face.

"I see," she says. "You haven't read Orwell!"

"So?" the detective prompts.

"That is *doublethink*," Julia says. "It means holding two contradictory beliefs in one's mind simultaneously, and accepting both of them. In Orwell that is a practice of totalitarian systems."

"No," Schilf says. It sounds like a cry for help. Julia takes his hand, looking concerned.

"What's the matter? Don't you think it works?"

"Yes, yes."

"There you go. And that guy there," she indicates Oskar, who is still pointing his finger and smiling devilishly, "thinks that guy there"—Sebastian, sitting next to the host, is flickering on the screen—"is particularly good at it."

"*Doublethink* must go," the detective says.

He can't stop staring at his girlfriend; his frozen gaze needs somewhere to land. His heart is beating like a drum. The black king has forced itself into the farthest corner of H8. The white king has fallen off the edge of the board. Chess pieces whirl around and sixty-four squares have torn themselves apart, clattering onto the hard ground.

Is the existence of mankind in the world not enough of a misunderstanding? the detective thinks. Must aural misunderstandings add to the confusion?

And: When branches surface at two different places in a pond, they can absolutely belong to the same bough.

He feels gentle fingers stroking his cheek. This time they are not his own.

"Have we solved the case?" Julia asks tenderly.

"Fuck, yes," the detective says.

[2]

TO SENIOR POLICEMAN SCHNURPFEIL, Rita Skura is the most beautiful woman in the world. There has never been a more beautiful woman and there never will be, unless they were to have a child together. Schnurpfeil does not think of himself as a clever person. He has not experienced much, and therefore has not much to tell. He also has no particular abilities that would distinguish him in a crowd. But he knows that he is good-looking and feels that, for this reason alone, he is a good match for Rita Skura. Besides which he has been exemplary in his loyalty to her. And she doesn't have a boyfriend. She is married to her ambition, and this quality, as Schnurpfeil's perusal of the pay-banding has told him, will bring her a considerable income one day. Rita will pursue her career and earn more and more, first enough for two, then for three or four. Schnurpfeil would not mind staying at home and taking care of everything for a woman like Rita; on the contrary, he would be proud of her. His plans are clear, well thought out, and quite flawless. He just hasn't found the right moment to present them to her.

The senior policeman leans back in the passenger seat of an Austrian police car and gazes at a landscape that looks as if it were shorn every morning by a lawn mower. When Rita had asked him if he fancied a trip to the Bregenz region, he imagined blue skies, white clouds, and green meadows, all of which are very much in evidence. But Schnurpfeil also thought of the safety belt between Rita's breasts, and of her brown eyes with the sun smiling out of them. He said yes so enthusiastically that Rita gave him an odd look. Schnurpfeil didn't mind this. Odd looks were the least of his troubles when it came to the detective.

However, now it is not Rita sitting next to him but an Austrian policeman whose stomach barely fits behind the steering wheel. He lets rip at the hordes of tourists on whom he and his countrymen depend. The town center in Bregenz is full of people who behave as if their visitors' taxes have paid for an all-day pedestrian zone, so reluctant are they to make way for cars. Schnurpfeil can at least be thankful that he does not have to find his own way to a place called Gwiggen. On the backseat, his green police cap and the Austrian's white one lie next to each other harmoniously, a symbol of international police cooperation.

When the car starts creeping up the foothills of the Pfänder mountain, swinging heavily from side to side on the curves, the Austrian releases a sigh that smells of *Jagdwurst*. He comments on the beauty of the landscape as if he had discovered it himself. Schnurpfeil does not understand how someone can be proud of a region that is too kitschy even for a postcard. Anyone not wearing lederhosen or a dirndl looks out of place here. This scenery might have been the right environment in which to discuss his life plans with Rita. But now he has no choice but to bring the detective the information that she needs: all of it, quickly and thoroughly, to her full satisfaction, as he always does.

The car finally judders over a dirt track and comes to rest in the shade of a thoroughly German oak tree. The Austrian wipes his neck with a checked handkerchief and puts his seat back, while Schnurpfeil gets out and walks toward the wooden house. With its wide balcony and its intricately carved gables, it looks like a giant cuckoo clock. In the meadow, a tower made of wooden posts, barrels, and cable rises up so mysteriously that the senior policeman does not even attempt to guess at the purpose of this construction. In the distance, a group of children is running along the edge of the forest.

Inside, the building smells of tea and shoes. There is no one at reception or in the dining hall. Schnurpfeil opens and closes numbered doors, and looks into room after room full of bunk beds until he stumbles upon a boy and a girl in a shabbily furnished office. His appearance throws them into some confusion. The fat boy stares at the police badge, his eyes bulging as if his head is bursting with sheer concentration. Schnurpfeil decides to address himself to the girl. Her hair is shaved at the sides and tied in a ponytail. When she speaks, the stud of her tongue piercing clicks against her teeth. Once the senior policeman realizes that these are not children on vacation but two of the group leaders, his tone becomes more formal.

They remembered Liam, yes, of course. His father had caused a stir when he came to pick up his son out of the blue. The girl had helped the poor boy pack. Head lowered, he had folded his socks one by one and insisted on making his bed exactly as they had all learned on their first day.

Who had brought the poor boy here?

The two group leaders look up at the ceiling and grimace. Difficult to say. On the first day, about a hundred children arrived in Gwiggen. It could have been the man who picked him up, but perhaps not. In any case, the man wasn't particularly tall. And wasn't especially short, either.

Schnurpfeil loses patience immediately. He has always found it difficult to take people with Austrian accents seriously. With an imperious movement he waves the fat boy away from the chair behind the computer, sits down, and grabs at a tattered ledger that is lying open on top of a pile of magazines. The book contains charts full of information: arrivals, departures, details of age, gender, illness, dietary requirements, details of deposits. All the entries are in different inks and different handwriting. Leafing through the pages, the senior policeman finds Liam's name under number 27. There is his date of arrival, but no other comments. As he is about to put back the book, a piece of yellow paper falls out from between the pages.

In round handwriting: *Stefan, no. 27, not coming because of flu. The father rang. F.*

Schnurpfeil asks the girl if she wrote this.

She shakes her head vigorously. F is another person. And the note was wrong. The poor boy was there. Just left early. Why does the officer look at her so strangely?

Schnurpfeil sinks back into the chair as the group leaders discuss the situation. He clenches and unclenches his fists, observing the play of muscles in his forearms. He thinks about the moment when he will report back to the detective. Perhaps he will claim that the forgotten note was lying hidden in the pile of magazines. Rita Skura will look up at him and push the hair away from her forehead, showing him her armpits. Thank you, Schnurpfeil, well done.

The silence in the room brings him out of his reverie. The fat boy is staring at him and the girl has disappeared to fetch reinforcements. A few minutes later, Schnurpfeil is surrounded by children who all look like Liam, whose photo he has seen in the file. High voices screech and sticky fingers reach out for the leather holster containing his weapon. Schnurpfeil does not like children, other than the ones he will bear with Rita Skura.

He jumps up and makes his way to a man towering over the throng. That's Stefan, the boss, the fat boy says. With his untidy beard, Stefan looks like an eternal conscientious objector. He speaks in a nasal tone that infuriates Schnurpfeil.

He couldn't leave the scouts alone in the field, so he brought them in. He knows nothing about a phone call or flu. There's a lot going on, he doesn't have eyes in the back of his head. And he doesn't understand what's so important about this now.

Schnurpfeil grabs Stefan by the arm and presses hard.

Yes, of course he remembers. A tall man brought the sleeping Liam to Gwiggen and carried him into the house in his arms.

The senior policeman strengthens his grip, whereupon Stefan remembers that the man had dark hair. And when the senior policeman adds the pressure of his other hand, he also remembers that the stranger had really piercing black eyes and a really arrogant face. He is really sure that this was not the same man who took Liam away a few days later.

Schnurpfeil puts away the yellow note, takes down F's full name, and wishes everyone good day in his purest German before he blazes his way through the babbling hordes of children and leaves the room.

The Austrian officer has fallen asleep in the car and wakes with a start when Schnurpfeil shakes him by the shoulder and asks him for the car phone. Of course it would be more pleasant to deliver the news in person. But Rita Skura does not joke about such matters. Complete. Thorough. Swift. Satisfaction guaranteed.

The senior policeman picks up the receiver and moves it as far from the car as the cable will allow.

"Mission accomplished, boss!"

"Enough of that Starship Enterprise crap," Rita says. "Spit it out."

It is precisely these retorts that Schnurpfeil most loves about Rita Skura.

[3]

"JULIA? IS THAT YOU?"

"Far from it, Schilf. Why do you always answer the phone with a question?"

This has never occurred to the detective before. It is probably just the way he is.

"And who is Julia?"

"My girlfriend. I told you about her, in a moment of weakness."

"Whatever you say!" Rita is in a good mood. "I probably didn't believe it."

"Same here."

"Very funny. I'm calling to lecture you."

"All right," Schilf says morosely. "It's an upside-down world."

Rita has not phoned at a good time. The round foyer has the acoustics of a cathedral. Schilf tucks himself between two pillars beneath a cupola painted with the constellations of a winter sky. Downstairs, people are milling about as they wait for the program to start. They peer into display cases set in the walls or stand in small groups chatting. The floor shakes when a train passes behind the building.

"The theme of today's lecture is: 'What it feels like to have a case snatched away from under your nose.' "

"Go on, then."

"Do you know who took Liam to scout camp after the supposed kidnapping?"

"Yes."

"You're bluffing."

"Certainly not."

Rita Skura sucks air through her teeth. The hissing sounds like a false bottom being moved aside. The conversation stagnates, while her good mood changes into its opposite.

"Then say who it is," she finally huffs.

"Oskar."

"How do you know?"

"Because it's the truth. How about you?"

"My people were in Gwiggen."

The detective can't help smiling. He knows that the role of Rita's "people" is played by Senior Policeman Schnurpfeil.

"I received a description from Gwiggen. It matches a photo in the murderer's desk drawer."

"What were you doing in Sebastian's desk?" the detective asks sharply.

"A search," Rita says. "That tried-and-tested tool of police investigations."

"For God's sake! Why don't you just stop this nonsense and leave him in peace?"

"It's perfectly simple, Schilf. He killed a man."

"He's confessed."

"I'm looking for a motive."

"Then you can call me!"

Startled by the loudness of his own voice, Schilf claps a hand over his mouth. Carefully, he leans over the balustrade. No one looks up at him. The two people he would like to corner are standing in front of a glass case containing globes of various sizes. A pyramid-shaped piece has been cut from each, revealing the colorful stripes inside.

"I'm not calling with questions anymore," Rita says, "but with answers."

When the two people turn away from the display case, Schilf lifts his gaze to the solar system hanging from steel cables in the middle of the foyer, turning like a giant mobile. Schilf envies the drive toward orderliness that keeps the planets on course. He has looked up the second law of thermodynamics on the Internet: In any system chaos increases constantly unless immense amounts of energy are used to stop it. Schilf has clearly not had enough energy even to protect Sebastian from Rita's search. His apartment must look as if a tornado had passed through.

"Anyway," he says, "I'm happy that you finally believe it."

"Believe what?"

When Schilf's targets stop in front of the next display case, a spotlight casts a halo of light around their blond hair. Two angels striding through space, the detective thinks.

"That you finally believe in the blackmail."

"For goodness' sake." The cheerful Rita has disappeared. It is the police officer who is talking: cool, unscrupulous, and efficient. "You don't seem to be up to speed. This Oskar person who brought the kidnapped boy to Gwiggen is Sebastian's best friend."

"The stuff of Greek tragedy," Schilf says.

"I call that being an accessory to murder, and very clever, too. The professor has to get rid of a rival. His friend fakes a blackmail. Much better than a shaky alibi. I knew from the start that this was a crime of passion."

"And that's why you proceeded from the opposite of this conviction, right?"

"In any case," Rita says, "crimes of passion are terrific. Crimes of passion have nothing to do with the hospital scandal."

"Listen to me!"

The panic that the detective has made such an effort to suppress bursts forth so strongly that Rita falls silent for a moment. Schilf leans his forehead against a sandstone pillar and forces himself to speak quietly.

"You're right, it could have happened that way. But I swear to you, Rita, that it didn't."

"Schilf . . ."

"It was a silly boy's prank, thought up by a particularly dangerous boy. It was a great love, the Many-Worlds theory, and a masterwork by the most ruthless criminal that exists on this earth: coincidence. So ruthless that I prefer not to believe in him."

"Detective Schilf?" Rita says. "Are you listening to yourself? Silly boy? Great love? Coincidence?"

"I can explain it all," the detective whispers.

The little angel has reached out an arm, and his fingertips follow the lines of text on a board. He is saying something. The grown-up nods.

"I'll bring the person who is the real culprit to you. He'll confess. You can tell the powers that be that the case has been solved. Stop trying to beat me, Rita—help me!"

"But what are you expecting me to do, Schilf?" Rita cries.

The detective holds the phone away from his ear so that he can dry his forehead and cheeks. There is a ripple of movement below. The first few people are walking toward the stairs. Schilf bends down and picks up the briefcase wedged between his feet.

"Are you doing anything tonight?" he asks.

"Of course not."

The two angels are floating up the stone staircase. Schilf retreats farther behind his pillar.

"I have to sort something out here first," he says. "Don't do anything. Be prepared."

"One more question. Do you think this case has anything to do with hospitals at all?"

"Not in the slightest."

"OK. See you later."

The detective slips the mobile phone into his trouser pocket and waits until everyone else has entered the auditorium. Then he, too, produces his ticket and slips inside.

IT'S DARK. There are no seats. Everyone is clustered together looking at the dome above them, which is lit with a bluish glow. A teacher tells her giggling class to sit down on the floor, as they can't keep their balance in the dark. The detective has some difficulty keeping his balance, too, as he pushes his way through the crowd. A giant spiral is beginning to turn in the artificial sky. $E = mc^2$ shoots across it like an asteroid. The children screech excitedly and duck.

"In the great play of Being, we are actors and spectators at the same time," a male voice announces to open the show.

Schilf has found his two angels and is standing directly behind them. Every time the taller one moves her shoulders, the smell of her silky hair rises. She smells quite different from Julia—even sweeter. The aroma, as that of lime-blossom tea, calls forth images from the depths of his memory. This is my new past, Schilf thinks. I'll remember this when I go: a man, a woman, and an excited boy turning their faces up to space. Perhaps a caress on the back, too, interlinked fingers, and a child's head that fits neatly under the palm of the hand. Schilf almost taps his two targets on the shoulder; he stops himself just in time. Here, right in front of him, are two people whose future he is responsible for. Fate has united them with him in a tiny speck on the outer crust of this planet.

The time for unconscious living is past, the detective thought, the detective thinks. In the last few meters, life can no longer be worn like a shoe that you don't notice as long as it doesn't pinch your foot.

For a moment, Schilf is filled with such happiness that he feels like crying. But like most people, he has long ago exchanged the ability to cry with the desire for revenge. He understands perfectly well that he can no longer build a true home for anyone. He can only punish anyone who dares to destroy something as precious as a true home.

The detective takes a step backward; he has to concentrate to avoid tipping over. He feels the pulse inside the bird's egg, and the way the second law of thermodynamics is working to throw him and his case into a state of increasing chaos. Soon he will no longer have the energy to fight against the dissolution. He has to make one final effort now. There is half a day and one night left. It is his last chance to put things in order. The two angels are holding hands. Images showing the collision of accelerated particles play in their hair.

"From all the possible outcomes, the one that has actually taken place is determined by the observer," says the male voice coming out of the loudspeakers.

"I'm here," Schilf says.

Maike's back stiffens and she turns her head slowly.

"I know," she says.

A violent explosion on the screen bathes the auditorium in white light. Every detail of Maike's face can be seen, cool and impenetrable, like an overexposed photograph. Liam turns around, too, and his eyes look hard, like pieces of blue plastic. When he recognizes the detective, he turns his narrow back on him in a deliberate gesture.

"I can't stand you following us," Maike whispers.

"But I'm not following you!" the detective says in a suppressed shout.

"No elementary phenomenon is a phenomenon until it is an observed phenomenon," the man's voice continues.

A cartoon cat paces across the dome: the children cheer and a forest of arms rises from the human undergrowth.

"I wanted to ask you how you are," Schilf whispers.

Maike laughs silently.

"Get lost. There's nothing else you can get from us."

The cat is shut inside a cardboard box. Schilf knows what is coming next. His reading on the Internet covered Schrödinger's cat. As long as no one looks inside the box, the cat is both dead and alive at the same time, in a state called quantum superposition. From Maike's point of view, Schilf and Rita are in just such a state. Maike cannot distinguish between them. Police work is police work. It is no use explaining that he has saved her husband the agony of remand, but that he cannot do anything about the way Sebastian is treated. Maike would certainly think he was lying.

The frantic ticking of a clock is getting on Schilf's nerves, but he is relieved when he realizes it is coming from the loudspeakers this time, not from inside his own head.

"I'm terribly sorry about the search," he says finally. "I must apologize on behalf of my colleague."

"What search? What do you mean?" Maike asks.

"Don't you know about it?"

"I haven't been in the apartment since yesterday."

"So . . ." Schilf says, feeling horror creep over him. "So you've left him?"

"He has left us, in both heart and mind. All we've done is move out of the apartment. A mere formality in comparison."

"No," Schilf says. "You're wrong. Sebastian would never—"

"Detective," Maike whispers, leaning toward him so that Liam cannot hear her, "did my husband murder Ralph Dabbelink?"

"Yes."

"Thank you," Maike says, and turns away. "It's good to get a clear answer."

"He didn't want to."

"No one does anything they don't want to do."

"He was blackmailed."

"You believe him?"

"Strange, isn't it? And you're the one who's married to him, not me."

"What I believe doesn't matter anymore."

"You're wrong there, too."

The detective shifts a little in order to look at Maike in profile. She is not smiling. She also shows no despair, no anger, no pain. She's a statue, Schilf thinks. Cold inside, outside pure form.

"Imagine three people walking along a beautiful road together," Maike says. "The road suddenly comes to an end. And one of them beats his way into the bushes and runs off without hesitation. Alone."

"That image is completely wrong."

"Could you stop blathering?" a woman standing next to Maike asks.

"Almost done," Schilf says, lifting his police badge up into view.

"Quantum physics opens up our thinking to an entirely different reality," the announcer says.

"Everything I'm doing is aimed at proving Sebastian's innocence," the detective says to Maike. "And what's more, to *you*."

"Why?"

"I want you to stand by him."

"Why?"

Because you belong on the postcard that I want to put on the fridge door of my memory, Schilf thinks.

He rubs both hands over his face. He is prolonging this conversation because he likes talking to this woman so much. He has to pull himself together and stop looking at her cloud of hair and her almost white eyelashes. He must make use of the seconds in which she is still listening, her arms crossed and her smooth face turned up toward the dome.

"Listen," Schilf whispers. "Give me twenty-four hours and I'll be able to explain everything to you. But I want the real guilty party to do that."

"This is not my battle. I was cast aside before it began."

"But Liam wants to know the truth. I promised him the truth."

Maike glances at him, leans down to her son, and puts a hand on the back of his neck.

"Liam," she says quietly, "do you still want this man to tell you anything?"

Liam looks over his shoulder and catches the detective's eye.

"Get lost," he says.

Schilf buckles as if he has been hit in the stomach. He turns the collar of his jacket up and presses the briefcase to his side.

"Our reality is like the smile of a cat that does not even exist," the voice from the loudspeakers says.

As the detective wends his away through the crowd, he feels his nose, his mouth, and his ears as if he were learning to recognize himself in the dark through his sense of touch.

"Pardon," he whispers. "I'm going now."

Again and again, as if he has to tell every one of the hissing spectators: "I'm going now."

[4]

THE BRIEFCASE MAKES IT DIFFICULT TO RUN. Schilf wedges it under his arm as he runs past the station and onto Stephan-Mayer-Strasse. The entire city seems to be fired up by his exertion. Passersby turn into multicolored streaks and buildings hold in their stomachs and lean forward to watch him hurry past. A boy runs alongside him for a while, shouting, "Giddy-up! Giddy-up!," and clapping his hands. It is only when Schilf reaches Sophie-de-la-Roche-Strasse that he slows down. His heart is pounding hard against his ribs. Beneath his feet the ground breathes, the pavement rises steeply heavenward. The detective half expects that he will turn into a murky fluid at any minute.

Bonnie and Clyde drop from the wall into the water and glide toward him, tugging a ripple behind them.

"Quick, quick, quick," they quack.

Schilf cannot speak, but raises his hand to thank them before he enters the building.

The walls of the stairwell mimic his panting. Schilf pulls himself up by the handrail, step by step. He has not given any thought to how he will get the door to the apartment open in case of emergency. When he gets to the second floor, the door is open. Schilf checks the lock; it is undamaged. Either his colleagues have made a very clean job of it or they were admitted voluntarily. In any case, the open door is no longer a technical problem, but an invitation.

Although Schilf first visited the apartment no more than two days ago, he has difficulty recognizing it even from where he stands in the doorway. Paper is strewn everywhere, the carpets have been rolled up, and the pictures taken off the wall. Everything gives the impression of forced departure and homelessness. Schilf does not have to think long about where to find Sebastian. Certain things always happen in the kitchen, which is the stomach of an apartment, just like the hallway is its legs, the living room its heart, and the study the convolutions of its brain.

All is still in the kitchen. The wire noose hanging from the ceiling casts a sharp shadow on the floor. The ceiling lamp has been removed and placed on top of the table like a suction cup. A chair had been knocked over and its legs are lying against the oven door. The contents of the drawers are scattered on the floor: cutlery lying between candles, string, plastic wrap, and cleaning cloths. Pots and pans are piled up on the windowsill. Sebastian's body blends seamlessly into the picture. He is sitting at the table, motionless, bent over like a question mark, staring blankly at an empty glass decorated with a picture of two nuzzling parakeets.

"Goodness gracious," the detective says.

He drops the briefcase and hurries over to Sebastian with both arms stretched out as if he is trying to take something heavy from him. Sebastian lifts his gaze, but does not quite manage to look the detective in the eye.

"Liam gave it to his mother for her birthday this year," he says, lifting his finger ever so slightly to point at the glass. "We stumbled upon it in a department store. Maike was very pleased with it."

"How lovely," the detective says.

"I thought it would be easier. It was quite simple with Dabbelink. Steel cable is steel cable, I thought."

"That is not just a bad solution," Schilf replies. "It's no solution at all."

"Oskar once said that life is an offer that you can also refuse. But I wasn't in a position to decide then. Same story my whole damn life." Sebastian's laugh turns into a coughing fit. "What brings you here?"

"I have a message for you."

Sebastian finally raises his head.

"From Maike?"

"No." Schilf clears his throat. "You'll find out very soon who it's from."

An ambulance siren draws closer, grows louder, and shrieks a high-pitched warning. Its frequency decreases as the vehicle passes.

"The Doppler effect," Sebastian says. "A great example of how everything is relative."

Together, they listen to the sound ebbing away. Schilf feels like a surgeon who is allowing his patient a few moments of peace before he cuts away an abscess without anesthetic. This abscess is a mistake. It is the final, the biggest, and the most painful mistake that Schilf wants to cut out and replace with the steel instrument called truth, which will function as a sterile foreign body in the organism of the patient. The detective wishes an anesthetist were present.

"This is going to hurt for a bit," he says. "Get ready."

Sebastian looks at him, waiting.

"*Doublethink* must go," the detective says.

"What the . . ."

Sebastian starts to jump up, but sinks back into the chair when the detective places two heavy hands on his shoulders.

"Listen carefully," Schilf says. "*Doublethink* must go."

At first nothing happens. Almost a minute passes before Sebastian lifts his head again and thrashes toward Schilf like a drowning man toward his rescuer. The detective bends over Sebastian and braces himself to withstand the attack.

"No!" Sebastian screams.

"*Doublethink* must go," the detective repeats.

"Leave me Oskar! Let the whole disaster at least make sense!"

The uproar ends as suddenly as it started. Sebastian has collapsed and is lying on top of the kitchen table, lifeless. Suicide would have been quite logical in his situation. A man who has lost everything throws his shoulders back, picks up his hat, and leaves the scene. Logic must mean honor. But now there is a new three-word sentence that is much worse than that. "Dabbelink must go" was the tragic command to destroy his own life. "*Doublethink* must go" is a farce. A grotesque coincidence, a poison that has made everything that resulted from it ludicrous.

The detective understands why Sebastian is so still. He is almost afraid he will find Sebastian's face transformed into a ridiculous caricature of itself. Schilf's hands are still on the man's shoulders. The only thing needed to complete the scene is the ticking of a kitchen clock. Just as Schilf has decided that the only thing he can do is make coffee for them both in the chaos of this kitchen, Sebastian starts laughing quietly.

"Vera Wagenfort," he says. "I recognized the voice right away. That's the brunette who sits outside the office of the greatest particle physicist in the world." He laughs again. "He probably expected that I'd recognize her. That I'd blithely ring him up and call him a scoundrel. Instead I murder someone. It's true, isn't it, that we always understand what we want to understand?"

"There might be some truth in that," the detective says cautiously.

"And I thought I was finished." Sebastian turns his head so Schilf can see his face, which is pressed into a lopsided grimace on the kitchen table. "Oskar was right. I know nothing of guilt."

The sob seems to come from somewhere else in the kitchen. It is small and quiet, as if a child has started whimpering. Sebastian puts his hands to his face, his fingers spread wide. His mouth stretches itself into a rectangular opening and releases a toneless scream that shakes his entire body. The detective holds the trembling man close, gripping his shoulders, feeling the shudders running through him. He cannot tell for certain if Sebastian is laughing or crying. There is a neutral point at which all opposites meet. This outbreak, too, is over within minutes. Schilf reaches for a kettle that has rolled under the table, fills it, and puts it on the stove.

"Tonight," he says, as the water begins to boil, "Detective Skura and I need your help. Can I count on you?"

"You have destroyed me," Sebastian says in a voice that seems to have been discovered for this moment. "I'm yours."

"Good," Schilf says.

He pours boiling water into the cups with one hand while the other takes his mobile phone out of his pocket and presses a key.

"Good evening," he says into the telephone. "This is Detective Schilf. There's another game that we have to finish."

[5]

RITA REALLY OUGHT TO HAVE KNOWN that this would be one of the strangest days in a series of strange days. This morning, the cat threw up on the kitchen table as she was having a hasty breakfast. In the vomit were pieces of the chicken salad that Rita had eaten the night before. She felt nauseous. She perked up considerably after Schnurpfeil called from Gwiggen. The case was solved, the evidence was in place, and, as ever, the final verdict would be a matter for a judge. Rita spent half the afternoon writing her report for the public prosecutor's office and the interior ministry, but the elation that normally came with the close of a difficult case escaped her. When the telephone rang, she knew the reason why. *She* might have thought that the whole thing was wrapped up. Detective Schilf certainly didn't think so.

It is impossible to ignore a cry for help. Rita did as Schilf asked and borrowed a police van. The walrus-mustached police chief had called her up once again and told her that her career depended on delivering a full report tomorrow, a report in which the words "doctor," "patient," and "hospital" did not appear. Now she is sitting on the backseat with an avowed murderer, in the full knowledge that her professional future is, as they say, hanging by a thread. When she starts thinking about what kind of net this thread belongs to, she can understand why the feeling of nausea has come back and won't go away.

The first thing Rita Skura and Schnurpfeil did was collect Schilf and the murderer from the house by the canal. The murderer had a blue and white cooler with him. He climbed into the backseat next to Rita without a greeting, proffering instead an explanation that the box belonged to his ex-family. After that, Schilf ordered them to stop at the cycling club, where he commandeered two racing bikes without any legal justification. The two bikes are now in the back of the VW van, as good as stolen property. The next stop was the forensic department. Their business there finished, the murderer was now looking ahead of him with a rapt expression, balancing the cooler on his lap and stroking the blue lid from time to time. Rita has to stop herself thinking about what the box contains and how it got in there, otherwise she will go mad. Schnurpfeil seems to be feeling the same way. Following Schilf's instructions, he is steering the vehicle through the city center, but takes the bends so swiftly and brakes so hard that his passengers bow toward each other simultaneously before righting themselves again.

But the worst thing of all is the voice of the first detective chief superintendent. Schilf is crouched on the passenger seat talking to the windshield about branches and ponds and parallel universes and other bizarre stuff. The crazed monologue makes Rita Skura wish that Schnurpfeil would draw into the next petrol station and throw everyone except her out, and simply drive off, out of the city, onto the A5 toward Basel, and go straight on until the sea can be glimpsed between the trees. Sadly, Schnurpfeil makes no move to do this, but is concentrating on the evening traffic. Nothing in his actions betrays the fact that he imagines throwing everyone except Rita out at the next petrol station and driving off with her, until he reaches the sea.

Rita's fingers drum up a storm on her lap. Schilf's cry for help has shaken her self-confidence somewhat. Her instincts tell her to call up the chief public prosecutor and request an arrest warrant for Sebastian. But if she is to proceed from the opposite of her instincts, as she normally does, she must stay where she is and follow the ideas of someone of unsound mind. Her method of working doesn't seem to be effective any longer. Or perhaps it simply cannot be applied to its progenitor.

When Schilf's babbling stops for a moment, Rita ventures to speak.

"This is madness." She leans forward and taps her forehead. "You're dangerous, Schilf. This is totally birdbrained."

The detective breaks into a sudden fit of laughter that fills the vehicle. He sounds like he is suffocating by the end of it.

"Birdbrained!" he splutters, also tapping his forehead. "That's a good one."

"I'm getting out at the next junction," Rita says.

"At the next junction," Schilf says to Schnurpfeil, putting his hand on the driver's forearm, "stop in front of the sports shop."

The van brakes. Schnurpfeil gets out and slams his door. Schilf passes him the briefcase through the open window.

"Two tops, two pairs of trousers, and two pairs of shoes," he says. "The jerseys in yellow. And take Sebastian with you for size."

Sebastian puts the cooler down at his feet as gingerly as if it were a newborn baby in a cot, and gets out of the van. Her mind completely blank, Rita watches him as he walks into the shop with Schnurpfeil. When the two men have disappeared, Schilf puts an arm over the headrest and looks back at her. They are silent. It feels good to be silent, even though Rita knows that this long stare is only Schilf's way of preventing her from getting out and walking away.

"All right, then," she finally says. "Give it to me straight, in simple language."

Schilf presses his thumb and index finger against his eyelids, as if he needs to concentrate intensely.

"Oskar created a parallel universe," he says, "in which Liam had been kidnapped and not kidnapped at the same time. Sebastian was supposed to recognize what it means not to be able to trust in reality. What it is like to have no 'either/or' but only an 'as well as.' "

"So much for the theory," Rita says. "Let's move on to the practice."

"In a way, the kidnapping was an experiment. But something went wrong. Another memorial to the horror of what we call coincidence was built. And that tangled up the worlds."

"I'm sorry. I don't follow you."

"Imagine two trains traveling next to each other for an instant, at exactly the same speed, totally parallel. At this point, it is possible to change trains. Oskar drew up the timetable, and coincidence created the disaster. And Sebastian slid from one universe into the other."

Schilf takes his hand away from his face at last. His eyes are glittering.

"Rita, my child, we're going to create a second parallelism, in order to enable Sebastian to return to his world."

"You can be really frightening sometimes."

Rita casts a glance at the cooler, tosses her hair back, and looks out of the window as if she is trying to convince herself that outside, at least, everything is as it was.

"This is what I understand," she says. "It's not about this nonsense of parallel universes, but about the fact that Oskar is the one who is really guilty. You're saying that he has fucked up his friend's life in order to teach him a lesson about responsibility. And he's sitting in Geneva pretending that this has nothing to do with him."

"That's exactly what I'm saying!"

Schilf's face lights up and Rita cannot bear to contradict him. She allows him to stretch out his hand and pat her on the cheek. Sometimes she wishes that her work still required her to wear a uniform. That would keep the world at a slight distance.

"You want revenge," Rita says, "justice, a moral victory. All things that have nothing to do with police work. That's what you yourself taught us in our seminars."

"I want to re-create a certain order of things," Schilf says. "Apart from that, you're right."

"You're overstepping the bounds of your responsibilities, and for your own personal pleasure, too. Give me one reason why I should play along, Schilf!"

"All right," the detective says. "I'll show you the reason."

Rita recognizes the documents that he is pulling from his briefcase. They are copies from the file on Dabbelink's murder. But Schilf is looking for something else. He flips back and forth, dips his hand into the briefcase again, and takes out a semitransparent photograph. The picture trembles between his fingers as he passes it to her. Rita lays the murky photograph against the window.

It shows a cloudy shape at least as wide as a hand—it is oval and so indistinct that it seems to be moving against the black background. Curved around the shadowy center is a tube, white as a maggot and filled with labyrinthine entrails. The whole thing is held together by two layers of skin on the outside: one thick and black in color and the other thinner and pale. Although Rita finds the sight repellent, she cannot tear her eyes from it. At the bottom of the picture is the detective's name in capital letters.

"Since you constantly seem to doubt my intentions," Schilf says, "why not simply look inside my brain?"

He rubs the top of his sparsely covered head, with its elephant face sitting loosely on the bone structure in front.

"Take a good look."

His index finger strokes the back of the maggot and traces the curling outline tenderly. At the bend, Rita notices a patch that looks like a bird's egg in both shape and size. Schilf taps it with his finger a few times.

"Good Lord," Rita says.

"No," Schilf says, "certainly not him."

Rita Skura sits there staring at the patch, silent, as if the connection between her brain and her body has just been severed. She knows that she should hug him. She would even do it gladly. He smiles bravely, a child turned into a grizzled old man, and Rita wants to hold him tight for a while and press her face against his, not to comfort him, but because she suddenly feels alone, abandoned, as if she is surrounded by marionettes and Schilf is the only other creature on earth who belongs to that dying species: the live human being.

But she can do nothing. She cannot find the right gesture, cannot even smile along with Schilf, although he is looking at her with such warmth.

"How long?" she asks, finally.

"Who knows? A couple of weeks."

Schilf takes the result of the MRI scan back and puts it in the briefcase at his feet. When he straightens, he and Rita are sitting one in front of the other like passengers on a bus. Rita sees his scalp showing through his thinning hair, and some flakes of dandruff.

"That's some ammunition, eh, Rita my child? Do you believe that I'm serious now?"

Rita nods. Schilf must have heard that. His smile causes his ears to lift.

A dove has been run over on the road. Feathers dance around the squashed remains whenever cars whoosh past. The traffic light turns red and the cars roll up to it with studied slowness, stopping at a well-calculated distance. A passing woman looks curiously at the police van. On the other side of the road, a young man is whistling for his dog. A cyclist rushes to get off the pavement, and nearly crashes into a child, who drops his ice cream and starts crying.

"A civil war will break out if we stay here any longer," Schilf says.

"What if he doesn't come tonight?" Rita asks.

"A man of honor turns up to a duel."

"How do you know that?"

Schilf turns sideways to look at her from the corner of his eye.

"Shall I take the photo out of the briefcase again?"

The minutes dawdle past, and the door to the sports shop finally opens. Schnurpfeil is laden with colorful plastic bags. Sebastian waves.

"Before I forget," Schilf says. "The police chief rang me. I'm supposed to go back to Stuttgart immediately."

Rita sits bolt upright, as if she'd had an electric shock.

"The hospital scandal has dissolved into thin air," Schilf says, blowing into the palm of his hand. "Puff!"

"What are you saying?"

"I'm saying that my time is limited, on all fronts."

While Rita huffs, as if she is an overheating computer about to crash, Schilf turns to her once more.

"It was a trainee nurse," he says. "She gave heart patients blood-thinning drugs before their operations instead of the prescribed tranquilizers. Apparently these pills all look the same. A stupid mistake."

Rita Skura sinks back into her seat, exhausted. What a ridiculous waste of a few weeks. Sleepless nights, visits to the hospital, neglecting the cat, being unfairly taken to task by her superiors—what had it all been for? Who on earth was interested in an exceptional performance to no end? There was only one way to see it: total failure. The thought has barely crossed her mind before she feels as if she has been declared cured, all without having an operation. She is floating in the air, she could sing out loud. She could kiss the detective or wring his neck.

She doesn't have much time to brood. Schnurpfeil wrenches the driver's door open and slips behind the wheel. While Sebastian gets into the back and puts the cooler back on his lap, the senior policeman sits motionless with both hands on the steering wheel, his head hanging like a schoolboy's.

"Stage fright?" Schilf asks.

"I don't think I want to go on," Schnurpfeil says.

Rita sizes up everyone in the van with an appraising look. All at once, she thinks she knows how Sebastian feels. And how Schilf feels.

Maybe even how Oskar feels. In the end, it's simply about confronting total defeat with a brave face. She stretches a hand out quickly and places it on the senior policeman's shoulder.

"Schnurpfeil," she says, "*I* am leading this investigation."

A smile flits over his face.

"What now?" he asks.

"Back home," Schilf says, "to wait."

[6]

JULIA RUSHES TO MEET HIM IN THE HALLWAY of the police apartment with such expectancy that Schilf is happy to have something to offer her. His girlfriend links arms with him as he introduces her to the murderer. Sebastian is lingering by the door that has just closed behind him, and seems quite helpless: too tall and angular for the narrow space. He grips the handle of the cooler. Schilf and his girlfriend are both smiling at him and he looks at them shyly, as if he is facing a court of law.

Schilf had not wanted to leave Sebastian alone again, so had asked him to spend the final few hours before the big event together. When Sebastian hesitated, Schilf turned the invitation into an order. Now Schilf realizes that a detective can no longer be an official when he is at home, in front of his girlfriend. Sebastian is suddenly presented with a stranger and his younger girlfriend, and is wondering what these two people think of him. In front of the police, a murderer is not ashamed of his crime, just as a patient seeing his doctor is not ashamed of his illness. But Sebastian does not have any practice in living with his crime in the personal realm. Like an accident victim, he must learn everything from scratch: speaking, hand gestures, looking people in the eye. The sooner you start, the better, the detective thinks.

Julia reaches out to shake Sebastian's hand and says that she likes him in person even more than she did on television, and he relaxes visibly. As the detective walks ahead of them into the living room, he realizes that the result of an important experiment has almost passed him by. While climbing the stairs, he was nervous about this meeting between Julia and Sebastian. He had imagined his girlfriend extending her hand to Sebastian and a lightning bolt striking at the same time, reducing her to a puff of smoke. Or, worse still, he had imagined Sebastian entering the apartment and simply walking through Julia as if she were simply not there. Schilf feels a fleeting prick of conscience. He is not sure why this fear surfaced at the crucial moment—because it was so absurd or because he now no longer cared whether Julia disappeared in a puff of smoke.

Sebastian looks around the apartment, and says something pleasant but untrue about it. The detective positions his girlfriend in the open-plan kitchen with her back against the wall and indicates that Sebastian should bring the cooler. Schilf has brought not only the murderer with him, but something special that more or less belongs to the murderer. This needs to go into the freezer, urgently.

"A picnic?" Julia asks.

She chats away, joking about ice cream and cold beer while Schilf lifts the blue lid off the cooler. Dabbelink's stare turns Julia's voice into background noise, as if someone has turned the volume down. The skin on the face has dried up and drawn tight over the bones, so the eyes are open and staring, as if the cyclist were speeding toward a taut steel cable for all eternity. The nose is out of joint and the mouth is stretched in an evil grin. The cervical vertebrae stick out of the tangle of severed tubes, white and clean like a handle. Sebastian pushes in front of Schilf; he wants to lift the head of his victim out of the box himself.

"Careful," Schilf says. "It's only held in place by skin."

When they had been standing over the large aluminum drawer in the forensic department, Sebastian bent down low as if to kiss his victim, then looked at the detective with shining eyes. Thank you, he said. Whatever you're planning, you've just saved me from going mad.

Now, although Sebastian takes hold very gently, Dabbelink cannot help grimacing between his hands. Schilf casts a quick glance at his girlfriend, whose gaze is fixed on the head of the dead man, this three-dimensional caricature that was once a living face. Julia does not look as though she intends to become hysterical.

"So that's what's left," she says.

Schilf nods at her. He is relieved to realize once again exactly why he liked his girlfriend from the moment he met her.

Dabbelink does not fit in the freezer at first go, so they scrape the lumps of ice off the sides of the compartment with a knife. Having succeeded, they feel quite comfortable with each other. Julia makes spaghetti and Sebastian lays the small table. Over dinner, they avoid talking about anything to do with Dabbelink, Oskar, Maike, Liam, or what could happen later that night. The only shared topic of conversation is the hospital scandal. Medical Director Schlüter has been suspended, not on grounds of bodily harm with fatal consequences, but because of inadequate supervision of his staff. The familiar public debate over poorly financed hospitals had started again immediately. Schlüter will pursue his career elsewhere. The rest is politics.

They don't talk much. Schilf is the only one who has a second helping. Never has a meal tasted so good to him.

JULIA INSISTED ON GOING TO BED AFTER DINNER. Why sit around endlessly at the table, weighed down by troublesome thoughts, when they might as well sleep for a couple of hours and wake up at a set time? Schilf envies her deep calm. Her head barely touched the pillow before she fell asleep, as if at the flick of a switch. Her ability to give her body clear commands means that she is as good at falling asleep as she is at sitting still for hours in a life-drawing class. She once said to Schilf that she could not understand the phenomenon of insomnia at all: you have only to turn on your side to embrace a temporary death.

Propped up on one elbow, Schilf watches his girlfriend sleep. She has kicked off the blanket but is holding on to a corner of it, which covers her shoulders, neck, and part of her face. She bears no resemblance to an unplugged machine that by day pulls the wool over Schilf's eyes. She breathes evenly, snuggled up in her own body warmth like a little planet with its own atmosphere. The longer Schilf looks at her, the more he thinks he has a miracle right in front of him. How can this be: a perfect system which, other than food, contains everything it needs for life!

The astonishment he feels rouses such a clamor within him that he is afraid the sound of his thoughts will wake Julia. He gets up quietly and closes the bedroom door behind him.

He stands in front of an open window. His head is clear, with no pneumatic drill trying to demolish the load-bearing walls. Behind him on the sofa is a large, dark shape: Sebastian, who is perfectly still, as if relieved he no longer has to come up with any answers. The zebra stripes across the room have grown sharper and the moon is tussling with the streetlamps over the color of the light. The street beneath is still covered with a carpet of wood shavings. Schilf remembers the feathery feel of it beneath his feet, and the smell of it, like a circus ring. He lights a cigarillo. The smoke casts shadows on the windowsill that curl around each other, fade, and then start swirling again when he blows the next puff out of his lungs. This is how he imagines the mysterious mesh of reality, the primordial soup at the heart of it all: shadows of a god smoking by a window.

In the kitchenette, the door of the built-in refrigerator glows like a white screen. Schilf crooks his fingers and casts the shadow of a panting dog onto its surface. Apart from the anticipation stirring in his stomach, he feels content. There is so little that a man can achieve in his life. Recognize the smell of a woman. Stroke a child's head. Beat an adversary in a duel. Think on the nature of things without forgetting that a man takes all his ideas with him one day, when he leaves the world through the well-used back door.

Schilf has gotten through his stock of happiness in the first few decades of his life, and has been operating on his current account since. Many years ago he stopped thinking that death was the worst thing that could happen to anyone. And Sebastian's explanations about long exposure time have eliminated once and for all any dizziness Schilf felt about standing at the edge of the final abyss. For this reason alone, he shall always be indebted to Sebastian.

Without fear, Schilf can think about his consciousness sinking painlessly back into the froth of information and transformation from which it once rose, and in which it thirsted all its life. He is not even afraid of having to leave an unpalatable block of matter behind, one that is just as hard and ugly as the deep-frozen Dabbelink. The recycling machine called nature will make sure that everything is used again. Whether he is hurriedly buried somewhere, cremated, or scattered over the sea, there are enough plants and animals around to find nourishment in the organic material that is currently still standing in human form at this window, emitting billows of smoke and thinking profound thoughts. They will turn him into something beautiful: green tendrils, blossoms, or colorful plumage. What had only yesterday seemed to him a depressing whirl of unsolved questions has transformed itself into a well-tempered score that has been preserved for millennia. The detective will take care of one last thing, and then go.

A lone dog passes beneath the window.

"What happened to the time-machine murderer in the end?" asks a voice in the darkness behind Schilf.

The detective turns around. Sebastian is lying in exactly the same position on the sofa, and there is no movement to indicate that he is awake.

"Life," Schilf says.

Smiling, he draws on his cigarillo. He is filled with a sense of well-being by having this man bundled up in a blanket in his apartment; he thinks Sebastian must be aglow inside. He imagines Sebastian sitting in his study thinking about the nature of time, holding a pencil between his thumb and index finger, a cap of sunlight on his head. He hears Liam playing in the next room, and hears the rustle of pages as

Maike flicks through an art catalogue in the living room. These images, or so he hopes, belong as much to the future as to the past. Memories that he can take with him.

A few streets away, the dog finishes his nightly walk, curls up on the mat in front of his owner's door, and thinks of nothing. He does not even speculate about the nature of time, which has no more meaning for him than the difference between being present or absent, something he can control by either opening or closing his eyes.

"He was convicted even though he believed that he was conducting a physics experiment?" Sebastian asks.

"They did not punish him for his convictions, but for his methods."

"If your plan works, what will happen to Oskar?"

"He will sacrifice a part of his life in order to give you back a part of yours."

The dog blinks and finds everything is in its place. His master's shoes are next to him and the mat he is lying on smells pleasantly of himself.

"Do you understand," Sebastian says, "that it is impossible for me to transform back into myself?"

"Yes," Schilf replies. "But if we don't try this, you will become like me one day."

"Turn into a detective?" Sebastian laughs. "From a murderer?"

The first detective chief superintendent raises his eyebrows. He stubs out his cigarillo and tosses it into the street.

"If Oskar confesses, there's a good chance that you'll be acquitted."

"A life behind bars seems quite desirable to me at the moment."

"You don't know what you're talking about."

"Detective Skura says that the people in Gwiggen recognized Oskar. You could convict him by conventional means."

"I'm amazed that a man like you understands so little."

"I have a very narrow specialty."

This time they both laugh. Sebastian shifts under his blanket. The detective grows serious.

"The worst always happens afterward," he says. "It happens when people think that the worst is already over."

"Go on," Sebastian says.

"When you visited Oskar in Geneva, he betrayed himself. In the process he betrayed you, too. He of all people offered you a parallel universe, a joint escape, what he most wished for himself. Betrayal weighs heavily on a man. No policeman or judge in this world can deal with it."

"Yes; go on," Sebastian says.

"Let's say you accidentally bump into a woman in the pedestrian zone. She stumbles and breaks her ankle. One week later she is in a car accident. Because of her broken ankle she cannot get out of the car and burns to death. No court will convict you of murder. The police won't even get in touch with you. But just think what your conscience will say!"

"You want Oskar to face up to his conscience," Sebastian says slowly.

"His conscience is the only judge who can really exonerate you," Schilf says.

Sebastian is silent. The detective shuts the window, sits down in an armchair next to the sofa, and spends the next two hours staring at the ceiling.

[7]

"IF YOU CALL UPON A MAN LIKE OSKAR to show up at a clearing in the woods at five in the morning, he will come. Even if he is not given the right to choose the weapons."

Doubtfully, Rita Skura holds the first detective chief superintendent's gaze, then she nods. The forest has not yet finished its morning routine: the leaves are moist with dew, glowing as if they have just been washed, and innumerable red foxgloves are yawning with tiny speckled mouths. In the orchestra pit, the birds are tuning their instruments. The human beings look pale in the midst of this collective awakening. The early morning light picks out their every physical deficiency; it shows the rings under their eyes and sharpens the lines around mouths and noses. This morning, Schilf's headache is not manifested as pain, but as a well-upholstered vacuum. He fingers his neck and touches the handle of vertebrae that is screwed into his skull. He touches the tubes and cables that connect the command center of his entire existence, the only place he ever resides, with the rest of his body below it. He thinks he can feel the skin already drying over his bones, and the corners of his mouth turning up into a diabolical smile that Rita will surely find repellent.

He signals to her; she goes up to Schnurpfeil, who is wearing the yellow jersey and standing forlornly next to a racing bike, and speaks softly to him. The senior policeman leans forward so that his ear is close to her lips. Rita's hand somehow ends up on his cheek, and her touch turns him into a beaming hero. Schilf watches as the detective and the senior policeman gaze into each other's eyes. A lovely couple.

The detective did not wake his girlfriend before leaving the apartment. He shook Sebastian by the shoulder, with a finger to his lips. Dabbelink was frozen hard in the freezer compartment. As quietly as possible, they had pried him free with a screwdriver and tiptoed out of the apartment.

Betrayal weighs heavy, the detective thought, the detective thinks.

But he also thinks: I have not asked her about her past. She doesn't ask me about my future. And that's what you call a deal. Sleep and death have this in common: they offer only single rooms. You can't take anyone with you.

Rita takes her hand away from Schnurpfeil's cheek.

"Go on now," she says, her tone sharp.

The senior policeman gets on the bike and pedals furiously to get uphill. Schilf watches him conquer the long, curving ascent and pass the inn at the upper edge of the hollow until his tiny figure disappears into the trees, where he will hide himself, bicycle and all. And wait.

Schilf turns away and checks the steel cable with one hand. Sebastian, the expert in such matters, has tightened it to maximum tension, even though that is wholly unnecessary for today's events.

Schilf signals again and Sebastian, who is wearing the same yellow jersey as Schnurpfeil, gets down on his knees. He stretches himself facedown on the pavement a few meters away from the steel cable so that his body is lying on the road. Rita Skura walks over and covers his head and shoulders, which are at the edge of the pavement, with branches.

When Schilf looks straight up he sees the second bike hanging from the treetops, dangling gently from an invisible nylon rope. On his second attempt Schnurpfeil had managed to loop the rope through the branches as if using a grappling hook. He raised the bike and tied the rope around the trunk of a young birch tree. Schilf now unties the rope, and has to brace himself with all his might against the weight of the bicycle.

Steel cord, dead body, bike.

He gives the final signal and Rita Skura steps behind the tree on the right-hand side of the steel cable, while he takes his position behind the tree on the left.

The orchestra of birds has finished tuning up and is whistling an aleatoric overture. Although Schilf is tense, his heart beats only reluctantly. At his feet, ants are carrying leaf fragments back and forth. No dead caterpillar this time, and no mosquitoes. Schilf's head expands into a wide room in which thoughts wander with echoing steps.

What if he doesn't come?

Then the story has no end.

And if it all makes no sense?

Then nothing new will have been said about human life, the detective thought, the detective thinks.

But here he is. He has thought it a good idea to wear a hat and carry a stick; they fit in with this romantic and somehow tragic charade. He looks like a man going for a Sunday stroll a hundred years ago.

Oskar checked into his room in the Panorama Hotel at the summit of Schauinsland late yesterday evening, and paid the bill in advance. He informed reception that, at dawn, he would be going on a long hike. Nobody found that strange. Patiently, he reciprocated the exaggerated smiles of the hotel employees.

He passed the night sitting on the balcony, watching a solid fog fill the crevices of the mountain landscape, thinking about whether the expression "a long hike" sounded strange. He had expected the police to get in touch ever since Schilf had come to see him. He hoped that they would be discreet enough not to visit him at work. He had prepared a reply for every possible question.

It was simply a joke between friends. No one was meant to come to any harm. Everything else that had happened could not, as the lawyers say, with all due and proper care, have been foreseen, so he could in no way be accused of it.

He had not reckoned on an invitation to take an early morning walk in the woods. It was very clear to him that his rehearsed replies would be of no use here. They probably wanted to confront him with Sebastian. Perhaps it was Sebastian himself who was behind the whole thing. Perhaps, Oskar thought, as he spent hour after hour staring into the dark, savagely silent mountain landscape, the detective is not a detective at all but a paid henchman. And Sebastian will shoot Oskar at the very scene of the crime. The question is: Will he toss Oskar a second weapon before that?

Oskar has not wasted a second asking himself whether it was sensible to accept the invitation. In a moment of weakness, he had a vision of himself standing opposite Sebastian in the dawn mist, each aiming at the other with an old-fashioned pistol before they hesitate, lower their weapons, and walk toward each other with arms held wide. He forbade himself this thought immediately. He knows he has lost his friend. Now he wants only to find out what these people have in store for him. He is longing to see how much he means to them. Is the intelligence of a chess-playing detective really equal to his? Nothing would be worse than losing to an inferior opponent.

If this mixture of anticipation and trepidation suited someone who was marching along an unknown path toward an unclear destination, the hike that Oskar had started on early this morning would truly be a long one.

There is a break in the forest. Oskar looks out over a broad hollow, dotted with sleeping cows, dark mounds of flesh in the grass. The road leads up toward the old inn, which looks rather put-upon with its blocked-up windows and doorways. Just before the building, the road swings around toward the left in a steep curve, disappearing between the trees after a hundred meters.

Oskar is happy to have the chance to walk a stretch under the open sky. Every dead tree in the forest is a shadowy man in a long coat, and the snap of every twig is a mysterious footstep. Enjoy the beauty of nature, the detective had said on the phone. Oskar counts his steps to avoid self-reflection. The seconds have slowed down, and are much slower than the tempo of his steps. One after the other they tip over the edge of the present in slow motion. Perhaps it seems that way because Oskar is striding forward so briskly. It happened down there. At three hundred his understanding of the situation begins to slip away. At four hundred he no longer knows what he is doing here at all. At five hundred he has reached the inn. He cranes his neck and squints into the distance. Something is shining in the half-light under the treetops where the road enters the forest.

A bell sounds and he nearly jumps out of his skin. He had not heard the cyclist coming from behind. He just manages to leap to one side as something yellow flashes past him. At the end of the curve the racing bike straightens its course and the cyclist pedals on with his head lowered. Oskar wants to scream. Barely a split second later, the bike reaches the forest. Something explodes onto the road and a shower of metal parts catch the light; screws and rods clink and clatter in every direction. Another split second, and all is silent. Deathly silent.

Oskar's leather-soled shoes are not made for running on slippery pavement. He slips and stumbles, ducks under the steel cord just in time, and slides to a standstill. He steps carefully over the wreckage of the bicycle. A man in a yellow jersey lies there, his upper body hidden in the undergrowth, his legs stretched out into the road. Oskar stares, incapable of taking another step, completely unable to think clearly. The eloquent inner monologue which has been with him since his childhood, always ready to pipe up, has been silenced. It's incredible how loudly the birds are singing.

Oskar senses rather than hears the movement behind him. He tears his gaze from the body on the road and turns around. The first detective chief superintendent is standing to the left of the steel cable, still as a waxwork. On the right-hand side is a woman in a flowery dress.

Two sentinels at the posts of a demonic gate.

The woman is holding a man by his hair, a man who consists only of a face and a neck. The eyes are wide open and staring shamelessly at Oskar. The woman starts walking toward him and seems to want to pass the severed head to him; a Salome, only without the silver platter. She stops in the middle of the road and puts the head on the ground. It tips over to one side and rolls toward Oskar, turns a semicircle on a vertebra, and lies still. Oskar realizes that he needs to breathe. His dizziness subsides after two breaths.

"I understand." He wants to cross his arms but they are hanging too heavily by his sides.

"Sebastian!" he shouts. Nothing in the tableau moves, so he lowers his voice. "You weren't the expert in doublethink. I'm afraid it was me."

If he had a saber, he would turn it around now and lay it on the ground in front of him.

[8]

HE EXPECTED THE ATTACK, so the shock from the bird's egg does not topple him immediately. A whistling in the ears, wherever they may be, a stabbing behind the forehead, wherever that has gone, finally a rip straight across the brain, whoever is using it. A rip through the whole body, cutting the detective in two. A person has two of almost everything—legs, hands, eyes, nostrils—so two people can easily be made out of him.

The first few seconds are not painful. Schilf uses both hands to support his head, in which a determined battle is raging. Something is struggling to break free of a prison in which it has been growing for far too long. A sharp beak pecks against the shell. Black dots dance rhythmically in the field of vision. His eyes are no use any longer, so he cannot see if Sebastian and Oskar are lying in each other's arms. If Schnurpfeil is pushing his bike up the road to stand next to Rita Skura. Instead he sees a fountain of water rising to infinite heights, and a broken rainbow in the mist. A boy whose hair is dotted with spray stretches his arms out toward the sky, laughing. When he turns around, his face is just as much Liam's as another boy's. My son, the detective thinks. They're all lying, the boy says, pointing at his watch. A blond woman looks down at the boy, smiling. Then she looks Schilf in the eye. We'll see, she says.

A trembling sensation starts under Schilf's skin. His teeth chatter violently, as if attempting to grind themselves to powder. He scrabbles in his hair with all ten fingers, looking for purchase. Pain finally scythes his legs. The shell shatters.

The detective keels over and does not hit the ground, loses himself in a fall with neither above nor below. He does not feel his hands and feet any longer, only a breeze on his forehead. His skull has opened, a twitching, a fluttering, something forces its way out. It shakes itself, spreads its wings, casts a rainbow of iridescent light that is more beautiful than anything Schilf has ever seen.

Good-bye, observer, the detective thinks.

A bird soars into the air. Finds its flock. Circles over the city.

[EPILOGUE]

AS YOU TAKE OFF TOWARD THE NORTHEAST, Freiburg looks less like a city than a carpet of colors flowing into each other. A shimmering rainbow mass. No one could say whether he is a part of it or it is a part of him. A mosaic of roofs on which the morning sun lavishes its golden tones. The quicksilver ribbon of the Dreisam winds its way through. You can float on the bluish air like it is water. The mountains call the birds home. The birds report their news.

It went something like this, we say.

A NOTE ABOUT THE AUTHOR

Juli Zeh's debut novel, *Eagles and Angels,* won numerous prizes, including the German Book Prize, and a nomination for the International IMPAC Dublin Literary Award. She has worked at the United Nations in New York and Kraków, and currently lives in Brandenburg. *In Free Fall,* her second book, is being published in seventeen countries and developed for film in Germany.

A NOTE ABOUT THE TYPE

This book was set in a digital version of Fairfield Light, designed by Rudolph Ruzicka (1883–1978) for Linotype in 1940. Ruzicka was a Czechoslovakian-American wood and metal engraver, artist, and book illustrator. Although Fairfield recalls the modern typefaces of Bodoni and Didot, it has a distinctly twentieth-century look, a slightly decorative contemporary typeface with old-style characteristics.